Also by Rachel Pollack

The Child Eater
Godmother Night
Temporary Agency
Unquenchable Fire

The Tarot of Perfection

78 Degrees of Wisdom

The Fissure King

A novel in five stories

Rachel Pollack

Underland Press

Copyright © 2017 by Rachel Pollack

This book was printed in the United States of America, and it is published by Underland Press, which is part of Firebird Creative LLC (Clackamas, OR).

Portions of this book first appeared in *The Magazine of Fantasy and Science Fiction* as stand-alone stories.

So Handsome Johnny was gone and he was himself again . . .

Book Design by Mark Teppo

This Underland Press trade paperback edition: May 2019.
It has an ISBN of 978-1-63023-098-2.

Underland Press
www.underlandpress.com

The Fissure King

To Vladimir Nabokov and *Pale Fire*, for the poet John Shade, and Richard Boone and *Have Gun, Will Travel*, for Paladin and the card on the silver tray, and Nancy Norbeck, who first came up with the title phrase and was gracious enough to let me use it in my own way.

The legend of the Traveler appears in every civilization, perpetually assuming new forms, afflictions, powers, and symbols. Through every age he walks in utter solitude toward penance and redemption.

—Annie Dillard, *For the Time Being*

I

In the Forest of Souls

Jack Shade, known in varied places and times as Journeyman Jack, or Jack Sad, or Handsome Johnny (though not any more), or Jack Summer, or Johnny Poet (though not for a long time), or even Jack Thief, was playing Old-Fashioned Poker. That was Jack's name for it, not because the game itself was antiquated—it was Texas Hold Em, the TV game, as Jack thought of it—but because of the venue, a private hotel room, comfortable, elegant even, yet unlicensed and by private invitation only, in the age of Indian casinos no more than a few hours drive from anywhere. Jack knew that most poker was played online these days, split-screen multi-action, or in live tournaments and open cash games held in the big casinos of Vegas, Foxwoods, or Macao.

Jack didn't like casinos. He'd never liked them, though for years he was willing to go where the action was. But after a certain night in the Ibis Casino, a game palace most players had never heard of and would never see, where "All in" meant something very different from betting your entire stack of chips, Jack avoided even the glossiest bright-for-TV game centers, and only played his quaint, private, no-limit match-ups. Luckily for Jack, though not always, luck being luck, there were enough serious money people who knew of Jack Gamble (or Jack Spade, as some called him, though not to his face) that he could more or less summon a game to his private table at the Hôtel de Rêve Noire, which despite its Gallic name was in New York, on 35th Street, a block from the J. P. Morgan Museum, where Jack sometimes went to sit with the fifteenth-century Visconti-Sforza Tarot cards.

Jack lived in the Rêve Noire (possibly why some people called him Johnny Dream), but no one in the game had to know that. Let them think he came in from—somewhere else. Jack didn't like people to know where he lived, an old habit that was still useful. The game, sometimes called Shade's Choice, took place on the eleventh floor, the top floor of the small hotel, where despite the larger buildings all around, the full-length windows looked out to the Empire State antenna (Jack was one of the few people who knew what signal that antenna actually sent, and the messages it relayed back to the Chrysler Building's ever-patient gargoyles), and in the other direction to a small brick house on Roosevelt Island, where Peter Midnight once played a reckless game of cards with a Traveler who outraged fashion in a black cravat.

Jack always dressed for poker. Tonight he was wearing a loosely tailored silk suit, deep-sea green, with a yellow shirt and a mauve tie, undone and draped around his neck. His ropy brown hair was cut rough, as if he'd hacked at it himself when drunk one night, or, as someone once said, as if he'd gone to a blind barber. The furniture in the room was old and carved, somehow heavy, graceful, and comfortable all at once, with influences both French and Chinese. The mahogany table and chairs carried so many layers, generations, of lacquer and polish that neither spilled drinks nor the sharp edges of those obscene good luck charms from Laos that some gamblers liked to fondle could possibly harm them. Even the drink stands by each player looked like they might once have held champagne flutes at Versaille (in fact, they'd originally served as writing platforms for a poetry contest a very long time ago).

Neither the drinks nor the furniture held anyone's attention right now. It was ten in the morning, twelve hours since Mr. Dickens, the white-haired dealer with the long spidery fingers, had given out the first cards. There were nine players—always nine in Jack's games—but everyone knew that only two of them counted. Jack Gamble and the Blindfolded Norwegian Girl. Jack thought of her that way because she'd once won an online tournament with a block up to stop her ever looking at her cards, playing the players instead of her hand. The Girl had been playing poker since she was fifteen, and pro almost that long, and yet she looked, Jack thought, all sweet and round, like she belonged more at a PTO bake sale than a game with a million dollars on the table. There were some who thought she might be that rarest of creatures, a Secret Traveler, but Jack was sure that whatever talent she had was rooted in poker.

Though he played in the highest stakes games Jack was not a pro. Poker just was not his only source of income. Some years it wasn't even the largest, though in others it was all that paid the bills. Pro or not, Jack knew something about cards. Right now he held a pair of tens, spade and club, a decent hand in Hold Em, where two cards was all you got, and you had to combine them with five face-up "community" cards on the table to try and make your own best five card hand. The five card "board" had come up ten, king, seven, all hearts, and then a nine, again a heart, and finally a second king, the king of clubs. So Jack had a full house, three tens and two kings, nearly a dream hand, but the Girl had gone all in, and now the *nearly* was making him crazy.

She could easily have a straight, or better yet, a flush, all she'd need for that is for one of her two cards to be a heart to go along with the four hearts on the board. Those were good hands, enough really for someone to ship all her money into the pot. But suppose she had a king-seven, or a king-nine? Then she'd have *kings* full, three kings and a pair, and there was no greater curse in Hold Em than for someone else to have a bigger full house. And she'd put her money in on the king, not the fourth heart. She could have just been waiting, but if he called, and lost, it would leave him with a long haul to get back even.

He glanced at Charlie, but the old man sat so still he might have been a clay dealer buried with a Chinese emperor. There was no clock for the girl to call on Jack the way she might have done in some casino tournament, but Jack knew she could ask Charlie and he would tell her to the second how long Jack had been deliberating. Jack leaned back in his chair, turned a single black chip over and over.

He was almost ready to fold—that damn tell seemed too obvious to be real—when he saw something that wasn't there.

Barely visible even to him, and just for an instant, a golden foxtail swept along the first four cards on the board, the hearts, lingering just for a moment on the king. Jack kept his face stone but he could feel a shock like an electric current in the long scar that traced his right jawbone. A flush! The Girl had the ace of hearts, and the four hearts on the table had given her a lock—if all she needed was a flush. She'd gone all in because how could you not, but she knew it was a risk—and now she'd lost.

Jack was just about to move in his chips when behind him the door opened. Jack's hand froze no more than an inch from his chips. *Just a few seconds more*, he thought, *just this one call*. But it was no use. He knew no one but the hotel owner, Irene Yao, would ever have opened that door without being summoned, and Irene would open it for one reason only. Someone had shown up with Jack Shade's business card. As if he needed any more proof, her soft voice, its rough edge of age worn smooth with grace, said simply, "Mr. Shade." It was only *Mr. Shade* when it was business.

"Miss Yao," Jack said, and turned around, and of course there it was, as always, on a small silver tray, a cream-colored card that contained only four lines: "John Shade," and below that, "Traveler," then *Hôtel de Rêve Noire, New York*, and in the final line no words, only a silhouette of a chess piece, the horse-head knight in the classic design named for nineteenth century chess master Howard Staunton.

Jack nodded to the Girl. "I fold," he said. *Just a few seconds more*. But the rule was simple: everything stopped when the black knight appeared. He stood up and nodded to the dealer. "Mr. Dickens," he said, "will you please cash in my chips and hold the money till I return?"

"Of course," the old man said.

Harry Barnett, a pork trader from Detroit, said, "What the hell? You're cashing in? Just like that? I flew in for this game. I had to wait two goddamn months for a seat. And now you're just leaving?"

The Girl stared at him, her apple-pie face suddenly all planes and angles. "Shut up, Harry," she said, and though Barnett opened his angry mouth nothing came out. To Jack, the Girl said, "A pleasure to play with you, Jack."

"You too, Annette," Shade said, then followed Irene out the door.

Jack Shade met his clients in a small office on the hotel's second floor. All that made it an office really was Jack's use of it. There were no computers or file cabinets, not even any phones. The only furniture was an old library table and three red leather chairs. The only amenity was a cut-glass decanter filled with water and two heavy crystal glasses.

The client's name was William Barlow, "Will," as he said to call him. Mr. Barlow didn't look whimsical enough for Will. With his thin hair and saggy cheeks and his small nervous eyes he looked about sixty-five but was probably no more than fifty. Overweight and lumpy, despite his expensive suit's attempt to smooth him, he breathed heavily, as if he'd just run up and down Irene's polished ebony stairs. It probably was just stress. People were never at their best when they came to see John Shade.

"Mr. Barlow," Jack said, "do you mind telling me how you got my card?"

"It was my wife's," Barlow said, and his head turned slightly to the left, as if he might find her standing there. "When she—when I was going through her things—I found it. In a jewelry drawer. It's not—not a place I ever would have looked when she was . . ."

Alive, Jack thought. He asked, "Do you have any sense of just why your *wife* had my card?"

"You must have given it to her. Some time ago? Do you teach workshops? I mean, Alice used to go to a lot of workshops."

"I don't teach," Jack said.

Barlow squinted at Jack. "What *do* you do?"

"You came to see me, Mr. Barlow. May I ask why?"

Now Barlow seemed intent on studying the grain in the table. "Strange things have been happening" he said. "Really—" He took a breath. "At first I thought I was dreaming—it was at night mostly—but then it started during the day, and I thought—" He stopped, stared at his hands in his lap. "I thought maybe I was— you know—" He didn't finish the sentence, but a moment later looked up. "But then I thought, maybe, what if I wasn't? What if it was all real? Alice was into all this—all this strange stuff. If anyone could find a way—but what if she was suffering? Mr. Shade, I couldn't stand that."

Jack said, "Do you mind telling me about the strange things?"

As if he hadn't heard the question Barlow went on, "I was supposed to go first. I mean, look at me. Alice kept fit, she watched what she ate. My biggest fear was always how she would get by, after, after I was gone. And then suddenly—it's all wrong. But at least, I thought, at least she won't have to stay on alone. But if she's *suffering*—"

"Tell me about the strange things."

Barlow nodded. "I'm sorry." He took a breath. About to speak again he glanced over at the water decanter, pressed his lips together. "May I?"

"Yes, of course," Jack said, relieved he would not have to find a moment to casually suggest his client drink a glass of water. "I'll join you" he said after Barlow had poured his glass. Jack poured himself exactly half a glass, which he drank down while keeping his eyes fixed on Barlow. The usual shiver along the spine jolted Jack, and he watched Barlow to see if he felt anything, but the client showed no signs of a reaction. *Blissful ignorance*, Jack thought, and realized how much time had passed, how many clients, since a man with a knife had called him Jack the Unknowing.

Barlow looked around for a napkin, then in his pockets for a handkerchief, and finally just wiped his lips with his finger as Poker Jack kept the smile from his face. The client said, "I guess the first thing was the voices. The whispers. That sounds, you know. But they weren't inside me. Or telling me to do things. It wasn't like that." He sighed. "It started a week or so after Alice's death. I was in bed, still not used to being alone there, and watching the news. Alice used to hate it when I did that, said she didn't want those images in her dreams. And there I was doing it, I felt so guilty."

"Mr. Barlow. The voices."

The fleshy head bobbed up and down. "Right. Sorry. Well, I heard sounds, voices. Like when you're at a conference, and there's whispering across the table or something, and you can hear them but you can't make out the words? I figured maybe it was on the TV, one channel bleeding into another, so I turned it off. And the whispers just got louder. I mean, really loud, like a whole building full of people, all whispering to each other."

Not a building, Jack thought, and he wished to hell that however Alice Barlow had gotten hold of Jack's knight she'd thrown the card away instead of keeping it somewhere her husband could pick it up and get the overwhelming urge to go see John Shade, Traveler.

Barlow said, "This went on for days, Mr. Shade. Every night I thought I was, you know, that the grief had gotten too much for me. I finally told my doctor and he said it was normal—it sure as hell didn't feel normal—and gave me some pills. To sleep. It worked for a couple of days but then I woke up, it was three in the morning, and the damn whispers were louder than ever.

"Then one night I got the horrible idea that they were really there. Not in the house, but in the backyard. I don't know why, but once I thought it I couldn't stand it, so I put on my bathrobe and went down to the kitchen. I made sure to make lots of noise to scare anyone away, but when I got to the kitchen everything looked normal. I mean, it was still dark, but the door light was on, and the moon was pretty bright, and I could see the patio Alice had me make, and the flagstones, and it all looked fine. Normal.

"But the voices! They were still there, louder than ever, but still whispers so I couldn't make out a word."

"And so you opened the door," Jack said. Barlow stared at him. "You thought, if you could prove to yourself once and for all that the whispers weren't real they would have to go away." Barlow nodded. "Let me guess what you saw. A forest?" Shaking now, Barlow nodded again. "Dense trees, with twisted branches and no leaves, going on as far as you could see. And flames. A kind of faint fire, so pale it didn't give off any light or heat or even burn any of the trees."

Barlow whispered, "Oh God. Oh my God. I'm not crazy?"

Jack managed to keep the regret out of his voice as he said, "No, Mr. Barlow, you're not crazy at all." Barlow sat back in the chair, mouth open. Jack said, "So you slammed the door and ran inside. Now tell me—is that when you found my card?"

Barlow half-whispered, "Yes." Behind him, for just a moment, Jack saw the flash of the golden foxtail as it brushed over Barlow's shoulders and then was gone. *A lot of good you are. You give me help on a hand too late for me to use it, but you couldn't warn me this was coming?* Out loud he said, "Mr. Barlow, what you saw was not a hallucination or a dream. It's a real place, though very few people actually see it." *At least not while alive.*

"Then why am I seeing it? I'm not anything special. I've never been, you know, psychic or anything."

"It's not about you, Mr. Barlow."

"But I'm—oh, God, it's Alice. Of course. How could I be so—" His hands began to twitch and he clasped them together. "Is she, you know, a ghost?"

"There are no such things as ghosts," Jack Shade said. "At least not the way you see in movies. But sometimes people get stuck." *Sometimes*, he thought, *they can't bear being dead.* And every now and then someone alive gets pulled in and can't get back. Or someone sends them there, and that was the worst of all.

Barlow said, "Mr. Shade, can you help her? Can you get her out? Is that why she had your card?"

"I don't really know why she had my card. But I will try to open a way for her."

"May I ask—what do you—" He looked away.

"My fee is fifty thousand dollars," Jack said. Maybe he couldn't actually refuse someone who had his card, but the clients didn't have to know that.

Barlow hardly seemed to care as he stared again at the desk. "This place. Where Alice is. Is it Hell?"

"No. It's actually just what you saw, twisted trees and cold fire."

"Does it have a name?"

"Yes. It's called the Forest of Souls."

8

Jack arrived the next morning at Barlow's house, just after dawn. Gone were Gambler Jack's silk suits and bright shirts and ties. In their place he wore a black shirt with black buttons, and black jeans over black boots. Black Jack Traveler.

He spent two days and nights in the Westchester McMansion, a house that reminded him of the bland food your mother gave you after stomach flu. The dull creams and light browns of the walls were matched by furniture that might have belonged in a conference room. Barlow had said that Alice took courses and workshops, and in fact there were large faceted crystals and stone incense holders on knickknack shelves in the living room, and a few books scattered aroun the paneled den with breathless promises of some imminent shift in "world consciousness" (clearly, Jack thought, if they had any idea what that term actually meant they would never dare to write a word) or promises to choose the "quantum reality" you want and deserve. Somehow it all seemed like dust floating on a deep impenetrable pool, a well of emptiness.

Only in Alice's dressing room did color manage to break through the dull fog, with yellow walls and light blue trim to match the bottles of perfume and vials and jars of European creams and makeup. The first time Jack went in there he just stood in the center of the room and breathed deeply, as if he could take the color into his lungs and spread it through his body. He realized he'd been closing himself down in the rest of the house, maybe even before he entered it, in a kind of psychic expectation. Only here could he find a place to begin his search for trace elements of Alice Barlow.

Jack spent a lot of time in that room, the door closed to his client, the lights full tilt as he touched and smelled Alice's clothes, her makeup, each elaborate bottle of perfume. He lined his eyes with violet kohl, and painted his lips dark smoky red, and probably would have tried on some of her clothes if Alice had not dieted herself down to a size two. A wedding picture in the living room had shown Alice at about an eight. By the time of her death, apparently, a significant part of her had already vanished.

Some women diet for social approval or self-esteem, but Jack was pretty sure Alice did it to diminish her place in the world. "What were you running from?" he whispered to the mirror as he held a silk camisole against his cheek. Was it Barlow? Jack shook his head. The man was as dull as the house. He wasn't the cause of Alice's desire to disappear, he was just part of her strategy.

Jack had made sure to warn Barlow not to come in during his "psychic investigatory procedures" in the dressing room. Subtle, even dangerous, energies ran through the room at such times, he said, and if Barlow just knocked on the door he could bring down the entire framework Jack was constructing. All of that was partly true, but mostly Jack did not want to repeat the scene of some years back, when a client had walked in on Jack Shade wearing his dead wife's clingy black dress.

Outside the dressing room, Jack talked with Barlow for hours about Alice, their marriage, the things they did together, Alice's hobbies and interests, which apparently came and went. She'd tried knitting, book clubs, French cooking, but gave them all up after a few months. The cosmic crystal phase had lasted longer than most, nearly a year when she died, but Barlow suspected it had already begun to fade. There'd been a lot more of the "dolls and things," he said, and then one day he noticed she'd gotten rid of about half of them. He'd never asked her what she'd done with them.

There were no kids. Alice had had "medical issues," Barlow said, and when she said she didn't want to adopt he'd just agreed. "Maybe I should have pushed it," he told Jack. "Maybe she would have been happier." Jack didn't know if that was true, so much of what Barlow said seemed layered over with guilt like archaeological sediment. Maybe if he'd done more, he said, read some of her books, joined the cooking classes, they could have traveled more. She always seemed to pick up on trips, especially Paris, she loved Paris. *Just like the song,* Jack thought.

Most of all, Barlow built palaces of guilt around the fact that Alice had died at all, at least before him. He was the one who broke his diet, whose numbers had crept up despite the statins and the dreadful low-salt food. All his preparations, the will, the retirement accounts, they all began with the same assumption, that Alice would outlive him.

How did she die? Jack asked. They were sitting at a brown oval dining table. Aneurysm, Barlow said. Undetectable and as unexpected as a thunderstorm when the weather bureau had promised a sunny day. "How could that happen?" Barlow asked.

"I don't know," Jack said. "I'm not a doctor. Or a theologian." He knew he was being hard, but he'd never get anything done if he had to hold the client's hand all day.

Barlow blinked, stared at Jack a moment, then said, "Mr. Shade—can you find her? In that place, that *forest*?"

"Yes."

"And release her?"

"Yes." Jack might have said "I can try," but in fact he'd succeeded in every case but one. And that one was special.

Barlow said, "And will I stop hearing those noises? And seeing the trees?"

"Yes."

Barlow looked down at the table. "When you release her—where will she go?"

"I don't know," Jack said. "I have no idea."

The first night Jack was there Barlow had asked if they should stay up together and wait for the whispers to "manifest," a term that probably came from one of Alice's workshops. It didn't work that way, Jack said. The Forest tended to conceal itself when a Traveler came to investigate. He told Barlow he'd have to go track it down himself. He didn't say that in fact he knew exactly where the entrance was, and it was a garage on West 54th Street.

Jack slept that first night in the guest room and realized almost immediately it was a mistake. Many women saw their guest rooms as a chance to indulge their more extreme decorating ideas, but this one looked like it was copied from a magazine, or even a furniture catalog. The white bedding, the dull peach colored walls, fake flowers in the fake antique pitcher, they were all as lifeless as a plastic doll house.

Despite what he'd told Barlow, Jack went down to the kitchen in the middle of the night. He walked past the butcher block counter and island stove to open the back door. With his head cocked slightly to the left he said quietly, "Alice? Where are you?" Very faintly he heard the whispers of the Forest, far away and nothing like the roar Barlow had heard. And when he stepped outside all he saw was the patio and lawn furniture, more dead than Alice Barlow.

The next day he told Barlow he needed to sleep in Alice's bed. At first he thought the client would object, but no, Barlow just nodded and that evening left fresh sheets neatly folded on the king size bed and went off to sleep on the couch. Jack smiled as he changed the sheets. William Barlow might have to surrender his bed but damned if he would change the linens. Jack was just done when Barlow came to the door with an armful of towels and what looked like shampoo and conditioner. He said, "If you want to step out a moment I'll freshen up the bathroom for you."

"That's okay," Jack said and reached out to take the towels and hair products. Barlow hesitated, then nodded, and left. Jack watched him a moment, then closed the door.

Earlier in the day Jack had pocketed a loose bracelet of silver tiles from Alice's dressing room. Now, as he held it, he thought about the fact that Barlow had kept everything intact in his dead wife's room. A check of the closets and drawers in the master bedroom confirmed his guess that nothing of Alice remained, the walk-in closet home now to a lonely rack of suits. So why the shrine in the dressing room?

It took no more than a few seconds to figure out which side of the bed was Alice's. It wasn't physical, Barlow hadn't left a trough in the firm mattress. But when Jack tried the left side he began to wheeze and cough, an effect that vanished as soon as he rolled to the right. On that side there was only a sense of lightness, a lack of any presence at all.

And yet she *was* there, he could feel her all around him, especially in the bracelet that pressed against his wrist as if Alice

Barlow was taking hold of him. That lightness, Jack realized, had been there all along, it was there before she died. It was what she left behind. "How did you get so lost?" Jack whispered in tears. "What happened to you?"

Then he held up his left wrist with the bracelet before his eyes. Louder than before he said, "I'm coming for you, Alice. My name is John Shade, and I will find you. I will find you and set you free."

Suddenly exhausted, Jack dropped his arm and settled his head against the too thin hypoallergenic pillow. For just an instant, heat flared in the bracelet, so intense Jack almost tore it off, but then it went cold again, as chill as moonlight. Tired as he was, he still didn't expect to sleep that night, so it came as a kind of distant surprise when his eyes pulled down, his limbs grew sullen, and then he was gone.

He dreamed he was walking in the Forest, only it was disguised, the way it so often was (even in the dream he remembered telling that to Barlow). This time it appeared as some kind of march or demonstration in a city that may have been Manhattan. All around him everyone was holding signs or shouting slogans. Only, he couldn't read the signs, or understand the loud chants, and then he realized, the souls, the lost, they were not the people in the march, the people were the *trees*. The souls were trapped inside the fake demonstrators, unable to speak, or to tell Jack what they needed. The fire, so cold, so pale, wound around the tree people with their signs, like a thin fog.

Jack tried to speak but his words came out all thick, as if his jaw moved too slowly, so he reached up to massage it, loosen his tongue. He was several seconds rubbing his lower face before he realized—there was no scar. He was back the way he was before—before everything fell apart. Back when he was Handsome Johnny, and being a Traveler was, well, something that made you better than other people, all the dumb William Barlows of the world. Disgust twisted his insides. He didn't want to lose his scars, he deserved them, he needed them. They made sure he never forgot.

All around him, the people, the *trees*, stamped and shook their signs. If they were trying to tell him something they were wasting their time, the signs meant nothing, the voices just scrambled sounds. Tree language. He remembered now that he was on a mission, and he called out, "Alice? Alice Barlow? Are you here somewhere? Can you show yourself?"

His eye caught a flash of motion to the right, and he turned in time to see a thin woman in a pale red dress dart behind the crowd of demonstrators and head toward a kitchen supply shop. "Alice, wait!" he called above the noise of the demonstrators. Pushing aside the tree people, who took no notice of him, he made his way in her direction.

It was only when he got free of the crowd and their signs, and could see that she had stopped in front of the show window full of knives, that he could see it wasn't Alice Barlow, it wasn't even a woman but just a girl. Fourteen years old. Arms and legs stick thin. Long straight hair, her mother's hair, dyed black, sharp and bright against the pale red dress that echoed the faint fire flickering through the forest.

"Oh God," Jack whispered. "Oh my God. *Eugenia*."

She turned around now, slowly, with that adolescent drama smile, and lowered her head slightly so she could look up at him as if she was just a child again. Softly she said, "Hello, Daddy."

And the store window exploded, and all those gleaming knives and cleavers came flying at Jack.

He managed to knock most of them out of the way, all the while shouting, "Genie! Don't go! I can help you—" But not all. A carving knife and a long-pronged fork hit his face and he screamed in pain. *No!* he thought, *Not again.* He looked away, lost focus, for just a moment, and when he turned back she was gone.

He touched his face to see how much damage the geist had done only to discover there was no blood, no fresh wounds, just the hardened scars of an attack long ago. So Handsome Johnny was gone and he was himself again, Scar-faced Jack, Johnny Ugly. Johnny Lonesome.

"Mr. Shade!" a man called, and when he turned to see who it was he discovered himself awake, back in the Barlow bedroom, with the client himself trying the locked door and yelling, "Mr. Shade! Are you all right? I heard noises."

Jack sat up and discovered books scattered on the bed and the floor around it, bestsellers and art books from the low decorator bookshelf opposite the bed. They must have flung themselves at him while he slept. Could a poltergeist operate from a dream?

"I'm all right!" he said loudly. "Go back to bed, Mr. Barlow. We'll talk in the morning."

When he heard Barlow leave, Jack lay on the bed, ignoring the books as he tried to steady his breath and lower his heart rate. "Eugenia," he whispered. He thought, as he did so often, of the early days, when cups or plates started crashing on the floor, and then the coffee table flung itself across the room, and all the drawers of his wife's dresser smashed into the wall above the bed. He remembered how Layla had screamed she couldn't stand it anymore, Jack had to *do* something, how he'd held her and told her, with all the reassurance of his great knowledge, his experience as a Traveler, that it was just a phase, that doing something would only strengthen it. If you left them alone geists just faded away. Lying in his client's bed, remembering, Jack felt the tears slide down his cheeks until they hit the dead crevices of his scars.

He lay there until dawn, eyes on the ceiling as he waited until first light would allow him to get up and take the final step before he could leave the gray house. Once he was sure the sun had come up he went into the oversize lifeless bathroom where he washed his face and got dressed, all but his shirt. On his way back from the bathroom he noticed something odd, a small black leather copy of MacGregor Mathers' translation of the fifteenth century manuscript, *The Book of the Sacred Magic of Abra-Melin the Mage.* He smiled. Maybe Alice had advanced beyond the dabbler stage. She must have hidden this behind the big showy art books, where she could count on William never noticing it. Softly Jack said, "You deserve better than the Forest, Alice. I'm coming for you."

Back at the bed he set down a small black rectangular leather case he'd brought with him from the hotel. Various instruments lay inside it, only one of which he needed. A black knife, unadorned, with a polished ebony handle and a double-edged carbon blade exactly five inches long.

He held it up and stared at it awhile as he turned it in the morning light. Then he cut a shallow line along the inside of his arm. There was a network of such lines, light scars, and Jack had often wondered if some doctor, or even a cop if Jack was ever careless enough to get arrested, might think he was a junkie. Or self-destructive. He watched the fresh cut slowly ooze with blood, then took a deep breath and finally spit into the wound.

Jack had to grip his thighs to keep from crying out. There was always pain, but *this*—

The action had begun when Jack had shared that simple glass of water with Barlow back in the office. There'd been nothing in the water but Jack had charged it to align the two of them, so that his own etheric pulse would hold some of the client's bond with his dead wife. When he spit into the cut he temporarily united himself with Barlow, so that the wound could call out to Alice. It was the surest way to find her in the confusion of the Forest.

The action was never easy—it was like injecting himself with someone's grief, or fear, or guilt—but he could never remember it hitting this hard. When the pain subsided enough that he could breathe a little easier he discovered his face wet with tears and sweat. He went into the bathroom and washed again, then put on his shirt, packed his knife, and left the house, hopefully without waking his client.

At 9:47 in the morning Lonesome Jack Shade stood on Lexington Avenue, north of 72nd Street, and watched a slim young man open the door to Laurentian Chocolates. Along with his all black

clothes Jack wore the carbon blade knife in a sheath up his left sleeve.

Jack knew he should go get what he needed before the shop filled with customers, but he hated what he had to do. He wondered, did chocolate-shop owners around the city all talk to each other? Would Monsieur Laurentian see Jack's knife, roll his eyes, and say, "Oh, it's *you*." Or would he just moue in fear, like the last poor truffle-maker?

Jack sighed. At least he could disguise himself. He pretended it was to escape detection, but knew it was really to lessen the embarrassment of what he was about to do. He slipped the knife from its sheath and stared at the point, so sharp it could cut sunshine. In two quick touches he lightly pressed the point against his forehead and then his lips.

He cried out, loudly enough that a woman walking five dogs turned around and stared at him, and a bike messenger reflexively shouted, "Fuck you, man!" Gently, Jack moved his fingertips around his face, feeling a smooth plastic quality that told him the trick had worked. Once it firmed up, his false face would look so bland that Laurentian would not be able to describe Jack at all. "I don't know," he'd tell the police if he even bothered to call them. "It was just one of those faces. You know. As if it wasn't really there."

On the street corner Jack touched his nose, his cheeks, the area around his lips. It still felt like some opaque plastic mask but it held firm against his prodding. He crossed the street toward Laurentian Chocolates.

He was nearly at the door when he felt a light brush against his legs. He glanced down and there was the golden tail, its tip just leaving his left knee. Unlike at the poker table, where the fox had vanished almost before Jack caught sight of it, it turned to sit on its haunches right in the middle of the sidewalk, its fur dazzling in the sun. No one but Jack could see it but people automatically walked around it, some squinting at the glare from the invisible fur. One young woman walked by, stopped, and turned to stare right at the spot where the fox sat, then shrugged and walked on. *You've got a future*, Jack thought. *With any luck it'll never find you.*

"Hello, Ray," he said to the fox, who bowed his head a moment. Jack Shade had met Ray on one of his first travels, when he found himself in a bad place, surrounded by, of all things, predator chickens. He did an action for help and Ray had appeared, a fitting protector, Jack supposed. Now Ray came to him mostly to warn him, or show him things. The name was Jack's choice, short for Reynard, of course, but also the correct pronunciation of Ra, the Egyptian Sun god, for in the catalogue of foxes—mountain fox, fox of the willows, fox of the stairways, tracker fox—Ray was a noon fox, a solar helper, bringing clarity and strength.

"Thanks for being here," Jack said. "You know I hate this part, it's so damn embarrassing. But what can I do? I've got to give the Door Man what he wants." Ray stared at him awhile longer, then leaped off the curb to vanish in front of a taxicab, whose driver hit the brakes then looked confused before he sped up again.

The owner of the chocolate shop appeared to be around twenty-two but was probably ten years older. In black creased pants, shiny wingtips, and gray vest over his pale blue shirt he looked as old-fashioned and immaculate as his glass display cases filled with exotic concoctions. He looked Jack up and down briefly, his expression confused as he tried to focus on the face that wasn't quite a mask, then more relaxed again as he let his eyes move back to Jack's muscular upper body and thighs. "Good morning," he said, with a smile. "You're my first. At least for today."

Blank-faced Jack pointed to a tray of dark chocolate truffles covered in chocolate powder. "I'll have one of those," he said.

Mr. Laurentian nodded his appreciation of Jack's good taste. "Certainly," he said. "Shall I put it in a presentation box?"

"Yes, thank you." Jack watched Laurentian carefully set the truffle in a miniature cardboard box, which he tied with a red ribbon and a slight twirl of his hand. "Thank you," he said. "That will be $7.95."

With a sigh Jack slipped the black knife from the sheath in his sleeve and pointed the tip at Laurentian's neck. "I'll just take it," he said.

"Oh! Oh God," the chocolatier said. "Take whatever I've got. I mean, there's not much. I just opened. But take it. Whatever's in the register."

"I just want the truffle," Jack said

The young man froze, as if stuck in the strange moment. Then he said, "Of course. Yes. Let me get a bag, I'll put all the truffles—"

"No. Just this one."

"What? Are you— it's only $7.95! I said you could—" He stopped himself, realizing he was trying to argue an armed robber into taking more than he wanted. It was a reaction Jack had seen before. "Here," Laurentian said. He thrust the small box at Jack, who grabbed it and ran from the store.

A principle of opposites governed the entryways to what an old German Traveler once called "non-linear locations." Opposites and doorways. In New York City, you entered the Forest of Souls in a garage on 54th Street, through a red metal door marked "Employees only." As with every other NLL entrance, you couldn't get through unless you paid the Door Man. In the Empire Garage this job fell to a white-haired gentleman named Barney. And Barney liked chocolates. Stolen chocolates.

When Jack began his travels Barney demanded nothing more than chocolate kisses. Just one each time. He used to pull the little ribbon top and smile as the foil came away. As he popped the brown cone in his mouth he would nod to Jack to go on through. The nice thing about chocolate kisses is that they were easy to steal. But then a couple of years ago Barney had gone upscale. Jack had heard that some Wall Streeter had taken up traveling after the credit swap bubble burst, and had ruined things for everybody by giving Barney his first dark chocolate delight. Now it had to be a truffle. Fresh. And it had to be stolen.

"Why can't I just buy you one?" Jack asked him once.

Barney had smiled. "Money comes and goes, Jack. Silver, paper, even beads sometimes. You got money, you never know what you got. But stealing is forever."

He found Barney, as always, sitting on a steel chair against the wall of the garage, alongside the door he protected. He wore a blue shirt and pants, with "Empire Garage" in italics on the right pocket and "Barney" in gold script on the left. He was short, about five-eight, and stocky, but not fat. He had a full head of fine white hair, cut short, and a square face with enough fine lines on it that it might have served as a map of the Non-Linear worlds. Jack had no idea how long the old man had served as Door Man. Fifty years? Five thousand years? Maybe the first Manahatta Traveler had found a white-haired man in a beaver cloak sitting on a tree stump next to a cave that served as entrance to the Forest. Or maybe Barney would get the job next week. Non-Linear employment.

One time, just to see what would happen, Jack had asked the cashier about "the old guy who just sits in a chair upstairs."

"Oh, that's Barney," the man said.

"Well, what does he do? He doesn't seem to ever leave his spot."

The cashier looked confused. In a tone that suggested Jack had asked a really dumb question he said, "I don't know. He's Barney."

Today, Jack walked up with a smile, waiting for Barney's usual "Hey, kid," but instead the Door Man tilted his head to the side slightly and squinted at Jack like he was trying to make out who he was. "Can I help you?" he said.

Jack stared at him. "Barney? It's me. Jack Shade."

Barney shook his head, then laughed. "Jack!" he said. "Sorry, kid. My old eyes ain't what they used to be, I guess."

Jack touched his face to make sure the mask was gone, and in fact, for just a moment he thought he felt smooth skin, but no, there were the scars. He said, "It's probably just me, Barney. I had to dupe my face for something and there's probably traces of the overlay still on it."

Barney nodded. "Ah, that must be it."

Jack said, "I've got something for you."

"Hey, you're all right, Jack," Barney said as he took the box and undid the ribbon. "Ah, Charlie Lawrence," he said. "You know he calls himself Charles Laurentian now?" He pronounced it "Sharl Lor-en-zhin" in the worst French accent Jack had ever heard. "I guess whatever sells product, right, Jack?" He smiled at the candy in its gold foil nest. "You know, Jack, you've got taste. That's what I tell the others. Jack Shade, I tell em. He knows what to bring an old man." Biting down, he waved Jack to the door.

The handle was hot, like the door to a furnace, and when Jack opened it all he could see was a red glow so intense his face felt on fire. As soon as he stepped through, however, and felt the dirt and leaves under his feet, a cold wind hit him. He gasped, as he always did, for knowledge of what's to come doesn't help much in the Forest. It wasn't really cold, just as before it wasn't really hot. If he'd had to guess the actual temperature he would have said around 60. But it felt like his bones would freeze so tight his toes would snap off.

Jack paid no attention, only took a piece of red chalk from his jeans pocket and marked "JS" on the door, which stood incongruously all by itself, surrounded by trees. Jack made his mark graffiti style, with block letters and a flourish at the end. Almost as soon as he finished, the door just faded away and all that was left were trees. Endless trees, all sizes and shapes, a few with dusty leaves or yellowed needles, but most bare, the branches black and twisted. Unlike an actual woods, where the trees grow densely together, blocking your view, here each tree stood by itself, as if they refused any contact, so that Jack felt like he could see for miles and miles with no horizon, only twisted trees, forever and ever. It was twilight, dim, the only color the faint fire that wound in and out of the branches like pale weightless ribbons.

Jack Shade closed his eyes and took a breath, and when he looked again everything had changed. A department store. He was in some kind of large store, standing in the watch and jewelry section, looking out toward various clothing sections for men, women, and children as shoppers moved in and out of mannequins displaying middle-of-the-road clothes, the kind you might see in suburban malls. People in winter jackets rushed about, some checking lists, and as if that observation triggered a next step, red and green ribbons appeared on the walls and displays, while voiceless holiday Muzak whined through the noise of the crowd. It all looked so real—except for the wisps of flame that snaked through the shoppers and the mannequins.

Jack moved slowly, careful not to touch anything, the people, the displays, the clothes on the racks. He knew only one thing for certain, that Alice had to be somewhere nearby, for part of the reason for the cut on his arm was to act as a kind of homing signal to bring him to that part of the Non-L Forest where Alice was trapped. But he couldn't begin to summon her until he could identify the *trees* in all this crowd of goods and shoppers.

He kept looking, staring, until suddenly he realized he was doing it all wrong. You don't *look* in the Forest, you listen. Jack was staring round corners, and through the crowds, and even under the counters in the unconscious hope he would spot Eugenia. Unconscious and useless. This wasn't his dream, after all, and if his daughter was even in this part of the Forest, she would show herself only if she wanted to. Right now he was here for Alice.

He said out loud, just to be sure, "Genie, if you're anywhere around, and you want to show yourself, I want to see you. Right now I've got a job to do, but I'm here. I love you."

Then, reluctantly, he closed his eyes. He took a deep breath, another. On the third exhale he heard the Forest. Voices, whispers, a roar of whispers, waves and surges of grief and loneliness, hurricanes of rage. Jack screamed, fell on all fours where he shook wildly, like a terrified dog, and it was all he could do to keep from howling. But when the voices subsided enough that he could stand up and open his eyes he knew.

The mannequins. The trees were the mannequins, the plastic bodies in absurd poses prisons for the dead. Jack could see it in the blank smooth faces, where underneath the plastic eyes something pulsed. He could hear, or just feel, the whispers in the rigid half-opened mouths.

Jack slipped his knife from its sheath and in one stroke sliced open the left sleeve of his shirt. Years ago, when he was first learning, Jack had laughed and asked his teacher why he couldn't just roll it up. "Oh, Jack," she'd said. "Carefree Jack. Don't you know you have to sacrifice something? Even if it's just a shirt?" These days Jack figured he'd sacrificed more than enough in his years as a Traveler, but you didn't mess with tradition. He held up his exposed arm like a signpost, the cut bright and shiny.

Slowly he turned around, like a lighthouse lamp. "I'm looking for Alice Barlow!" he shouted, then, "Alice! I'm carrying your mark. Your memory. Show yourself! I've come from the Old World to release you to the New. You don't have to stay here any more. I'm here to help you. Alice Barlow! *Show yourself!*"

For a long time nothing happened, and Jack wondered if somehow, some way, he'd made a mistake. Why didn't she respond? Usually, all the dead wanted was to get free of their tree prison. Could he possibly have screwed up the action and took himself to the wrong part of the Forest? He thought back over everything he'd done and it was all correct, he was sure of it. There was Barney's odd reaction when he first saw him, but that was just—

Then he saw it. In the men's sportswear section, a mannequin dressed in jeans and a checked shirt and one of those denim jackets with a corduroy color gave off a faint pulsing light.

Jack walked over to it, still with his arm up and held so that the cut faced the mannequin's face. "Hello, Alice," he said gently. "I'm very glad to meet you. I've been searching for you for some time." The mannequin—the tree—didn't move, of course, but Jack thought he saw a glow of heat in the smooth plastic and even the sweatshop polyester clothing. "It's okay," Jack said. "I know you're scared. And angry. That's always the way it is. But now I'm here, Alice, and it's all going to end. Here's what I'm going to do, Alice. I'm going to bring you out, and once you're free, I will open a gate so you can leave here. Are you ready, Alice?"

Not just a glow this time, but a real flash of light. It lasted only a second but there was no mistaking it. He nodded. "Thank you, Alice. Thank you for showing yourself."

Without turning his back on her he moved a few feet away, far enough that he could draw a circle with his chalk on the floor in front of the mannequin. Jack sometimes thought that in all his Traveler training the hardest thing had been to learn to freehand a circle. Now he looked at his work and couldn't help but smile a moment. Taking Alice as due south he marked the compass points, then drew various signs in the cross-quarter. Using the various points to guide him he found the circle's center, where he drew an eight-pointed star. It was a little awkward because he had to make sure he didn't actually step inside the circle or touch the rim. "This is your mark, Alice," he said. "This is where you'll go. It won't be long now."

He stood up and took a position behind north so he would face the mannequin, with the circle between them. He reached in his jeans pocket and took out the silver bracelet he'd worn in Alice's bed and held it up high. Slight shocks ran from the bracelet to the cut in his arm, but he ignored them. "Remember this, Alice?" he said, his eyes fixed on the blank plastic face and the fire he could sense under it. "It holds the genuine you. Your existence here isn't real, Alice. *This* is real. I'm going to open a kind of door. You're going to feel it more than see it. And when you do you'll know the bracelet is calling to you. Just like I've been calling you. I'm going to start now, Alice. Are you ready?"

As Jack leaned over to lay the bracelet on the chalk star a strange smell almost made him stumble. For a few seconds the air stank of dead meat and wet fur, of layers of urine and feces. Some kind of animal den, large, like a bear. Was that how Alice experienced her imprisonment? Not what Jack saw, not a mannequin or even a tree, but the prey of some wild animal?

The smell faded, and with it Jack's attempts to figure out what it meant. It was time to do what he'd come for. Jack pulled out his knife and raised it in his left hand to point at the ceiling. Then as hard as he could he brought it down to slice the air inside the circle. "Alice Barlow! " he shouted. "The way is open!"

All around him the shoppers, just props after all, paid no attention but continued to chatter and check their lists and hold clothes up against their bodies. The Muzak, however, crackled, then sputtered out halfway through "Hark, the Herald Angels Sing." Within a range of twenty feet or so the mannequins all turned dark then suddenly flashed with light so brightly Jack had to shield his eyes to prevent retina burn.

He kept his focus on the blank manly face of Alice Barlow's prison. The expression didn't change, of course, or the pose, but the whole thing shuddered and swayed, as if something was shaking it. From the inside.

Slowly something began to emerge, first a vapor so fine Jack wasn't sure he was really seeing it, then more pronounced, an ooze that came out of the mannequin so slowly it might have been sweating. The sweat turned to a thick mass, the colorless gelatin that a French Traveler in the nineteenth century called "ectoplasm."

Jack held his breath. This part was tricky, for the dead person could emerge as anything, and he had to be ready to welcome it. Usually they ended up as who they were in life (though sometimes idealized, with bigger breasts, say, or poutier lips), often naked but sometimes so dressed up they looked like they'd stepped out of *Downton Abbey*. But sometimes they emerged as something else entirely, a different person, some other kind of creature, even an object. Once, Jack brought forth a child who'd died too young, but instead of a boy there was a school composition book, full of handwriting in some alphabet Jack had never seen.

This time it was going exactly right. The ecto was firming up, becoming recognizable, first as arms and legs with overly long hands and toes, then a torso, then at last the head, and it was her, Alice Barlow. She came out naked, thin, the body all tensed, the eyes squeezed shut as if afraid to look, the skin darker and rougher than in her photos, the hair longer and wilder, the muscles in her arms and legs more defined. She wasn't quite the same, but she was who, and what, she was supposed to be, and that was all that mattered. Jack let out a breath he hadn't known he was holding, unsure why this woman he'd never met could have such a powerful effect on him.

With a sudden violent twist Alice broke fully from her mannequin prison and pitched forward into the circle, where she landed on all fours. She trembled wildly, like a terrified dog.

Jack became aware that the whispers had risen all around him, drowning out the fake sounds of the store. If the souls in their trees could witness this, what were they thinking? Did they know, or sense, someone had broken free? Were they proud? Hopeful? Jealous? He looked down at the only one who mattered. "Hello, Alice," he said. "Welcome back."

She didn't get up, didn't move from her spot. Only her head moved, tilting up to look at him, and as it did so it changed.

The cheekbones stood out, so sharp they almost cut through the skin. The eyes became bigger, the pupils flat and dark, the chin narrowed, became almost triangular, the lips stretched thin. And when she opened her mouth the teeth had grown long and sharp.

Jack stared at her, no idea what to do. "Alice," he said, "it's going to be okay."

She sprang at him. Leaped from all fours directly at his face. No, not his face, his throat. The long sharp teeth nearly tore out his trachea. Jack grabbed her, he wasn't sure where, and somehow managed to fling her wildly twisting body away from him. He tried to get her back in the circle, where he might hope to contain her but she managed to break away and land on all fours just to the left of it. Immediately she spun around to face him again, shaking her head and growling. Strangely the Muzak came back, and "Rudolph The Red-Nosed Reindeer" bounced cheerfully above the snarls of the creature on the floor.

Jack reached up to touch his neck and face and feel the damage. As soon as he did so he forgot all about blood and wounds, for instead of his own tight skin and scars his fingers found a soft fleshiness. Wrinkled middle-aged skin over sagging jowls. And in that instant, with Alice about to spring again, Jack knew what had happened. He understood, finally, too late, what William Barlow had done to him.

In *The Traveler's Bestiary*, or "guide to Non-Linear fauna," as Jack's teacher once called it, there were many pages—files in the smart-phone version—devoted to Beasts of Fury. This is what Alice Barlow had made of herself. Enough human to hold on to her purpose, and enough animal to rip Jack apart. And when she was finished? Would she realize what had happened, what her husband had done to her as well as Jack?

Twice more Jack managed to fling her away, and both times she landed on all fours and turned right around to bare her teeth before her next leap. Both times Jack considered running, but knew he'd never make it. The watch and jewelry section was only twenty or thirty yards away, but it would take time—and energy—to open the door. And Alice had cornered the market on both. Powered by all the rage in existence, from jealous lovers to hungry babies to dying stars, a Fury could go on forever. But not Jack Shade. Everything he did in the Forest, even just seeing through its masks, drained him.

One more time. He could throw her off once more—maybe— and then she would take him. "Goodbye," he whispered. Goodbye to everyone, his daughter most of all, but also Irene, Mr. Dickens, to Ray, who'd tried to warn him but couldn't follow him into the Forest, and even the Blindfolded Norwegian Girl. And Alice, whom he'd tried to help but got it wrong.

As if she could feel his thoughts, Alice shook wildly, screamed, and threw herself through the air. Jack braced himself. His clothes were in shreds, his arms and chest bleeding. Alice leaped, arms straight out, clawed fingers spread wide for greatest impact, teeth bright in the holiday lights. And then she stopped.

As if she'd hit an invisible net set up by some Fury hunter, she twisted wildly in midair, screaming in frustration. No, not a net, and not invisible. A yellow cashmere scarf had come off a counter display to wrap around Alice's abdomen, and even though it was attached to nothing, hold her above the floor. She thrashed and clawed and managed to cut herself loose, only to have two more scarves, cheap nylon this time, spin around and once more hold her suspended.

Jack spun around, searching, looking. "Where are you?" he shouted above the Muzak, which now played "Santa Claus Is Coming to Town."

"Genie!" Jack called to her, and then he saw her, small in her red dress and pink sneakers, her hair in pigtails. The only living resident—prisoner—in the Forest of Souls stood among a display of fake leather luggage. It was all fake, of course, the whole place. Everything in it was a prop. Except for Eugenia Shade. And Alice Barlow.

Jack started toward his daughter, only to have her shout, "No! You have to go, Daddy. I can't hold her. Hurry!"

27

For just a second he hesitated, but he could see she was right. Alice was already pulling loose, and Genie was swaying with the effort to contain her. He ran to the watch counter, dropped to the floor, and frantically drew a threshold with the blue chalk. Then he used his knife to trace the form of a door in the air.

Three of them appeared, lined up in a row, identical—except the one on the right bore the graffiti "JS." With his hand on the knob he turned around. If he could somehow grab Genie before Alice broke loose, could he take her with him? But he'd already tried that, more than once, and he and his daughter both knew the door would let him pass, and no one else. "Genie!" he called out. "Sweetheart. I'll find a way to bring you back."

He had the door half-open, he could even smell the oil and grease air of Empire Garage, when his daughter called to him. "Daddy?" she said in a voice that sounded like she was eight. "Daddy? Did I kill Mommy?"

"No, baby," Jack said. "It wasn't you. It was the geist." And at that moment Alice fury broke loose to fly at him, and it was all he could do to slide through the door and slam it shut before Alice crashed into the back of it.

Jack didn't realize he was on the floor until Barney reached down to help him up. And then the shock of that, Barney getting off his chair, helping him, touching him, shocked Jack back to where he was.

"Hey, Jack," Barney said. "Looks like you had a rough time of it in there."

"Yeah," Jack said as he got to his feet. He looked down at his torn shirt and jeans, the bloody scratches and bites on his chest and arms. Holding his breath, he reached up to touch his face. His fingers came away with more blood on them, but he was pretty sure he was himself.

"You want to sit for a moment?" Barney said. "You look a little wobbly." He gestured with his head toward the gray metal chair against the wall.

Jack smiled, surprised he could do it. He said, "So if I sit down does that mean I become the Door Man? And you wander off, and what, go get laid for the first time in a thousand years?"

Barney laughed. "Ha. You wish, kid. You don't get to guard the door just by sitting in my seat. We've got standards."

"Barney," Jack said, "you knew, didn't you? That's why you didn't recognize me at first. You saw the other face, overlaid on top of mine."

Barney shrugged. "Yeah. I saw it."

"Then why the hell didn't you tell me? I almost died."

"Not my job."

"What? Do you guys have some kind of union or something?"

"Kind of like that" Barney said.

Jack burst out laughing, then stopped, afraid he couldn't control it. "Jesus," he said. "I've got to get home somehow. Without attracting any cops or ambulances."

Barney said, "You can use the employees locker room, sixth floor. There's a shower. I figured you might need a change of clothes so I put out an Empire uniform for you. But don't worry, putting it on won't trap you into parking cars for all eternity."

Jack smiled. "Thanks, Barney. You're all right."

Jack was at the stairway door when Barney called to him. He turned, and Barney said, "I've got something for you. Might come in handy." He tossed a small bright object at Jack who caught it in his right hand. When he looked in his palm, Jack saw it was a gold skeleton key, about three inches long. The head consisted of three flat circles, while seven short prongs formed the lock end.

Jack stared at it a long time. Finally he looked up at Barney. "Holy shit," he said.

Barney's face turned hard, and when he spoke the old-man folksiness had vanished from his voice. "Jack Shade!' he said. "You give that sonofabitch what he deserves!"

Jack stood across the street from William Barlow's house. It was early evening, and Jack might have worried that Barlow would spot him, except it was Jack Shield time, and he was good at that. After cleaning up as best he could at the garage, Jack had not returned to the Hôtel de Rêve Noire. Long ago he'd made it a rule not to go back until the job was finished, and this William Barlow assignment was a long way from over. So he'd gone to a small office he kept, where he changed clothes, treated his cuts, and packed up a few supplies. Before he'd set out for Barlow he'd spent a long time staring at the key. Could he use it for what he really wanted? Would it obey him? Or did Barney charge it for one purpose and one purpose only?

He was half deciding to try it when Ray appeared in the small office, standing in front of the door. Slowly, the fox shook his head. "Oh hell," Jack said. "Yeah, I know." When he put the key back in his pocket Ray vanished.

Now he watched Barlow's McMagic Mansion and debated the best way to get inside. He imagined kicking in the door and catching Barlow in the act of sacrificing some small creature. In the end he just muttered, "Fuck it" and walked up and rang the bell.

William Barlow opened the door wearing a green sweat suit and holding the *New York Times* Auto section. The moment he saw Jack his mouth fell open and he stepped backward. With his free hand, the left, he made a gesture to bar the threshold.

"Oh, William," Jack said. "Really? You think you can keep me out?" He snapped his fingers and a small capsule he'd been holding broke and scattered bright green powder in the air. The green flared as the powder absorbed the blocking spell, then fell dully to the floor.

Barlow's face visibly composed itself into a friendly smile. "Keep you out?" he said. "Why would I do that? I've been waiting for you. What happened? Did you find Alice? Could you help her?" Jack walked around him, once, twice, counterclockwise, always keeping his eyes on Barlow, his face, his feet, but especially his hands. "What are you doing?" Barlow said. "Why don't you tell me what happened? Is she—" In the middle of talking he brought his hand up for a blinding spell.

Jack stiffened his fingers to dagger Barlow's hand, then kicked the man's legs out from under him. As Barlow fell Jack said, "You stupid sonofabitch. Do you think you can attack *me*? You may have been good enough to cloak what you were doing when you sent me to the Forest, but in an open fight? I'm a Traveler, Willie. Do you have any idea what that means?"

Barlow didn't try to get up. Lying on his side on the floor he moaned, "Please. I have no idea what you're talking about."

"Still?" he said. "Still playing Dumb Billie? Then let me tell you, so you'll know it's too late.

"I'm going to guess something—in all your lies there was one thing that was the truth. When you said you were supposed to go first. You could tell, couldn't you? Was it just your EKG, or did you find some blind seer? Hell, maybe you did a casting yourself. And there it was. William Barlow, dead in six months. Am I right, Willie?"

Barlow said nothing, and Jack went on, "You just couldn't stand it. The great magician, the scholar, dead, and your slow dumb wife gets to live. Gets your money, too. Waste it on her stupid feel-good workshops."

"Please," Barlow said. "It wasn't like that. I loved her."

"Sure you did, Willie. You just loved yourself a lot more. So you killed her. Took all that healthy life force for yourself."

Barlow began to cry.

"Problem solved," Jack said. "Only, Alice started coming back. The Forest appeared to you. All those voices. And one of them was hers. Did you imagine you could hear her? Was she calling your name?"

"Please," Barlow said, "I would have lost—"

"*Lost*?" Jack yelled. "You sonofabitch, I lost my wife and my daughter on the same day! My daughter killed my wife, and then I—" He had to stop, his whole body was shaking.

When Jack spoke again his voice was hard and measured. "Yeah, you didn't want to lose. All that great juju you'd built up wouldn't help you at all if Alice could get hold of you. You needed to get her off the scent, and what better way than to send in a substitute? A fake Billie who would go right up to her and she could tear his throat out and go off all satisfied."

He squatted down to put his face close to Barlow's. "It was the water, wasn't it? I wanted to link us—you and me—so I could find Alice. But you charged the water so it would begin something else. Lay your face on top of mine. And then the dressing room—that was to keep the link open, right?" He stood up again, said, "How long did it take to build up enough mojo to make it all work?" Barlow said nothing. Jack kicked him in the ribs. "How long?"

Barlow cried out then said, "Three months!"

"And God knows what you did in those three months to get yourself ready. A whole lot of nasty."

"Please," Barlow said. "What—what are you going to do to me?"

Jack grinned. "Do, Willie? I'm not going to do anything to you." He watched the hope flicker in Barlow's face. Then Jack took out the gold key and held it up by its three-ring head. In the dim entryway the seven prongs sparkled with their own brilliance. Jack said, "*Hey! Magic boy!* Do you know what this is?"

For just a moment, Barlow stared at it, confused. Then he screamed. Jack nodded. "Did your research, did you?"

Barlow scrabbled backward along the floor until he bumped into a table along the wall. "Please," he said. "I can help you. I can give you things. I'll work for you. I've got money. I know things. *Please.*" Jack said nothing, only took out his chalk and drew a blue threshold on the polished wood floor. "Oh my God," Barlow said. With his knife, Jack traced the outline of a door in the air. A faint image appeared, and when he held up Barney's key an actual door appeared in the room. No rough garage metal this time, but proper suburban polished wood and frosted glass, with a keyhole rimmed in gold. Barlow gagged, as if he was trying to scream but couldn't get it out. Finally he cried, "Shade! I'll give you everything."

"Oh, Willie," Jack said. "Don't you get it? You don't have anything. You're finished."

"No! You're wrong. I can help you get your daughter back."

Jack went up to him, and for a long moment stared at Barlow's frantic face. "You're a liar, William Barlow. A liar to the end."

"No, no, no. I can do it. Really."

Jack wasn't listening. He shoved in the key harder than necessary, and for a moment worried it night have jammed. But no, the prongs meshed into the tumblers, which Jack knew were layers of reality, entire worlds. The key turned and the worlds shifted into place, and when Jack opened the door he saw darkness, lit only by pale tendrils of fire.

The whispers roared in the room, nearly drowning out Barlow's desperate cries. When they died down Jack could hear the mixed growls and laughter of the wild beast that once was Alice Barlow.

He didn't stay to watch, there was nothing there he needed to see. He walked out of Barlow's house, leaving behind wild thrashing sounds and the smell of blood.

When he got back to the hotel, Jack entered through the basement and went up in the service elevator to get to his room. He took a long shower, then sat on his bed even longer, trying not to think. Finally he got dressed, a blue oxford shirt, tan pants, and a blue silk jacket. He stared for a moment at the pile of black clothes lying on the floor, then left the room and went back out via the service elevator.

He entered through the front door now, and there in the lobby stood the hotel owner, carefully setting roses, one by one, in a green vase. He watched her for a while, admiring the grace and economy of her movements in a gray wool dress. "Hello, Irene," he said.

She turned quickly, with a bright smile. "Jack! Welcome home." She wore a small gold pendant of an owl he'd once given her, on a thin gold chain. "Would you like a drink?" She set down the final three roses in front of the vase.

"That would be wonderful," Jack said.

In Irene's small office, with a glass of brandy before each of them, Irene said, "Annette called. She asked me to invite you to a game in Philadelphia. Next Tuesday. Old-fashioned, she said, the way you like it. And then she said the oddest thing. I wrote it down to make sure I got it right." She picked up a small piece of paper. "It was two things, actually. She said blindfolds would not be necessary." Jack smiled. "And she said to tell you she would prefer it if you would leave your fox at home."

Jack stared at her for a moment, then burst out laughing.

On September 17th, 2004, the fourteenth birthday of one Eugenia Shade, a bottle of beer flew off the kitchen table and smashed itself against the wall. Eugenia's father, a Traveler named Jack, sometimes called Care Free Jack, or Johnny Easy, had just told his daughter she could not drink beer, and so she laughed at the broken glass and the amber puddle on the floor.

Over the following weeks more and more things surrendered their stationary lives to take flight. A personal CD player smashed through a window. Chairs rearranged themselves in a wild dance. Any jar of food left out on a table or shelf was likely to destroy itself.

Eugenia's mother, Layla Shade, originally thought some action of her husband's had backfired, or worse, some spirit he'd angered had invaded their home. No, her husband told her, it was Eugenia herself, or rather an energy configuration, a poltergeist, that sometimes entered teenage girls. He told her their daughter was just an innocent host, but he knew it was more complicated than that. Geists, Jack knew, fed on the confusion, anger, and surging desires of adolescence. Eugenia wasn't doing it, but probably liked the fear and confusion she saw in her mother.

Weeks, then months, went by, and Layla begged Jack to do something, an exorcism, a spell, *something*, she hated being so nervous around her own daughter. Her husband assured her that geists were basically harmless, that teenagers almost always outgrew them, and that aggressive action might only make things worse. Not nearly as certain as he pretended, Jack secretly spent many hours online, especially in the Travelers Archive, a collection of research and first-person accounts that once was stored in underground vaults. Pretty much all of it confirmed what he'd told his wife.

Still, Jack went so far as to consult his old teacher, whom he had not seen or spoken to in years. "So the archives are right?" he told her. "I do nothing?"

Anatolie, as she was called, was a large woman with long thick dreadlocks that coiled around her massive belly like protective snakes. Despite her size, she lived in a fifth-floor walkup in Chinatown, in an apartment Jack always thought was too small for her, let alone a visitor. She agreed with his assessment, but then mentioned, in an offhand manner, "You might want to build up credit."

"Credit?"

"Yes. A conditional vow in case you need help and don't have time to perform the necessary appeasements. If everything goes smoothly you will have no need to invoke it."

"What kind of help?" Jack asked. And, "Help against what?"

Anatolie didn't answer. By her expression she seemed to have lost interest in Jack entirely.

Down in the street, outside grocery stalls filled with bitter melon and *gai lan*, Jack called his wife to tell her he had to go out of town for a couple of days. Layla was not happy. "You're going traveling?" she said. "Leaving me alone with this?"

"It's not a job," Jack said. "It's to get help."

Layla was silent a moment, then said, "So if you—do whatever it is—will that stop it?"

"Probably not. Or not exactly. But it will give us some insurance."

Layla sighed. "Come back as soon as you can," she said, and hung up.

Jack rented a car and drove upstate to a place he knew in the woods. The site was not an original but a cognate, a spot with the right configurations to stand in for a location where ceremonies were enacted thousands of years ago. There he lit four small fires, to mark out the action, but also because it was March and he would have to strip naked. Once his clothes were off he used an all-black knife Anatolie once gave him to draw a cross in the dirt connecting the fires. Now he drew the knife down the center of his body from his forehead to his groin. A charge ran through him and he gasped in the chilly air.

Setting aside the knife he picked up a business card he'd designed for himself, and a magic marker, then stepped into the circle to lie down on the axis between the two largest fires. Beyond the circle he could hear an owl, a deer crashing through some low branches, and a brief high-pitched cry that sounded like a woman's scream but probably was a coyote. He thought about what he was about to do, wondered if there was some other way. It was still likely the geist would just retreat and his vow would come to nothing. But if his daughter needed him . . .

Jack Shade was a freelancer. Jack Choice, as another Traveler once called him, liked to pick his cases, liked to turn away clients who annoyed him. It was one of the reasons he'd broken with Anatolie, who considered Travelers "servants of the soul." But when you ask for help you have to offer something precious.

He held the card up high in his right hand. "I, John Marcus Shade," he said, "make this vow in honor of my daughter, Eugenia Carla Shade. If she ever needs help, if she ever needs a path to open for her, I make this promise. From the moment I should invoke this vow, anyone who finds and brings *this* card may compel my service. I may not refuse them, I may not turn them away. I offer this for the sake of my daughter Eugenia. May she never need it. May this vow never be invoked." Then he stabbed the card down onto his solar plexus.

The fires all flashed high then burned out at the same moment. Even as he lay on the dark cold dirt Jack realized he could not feel the card on his body.

Too exhausted to drive further than the next cheap hotel, Jack got home the next day. The moment he stepped in the house Layla ran up and grabbed his arms. "Did you do something?" she asked, "Did it work?"

Nervously, Jack said, "I did something. But we won't know. Not for a while."

Layla pulled back from him. "No," she said. "You were supposed to fix this. I can't stand it anymore." Jack looked past her to see his daughter on the wooden stairs to the bedrooms. She was wearing a too tight halter top and too short miniskirt, and spike-heeled sandals—everything her mother would have forbidden if Layla wasn't afraid of her. She raised her middle finger toward her mother, and then clumsily walked upstairs with an exaggerated sway of her narrow hips. They'd reached a dangerous stage, Jack thought. The poltergeist wasn't Genie but she wanted to believe it was. She liked the power.

Jack spent the night on the couch. When his wife told him she wanted to be alone he did not contest it.

He slept late, woken finally by the sound of his wife's voice, high and tight as she shouted at her daughter. Jack ran into the kitchen. The date was March 9, 2005.

The first thing Jack saw was his wife, dressed in a blue sweat suit, shouting at their daughter, who was laughing as she leaned back against the doorway to the dining room. Eugenia wore a red dress and her old faded black Mary Janes. And then Jack ignored them, suddenly focused on everything else he saw in the kitchen. Iron pots. Large ladles. *Knives.*

Eugenia said, in a singsong taunt, "Good morning, Daddy. Mommy seems all upset about something."

Jack ignored her. "Layla," he said, trying to keep his voice even, "what are you doing?"

"I'm making lunch!" his wife shouted. "I'm making lunch—for my family—in my own fucking kitchen."

Jack said, "We agreed—"

"No! You agreed. You gave the order. The great Jack Shade the Traveler. I won't live like this any more. My husband and my *daughter* don't get to boss me around in my own kitchen."

Jack turned to Eugenia. In that same steady voice he said, "Genie, I need to talk to your mother. Please leave the kitchen."

His daughter laughed. "Whatever," she said, and moved from the doorway. Then, "Nah, I think I'll stay," and she went back to where she'd been standing. "This is too much fun."

Layla said, "Goddamn it, do what your father says. I don't care what *thing* you've got inside you. You're fourteen years old and he's your father. If he tells you to do something you do it."

"Please," Jack said. Later he would wonder if he'd been speaking to his wife, his daughter, or the "thing." It didn't matter. None of them was listening.

A pot flew past Jack's head to hit the wall opposite the stove. Hot tomato sauce spilled down to cover a framed photo of the three of them at Disneyland when Eugenia was seven.

Layla screamed. Eugenia jumped up and down and clapped her hands. "Good one!" she said. "Let's see what else we can do."

"Genie!" Jack cried. "This isn't you. You can fight it."

"Why?" she said. "It's fun."

Then the knives started. They came at Jack, all different sizes, end over end or straight toward him. He flailed his arms like a windmill, spraying blood even as he batted most of them away. It was the smaller ones that got through his defense. Two small paring knives and a long-tined fork caught his right jaw and the side of his neck.

And then it was over. Jack was on his knees, his left hand pressed against his neck to stanch the blood. He saw his daughter first. She stood frozen in the doorway, ludicrous in her cheerful red dress, her mouth open but unable to make a sound. He looked at her for a long time, afraid to turn his head. When he finally did he saw his wife, and there she was, his beloved Layla, on the floor in a thick puddle of blood. The vegetable cleaver that lay next to her had cut right through her jugular. He crawled over to her and cradled her empty body.

"Daddy," Eugenia whispered. "I didn't—it wasn't—"

"I know, baby," Jack said. "It wasn't you. It's not your fault."

Eugenia said, "Help me. I don't think I can hold it." The knives had begun to swirl around her legs, a few inches from the floor.

"I know," Jack said again. His voice wet, he called out, "I, Jack Shade, invoke my vow. I demand payment!"

"Daddy?" Eugenia said. "What are you doing?"

Ignoring her, Jack said, "Take her somewhere. Somewhere safe, where she can't hurt anyone."

For months afterward Jack would wonder—did he want what happened? Was he trying to punish her? He would lie in bed and try to bring back that exact moment. He could never decide.

A door appeared in the room. Stone, unmarked. "Oh my God" Jack whispered. Then, "No! *That wasn't what I meant.*"

Eugenia just stood there, looking up at the door that somehow stood taller than the room. Jack called out "Genie. Get away from it. You don't have to go there." But she didn't move, and neither did her father, though he fought to get up against an invisible hand that pressed him to the floor, even as he yelled to his daughter to run.

The door swung open, and Jack heard the Forest before he saw it—wind first, then voices, swirls of hushed voices. As it opened wider, so that his daughter stood framed in clouds of trees, Jack tried once more to move, but now he couldn't even speak, not to tell Eugenia to fight, not to try once more to take back his vow. He could only watch as his daughter walked, robot-like, into the world of whispers.

And then the door closed, and a moment later vanished, and he was all alone, Jack Shade with his dead wife in his arms— Johnny Lonesome, on the floor of a kitchen covered in blood.

2
THE QUEEN OF EYES

J ACK SHADE STOOD WITH A GLASS OF LAPHROAIG SINGLE malt and looked out the window of his room in the Hôtel de Rêve Noire, the small Art Deco building on 35th Street where he'd lived for the past seven years. Down below, people were hurrying through the streets, clutching their coats against their bodies to shield them from the gusts of wet November wind as New York prepared for yet another "freak" storm. In the press and on TV, people argued over whether it was global warming or just unlucky coincidence, and what, if anything, should be done about it. Jack didn't know much about climate change. What he did know was that this particular string of storms came out of a really bad contract a foolish magus had signed half a century ago, up the Hudson in Tarrytown. How naïve did a wizard have to be to make a compact with a storm elemental?

Jack sipped his whisky. Right now NYTAS, the New York Travelers Aid Society, of which he was officially a member, would be gathered down by South Street Seaport, chanting, casting spells, laying down sigils and vêvés, in other words, doing whatever they could to protect the city. Jack knew he should be there. Arthur Canton, the current Chief of NYTAS, considered Jack a weak link and blamed him for how ineffective their configurations seemed to be, how the city still got flooded and houses still got blown down.

Callous Jack, they called him. The nickname originated in a knife fight Jack had gotten into outside the Bronx Gate of Paradise (every borough had a gate, with two on Staten Island). The name had stuck beyond its origin, and now the New York Travelers used it whenever Jack refused to help them.

It wasn't true, of course, the idea that Jack didn't care. The fact is, every Traveler has limited resources for this sort of thing, and if Jack was going to take on the role of Fairweather Johnny and become a weather witch, he had to choose—give his small energy to help spread what little protection NYTAS could muster for the whole city, or focus everything he had on guarding the hotel.

Travelers don't take much to witchery. They might struggle with elementals, or the endless visitors from Above or Below that seemed to find our world so fascinating, but they didn't like to mess with such things as hurricanes or droughts. With every storm, Jack waited until it was nearly on them, telling himself that this time it would be okay to join the others. Sometimes he even got everything ready to go help. But then he would always remember the year a blizzard had shattered the windows on three floors of the building's north side, and how Irene Yao, the hotel's owner, had just stood and stared at the smashed Hepplewhite chairs, the ruined Mantegna print, the stained rugs. And then he would sigh, realize he was stalling by constantly checking the Traveler meta-weather app on his iPad, and just head up to the roof to guard the Rêve Noire.

So now Johnny Witchboy had cast his protective net over the hotel, and was back in his suite drinking whisky , and thinking he might go wander among the crowds stocking up on batteries and candles. He felt a slight brush against his right leg and looked down to see the subtle red glow of Ray, his fox spirit companion. Jack raised his glass in a toast. "We did our best," he said, "Let's hope it works." Ray sat back on his haunches and dipped his head. Spirit foxes come in various forms, but Ray was a Fox of the Morning, a solar emanation, useful for weather work, and he'd been with Jack when Jack had been doing his work up on the roof. "Thanks," Jack said, and took a drink.

Ray vanished as a soft knock came at the door of Jack's suite. *Oh hell*, Jack thought. He knew that sound. "Miss Yao," he said as he opened the door, and there she was, in a pale lavender wool dress and gray, low-heeled pumps, her smooth, almost translucent face carefully without expression as she held out the silver tray with the cream-colored business card. "Mr. Shade," she said. It was only *Miss Yao* and *Mr. Shade* when she brought the card.

There were four lines on the card: *John Shade,* followed by *Traveler,* then *Hôtel de Rêve Noire, New York,* and finally the black horse head knight from the Staunton chess designs.

Jack picked up the card. "Thank you, Miss Yao," he said. "Who have I got this time?" Due to a self-inflicted bad bargain that only made a tragedy worse, Jack Shade could not refuse any client who came to him with his business card.

"A woman. Mid-forties, I would say. She looks . . . suburban. Like a soccer mom, if one still uses that expression." Jack nodded. Irene's voice was never less than elegant, with hints of her long-ago operatic career, but Jack knew her well enough to catch the worry under the surface. He doubted she knew much about what he did, what "Traveler" meant, but he suspected it was more than she pretended.

"Did she give her name?" Jack asked.

"Yes. Sarah Strand." She hesitated, then said "This is foolish, perhaps—she certainly sounded genuine when she said it—but I had the oddest sensation that the name was fake."

"An alias?"

"I'm not sure. More as if she indeed uses that name, yet somehow it is not entirely who she is." She looked down. "I'm sorry, I'm being anxious. And interfering in your business, which is worse."

Jack smiled. "Not at all. But I guess there's only one way to find out. Is she in the office?"

"Yes, of course."

Jack nodded to her. "Thank you, Miss Yao."

"Good luck, Mr. Shade."

Jack's office, a converted guest room on the second floor, had no computer or other office equipment, nothing more than an old library table and three red leather chairs. Jack used to keep a decanter of water on the table, with two of Miss Yao's crystal goblets, something for nervous clients to do with their hands, but even more, a chance to work an alignment if he might need to search the client's memories. After a recent incident, however, with a man named William Barlow, Jack no longer trusted such tricks. If a client's throat got dry, he or she could always get a drink from the bathroom.

Sarah Strand, or whoever she was, sat on the far side of the table, facing the door, her hands in her lap holding the clasp of a nondescript black leather purse, something she might have bought at any suburban mall. Jack guessed you could say the same for her tan pants suit, and tailored white blouse open at the neck, and her dark red synthetic wool coat draped over a chair. Her face was somewhat square but not enough to make her look heavier than her hundred twenty-five pounds or so. Her brown hair was neck length and cut in layers to try to give it more body than it actually had. She wore no wedding or engagement ring, but her right pinkie held a small but good quality sapphire in a simple gold setting. Jack wondered if it had belonged to some relative.

"Mr. Shade?" she said, half rising until Jack waved her down again.

"I'm Jack Shade," he said, and took the chair opposite her.

"I'm Sarah Strand. Thank you for seeing me." When Jack said nothing, she took a breath and went on. "It's about my mother, Mr. Shade. She's missing and I'm very worried about her."

Jack stared at her a moment. Not his kind of case, but then, she did have his card. "How long has she been gone?"

"It's only three days, and yes, I know that's not very long, and maybe you're thinking she probably just wanted to get away by herself for some reason. But it's not like her. We're very close, she would tell me."

"Does your mother live with you?"

"No, but her house is only a mile or so away. We see each other all the time."

"And where exactly is that?"

Sarah Strand's eyes darted to the side a moment. The question bothered her for some reason, though it seemed harmless enough to Jack. She said, "We both live just outside a small town upstate. Gold River."

Jack's eyes narrowed a moment. He *did* know that name, though he could not remember how. Ray appeared on the table top. He stared at Sarah Strand, or rather her hands, still holding the clasp of her purse. Ms. Strand, of course, took no notice, and a moment later Ray vanished.

Jack said "Perhaps you'd better tell me your mother's name."

"Oh, of course," she said, but there was the slightest hesitation. "Margaret Strand."

Jack took out a small black notepad and a retractable Japanese fountain pen from the jacket's side pocket and wrote down *Margaret Strand. Gold River, NY (??)* He said, "Does she live alone?"

"Yes."

"How about you?"

"I have a daughter. Julie. She's fifteen."

Dangerous age, Jack thought. Just a year older than his daughter Eugenia had been when a poltergeist entered her. He noticed that Sarah hadn't mentioned any men. Could the Strand women be Matriscas, mage-women who took male lovers only to get pregnant, making sure they only gave birth to girls? Was that why Ms. Strand had come to him rather than the cops or a regular P.I.? But wouldn't a Matrisca go to a female Traveler? And Sarah didn't look much like a sorceress.

He said "Ms. Strand, do you mind telling me how you got my card?"

"My mother had it. Years, I guess. It was propped up against a small netsuke carving of a frog."

Despite himself, Jack's eyebrows shot up. How did this Margaret Strand know about *that*? Jack's involuntary service with the Council of Frogs was something he never told anyone. He wrote *CF?* on his pad, then said, "Have you spoken to the police?"

"No. They wouldn't—they wouldn't understand."

"How about the hospitals? I don't want to alarm you, but perhaps your mother was in an accident."

She stared down at her hands, and something stirred in Jack's spine. *Hands*, he thought, but couldn't make the connection

"No," she said. "It can't—I would know if something happened to her. If she was—" She looked up at him. "Believe me, Mr. Shade—I would *know*."

47

Jack turned his business card over in his hands. He couldn't refuse her if she really wanted him, but he could try to make her understand it was pointless. "I'm sorry, Ms. Strand, but I don't really see what I can do for you. I don't know what impression your mother gave you, but I'm not a detective. And I'm afraid that's what you need. I wouldn't even know where to start with a missing person case."

She sighed. "Mr. Shade," she said, "I'm afraid I haven't been entirely honest with you. Margaret Strand is not my mother's real name. Well, it is, it's the name on her driver's license, the name on her checkbook. But it's not actually who she is. Her true name, Mr. Shade, is Margarita Mariq Nliana Hand."

Jack jumped to his feet, knocking the chair over behind him. "Holy shit!" he said. "*Your mother is the Queen of Eyes!*"

Jack had met the Queen once, on a California beach just before dawn.

After all his years as a Traveler, after the poltergeist killed his wife and got his daughter banished to the Forest of Souls, after he came close to losing himself in the Ibis Casino, Jack had thought he'd seen everything. Implacable Jack, some called him. But it wasn't until he met the Queen that Jack understood what it meant to *see* at all.

It was right after the Sibyl War, the battle between oracular email services that Jack got stuck adjudicating. Jack hadn't wanted to be involved. These things always ended badly, he told himself. Hermaphrodite Teiresias having to tell Zeus and Hera whether men or women enjoyed sex more—Paris of Troy having to judge a goddess beauty pageant—disasters no matter which side you picked. So he'd really wanted to say no, and in fact, no one had come with his card that time, so theoretically he could have, but the case had come from COLE, the Committee Of Linear Explanation, and they didn't need his card. Jack owed them. After Layla's death, and Eugenia's disappearance into the Forest, Jack had had no choice but to contact COLE to cover it all up so he wouldn't have to tell any Normal Police what had happened to Mr. Shade's family, and where did he get that very nasty cut down the right side of his jaw? So when the Shadow Man stood in Jack's bedroom and told him the Committee would very much appreciate it if Mr. Shade would act as judge in the conflict between Ghostmail and Jinn-net, what could Jack do? Luckily he'd managed to survive the experience, suggesting that the two systems each launch an IPO and let the market decide. Grateful to not have his insides boiling, or his eyes turned to cockroaches, Jack had left the Night Castle, the Travelers' hostel on the coast just south of San Jose, and decided to take a walk along the Secret Beach.

He'd been up all night, and the sky was just growing light enough to streak purple and orange and reveal the odd little figurines hidden among the pine trees, when Jack heard a wail, a short, high-pitched blast of sorrow that knocked him backwards. He'd looked all around until he saw a young woman in a tattered black dress kneeling before an older woman whose long hands rested on the young one's shoulders.

Jack stared and stared at the older figure. She kept *changing*. One moment she seemed a 50s suburban housewife with brassy hair, the next a businesswoman in a light blue pantsuit, and then something else entirely, dull and wood and covered in leaves, or else with water constantly running down her body, like one of those urban fountains where water streams down a marble wall only to be pumped back to the top to do it all over again.

Jack couldn't look away. His teacher, Anatolie, had always told him that the main attribute of a Traveler was True Sight, the ability to see things as they really are, and after her training, Jack had considered himself pretty good at it. During his apprenticeship she would send him places—Macy's ground-floor escalator on Christmas Eve, Herman Melville's house on Long Island across from the Walt Whitman shopping center, a biker bar on N. Moore Street—and tell him to say what he saw. If he'd reported frantic shoppers checking their lists, Anatolie would bark into his bluetoothed ear "Look again!" and, "Again," and, "See what there is to see," the first line of the ancient Traveler's

Directive: *See what there is to see/Hear what there is to hear/ Touch whatever you touch/Speak the thing you must speak.* Only when he could tell her that for some riders the escalator did not end at the 2nd floor, but rose and rose until they were swallowed in a green cloud would Anatolie grunt and say, "Good enough, Jack. Come home now."

So Jack had stared at the woman, trying to figure just what the hell she was, until the younger one, the one on her knees, the one who didn't change shape but only bent forward and wept, suddenly cried out, as if something had burned her. "Hey!" Jack called, "what are you doing to her?"

The young woman didn't move but the older one lifted her head, and without looking at him, she'd said, "John Shade, you have no stake here. Leave now, without blame."

Confused, Jack had wondered if he'd met her. It was never good when someone knew your name and you had no idea of theirs. Was she some kind of Power? But it didn't matter, he'd decided, he couldn't just walk away. He'd done that too much in his life.

"No," he'd said, and hoped he sounded confident. "Not until you tell me what is going on."

For a moment, the woman had stayed still, but then she nodded, as if to herself, and turned to face him. She looked now like some ancient forest creature standing on its hind legs, for leaves swirled all around her body. Then she raised her hands to frame her face, palms facing Jack, with her fingers together pointing at the sky. "John Shade!" she called, and her voice had cut him like the wind on the stretch of Avenue D that Travelers called The Empty Window. "*See what there is to see!*"

Jack stared at the hands. The skin appeared to move and shift, to reveal something hidden. Eyes. A large, unblinking eye watched him from each palm, and he wanted to turn away but he couldn't, he could only look, until eyes appeared within the eyes, and more eyes on the fingertips, and Jack discovered he could see out of every one of them, see everywhere, everything, all at once.

Around the world, so-called psychics were looking, searching—cards laid on silk cloths, hungry faces staring into crystal balls, nervous hands casting cowrie shells or bamboo sticks, fingertips on photos or trinkets of the dead—they were all trying to see. And most had no idea that it all passed through her. The open channel, the transformer. Mariq Nliana. The Queen of Eyes.

When Jack tried to look away, he'd discovered the eyes were all over his body, like a swarm of spiders. He wanted to swat them but didn't dare, for fear of what they might show him if he got them angry. And then it was over. He was himself again, standing on a rocky beach with pine trees behind him, and hidden in the high grass the small grimacing figurines that may or may not have been carved, but were certainly far older than the trees.

The Queen had settled on her corporate woman-of-the-world-look. Pant suit, smart, expensive shoes, shoulder-length blonde hair. She looked, oddly, like a former Secretary of State. The young woman was still on her knees but now rested her head against the Queen's belly while the Queen stroked her hair. Looking past the girl, the Queen said gently, "You did well, Jack. Go home now and rest."

In his office in the Hotel Rêve, Jack calmly picked up his chair and sat down again as if his outburst had never happened. He observed Sarah Strand a moment. She appeared unperturbed by his reaction, and it occurred to him that if the Queen had kept Jack's card on display (*no wonder she knew about the frogs,* he thought, *she's the fucking Queen*), then her daughter would simply trust him, no matter how unprofessional he seemed. The real question was, how could the Queen of Eyes be missing? He said "Are you sure she's not just doing her duty someplace beyond reach?"

Sarah shook her head. "No, she always keeps in touch."

"How? Some sort of psychic eyespeak?"

Thin smile. "Only if there's no cell coverage."

"And you know she's alive because you would—"

"Become Queen as soon as she died."

"So until then, do you have any power of your own?

"No. Oh, I suppose maybe I can sense certain vague things, like whether someone's going to call. But many people can do that. To be honest, Mr. Shade, being the Queen of Eyes is pretty much all or nothing. And there's only one."

"Does that excite you? Becoming Queen?"

She frowned. "Excite me? I remember when my mother became Queen—when my grandmother died. It was a Saturday, of course." Jack frowned at the odd statement but didn't interrupt. Sarah said, "We knew Grandma was sick, but really, we didn't expect—we were home, taking a break from the hospital. And then, out of nowhere, the strangest look came over my mother. She kind of gasped, and then she turned over her hands and stared at her palms, and suddenly she started crying, and whispered to me, 'Grandma is dead.' So am I excited at the idea of becoming Queen? No, Mr. Shade. I would rather have my mother."

Jack blurted out, "I met her."

"Really. In her aspect?"

"Yes."

"Then I'm sure you can't think of her any other way. It's very impressive, I know. But she's my *mother*. When I think of her it's not what she can do, not what I will have to do after—it's how she kissed my forehead when I had a fever, or the video games she played with me on rainy afternoons. In the weekend I graduated college, she'd off in South America somewhere, doing God knows what for some group of defrocked shamans or something. But she made sure to come back and sit in the front row and embarrass me by yelling and releasing a flood of owl-shaped balloons when I got my diploma." She stopped, took a breath. "Please, Mr. Shade. You have to find her."

"What about your father?"

"I'm sorry?"

"Did you have one?"

"Of course. We don't reproduce parthenogenetically."

"Then what about him? What did *he* do when you had a fever?"

"The fathers—they don't last long. It's not as if we deliberately push them away or anything. When I met . . . Julie's father, I told myself I would be different. My daughter would grow up knowing her dad for more than a few innocent years." She'd been looking away but now she stared at him. "It's just not possible. No matter how hard we try, there are things they can never know. Things our daughters *have* to know."

"What if you found someone who already knew?"

She laughed. "You mean a Traveler?"

"Or a mage. A seer."

"Mr. Shade, you met my mother. She let you see her. Did that leave you with the yearning to marry her?"

Jack didn't answer. It was all he could do just to hold her gaze without blushing. And yet, he found himself wondering how much this woman had lost in her life because of who her mother was. And how much she would have to change when her mother died, and she took over the family business. Did it terrify her? Thrill her?

He said, "I'll need to come out and see the home. That is the last place you saw her, right?" Sarah nodded. "All right, then. I'll go back with you tomorrow morning. You'll have to stay here tonight—the hotel will be safe but the roads won't be. Will your daughter be all right alone?"

"She's fifteen, she'll be thrilled."

"Good." Jack sat up. "I'll ask Miss Yao to give you a room. Assuming the roads are okay, we'll leave at nine." He walked out.

Jack headed for his room, but changed his mind and went up to the roof. Standing in the protective calm of his spell he watched the few people still on the street try to make their way through the rain. What would happen if they started to see what was really going on? There—that man yelling at a cab because it wouldn't stop for him. Suppose, just for a moment, he saw that Yellow Taxi as it really was, a Piss-Lion escaped from the Alchemical Zoo on top of the Metropolitan Museum of Art? Jack could see, but even he needed to concentrate.

There were people who thought Jack Shade didn't care about anything. Callous Jack, but also Jean Oui, a name given to him by the Societé de Matin, a group of gangster magicians formed in Paris in the eighteenth century. The American branch turned the pun around as Johnny Non. But it wasn't true that nothing mattered to Jack. It was just—seeing your wife cut apart by a poltergeist and your daughter taken out of the world made the things most people care about not very important.

He watched as a homeless woman pushed her stolen shopping cart furiously up the street, as if she had somewhere to hide from the snow. Across the street, a skinny ehite kid bumped up against a middle-aged businessman, also white, and picked his pocket. Storms were good for pickpockets, the marks having their minds on other things. When the businessman made it home and discovered his wallet gone, would he remember the kid but think he'd been black? Racism was a kind of magic, Jack knew, affecting what we see, or think we see.

You could cast a glamour over yourself and people would look right at you and see something completely false. The Societé de Matin operated that way. That, and spells of cruelty and raw violence. The Society of the Morning had come to America not long after its French beginnings. Some said Lafayette had been a member, others that Ben Franklin had brought it back from Paris. Its everyday schemes and crimes were run by the DHO, Deputy Head of Operations, who traditionally took Matin as his last name. Usually the American DHO came from the head office in Paris. The real power, however, lay with a figure called the Old Man of the Woods, a hermit sorcerer who lived in a stone cabin hidden in the French Alps. Recently, Jack had heard stories that the DHO had tried to stage some coup against the Old Man. He didn't know any more than that, and didn't want to know.

Down in the street, a woman in her thirties rushed her young daughter into a building. The little girl wore a red coat and yellow rain boots, and Jack was sorry to see that bit of brightness leave the street. He sighed and headed for the stairs down from the roof.

In the morning, it turned out that Sarah had come to New York on the bus, so Jack got his black Altima out of the hotel garage and they headed up the Thruway. Due to certain hidden design features, all Travelers drove Altimas. Happily, the only special feature Jack needed today was cruise control.

They rode mostly in silence. About halfway, Jack said, "So how did it begin?"

Sarah hesitated, then asked, "Begin?"

Jack was pretty sure she knew what he meant, and was sorry he'd said anything, but it was too late now. "Being the Queen," he said. "It goes from mother to daughter, but how did it start?"

Sarah didn't answer for awhile, then said, "Have you heard the stories?"

Every Traveler knew the various theories. One version said the Lord of Night fell in love with a human woman. Maybe the first human woman. When she slept with him, he granted her the power to see as a reward. Or a way to survive without him, since he knew how fickle he was. Or maybe she refused, and he gave her the sight as a curse that she would pass down through all her daughters.

Another claimed that the Shaper brought three women out of the rock and asked each one what she wanted. One looked at the flowers and the animals, and said she wanted children to love and to fill the Earth. The second watched birds mating in the sky, and said she wanted beauty, and desire that could never be contained or controlled. But the third looked at all the strangeness of the world, and then up at the stars, and said, "I want to *see*."

A third theory described a starving woman who'd been cast out of her tribe for disobedience, how she'd faked experience as an apprentice mage, and was hired by a sorceress to help stir up a batch of pseudo-immortality elixir to sell to some gullible king. Having no idea what she was doing, she burned her hands and thrust them into what she thought was a bucket of water. When she lifted them up again, she discovered they were covered with eyes.

"Sure," Jack said. "I've heard a whole slew of stories."

Sarah said, "Then you know as much as I do."

The moment Jack saw Margaret Strand's two-story house at the edge of Gold River, he realized he'd expected something different. More fake. Despite Sarah's insistence on her mother's off-duty life, Jack had expected to see a façade, an All-American front. But there was nothing Hollywood about the hundred-year-old house, with its white paint and green trim that would need a touch-up in the next year or so, or the weather-worn chairs on the front porch, or the remains of Halloween decorations, the not quite rotten pumpkin, the droopy, fake cobwebs, the plastic skeleton bent forward as if asleep, or maybe passed out after a party.

Sarah noticed Jack's stare and smiled. "My mother loves Halloween," she said. "She dresses up as a witch, pointy hat and all, and keeps a cauldron full of candy next to the door."

Inside, the house had that same comfortable realness. In the living room, a slightly sagging brown sofa and two maroon chairs were angled to face a forty-seven inch LED.

"New TV?" Jack asked. Sarah nodded. "What does she watch? Please don't say *Ghost Hunters* or that one about the Long Island psychic."

"No," Sarah said, looking around the room rather than at Jack, as if her mother might suddenly walk in with a jug of cider and a plate of homemade donuts. Except, of course, that Margaret Strand probably just bought her donuts at Krispy Kreme like everyone else. Sarah said, "She likes cop shows, mostly. Oh, and this time of year she gets all excited about those Christmas movies on Hallmark." Jack nodded. He knew the ones she meant, where a struggling single mom discovers that Santa has left the North Pole and is running a deli in Jersey. Layla used to watch them.

He looked about the room. An old oak table held a gallery of photos showing Margaret's daughter and granddaughter at various ages and life-events. A woman who was obviously

Margaret herself appeared in two or three of them. Jack picked one up and stared at it, trying to remember the different forms the Queen had taken that night on the beach, and if any of them looked like the proud grandma. He realized he was doing it again, trying to see the middle-aged woman in the photo—slightly overweight, not exactly stylish but not dumpy either—as a fake, a disguise. Maybe the changes were the disguise. The Queen was human, despite her powers. He put the photo back with the rest.

Sarah said, "Did you get anything?"

Startled, Jack realized she thought he'd been trying to absorb her mother's vibrations, as if he could sniff her and follow the trail like some psychic bloodhound. "No," he murmured, and wished he just hadn't answered.

He was about to leave the room when he spotted the small jade frog on a narrow ledge above the simple fireplace. When he walked over and picked it up he discovered it wasn't jade but emerald, and very old. It was probably worth more than the rest of the room, new TV included. He said, "This is where she had my card?"

Sarah nodded. "Yes, that's right."

"How long did she have it there? The card."

Sarah started to speak, then stopped. "You know," she said, "I wanted to say forever, that it was something I'd seen all through my childhood. But now I'm not sure." She frowned. "It could be—just a month? A few weeks?"

Jack put back the carving. So, he thought, she knew something was coming and wanted Sarah to find the card but think of it as automatic, something she'd known her whole life, as if her mother had said to her back in kindergarten, "If anything ever happens to me, sweetie, go find nice Mr. Shade. Don't forget, now."

Jack made a cursory search of the rest of the house but knew he wouldn't find any more signs of what he still considered Margaret's—*Margarita's*—true self. *Now what?* he thought. He couldn't just stand there. "Let's go look at your place," he said

When they got back in the car and drove a mile to Sarah's house, closer to the village, it was more of the same. The house was newer, a 1960s ranch with the same white and green paint scheme as Margaret's, but without the porch or Halloween decorations. It stood on a quiet street with other houses from roughly the same period, except for a McMansion that loomed over the rest of the block like an overdressed lottery winner at a neighborhood picnic.

A strictly clipped lawn went around the front and sides of Sarah's house. It looked absurdly green for mid-November. He glanced sideways at her. Did she get wood sprites in at night to water the grass with their golden-stream fertilizer? A lot of sprites were meth addicts and would do pretty much anything for a few bucks. Looking at the house again, Jack could see a white fence in the back, and the corner of a large propane barbecue. Somehow, the thought of the Queen of Eyes munching a hot dog made him queasy. A couple of maple trees and a young oak broke up the flawless lawn. The branches were bare, of course, but Jack didn't see a single leaf on the grass. He smiled a moment, remembering how hard it had been to get Genie to do any yardwork. He'd guessed it was Sarah who'd done all that raking. Or sprites.

"How long have you lived here?" he asked her.

"Eighteen years. It was Sam's—my husband's—idea. To get our own place, I mean."

Jack smiled. "He didn't want to live in his mother-in-law's house?"

Sarah looked away a moment. "I told him it was our ancestral home or something like that. But he insisted, and to tell you the truth, Mr. Shade, I didn't really mind having my own home."

"Yeah, and a whole mile from your mother. Sam must have loved that."

She laughed. "He used to say that my mother didn't have apron strings, she had steel cables."

"How long did he last?"

"Julie was four."

Inside, the house was a more up-to-date version of Margaret's, just as comfortable, just as anonymous, but with an Xbox hooked up to the TV, a couple of Impressionist posters, and a handful of teen gossip and sex magazines scattered around the gray carpeted floor. Looking at the magazines, and their owner, who sat cross-legged on a dark gray couch, fingers flying over her iPhone, Jack felt nostalgia stick a knife in him. He could see them so clearly, Layla screaming at their daughter to pick up her "trashy magazines," Genie rolling her eyes with that look that suggests all teenagers are prisoners of war.

"Julie," Sarah said, "this is Mr. Shade."

Julie didn't answer. Tall and thin, with long straight hair dyed black with pink highlights, she wore tight jeans tucked into black UGGs, and an open Gold River High hooded sweatshirt jacket over a pink top cut low to show off the skinny girl's brave attempt at push-up cleavage. She didn't look up.

Sarah's face took on a harried cast that once again reminded Jack of Layla. Sarah went on, "Mr. Shade is here to help us find out where Grandma has gone."

With a sigh, Julie looked Jack over as if he was auditioning to strip at her Sweet Sixteen party. "Yeah, I know," she said. "*Jack* Shade," she pronounced, in a tone that made his first name an obscenity her mother had always forbidden her to say. With a glance at his crotch she said, "Are you a private dick?"

"No," Jack said. "I'm a Traveler."

"Whatever." She started working her phone again.

Sarah said, "Honey, can you think of anything that might help Mr. Shade—Jack—find out what's happened to Grandma?"

Shrug. "He's the dick. Let him figure it out."

"Please. It's important."

"Why? Grandma's the damn Queen, isn't she? If she wants us to *see* her, she'll reveal herself."

"This is your grandmother," Sarah said sharply. "And being Queen is important. Very important. I thought you understood that."

Julie stood up now, even skinnier than Jack had thought. She raised her hands to the sides of her face, palms out, and wiggled her fingers as she rolled her eyes and made woo-woo noises. "Ooo, the Queen of Eyes." Abruptly, she dropped her arms. "I can't wait till it's my turn. I'll get to see geese shit in California, and fags screw in Philadelphia, and old men pissing themselves in the woods. Whoopee." She picked up her phone. "I'm going to my room. If Mr. Shady Dick wants to search me for clues, I'll be on my bed." For just a moment as Julie left the room, Ray appeared behind her, then flickered back out of existence, or at least out of sight.

Sarah looked down at the floor. "I'm really sorry about that," she said.

"Don't be," Jack said. "I have a teenage daughter myself." *Had*, he corrected himself, then immediately changed it back to *have*. Genie wasn't dead, she was just—out of reach. He tried to think smugly how even at her worst, his daughter had never been nearly as obnoxious as Julie Strand, but the thought of Genie was too painful. He brought his attention back to his client. "Can I look around the rest of the house?"

Sarah tried to smile, with limited success. "Sure. Hopefully my daughter won't leap out and bite you."

The house was a bit larger than it looked from the outside, with a dining area off the living room, three bedrooms, and two baths. A door in the hallway between the kitchen and the bedrooms led out to a simple cement patio with a wrought-iron table and chairs and the barbecue Jack had spotted from the driveway. Weren't they supposed to put a tarp over it? *City boy*, he told himself. Johnny Urban, knows the secret language of the Chrysler Building gargoyles, but not what you do with a barbecue in winter.

He glanced in at what was obviously Sarah's bedroom, his eye falling on the framed photo of Julie graduating Middle School. Jack had one of those. He went on to the guest room, which didn't look like it saw much use, and the bathrooms, where he opened the medicine cabinets and examined the prescription bottles, finding nothing special. He didn't bother to knock on Julie's door, though he did stop and listen to her muttering something into her phone. When he couldn't make anything out, he shrugged and walked on.

The fact is, Jack had no idea what he was doing. The best he could manage was to try and look professional so Sarah wouldn't lose confidence in him. He went back to the living room and kept a straight face as he said he had some "leads" he wanted to "follow up." Sarah was so desperate, she just nodded.

Jesus, Jack thought as he drove away from 19 Holly Drive. *What a disaster.* What the hell did he know about leads? What would he do next, go down to sleazy dives by the waterfront and knock back a few shots while he asked pointed questions until a couple of goons roughed him up and took him to see Mr. Big? He almost turned around when he realized he'd forgotten to ask Sarah for a photo of her mother. But what exactly would he do with it if he had it? "Oh, for fuck's sake," he said out loud, and swung the Altima onto Route 17 East, heading back to the Thruway. If in fact the Queen had placed his card there so he would be the one to investigate if "something happened" to her, he sure as hell couldn't figure out why.

He had just passed Goshen when something caught his eye. A billboard advertising one of those fake 1950s diners blocked most of the view toward the south, but he could still see a cone-shaped hill behind it, and at the top three pine trees, evenly spaced in a triangle. He grunted, then pulled off the road at the next exit, close enough that he could get out of the car and stare at the hill. Ray appeared alongside him, tail stiff, hair on his back standing up. Jack smiled down at the spirit fox. "Yeah, I see it," he said.

The one thing Jack had said that was completely true was when he'd told Julie Strand that he was not a detective, he was a Traveler. Maybe he knew nothing about how to search for clues but he knew how to ask for help. He got back in the car and drove as close to the hill as he could, then parked on the side of the road.

Up and down the country road Jack saw neat houses, a couple of anchored mobile homes, a small autobody shop, but right here, at the base of the hill, there were no signs of ownership. Only, the grass and weeds had obviously been cut, and the dirt and pebble path that snaked to the summit was clear of the rubbish and trash that tended to accumulate on unused property. As he walked to the top, Jack wondered if the land had passed from father to son for longer than anyone could remember, and every generation or two, someone would wonder why they never did anything with it. Or maybe it belonged to the town, and somehow any plans for a park, or offices, or senior housing just never went anywhere.

At the top of the hill, Ray held out a paw, like a dog trained to shake hands, then vanished before Jack might take hold of it. Jack frowned. He'd never seen Ray do that before, but he knew why the fox had to leave. Jack needed to stand in the exact center of the triangle and anyone else present would distort that, even an NT, a Non-Tangible.

One of the first things Anatolie had taught Jack was how to locate the center of an irregular plot of ground. Jack found the spot and nodded to each tree as if to a helper. Though they didn't look older than six or seven decades, the trees were probably old when the Seneca, or the Wampanoag, or the Mohegans first showed up here.

He inhaled deeply, in search of a certain smell, and there it was, cinnamon and cloves. Travelers called the long-lost people who created such places "precursors," and the conical hills "Pics," precursor information centers. Pics varied from place to place, but there was always the aroma, as if Pics were part of an office Christmas party. Down below, the sky had appeared gray, streaked with muddy-looking clouds, but here the sun shone.

For a moment, doubt stopped him. Was he really expecting to use an oracular hot spot to find the Queen of Eyes? If the Mother of all oracles had gone missing, how could he expect to find anything? But then he realized, he'd seen the Piss-Lion taxicab, he could still see Ray, and hadn't he spotted the trees?

Jack lay down on the damp grass. Well, it wouldn't be the first time he'd have to wander around in wet clothes. As usual when on a case, Jack had slipped his black knife into the sheath at the back of his right boot. Now he pulled it out to set it on his belly. The carbon blade glowed slightly, as if excited. Jack placed his palms flat on the grass, closed his eyes, and breathed deeply. He became part of the ground, his head and limbs like roots or a mud bank. The smell of cinnamon and cloves filled his blood.

Jack had no idea how much time passed before a slither on his belly brought him back to himself. When he opened his eyes, an albino snake, about two feet long, looked up at him from the middle of his chest. Jack reached for his knife.

This next part was tricky. You were supposed to kill the snake, but years ago, when Eugenia was seven, Jack had made the mistake of bringing her along on a Snake Enactment. He'd told her to stay in the car, but what kid would listen when Daddy was doing something mysterious? So she peeked, and became hysterical when Jack cut open the snake (green and yellow that time), and wouldn't calm down until Jack promised he would never ever do that again.

That was long ago, but for all Jack knew Genie could still watch him from the Forest. And besides, the one thing a Traveler must never do is break a vow. So now Jack looked at the snake, and said "I need a drop of your blood but that's all, I promise. Okay?" Ray appeared now and inclined his head towards the snake, as if to translate. The snake reared up and tilted back its head, as if to offer its neck.

With the tip of the knife, Jack made a small incision. A thin sheen of green ichor oozed out, almost fluorescent against the rubbery white skin. As soon as Jack had pressed a drop onto his finger the wound closed up, dry even before the snake darted back into the grass.

Jack stared at the bright green on his finger. Curiously, this particular bit of Traveler tech had leaked out to the outside world more than most, with anthropologists and folklorists going on about snake blood and "the language of birds." When Jack read these garbled accounts, he always got the impression this was supposed to be a glorious experience. Well, he thought as he placed the ichor on his tongue, they should try it.

It wasn't pain, or nausea, it was just that the very thing all those writers thought was so great could drive you crazy. Voices. Voices everywhere, nearby, across the globe, maybe on other planets. Loud, soft, subtle, blaring, and all of them chirping, singing, honking, squawking, tweeting. All over the world, in the sky, the forests, on the roofs of buildings, the birds were talking. And Jack Shade could hear them all.

He wanted to scream, to cover his ears, to yell at them to shut up. *God*, he thought, he'd forgotten how much he hated this. But all he could do was lie there, and wait. Sure enough, after a time it died down to a kind of background noise. Theoretically he could understand them all, that was the whole point, but in reality you had to wait for some single visitor to come talk to you in person.

All those anthros and linguists have come up with all sorts of reasons for the high value attached to understanding bird speech. Birds make beautiful sounds (*oh really*, Jack thought, *try discussing politics with a goose*), birds fly up to heaven and come back with messages from the gods (why would the gods build heaven where it was cold all the time and you could hardly breathe?). The simple fact was that birds are just incessant gossips. They can't resist telling you things.

More time passed, and then a large bird with brown feathers, a white chest, flattened head, and a crooked beak came and perched on Jack's chest. The claws hurt but he did his best to hide the pain. Birds could be very sensitive and fly off if he appeared to complain.

Some Travelers prepared for these things. They studied bird books, they practiced calls, they even carried baggies of seed. Jack just, well, winged it. The bird stared at him and he wished, not the first time, that birds could blink. He said, "Umm, thanks for coming to talk to me."

"Ach," the bird said, "it's not every day you get to speak with the great Johnny Shade."

Wonderful, Jack thought. *A sarcastic bird.* To make things worse, it spoke with a thick accent of some kind. "Noot ivery dee," that sort of thing. "The honor is mine," Jack said.

"How can I help you?" (Hoo kinna hoolp ya?)

"The Queen of Eyes is missing," Jack said. "I'm trying to find her."

The bird gave a shriek that made Jack want to cover his ears. The feathers stuck out in all directions, and for a moment, the creature lifted off his chest, only to dig deeper into his skin when it came down again. "We know, we know!" the bird said. "What d'you think everyone is talking about?" (Tawkin aboo.)

"Well, can you help me?" Jack said. "Do you know where she is? I'm pretty sure she's alive, but that's it."

"Aye, lost, lost. Think, Jackie. If Mother Nliana dinna wan' to be seen, d'ye think the whole clan could find her?"

Shit, Jack thought, *all that trouble and a ruined shirt for nothing.* But then the bird said "But I know what can help you." (noo whut kin hoolp yuh.)

Jack waited, then realized he was supposed to ask. "What?"

"Yuh nid to find the nude owl."

"I need to find what?"

The bird tilted back its head in what Jack guessed was the avian version of rolling its eyes. "The nude owl!" it repeated.

"I don't—oh! You mean the Know-It-All."

"Ay," the bird said with a kind of long-suffering sigh that its advice had penetrated the fog in Jack's brain.

The Know-It-All was a Knowledge elemental who lived in a homeless shelter, or else on the street, in New York. People thought of elementals as limited to the classic Fire, Water, Air, and Earth, but any discrete part of the world could generate its own elementals. There were politics elementals, sales elementals, talk-show elementals. But even though there were various knowledge elementals scattered across the world, there was only one Know-It-All. Or Nude Owl, as Jack was already starting to think of him. "Him" was really a term of convenience, for the Owl—the term somehow fit—wore so many layers of clothing, winter or summer, and talked so softly it was impossible to determine if "he" was male or female. Maybe those categories didn't apply to a Nude Owl.

"Thank you," Jack said. "That was a wise suggestion."

The bird fluttered its wings. "Tuuk lung enuuf," it said, then flew off. Jack stood up to watch it fly towards the weak November sun. Then he dusted himself off and headed back to his car, Ray loping alongside him.

The Risen Spirit Shelter occupied a former furniture store on 11th Avenue north of 54th Street. A brown sectional couch, a Formica-topped dining table, and a skinny floor lamp without a shade stood scattered in the window, as if the remains of a defunct business. The place was glammed, of course, to prevent people from seeing what really went on inside, but props never hurt. The group in charge of the place, the AADE, or Association of Angels, Demons, and Elementals, consisted of second-level Powers ("derivatives," as some Travelers called them) who found themselves more or less stuck on Earth by nature, choice, or exile. In their proper realms, angels and demons would never meet, and neither would ever consort with elementals. Stuck in the Outer World, however, they had no choice but to work together. The most common complaint at AADE meetings—besides the constant bickering over the order of the words in the title—was how cluttered and complicated the human world had gotten. When some overwhelmed derivative just couldn't take it anymore, just lost it, like any over stressed human, he or she or it often found themselves at Risen Spirit.

Oddly enough, the place was run by a human, a former venture capitalist named Andrew Martin. Martin had apparently realized the emptiness of his profession—some said the head of a company he raided had killed himself, others that his own company forced him out—and decided to "give back," or whatever the current buzz term might be. Right around that time, the AADE was having to admit that rotating the management of the shelter between the three constituencies just wasn't working. A simple rune-casting had led them to Andy Martin, who, like many corporate raiders, was a low-grade magus and could handle the culture shock of his new job.

Jack returned the Altima to the hotel garage and took a taxi to 11th Avenue. He could have glammed an illegal parking spot, but why bother? He told the Sikh driver to let him out at the corner and waited till the cab had gone a block before he walked to the shelter. An unnecessary caution, but what the hell. As he approached the building, he noticed a woman sitting on the curb, muttering as she sorted through a pile of crumpled newspapers. She obviously belonged to New York's army of crazies. Slightly less obvious was the fact that she wasn't human. Her night-black skin might be construed as pure African, but what of the gold eyes—literally gold, smooth metal without any pupils? Or the hair that braided and unbraided of its own accord? Pedestrians averted their eyes but at some point a Natural would walk by. Naturals were raw Travelers, unschooled, and unknown even to themselves. They could cause a lot of trouble.

Jack kneeled down beside her. Angel or demon, it was hard to tell when they got like that. "Hey," he said. She glanced at him, then returned to her papers. "I'm Jack."

She smiled, or maybe grimaced, then said, in a high, thin voice, "I know. Everyone knows. You're Johnny Non."

Great, Jack thought. *Thanks, Societé.* He made himself grin. "Yeah, that's me. What are you doing?"

"Going home. It's all here. I just have to find the right order."

"Yes, of course," Jack said. "But you know, you'll probably find it quicker if you go inside."

She looked at him, eyes suddenly open wide, so that the sun bounced off the gold and made Jack squint. "You think so?" she said.

"I'm sure of it." She nodded and let Jack put his arms around her and lift her gently to her feet.

Inside, a large man in jeans and an old-fashioned blue workshirt with rolled-up sleeves put his arm around "Aggie," as he called the Lost Lady, and led her to a cot where he told her to sit quietly and he would bring her crackers and her "maps," which Jack suspected were just old circulars, take-out menus, and any other loose papers lying around.

"Thanks for bringing her in," the worker said as he moved past Jack to his next task. This one could pass for human even better than Aggie, Jack thought, with his pleasant but not overly handsome face, his muscular six-foot-five frame, and his large, graceful hands. He struck Jack as the kind of man women looked at it in the street and he didn't even realize. If they noticed his orangey skin they could think it a bad tan. And the overly long fingers? Well, that was part of the attraction. Of course, he wasn't a man at all but a service golem, part of a set created by AADE to help the shelter's manager. The original golem, centuries ago, was made of good Prague dirt by a Traveler rabbi named Judah Loew. These days golem makers tended to use trash, because why not, there was just so much of it. Food thrown out by restaurants and medical waste were the favorites. Modern golems didn't last as long but they looked better.

Jack glanced around for the Know-It-All, or at least Andy, whom he knew slightly. The shelter was mostly one big room with a gray cement floor (easily washable), overhead fluorescent lights that probably stayed on night and day, and high air vents covered with dense copper mesh to prevent sylphs clogging the openings. Similar shields kept the salamanders out of the heating system, but what of undines and other water spirits in the toilets? And those were just the classics. Jack had heard of a shelter in Cincinnati where they had to go into full lockdown every garbage day to stop a trash elemental from eating everything.

Jack was wondering where Andy might be when a cold wind whipped around the room and all the lights dimmed. "Jeremy!" a voice called out. "Wings folded. You know the rules." Shivering, Jack turned to see three golems, two men and a woman, grabbing at an ice demon whose leathery wings banged against the ceiling. "Jeremy!" the voice said more sharply, and Jack turned to see Andy Martin, furious, his right arm straight out and holding what looked like an iPhone. "House rules! Right now, or I'm calling your principals. You want them to come get you?" The demon thrashed towards Andy, but Jack could see the fight had gone out of him. The wings became almost transparent as they slowly dropped down and folded into his body. A moment later he looked like a tired, white-haired old man who'd been on the street for too long. He let the golems lead him to a cot.

Andrew Martin, five-foot-eight, 175 pounds, mid-forties, wearing jeans, black high-top sneakers, and a cream-colored shirt that might have been left from his corporate days, walked over with a smile. "Jack," he said. "Good to see a human in here. Come to volunteer?" He spoke in a bland Midwestern accent that Jack could never pin down to a particular state. For some reason, this annoyed him.

Jack smiled and shook Andy's outstretched hand. "Not today," he said.

"Hey, can't blame a guy for trying. Want some coffee? I've finally trained the golems to brew a fresh pot every two hours."

He led Jack to where a glass carafe of coffee rested on a hot plate behind a trio of white mugs. "Milk? Sugar?"

"Black is fine," Jack said. He took the cup and, as always these days, psychically scanned it for potions, mind formations, or other traps. It was clear, as he'd known it would be. Didn't taste too bad, he thought when he sipped it. He followed Andy to a bare metal table and a couple of folding chairs. He nodded toward the ice demon on his cot. "Jeremy his real name?" he asked.

Andy laughed. "Course not. That's just what it sounds like to my dumb human ears. You think I have time to learn all their languages? Even if I could."

Jack nodded. "Human mouths are not built for some of those sounds. Maybe some day I'll tell you what it's like to play cards in the Ibis Casino. Understanding the dealer's the hardest part."

Andy said, "You know, back in the old days, learning odd languages was something I'd have my 'people' do. Funny, isn't it? I used to have all these men and women serving me and I never learned their names. Now I'm the one serving, and it's definitely not humans. But it *is* service. You know?"

"Yeah," Jack said. He thought of the days when he was young, and people called him Jack Easy. And then the geist took his family and everything changed. Maybe he and Andrew Martin were not so far apart. He said, "Do you miss it? The old days?"

Andy grinned. "Look around, Jack. I'd be a fucking liar if I said this was how I wanted to live out my life. Do you know we had an honest-to-God shit elemental here last week? Thank God her principal came and collected her. That was not fun, let me tell you. But you know, there's something about doing this. Being of use. It's hard to describe."

"So how did it happen? Leaving your life like that." Immediately, he added, "Shit. Probably you get asked that all the time."

"Oddly enough, no. There's usually too much going on." He gave Jack a sharp look, as if to say, *And I know you're not here just to find out about my history.* But all he said was, "There wasn't any great crisis. I didn't just wake up in the morning and decide to throw everything over."

Jack frowned. There was something odd about what Andy had just said, but he couldn't seem to place it, so he let it go.

Andy went on, "It wasn't like we were doing horrible things. Sure, sometimes people suffered when we took over a company. Sometimes they did great. We weren't cold-hearted bastards out to destroy people. We weren't *anything*.

"At first it was to get rich. Then it became a way to keep score. And then—it was nothing. Just what we did every day. So finally I decided I wanted out. Do something useful for once."

Jack heard a moan somewhere to the left, and then it rose to a howl before it plummeted to a series of grunts. "Oh, hell" Andy said, and rolled his eyes.

Jack turned to see some kind of ape in a long red wool dress that hid all but the brown chittering head. As Jack watched, the head changed to a deer's, and hooves stuck out from the sleeves.

Andy didn't get up or even set down his coffee, just called out "Maribeth, we've talked about this." He sounded like Mr. Sylvio, the assistant principal from Jack's high school.

The deer stared at Andy a moment, then seemed to collapse in on itself, and a second later became a middle-aged Korean woman with silver hair. She looked down at the floor, and said "I'm sorry, Mr. Martin." She had some kind of accent so that his name came out "Mahtin."

Andy's eyes narrowed, then he turned back to Jack. "It's hard for them," he said. "They're used to such freedom, and then the world changes and they get stuck."

"How'd you get started?" Jack said.

Andy poured himself more coffee. "No big drama. The Powers keep track of people, you know that, right?"

"Sure. I think these days they have an app for it."

Andy laughed. "Apparently my attempts to find a worthwhile cause caught someone's attention. I was walking to my apartment one night when this *thing* appeared in front of me. I found out later he was an emissary."

"Which one?"

Andy grinned. "Well, he was twelve feet tall and green."

Jack laughed. "Oh God, the Ur-Leprechaun!"

"They wanted to impress me and they sure as hell did. Do you remember back before the financial crash people like me called ourselves 'masters of the universe?'" Jack shrugged. "Now I actually met one, and the difference was pretty amazing. He offered me a choice. Take this job and be of service or have my memory wiped and spend the rest of my life drifting from cause to cause. Pretty simple decision, don't you think?"

"Guess so," Jack said.

"Good." He set down his coffee. "You've paid the price, Jack, let the Ancient Mariner tell his tale. Now the reward. What can I do for you?"

"I'm looking for the Know-It-All. Is she staying here?"

"She? Have you decided the Knower's a woman?"

"Who knows?"

"Presumably *she* does. Sorry, Jack. You listened to me for nothing. The Know-It-All hasn't been in here for a few weeks." Jack sighed and stood up. "But I did hear that someone had seen him—her—up by the Museum of Natural History. Sleeps in the park, I guess."

Jack nodded. Better than nothing. "Thanks, Andy." He looked around, at the bare, antiseptic walls, the stained floor, the golems who stood together like robots at rest, at Jeremy, Maribeth, and the handful of others sitting quietly or standing around, staring at nothing or leafing through magazines, all of them strangely silent. "Good luck," he said.

"Thanks, Jack. Same to you."

It took Jack three days to find the Nude Owl, and in the end she was just where Andy had said, in Central Park, outside the Museum of Natural History. During those seventy-two hours of looking, Sarah Strand called Jack's cell four times. He answered the first two with platitudes and promises, and after that let voicemail take it. As he searched the park, he wondered why he'd been so sure the Owl was a woman, or at least female. It was because of the Queen, he decided. They were so much alike. The

Queen saw, the Owl knew. And Jack Shade stumbled around searching.

He spotted the Owl on a raw, drizzly day, with gusts of wind that bit your face. Just over five feet tall, she was wearing so many layers—sweaters, jackets, coats, at least two pairs of pants tucked into over large brown rubber boots, scarves, and an old-fashioned Russian hat with ear-flaps—that she was nearly as wide. A round, red-cheeked face, with small hazel eyes, wide nose, and a prim pink mouth peeked out from beneath the heavy hat. Jack glanced down at his own long double-breasted black coat, his worn black riding boots, and felt under dressed, exposed.

For a few minutes, he stood some fifteen feet away, hands in pockets, and watched the Owl, who appeared to take no notice of him. She stood very still, arms straight but held a little away from the body, head tilted back, and hummed. There was no actual tune, rather a hint of melody in the slow moans punctuated by occasional grunts or high-pitched monotones.

People walked by, eyes averted in that relaxed New York way. A little girl tried to stop and listen until her mother pulled her away. Half a minute later the girl ran back and her mother had to come get her, this time with stern whispers of, "Not nice," and murmurs of, "people who can't help themselves," even as the girl continued to look over her shoulder. *Natural*, Jack thought. He half-considered taking one of his cards, writing, "Call me when you're ready," and following them to slide the card into the girl's backpack. But just then a soft voice behind him said, "Hello, Jack. It's good to see you."

He sighed and walked over to the Nude Owl.

"It's all right," she said. "When the time comes, she'll find her way without your card to guide her."

Well, this should be fun, Jack thought. Could she read his mind? He hoped she only knew about events and not the thoughts that triggered them. He said, "Were you singing?"

"Not exactly." She turned her head to look up at the Planetarium, a large globe in a glass cage. "The children are playing recordings of the Andromeda Galaxy. That name is so sweet, don't you think? If they knew its real name . . . The sad

THE FISSURE KING

thing, you see, is that their poor little radio telescopes distort the sound. I just thought it deserved something a bit more faithful. You understand, don't you, Jack?"

Oddly enough, Jack thought he did. He discovered he liked the Owl. People who knew about the Travelers often assumed their power lay in "magic." Spells, conjuring demons, turning lead into gold. But all that was secondary. What mattered was knowledge. Knowledge and sight. Travelers knew things about the world, why and how things exist, and this enabled them to see.

Jack walked to a bench facing Central Park West. "Shall we sit down? You can still watch the globe."

"That's not a problem," the Owl said as she stood with her back to the bench, placed both hands on the slightly mossy wood, and hoisted herself onto it. "It won't vanish if I don't look at it. Thank goodness, seeing is not my responsibility."

"Ah," Jack said, "so you know she's missing."

"The Queen. Yes."

A trio of Asian girls about Julie's age walked by. They stared a moment at Jack and the Owl, followed by whispers and loud laughter, the kind meant to cast a net of shame over its objects. Jack realized what an odd couple they made, a tall man all in black, with rough-cut hair and a deep scar on the right side of his jaw, and a short person of indeterminate gender, wearing half a thrift shop's worth of clothes.

Jack said "Does it bother you? People like that?"

The Owl shrugged. "Like everyone, they do their best with what they know." Now she looked at him and there was no doubt she was smiling. "I like that name. Nude Owl. So much nicer than Know-It-All. Perhaps I shall perch in a tree tonight."

Jack said, "I need to find her."

"Yes, I suppose you do." As if there'd been a lull in the conversation, she said, "Have you wondered about the name?"

"I don't understand."

"Margaret Strand. It's so close, don't you think? Magarita Hand, Margaret Strand. She might have called herself anything. Alice, Jessica, Elaynora."

Despite his frustration, Jack thought a moment. "Maybe it's continuity. Sarah said her mother's life as Margaret was real, not a disguise."

"Ah, so people who must change their name prefer to hover close to the original. You might want to remember that, Johnny Non." Jack couldn't think of what to say, so he just sat there and hoped she would get onto something useful. Instead, the Owl said "Do you know what day it is?"

"What, you mean some holiday?"

"No, no, the day of the week."

"Jesus," Jack said, "you know the real name of the Andromeda Galaxy but not the day of the week? It's Tuesday. A dreary November Tuesday, and I'm searching for the Queen of Eyes. Can you help me?"

The Owl stared down at the ground as she whispered, "It's always good to know what day it is. You never know, it could be important."

"Hey, I'm sorry," Jack said.

Suddenly bright again, she lifted her head and said, "Do you like toys, Jack?"

Jack thought of the happy afternoons in toy stores when Genie was a child. "Sure," he said.

The Owl said, "Toys can form their own world, you know. For the right child. Or maybe it's a doorway. I wouldn't know, I've never had children."

Jack stared at her. "Really?" he said. "The Toy Store? It's that simple?"

Just above a whisper, she said, "Only a *little* knowledge is ever simple, Johnny."

"Yeah, but—" Impulsively, he leaned over to hug her but she reared back and held up her arms in an X in front of her body. "No!" she said.

"Sorry," Jack said, and stood up. "I didn't mean—thank you. Thank you so much." He walked to the curb and hailed a cab.

"Jack!" she called as he was opening the taxi door. He turned to see her standing as still as some figurine from the Secret Beach. She said, "Why do hurricanes bear women's names?" When he didn't respond, she said, "Because they have eyes."

As the car pulled away from the curb, the driver looked in the rearview mirror and said "Ain't he hot in all that crap?"

"She," Jack said.

"Huh?"

"She's a she."

The cabbie squinted again in the mirror at the now small form, like a soft fireplug with arms. "Jesus," he said, "how can you tell?"

"You just have to know," Jack said.

The Toy Store had an official name, of course, that of its famous founder, and most Normals called it that, but Travelers only cared about his son-in-law, known as Emil S. Emil had had the bad fortune to bring the legendary store to the brink of being swallowed by some corporate serpent. Luckily, one of the ways he'd avoided business school was to dabble as a mage, enough that he knew of the existence of the New York Travelers Aid Society. "Please," he'd said to the Chief back then, a man named Sebastian Elkiado, "I'll give you anything." Then, as if he'd realized what he'd said, he'd added, "Except, I didn't mean my soul."

Elkiado had laughed. "Whatever would we want with *that*?" he'd said. "All we ask, really, is that you take on a certain new attraction. It will be quite nice, I promise you. The children will love it."

Jack wasn't sure why later owners had never dismantled the exhibit, which had stood now for half a century. Part of the contract? Or maybe it was gratitude for saving the family business. Maybe if Jack spent more time at NYTAS he would know such things.

It was a Tuesday afternoon, and well before the Christmas shopping season, yet children and adults, not necessarily together, filled the store. At least there was no line outside the door, as there would be in a couple of weeks. He made his way past video games, and home robots, and life-sized stuffed animals, and animatronic ring-bearers with furry feet until he reached the escalator to the second floor. And when he got to the top, there it was. The Witch's Cottage, a dollhouse big enough to walk inside, and made to look like a mix of cobwebs and gingerbread.

A short line, mostly of young kids with their parents, waited patiently behind a red rope that kept people ten feet from the door until their turn came. As Jack took his place at the end he felt a movement against his leg, and when he looked down, Ray stood beside him. *Thanks*, he said without words. *Too bad you can't show yourself to the kids, but the store probably has an anti-fox policy.* A guard dressed as some costumer's idea of a fairy-tale prince—gold velvet tunic and trousers, shiny boots, and a red cape—stood at the rope to let people in. Jack wondered if he should have borrowed a child, make it look good. Miss Yao had a grandson. He thought of the times he'd taken Genie to Macy's to sit on Santa's lap, and how odd it had felt, since unlike all the other grown-ups, Jack had known the origin of that strange practice.

When Jack stepped up to the rope, alone, the guard narrowed his eyes at him and said, "You know this is supposed to be for kids, right?"

"I know," Jack said in what he hoped was a wholesome tone. "I won't go in for long. I used to bring my daughter here and I miss her."

The guard made a noise. "What'd she do, run away? Find friends her own age?"

She killed her mother and was sucked into the land of the dead. "She was taken from me."

"Oh, Jesus," the guard said, "sorry. Go on, take as long as you like."

"Thanks," Jack said, trying to sound like one divorce victim to another. Ray vanished as Jack passed the rope line.

The doorway was large, out of proportion to the rest of the cottage, but even so, at six-foot-one, Jack had to bend slightly to go inside. The rustic look continued indoors, with plastic walls made to look like logs, more fake cobwebs and a large plastic spider around a misshapen window, a small distressed rocking chair behind a spinning wheel with a shiny gold spindle—real gold, Jack knew, you needed gold somewhere in the room for an enactment to work—a black iron oven, open to reveal fake flames, and against the back wall a short, narrow bed with a multicolored quilt, as if waiting for Goldilocks.

In the center stood the main attraction, a triangular iron table with three life-size dolls seated around it, a classic hook-nosed witch dressed all in black, and a boy and girl in bright peasant clothes. The artist who'd painted the children's faces had captured a dual quality of excitement and terror, the source of people's love of fairy tales, the union of the cortex and the amygdala. Plastic mugs made to look like crockery stood in front of the children, along with plates of plastic cookies. A small iron cauldron squatted on the table in front of the witch.

The child dolls sat frozen but the witch showed some minimal animatronic life signs. She cackled, and the head turned stiffly through an arc of about sixty degrees, and her right hand stirred the cauldron with a wooden spoon. Jack stared at the witch. It was just a toy, he thought, and yet his arm nearly spasmed as he reached for the knife in his boot. Just a doll. The cackle sounded shrill in his ears as he held the knife with his arm extended all the way out so he could swing with maximum force. Jack had never done this but he knew the rule, you had to lop off the Guardian's head in one stroke or the way would refuse to open. He took a deep breath, thinking of Genie and the creaky voice she would use when she pretended to speak for the Barbie doll she'd dressed as a witch. He stiffened his arm.

A high, soft voice to his left said, "Would you like some tea, Mr. Shade?"

Jack grunted and spun around. It wasn't the witch, it was the *girl*. The doll had come alive and was stirring the thick, dark liquid in her mug with the golden spindle. No, not really alive, for the face stayed plastic, and the hand remained stiff as she held up the mug. In that same gentle voice, with a hint of a German accent, the doll said, "My auntie made it herself. She's ever so good at brews. Aren't you, Auntie?" She looked at the witch, who just cackled and stirred the cauldron.

Jack said, "You know what I came here to do, don't you?"

The plastic head tilted forward and the eyes looked down with either resignation or modesty. "Yes, of course," she whispered. "But we don't need to become monsters. We can still be nice, can't we?" Abruptly cheerful again, she lifted her head and smiled as she once more held up the mug. "Here," she said, "drink this and I promise not to run away."

Jack doubted very much she could get out of the chair, let alone leave the cottage. He took the mug in his right hand, the knife still in his left. He sniffed it, of course, and did not pick up any poisons, physical or otherwise. "Once you learn how to see," Anatolie had told him long ago, "I'll teach you how to smell." He took a sip.

Bitter and sharp at the same time, it cut into his tongue and the roof of his mouth. He began to feel dizzy, confused. He set down the mug to grab ahold of the triangular table alongside the boy doll. He said, "I didn't—there was no—"

"Nasty smell? I told you Auntie was good, didn't I? Dear, dear Mr. Shade, you always think you know everything. But how can you become an Owl if you never want to get naked? And how can you see until you find the Queen?"

Jack tried to raise the knife. "I can still—"

The doll whispered, "It's not necessary, Mr. Shade. Not this time. You don't have to be the killer. You can just rest."

As if commanded, Jack glanced over at the cheerful bed, so inviting, so calm. He thought he was a bear, but maybe he was nothing more than Goldilocks. But when he lay down, his feet stuck out over the edge of the bed. Somehow this felt comforting. He glanced over at the table and saw that the witch and the boy had vanished, and the girl herself had changed. In her place sat a perfectly carved lifesize wooden figure of a woman, impossibly old, the face so covered lines it might have been a map of all the Worlds laid one on top of another.

"The Ancient Doll," Jack whispered, and then he couldn't help himself, he said a prayer. He knew who she was. All Travelers knew of her, but very few ever saw her. The Doll was a puppet avatar of The Bride of the Earth, who sustains all life, and to see the Bride in any form was a gift beyond all merit. "Thank you," Jack managed to say, and then he closed his eyes and fell asleep.

He woke, groggily, to a chorus of birds, hundreds, and the first thought that came to him was that the snake blood must have worn off, he couldn't understand a word. Genie's fault, he decided, a single drop just wasn't enough. This seemed funny, somehow, or maybe just the thought of his daughter made him happy. He felt drowsy, and he almost fell asleep again. Instead, he shook his head to clear it, an action that banished the birds, as if they'd been lodged in his skull. He managed to stand up and looked around.

The dolls were gone, and the table, but the chairs remained, as if set up for a triangular séance. The cottage seemed brighter somehow, more substantial. He glanced back at the bed, half-expecting to see it had remade itself, but no, the sheets were rumpled, the blankets half on the floor.

He was stalling. There was only one thing to do, and that was to go look. So he took a breath, ducked his head, and stepped outside. And there she was.

"Hello, John," the Queen of Eyes said. "I thought you might come."

Dressed in loose jeans, a light-blue cotton sweater with the sleeves half rolled up, and low sneakers with white socks, she sat in an old-fashioned wooden lawn chair, the kind with a fan-shaped back made of wooden slats and armrests wide enough to accommodate a glass of lemonade and a dish of ice cream. A second chair stood to her right. The Toy Store was gone, of course, and so was November. Behind the cottage stood a group of trees that got denser the more you stared into them. Jack was glad he didn't have to go searching in those woods.

If what lay in back of the cottage appeared impenetrable, the front offered as wide a vista as could be found in any brochure advertising a country holiday. The cottage perched on a flower-strewn hill, which sloped gently down to a wide, bright river, and beyond that layers of mountains, the nearest ones gentle and green, with larger, darker peaks rearing up behind them like their nasty big brothers.

"*Thought* I might?" Jack said. "Didn't you see it?"

She smiled slightly, and it was definitely Margaret, not any of the visions he'd seen that night on the Secret Beach. Her hair looked a bit longer than in the photos Sarah had shown him, as if she'd recently decided to let it grow. She said, "I try not to see myself too much. It can be rather frustrating. But please, sit down."

Jack turned the empty chair to face her more directly and kept his eyes on her as he sat down. He said, "Still, you must have known I would come looking for you. You put my card up so your daughter would find it."

The Queen—Margaret—frowned a moment, then said softly, "I'm sorry, John. That wasn't me."

A tingling moved up Jack's spine. "Someone did it," he said, "with some kind of working to make Sarah think she'd seen it there for years." Margaret didn't answer. "If it wasn't you, and you didn't see it, why did you think I might come?"

"Well, obviously because if I needed to find someone *I* would go to John Shade. You are quite good, you know."

Jack didn't answer at first, then said, "Where is this place?"

She waved a hand, then said, "Just somewhere to get away."

He glanced out at the view. "Very nice," he said, and was about to turn back when he noticed something about twenty feet from where they were sitting. If he glanced at it casually it looked just like any other mix of dirt and grass and weeds, but if he stared at it—at first he discovered he could see every rough edge of every blade of grass, the exact contours of each nubble of dirt. But if he looked a bit longer it changed. He could see images, scenes, people. A man in a hotel room weeping silently as he watched his sleeping son. A woman in Chicago clutching a homemade Ancestor Bundle as she tried to summon a spirit she had read about in a book. A dog whimpering, confused, outside a tornado-flattened house. Child soldiers marching, terrified, on a shabby presidential palace and its rows of shiny guns. On and on it went, until all Jack could do was squeeze shut his eyes and pray for it to stop. And so it did. When he dared to look again, the hill had come back, pleasant and dull.

He said, "How can you stand it?"

She shrugged. "You learn. My first days were rather difficult but it's the same for every Queen. And my mother had helped prepare me in the weeks before her death."

"You know it was your daughter who sent me. However she got my card." Margaret didn't answer. "If you wanted to get away—or whatever the hell you're doing—why didn't you just tell her?"

"It's hard to explain, John. Please believe me that I am truly sorry for any suffering I might cause Sarah or Julie. Or you, for that matter."

Jack laughed. "I'm not suffering. I'm just pissed off. I feel like I'm being used, but I'm not sure how." The Queen didn't answer. "Shit," Jack said, and leaned back against the chair. "I saw the Ancient Doll before."

"Oh, really?"

Jack couldn't tell if her surprise was genuine. He said, "That wasn't you, was it?"

She laughed. "I'm not *that* old, Mr. Shade."

"But you change. I know, I saw you on the beach."

"Well. That was something of a special occasion. But I assure you, however I might appear, I am definitely human. It's a rule. The Queen must always be fully human. No hybrids. And the Doll—well, the Bride of the Earth is one of the Great Powers." When he didn't answer she said, "She's the one who brings you your third soul every Saturday."

Jack nodded. He knew the theory, though he couldn't say he ever felt it. Everyone possesses two souls all the time, physical and mental. Without them, we couldn't function. At midnight on Friday, when it turns into Saturday, we get what some call a spirit soul. As far as Jack was concerned, all that that meant was there were certain incantations and enactments you could only do on a Saturday. "That's very interesting," he said. "But tell me something. Why are you here? Why now, and why didn't you tell Sarah?"

Without looking at him, the Queen said, "I needed some time away."

"Really? You could have taken the family to Disney World. November's a good time for that."

"I needed to spend some time with my daughter."

"Your daughter? She's the one who's worried sick over you."

"Not Sarah."

Jack frowned. "Julie? She doesn't seem to care much about anything that doesn't come on a five-inch screen."

"No, Jack. Not Julie."

"Then what—" He stopped, felt his jaw drop and closed it. "The girl on the beach," he said. "That was your *daughter*?" The Queen looked at him but said nothing. "Does Sarah know?"

Margaret shook her head. "It was before Sarah, before my marriage. I was quite young, actually. My turn at youthful rebellion. We all have them, the Nliana girls' reaction to all that responsibility. Well, all except Sarah. But I suspect Julie will make up for her mother's mildness."

"But wait—if you had this other girl first, won't she become Queen? After you, I mean."

"I told you, Jack, the Queen of Eyes must always be fully human."

It took him a moment, then he laughed. "Wow. You had an affair with a Power?"

Margaret allowed a slight smile to lift the right side of her mouth. "I was not always so . . . comfortable-looking."

"I'll bet," Jack said. "Which one?" Her smile widened a little but she said nothing. Jack had the sudden thought he might have made a mistake about the Owl's gender. He said, "It wasn't the Know-It-All, was it?"

She laughed. "Good lord, what an idea. No, John, it was definitely not the Owl, nude or otherwise."

Behind them, from the door of the cottage, a man's voice said, "What a jolly scene. Little Jack Riding Hood and Grandma. I guess that means it's time for the Wolf."

Jack jumped up; the Queen rose more slowly. "Andy?" Jack said. "What the hell are you doing here?"

Andrew Martin had ditched his frayed work clothes for what looked like a designer suit, dark blue with a double-breasted jacket, a light blue silk shirt, and a yellow tie with thin red stripes. Italian handmade shoes had replaced his sneakers, and his hair looked freshly cut and gelled. When he spoke, his voice sounded different as well, sharper, more in control, the bland Midwestern tones replaced by a trace of an accent Jack couldn't quite place.

Andy said, "I followed your scent, of course. Oh, it was a bit difficult at the end there, all those children with their misformed psyches blurring the trail. But the tracer held, and, well, here we are."

Jack's mind raced over his time in the shelter. Ever since William Barlow and that damned glass of water he'd automatically scanned any touch, any gifts he accepted, anything he ate or drank during a case. He said, "You didn't plant anything on me. Not when you touched me, and not in the coffee."

"Oh, nothing physical. I knew you'd be too good for that. But do you recall when poor homesick Jeremy opened his wings?"

"Yes, and you told him house rules and he closed them."

"Well, yes, rules are indeed rules. But it was the wings that did it. They formed a rather elegant configuration that settled on you like a very fine psychic coat. I confess I'd worked with Jeremy for several days to get that right."

Jack had to fight the urge to brush himself off. He was about to ask what this was all about when suddenly he understood. For it was at that moment that he recognized "Andrew Martin's" accent. It was French. He remembered the Owl telling him that people who change their names usually choose something close to the original. And he thought of that odd thing "Andy" had said, not, "I woke up one morning," but, *I woke up in the morning.* It was the expression used by initiates in the *Societé de Matin*, the Society of the Morning, an organization whose chief officers took its name as their own.

Jack said, "You're André Matin. The Society's former Deputy Head of Operations."

André inclined his head. "Bravo, Jean Oui. You deserve your reputation."

"So all that crap about being a vulture capitalist and discovering the emptiness of it all was just a cover story. You were running the shelter as punishment. The Society loaned you out like an indentured servant after you tried to knock down the Old Man of the Woods."

André shrugged theatrically. "Oh, it wasn't so bad, Jean. The shelter gave me time to plan. And form alliances."

"Plan what? Alliances with whom?" Jack waved a hand at the hillside, the cottage. "What's this all about?"

"The Queen, of course. What else? I just needed to find her, which of course you did. *Merci.*"

Jack stared at him, then laughed. "You think Mariq Nliana is going to form an alliance with *you*?" But when he glanced at Margaret he saw her face had become stone still. His voice hardly a whisper, he said, "Oh no."

"Not her, of course," André Matin said. "Her *successor*." And then he raised his hand and a gun appeared in it.

As a rule, Travelers do not deal much with guns. In the places they go, and the situations they face, guns don't often work very well. *This one,* Jack thought, *shouldn't work at all here.* But Matin apparently believed in it, and so did the Queen. He noticed designs painted or carved on the barrel, sigils and signatures, marks of summoning, and he realized the gun itself was keeping open the channels back to the everyday world of cause and effect. A world where bullets could kill a middle-aged woman whose daughter had sold out to a psychopath.

He said to Margaret, "So that's why you didn't tell anyone where you were going. You must have seen what was happening. And that's why Sarah was so desperate to find you." As he talked, his hand moved down his leg toward his knife. The knife was bound to him and would rise into his hand. He just needed to distract André. He said, "She couldn't send her boyfriend after you as long as you were out of the world. So she hired me. Margaret, I am sorry, I am so—"

He threw the knife the instant it came into his fingers. It was a good throw, right at Matin's throat. But Matin was shielded, and the knife swerved and ended up stuck in the cottage wall, alongside the door. Jack had guessed that might happen. He had to try.

As if the throw hadn't even occurred, the Queen said to Jack, "No, John, you did exactly what you needed to do. There is no blame."

André Matin said, "There. You see? She forgives you. You're a lucky man, Jean Oui." And then he shot the Queen of Eyes three times, twice in the chest and once in her face.

"Margaret!" Jack screamed, and lunged to grab her body as it thrashed in the air. Blood and tissue splashed him but he took no notice. He set her down and tried to hit Matin with something, a spell, an energy burst, a word of power. Useless. He might have been a bee stinging a statue. He fell to his knees, gasping.

Matin stopped in the doorway of the cottage. "You've served me well here, Jean Oui, so I will give you a small word of advice. The doorway is still open but not for long. I suggest you leave her and go back."

"Fuck you," Jack said. "What now? You and Sarah go celebrate?"

Matin laughed. "Sarah? Weak, loyal, precious Sarah? Please." He laughed again and vanished into the cottage.

Jack stared at the doorway, then at the Queen's torn body. Something was wrong, something didn't make any sense. Did André know of the other daughter? But then wouldn't he know she wasn't eligible?

And then it came to him. A memory, a voice, as clear as a download. *Ooh, the Queen of Eyes . . . some old man pissing himself in the woods.* The Old Man of the Woods. Julie Strand had been talking about the chief sorcerer of the *Societé de Matin.*

Jack grabbed his cell phone out of his pocket. Could it possibly work here? André had said the way was open. The gun had done that. If a body could pass through, could a satellite signal? Yes! It was ringing. In his mind he begged Sarah to pick up, pick up the phone.

"Jack?" she said. Jack closed his eyes. *Thank God, there's still a chance.* "Jack," Sarah said, her voice distant and echoing. *Speakerphone*, he realized. "I can see—it's everywhere—oh, God, is my mother—*please.*"

There was no time to soften it. "She's dead. Killed. Sarah!" She was wailing, a high-pitched choking sound, as if she was trying to hold it in but couldn't do it. Jack said, "You have to listen to me. Please, Sarah. There's no time."

"Sarai," she said distantly.

"What?"

"My name. My mother said I would have to claim it when I—Sarai Cassini Nliana Hand."

"Sarai, please! You have to get out of there. Right now! *Your daughter is sending someone to kill you.*"

Too late. The new voice that sounded in his ears was so cold, so cheerful, Jack almost dropped the phone. "Oh, private dickie, so nice of you to think of my mother. But why would I send someone when I can do it myself? Take responsibility. That's what my mother and grandmother have always taught me."

"Oh my God," Sarah Strand said. "Sweetheart, what are you doing?"

"Claiming my own. Be honest, *Mommy.* You never wanted to be Queen."

"Julie!" Jack cried. "You don't have to do this. André doesn't care about you, he's using you. For God's sake—"

"Guilielma," came the excited voice. "Guilielma Callista, and of course, Nliana Hand."

Sarah—Sarai—whispered, "Sweetheart . . ."

And then the soon to be new Queen, "Goodbye, Dickie." The line went dead, cut off.

That was it. Jack tried three times to redial but knew he wouldn't get through. Even if someone might have answered, the signal was fading, the line between the worlds breaking down. He knew he had to get back—what was that old Traveler line, "Never overstay your welcome"—but he couldn't just leave the Queen. If there'd been any chance to stop Julie then yes, but it was too late for that. It had always been too late, right from the beginning.

He squatted down next to Margaret's body, forcing himself to look, at the bullet holes, the blood. Jack had seen bodies ripped in half by conjurings, or eaten by Half-bears or other creatures, but there was something about guns that filled him with a wild revulsion.

He picked up the body and held it against him, like a lover might, or a father. "I'm so sorry," he whispered. Even as he rocked back and forth he could see the land all around him begin to change. The color was draining out of the flowers and the grass. The very forms were changing as well, the mountains becoming lumpy, the chairs like sculptures that had half-melted and then solidified into uselessness.

Should he try to take her back? Where do you bury a murdered Queen of Eyes? No. Something told him she had to stay here. He didn't know why, but he'd learned long ago to trust such feelings. God, he thought, if he'd trusted his feeling that he knew nothing about missing-persons cases none of this would have happened. Too late.

With a last look back at Margaret, he stepped into the cottage.

As often happens, the way back was quick and easy. No potions, no falling asleep, no birdsongs. All he had to do was look around, close his eyes, and when he opened them it had all returned, the table, the robot witch, the Hansel and Gretel dolls, and the lights and noise of the store. Long ago, the Traveler Peter Midnight had said, "You conjure, or scheme, or buy your way into Paradise, and when it pleases the Masters, they spit you out again."

He staggered from of the cottage and into a room of screaming children. At first he thought they must know what had happened, how a power-mad gangster and a psychotic teenager had killed the Queen of Eyes—twice—and all the world was wailing in pain. But then Ray appeared, and pointed a paw at him, and he looked down at himself and said, "Fuck," because he'd forgotten to cast a glamour to hide the mess.

Jack wasn't very good at glams. He pretended some sort of moral objection, but really, he just liked himself too much. When he was young, he'd counted on his good looks to get him through life. And they'd brought him Layla, so he was right, wasn't he? And after Layla's death, and Genie's banishment, Jack had wanted to see the scars the geist's knife had cut into his face, the mark of memory. So he didn't like glamours and didn't use them much. But he could, at least long enough to get away from the guard yelling into his housenet phone, and race down the escalator and out of the store.

Don't run, he ordered himself, but he walked quickly, slipping between people without touching them, until he made his way to Madison and 47th Street, and the innocuous entrance to NYTAS, the New York Travelers Aid Society.

The glam fell away as soon as he'd stepped inside, no match for the anti-spell tech that ran through the building. He would have dropped it anyway. Who was he to hide the blood of the Queen of Eyes?

Carolien Hounstra, all six feet and one hundred sixty pounds of her, was standing door that day. "Jesus, Jack," she said in that cheerful Dutch accent, "what the fuck did you do to yourself?" A smile twitched at her generous mouth. "You didn't take on one of those Beasts of Legend safari jobs, did you?"

Jack said, "I've got to see Arthur. Right now." The last time Jack had seen Arthur Canton, the NYTAS Chief, they'd spent a good seven or eight minutes yelling at each other.

"Oh, really?" Carolien said. "Just like that." She snapped her plump fingers, then folded her arms across her magnificent breasts, the subject of much Traveler discussion and not a few dreams. She was wearing a tracksuit of soft purple fleece, and she'd woven her knee-length blond-hair into a thick braid.

"Let me check," she said, and turned around, somewhat dramatically, to walk down the long marble corridor lined with ornately carved story pegs, like miniature totem poles, each around three feet high. The pegs represented the history of NYTAS in some complicated mnemonic system Jack had never bothered to learn.

Jack spent the next few minutes trying to calm his breathing, with his arms folded to keep his hands from shaking. Finally, Carolien strolled back to say "Dr. Canton will see you now," and then, with a smirk, "God help him."

According to the NYTAS website (strictly guarded, though spirit-hacked at least twice that Jack knew of), Arthur Canton had been working as a resident cardiologist in NYU Medical the night he discovered the Real World. Something about an ER patient with two hearts, and the green, scaly next-of-kin who'd shown up to claim the body. Canton, so the bio went, "dedicated his life to uniting the best of modern science with the ancient lore of the Traveler." Jack had always thought that Canton's primary allegiance was to his own self-importance.

Canton had moved the Chief's office from its original ten-by-twelve space to what had been a ceremonial chamber, a room whose black marble floor was inlaid with gold and silver ovals marking the orbits of the planets, and diamond arrows showing the "fault lines" that allowed Travelers to move between the "Palaces," as the planetary realms were called. Canton's large ebony desk bore a similar design. According to rumor, probably started by Canton himself, the desk had once belonged to Tycho Brahe, the sixteenth-century astronomer and secret Traveler.

Chief Canton stood up when Jack entered, then quickly sat down again without offering to shake hands. He wore a dark blue suit with a light blue tie. He'd gotten hair plugs since Jack had last seen him. That, or made a deal with some growth demon. He looked, as always, as if he could give you five minutes before he had to go meet the mayor. "Jesus, Jack," he said, "you look like shit."

Jack said, "The Queen of Eyes has been murdered. Twice. André Matin did it. To get back in power."

Canton's mouth twitched. "Well, that's certainly rather vile. What exactly does it have to do with us?"

"Are you serious? It's a power grab. And he didn't just kill the second one, he got her own daughter to do it. So he could control the new Queen. For God's sake, Arthur—"

"I see," Canton said, with just enough of the Command Voice to stop Jack in midsentence. "A power struggle within a wretched organization has resulted in a double murder. Possibly more to come, since presumably the Old Man of the Woods will resist André's efforts. And now Jack Shade, the Traveler who can never be bothered to work with anyone—what is it you call yourself, Lone Wolf Jack? Johnny Singleton?—thinks he can come in here and rally all of NYTAS to his side. I don't think so."

"Arthur, a gangster has created a puppet Queen of Eyes. You don't think that concerns the Travelers?"

"There have been puppet Queens before. And assassinated Queens as well. Read the archives some time."

"Goddamn it—"

"Enough! Go home, Jack. Go sulk in your precious hotel."

Jack started to say something, then realized it was hopeless. He turned and was almost at the door when Canton said, "Clean yourself off before you leave."

"Screw you," Jack said. He reached for the door handle and discovered his hand frozen in midair.

The Chief said, "That was not a request. We do not call attention to ourselves."

"I'll glam myself."

"You can't be trusted."

The thought of washing Margaret's blood away nearly made Jack weep, but he managed to control himself. "Fine," he said. "Fresh clothes in the locker room?"

"Of course," Canton said. "The usual charges." He released control and Jack's hand yanked open the door.

Jack didn't return to the Rêve Noire that day, or the next, or the day after that. He didn't plan to keep away, he just couldn't seem to make himself go home. They'd given him jeans and a turtleneck and an old-fashioned pea jacket, so he was warm enough, though he hardly noticed. And he had some money, so he could eat, or get drunk, or even rent a room somewhere. Instead, he just walked through the city, hour after hour, until he got so exhausted he just fell down somewhere and slept. The first time he lay down on the sidewalk he thought of casting a look-away glam so no one would notice him, but it wasn't necessary. He never slept for more than ten minutes before the horror in his head jerked him awake. Ray would always be there, squatting alongside him.

Wednesday afternoon he gave all his cash to a hollowed-out young woman crouched in a doorway. Wearing only a cotton dress and sneakers without socks, she had her arms wrapped tightly around her knees, with her head bent forward. "Here," Jack said, and placed a couple hundred dollars in front of her. "Get yourself a coat. And some food." He walked away, but when he turned and saw she hadn't picked up the money, he went back and put it in her hand. At the corner he looked again and the money was gone. Jack hoped she'd hidden it away and no one had stolen it.

He kept wanting to call Miss Yao, to tell her he was okay even if he wasn't. But suppose they were watching her, waiting for his call? He couldn't bear it if he brought the Societé down on Irene. The fear was ridiculous, of course. André had the new Queen of Eyes, he hardly needed surveillance, electronic or magical.

For a while Jack stared at every billboard poster or newspaper photo, even statues, any image with eyes. Were they her? Was she watching him? Right now?

A couple of times he wondered if he should go to the Risen Spirit Shelter. He was their kind of guy now. But who was running it with "Andy" gone? And what would Jack do if he saw Jeremy? The fact was, of course, they wouldn't take him. He wasn't an angel, elemental, or demon. He was just a poor screwed-up Traveler. If Guilielma Callista was "fully human," what the fuck was Jack Shade?

In his more lucid moments he wondered about this overwhelming grief he felt. After all, he'd only spent a few minutes with her. He kept telling himself it was the horror of it, seeing her shot right next to him. And his own part, the fact that he'd led André right to her.

But there was something else. A couple of times, when he closed his eyes, he found himself back in his kitchen all those years ago, his wife's cut body bleeding out in his arms. Maybe that's all it was, the resemblance, the way Margaret's death seemed to wipe out all the years since he'd lost Layla. And Eugenia.

No. It was more than that. There was something about Margaret that had touched him in just those few minutes. Something about her he couldn't quite figure out. Was it the sadness in her face? The resignation? Did she see it coming and realize she couldn't stop it? All Jack really knew for sure was the pain that drove him through the streets.

Thursday night a woman came to him. He was sleeping in the doorway of some wholesale bead and findings shop on 38th Street when he heard someone call his name. At first he thought he'd managed to sleep all night for he opened his eyes to brightness. When he focused, however, he discovered it was still nighttime but the woman before him gave off a kind of radiance. She was kneeling down, so it was hard to tell, but she appeared tall and slender, with long hair that was actually black under the golden light that shone all around her.

"You're her," Jack blurted out. "The Queen's other daughter. The hybrid." Jesus, he thought, had he just insulted her?

"Yes, yes," she said, and waved a hand, as if to swat away such matters. "Jack, she needs you."

Needs me? Jack sat up and squinted at the light that shimmered all around her. She wasn't like this that other time. He said, "I saw you once. On the Secret Beach. The first time I saw your mother."

"Jack, please. Try to listen to me."

He knew he should keep quiet, but it was important somehow to understand. "You weren't all lit up then."

She shrugged, and flashes of sunshine seemed to splinter in the air. "I work for my father now," she said.

Despite everything, Jack almost whistled in admiration. *Wow*, he thought, *Margaret scored a Sun elemental?* He noticed suddenly that Ray, who hadn't left his side the whole time, was lying down next to the daughter and staring up at her in adoration. But what did it matter? What did anything matter? The Queen of Eyes was dead.

"Jack!" the woman said. "Please. You have to help her."

"Help her? Are you crazy? She's dead. I *helped* her murderers."

"She needs you."

"Stop saying that! What, are you feeling guilty?"

For the first time she looked startled. "Guilty?"

"Yeah. She told me she went there because of you. You needed help or something."

"Oh, Jack, it wasn't about me. Yes, we needed to talk, and in neutral territory. My mother and I, we had issues. She didn't like the work I was doing."

"For your father."

She ignored him. "But the whole thing, it wasn't—it was never about me. It was Julie."

"What?"

"It was always Julie. It was the only way my mother could save her."

"Save her? By letting her murder her own mother? Are you crazy?"

"Please, Jack. My mother needs you. You're the only one who can help her."

"For God's sake, she's already dead! *It's too late!*"

And at that he woke up, in the dull yellow glow of streetlamps and neon, and occasional headlights. Three in the morning, he guessed. He must have made a noise, for some elderly drunk in a shabby brown coat was crossing the street. Basic rule of New York life. Avoid the crazy guy yelling in his sleep. Jack leaned his head back against the doorway and to his amazement he began to cry. Maybe it was all very simple after all. The Queen of Eyes was dead. And Jack Shade had killed her.

That afternoon he came upon the Nude Owl. It was on Broadway by Herald Square, the stretch given over to chairs and tables to act as a sidewalk café in summer. Post-season, the furniture remained but no one used them, especially on a day like this one, gray and damp, with a harsh Hudson River wind. No one, that is, except a crazy homeless elemental dressed in so many layers she might have been an art exhibit. Of course, she might not be a "she" at all. At one time Jack might have found that question fun to think about. He could have debated it with his teacher, Anatolie, or maybe Carolien Hounstra. Right now Jack didn't care about what the Owl might look like actually nude any more than he cared that the chair was wet when he sat down next to her.

People walking along Broadway did that automatic swerve people did when they spot homeless people holding a meeting. Jack didn't care about that either. He said, "Why couldn't you tell me? You knew, you had to know, it's what you do. What you are."

For a long time she didn't answer or even look at him, just stared up at the Empire State Building. Maybe she had no idea he was there. Maybe he appeared to her as no more than a tangle of quantum vibrations.

Finally she turned and looked at him as if he had just materialized out of nothing. "Know," she said in a harsh whisper. "Not tell."

Jack said, "Oh, you've got to be kidding me. You're a Know-It-All, but the job description doesn't include telling? Should I have hunted down your twin sister, the Tell-It-All? Oh, God." He felt his anger burst and bent forward, arms tight against his chest. He kept seeing the bullets smash into Margaret's body.

The Owl whispered, "She didn't leave."

Jack was about to say something sarcastic but instead let out a breath. He'd thought about that. Didn't Mariq Nliana *see* what was happening? Wouldn't she have watched it all along? André must have spent weeks, if not months, cultivating Julie. Why didn't Grandma see that? And then to sit, and just *wait*. She said she'd gone there to help her daughter, the hybrid. But whatever they'd needed to do was over, and Margaret just stayed. The daughter herself said it was all about Julie, but that didn't make any sense. And besides, that was a dream. You can't trust dreams.

Margaret had said she didn't use her power to look at her own time-line, but Jack didn't buy it. She wasn't surprised when Jack appeared, she wasn't even surprised when André showed up with his goddamn gun. Why didn't she stop it?

"I don't understand," he said. "I don't get it." He bent forward, hands on his knees, too tired to sit upright.

To his surprise, the Owl reached out and touched his shoulder. It was only the tip of a finger but it made Jack sit up and stare at her. In a gentle, sweet voice, she said, "Jack. What day is it?"

"What?" He stared at her. "It's Friday."

"What day is it?"

"I just told you, it's Friday."

"Jack, what day is it?"

"Jesus," Jack said, and threw up his hands. That was all he needed, for the Owl to devolve into some fugue state. "It's Friday. All fucking day. At midnight it becomes—" He stopped, mouth open, hands half-raised in the air. And then, slowly, he stood up and lowered his arms as a great joy spread through his body. It felt like the antidote to a toxin that had paralyzed him for days. "Oh, sweet God," he said. "*They killed her on the wrong day!*"

Jack went back to the hotel just long enough to shower and change clothes. He didn't want to, he was afraid he'd see Mrs. Yao and have to explain why he looked the way he did, but he needed help, and smelling like a construction site Dumpster wasn't the way to go ask for it. He could glam something respectable for any hotel guests he might pass, but he hated to deceive Irene.

Luckily, he made it to his suite without anyone seeing—or smelling—him, and immediately stripped naked. Later he would burn the clothes, but for now, if they contained hidden NYTAS beacons he was just as happy to have Arthur Canton or whoever else who might be watching believe that he was staying at home. He didn't think Arthur would actually try to stop him, but caution never hurt.

The real question was André. Now that he had what he wanted, would he have bothered to keep tabs on Jack? Could Jack assume that André would consider Jack's part finished? No need to watch him? Jack took a long, hot shower, scrubbing himself with a counterspell pumice stone to remove any last traces of the configuration Jeremy the Ice Demon had cast on him. On a certain level it was all useless. André had the new Queen of Eyes on his side. Jack would just have to hope that the inexperienced Guilielma would have be giving all her attention to André's fight for control of the Societé.

After the shower, hunger hit him like a sudden storm. He found some leftover takeaway in his mini-fridge and gulped down Pad Thai, fried chicken, and half a pastrami on rye. Finally he got dressed. Usually when he worked, Jack wore all black, but this wasn't about work any more, and he needed to impress a prominent businessman. He held up a couple of sport jackets before deciding to go all the way and put on his light gray suit, with a pale yellow silk shirt, no tie. He considered dress shoes but decided to keep his black boots. He wanted his knife. He put on his tan cashmere coat and headed out.

It was 4:22 when he left the hotel, relieved once again not to see Miss Yao. Ray helped with that, guiding him to which elevator to take, which door. Outside he hailed a taxi to take him up to 58th

Street, between 5th and Madison. Jack breathed a small prayer of thanks that Emil S.'s grandson did not have his office in the main building of the Toy Store.

This was the trickiest part. Was he right about the family? Did they keep the Cottage out of gratitude? Or even better, because they liked the idea of it?

Somehow, Jack had expected a slick corporate office, maybe with classic toys on display, the kind of place Arthur Canton might have set up if he'd inherited the world's most famous toy store. Instead, he stepped from the elevator into an innocuous reception area, businesslike and unmemorable. A plump woman in her forties asked Jack if he had an appointment and looked a bit confused when Jack just said, "Tell Mr. Hessen I'm here on behalf of Emil S." Her confusion only increased when she conveyed this message into her Bluetooth, and her boss stepped forward with a big smile and his hand out to greet the visitor.

As with the office, Jack realized he'd expected some grand figure, perhaps in the pinstriped cutaway suit the rich wore in old cartoons attacking Wall Street. Malcolm Hessen wore jeans, a white shirt open at the neck, no tie and no jacket. Casual Friday. A white man about fifty-five, five-foot-ten, he looked like he worked out at the gym three or four times a week but just couldn't resist that late-night slice of cake. His hairline hadn't receded too much, and had kept most of its light brown color, gray only at the temples. He wore a neat mustache that seemed to accent his excited smile. "I'm Malcolm," he said. "Emil's grandson."

"John Shade," Jack said, and gave him his card.

Malcolm looked at it and shook his head. "Traveler," he quoted. "Wow. I never thought—" He noticed his receptionist staring at him and held open his office door. "Come inside," he said.

The inner office was as functional as the reception area with a long metal desk holding a Mac and piles of printouts, charts, and brochures, an executive "action chair" in green nylon webbing, and three polished oak chairs with dark green leather seats and armrests. Two large windows looked out over 58th Street. Hessen had crowded the ledges with family photos, a blonde wife and three children at different ages. The largest photo showed a young man in the uniform of some Minor League baseball team, looking very serious as he held his bat ready.

Hessen waved Jack to one of the chairs and perched on the edge of his desk. He said "What can I do for you, Mr. Shade? Seriously," and before Jack could answer, he added, "You have to understand, this is a special moment. In our family we call it the Great Debt. To have a chance to repay some small part of it—"

Enough, Jack thought. He had hoped the man would feel that way, but now it was time to act. He said, "I need to get into the store tonight."

Hessen looked disappointed, as if he'd expected Jack to recruit him for a full moon ritual, but all he said was "Yes, of course. What time?"

"Eleven-thirty."

"I'll tell the guards to expect you. No, I'll let you in myself."

"And then I'll need to spend some time in the Witch's Cottage. I'm not sure how long."

"Ah. I head something about—what happened on Tuesday. Was that you?"

"I'm afraid so."

"I should have guessed. It was the Cottage, after all. You caused quite a stir."

"I'm sorry. I never meant to bother anyone. Especially the children. I was—" He stopped, uncertain what he could say.

"No, no," Emil S.'s grandson said. 'I'm sure that whatever it was, it was necessary."

Jesus, Jack thought. *Necessary*. He stood up and offered his hand. "Thank you, Mr.—"

"Malcolm."

"Thank you, Malcolm. I'll see you at eleven-thirty?"

"By the front door." They shook hands and Jack left.

He walked back to the Rêve Noire, his collar up against a snow shower. Would snow shield him from Guilielma? Or did the flakes have eyes? Was she watching him right now? Had she seen him through the photographs in Hessen's office? There was nothing Jack could do about it. He just had to hope they didn't think he was worth watching. Maybe they'd be right.

When he walked into the hotel, Miss Yao was there, talking to the man at the desk, Harold. She smiled when she saw Jack. "Jack?" she said, which was her way of asking if his job had finished.

"Miss Yao," he said, which meant no. It wasn't really true, there was no job any more, but it was too difficult to explain.

Sadness and worry flickered across her face, but all she did was nod as he went past her to the elevator.

Back in his room, he made himself a cup of coffee and sat down at the table that served as his desk. What should he do? Nearly six hours, and everything he needed was already in place. Sleep. Anatolie had taught him to sleep whenever he could, under any circumstances, the chance might not come again for quite a while. He took off his boots and jacket and lay down on top of the comforter. Instead of closing his eyes, however, he picked up the framed photo from the nightstand next to the bed. Layla and Eugenia, splashing and laughing at the shallow end of a lake in Vermont. Genie was seven at the time, long before the geist. They'd been playing some silly game and Jack had been lucky enough to catch them at a perfect moment. He looked at it a while then pressed the picture facedown against his chest and closed his eyes.

He woke up at 10:22 with the photo still tight against his heart.

Malcolm Hessen was already there when Jack showed up precisely at eleven-thirty. Dressed in a brown wool coat with deerskin gloves, Hessen nearly glowed as he let Jack inside and called down the two guards on duty to tell them Mr. Shade needed to "check on some things in the Witch's Cottage" and was not to be disturbed "under any circumstances." Jack feared Hessen might say something about "strange sounds or lights," but Hessen restrained himself. Nor did he try to tag along. He and Jack shook hands and he left. Jack nodded to the two guards then walked to the back of the store and up the switched-off escalator.

Without the main store lights on, let alone the fake oil lamps inside the Cottage, it was hard to see anything clearly. Should he ask the guards to turn on some lights? And what about the Witch? She sat frozen with her arm poised over her mini-cauldron. It all looked so dead. He looked at the Gretel doll, lifeless as a stick. He'd guessed it would be up to him this time, and apparently he was right.

He took out the knife and laid it on his left palm. The dim light rendered the carbon blade almost invisible. He couldn't see his hand very well, and he was wearing black, so it was almost like he wasn't there. He sighed and slipped the knife back into his boot. No violence, he decided, not even to dolls.

He reached in his coat pocket for a stub of blue chalk and a clear packet of white powder. Walking counterclockwise with the chalk he drew a snake on the fake wood floor. He began with the tail to the left of the doorway, went around the triangle table with the dolls, and ended with the snake's head to the right of the door, its mouth open as if it was reaching to bite its tail but couldn't cross the doorway.

Jack cut open the envelope and poured the powder on the floor in the gap between the tail and the mouth. With the tip of his knife, he drew the Mark of the Opener in the powder then put back the knife and stood up. From the left pocket of his jeans he took out a small box of "conjure" matches, made in the old style by a family of fire witches somewhere in West Virginia. Jack allowed himself a smile as he remembered how the family had all dressed up as old-timey mountainfolk for the home page on their website. He glanced back now at the Gretel doll. As far as he could tell, it hadn't changed, but he still said, "See you on the other side," then lit the match and dropped it on the flash powder. In the brief flare of light he stepped through the doorway.

The first thing he saw was Margaret's ruined body. Lumpy, gray, the bloodstains as dull as dirt in February. For a moment, it was as if the last days hadn't happened, and he'd just watched André murder her. But no, it was Friday evening. The Queen of Eyes had died on a Tuesday, and now it was Friday, and in twenty minutes it would be Saturday.

It was a Saturday, of course. Sarah had said that. Talking about her grandmother's death. Jack had thought it strange at the time, and then he'd just forgotten.

Suddenly nervous, he glanced at his watch. What if time didn't work here, what if it stopped on Tuesday afternoon? No. His watch said 11:43. Most important, the second hand continued its implacable sweep.

Jack squatted by Margaret's body. The bullet had torn open the left side of her face. The right cheek, when he touched it, was cold and smooth, with a rubbery texture. When he pressed his finger against the skin it sank inward, and the shape didn't return when he took his finger away. Jack thought of the cheap plastic "modeling clay" Genie used to play with in day care.

Beyond Margaret the entire world had lost its shape and color, all of it as gray and lumpy as the body. The flowers were gone, the river had vanished, replaced by a meandering indentation. And beyond that, the mountains had collapsed in on themselves, like some disastrous soufflé made of gray mud.

Panic tried to propel Jack to the door, back to a living universe. What the hell was he doing here? If he didn't get out now the gateway would collapse and he would die. There was no air, why didn't he realize that? He could only breathe now because he'd brought a kind of bubble with him from the real world. But it was going fast, he could hardly get any air in his lungs.

He placed his hands on his knees and forced himself to breathe out, a slow hiss of air until he was empty. He waited a few seconds then slowly took another breath. Okay. There was air. Whatever else, he wasn't going to suffocate.

He had to stop himself looking at his watch every few seconds, as if he could will it to spin faster and get to midnight. So instead of looking, he thought about the Ancient Doll. And the days of the week. And souls.

He'd thought Margaret had been, what, conversing when she'd reminded him of the three souls, how everyone stumbles along six days a week with an animal soul to keep our bodies alive, and a mind soul to let us plan, and worry, and obsess, and maybe love. And then on Saturday the Bride of the Earth, who sometimes appears as the Ancient Doll, brings us something extra, a so-called spirit soul. No one understands too much about this, what it's for, and that was probably because most people don't use it. Don't know how.

But the Queen of Eyes does. It's the spirit soul that activates sight and makes what she does possible, even after it's gone, for the power it generates stays with her for the six days until the

Bride returns to charge her up again. More than anyone else, the Queen comes fully alive at midnight Saturday. And because of that she can only *die* on a Saturday. For the rest of us, who don't use our third soul, if we die—if someone kills us—on a Tuesday, or maybe a Monday, the day the geist killed Layla, we're gone. Finished. But not the Queen of Eyes.

It was a Saturday, of course.

At least, that was Jack's theory. But would it work? Had anyone ever tried anything like this?

11:48. Jack liked that number, it added up to fourteen. If thirteen was the number of death, then maybe fourteen promised resurrection.

11:52. 11:55.

At 11:57 Jack saw something. A flower. Tiny, on a stem only a half-inch high, with a blossom no bigger than his thumbnail, it shone bright yellow in the cold air. A city boy most of his life, Jack had no idea what flower it was, but he stared and stared at it. Others appeared, always when he was looking somewhere else. Yellow, black, pink. Soon the hillside had returned, and below it the river, and despite the dim gray sky Jack could make out the form of mountains. But on the ground beside him the Queen lay as lumpy and empty as before.

11:59.

Jack had assumed the Ancient Doll would appear, maybe in a blaze of light. Instead, as the hour and minute hands of his watch finally united on the twelve, a shadow seemed to settle all around him. Not fog or smoke, but just as impenetrable.

What was happening? Had he failed? Maybe André had sent the cloud. To block him. He stood up and called out a Spell of Disbursement. No change. Next he tried the Fundamental Command of Negation against "any and all malevolent entities." Nothing. Desperate, he looked at his watch. Nearly a minute after midnight. How long a window was there?

Then it struck him. Maybe the shadow had come to *protect* him. After all, who was Jack Shade to see the Bride of the Earth? He called out, "Ancient one! We welcome you. We greet you and honor you and thank you for all your gifts."

A shape took form in the shadow. Not the Ancient Doll but her counterpart, the Gretel doll from the Cottage. She was on her feet now, wearing pink Mary Janes, and she looked towards the Queen with her right arm out, palm up. Jack couldn't see anything in her hand but he could feel it, a pulsing brilliance.

He looked again at the Queen. Lifeless! Why hadn't she changed? He looked back at Gretel and she was staring at him. Him, not Margaret.

Quickly he bent down and picked up the heavy gray form that had been Margaret Strand. Fixing his eyes on the Bride, he proclaimed, "I, John Shade, Traveler from the New York Territories, offer myself as vessel and conduit for Margarita Mariq Nliana Hand. I give myself to the life and restoration of the Queen of Eyes!"

Fire surged through him and he yelled out, but not in pain. It was what he saw. Vast swirls of scenes came and went in an instant, all over the world, endless variations on love, despair, rage, sacrifice. He saw presidents and paupers, murderers and saints. For the briefest moment he saw himself, years ago, as he held his wife's body and watched helplessly as his daughter walked through a stone doorway into the Forest of Souls. "Genie!" he called to her, and she turned, mouth open, as if to tell him something. Then it was over, the stone door replaced by the Witch's Cottage, once again bright and cheerful, surrounded by a soft night sky scattered with stars.

He looked down now at the woman in his arms, hoping that it was Layla, that the Bride had taken the Queen and brought his wife back to him, and now he could carry her through the Cottage and back to the World of Disguise, which is to say, everyday life. But of course it wasn't Layla, it was her. Margarita Mariq— No, he realized. Margaret Strand. Mother and grandmother. A woman who would do anything, take any chance, to save her family.

She looked up at him now, and smiled. Tired, weak, but also kind, and grateful beyond tears. "Oh, Jack," she whispered. "Thank you. I knew I could count on you."

Jack Shade leaned against his Altima on a dead-end street just outside Red Hook, NY, ninety miles up the Hudson from New York. Red Hook was a little bigger than Gold River, a little fancier, with a couple of "nouvelle" restaurants and regional art galleries alongside the pizza joints and Chinese take-away.

None of that concerned Jack Shade on this late Saturday afternoon in early December. He was watching a house that stood by itself at the end of the street. There wasn't much to see, at least without a certain concentrated effort. Dark, its white paint and green trim chipped and faded, a few shingles gone from the roof, the front gutter hanging down at the corner, it looked like the bank had foreclosed on it during the crash and never got around to selling it.

It was all a glam, of course. If he'd felt like really looking, Jack could have pierced the illusion to the fresh paint and lights. When it came down to it, glamours depended on people not knowing they were there. But why bother when Jack knew what it was, and who was inside?

It had taken a bit of effort but Carolien Hounstra had helped him. She enjoyed it, speaking in whispers over the phone, calling him "Jack Spy," and wearing an honest-to-God trenchcoat when they met in Trader Joe's at Union Square.

27 Beech Grove was a NYTAS safe house. Right now it was being used as a combination prison and one-person therapy center, and no doubt would continue so for months. The focus of all this effort and attention, the single prisoner/patient, was Juliana Strand.

So, Jack had thought when Carolien had brought him the news. Dr. Canton was not above helping the Queen of Eyes after all, at least not if he didn't have to pick a fight with the *Societé de Matin*. The Deputy Head of Operations, the one who'd replaced André, and of course the Old Man of the Woods himself, had probably found some way to reward NYTAS (or Arthur personally) for helping to tie up loose ends to a failed coup. The *Societé* wouldn't have demanded punishment for Julie. It was André they cared about. And André's end, Jack knew, would not have been loose at all.

As Jack stared at the house, he wondered what they would do, what combination of drugs, family therapy (was Margaret there now? Sarah?), lower-level journeying, brain leeches, or mud-puppet surrogates would be used to break down the configurations that probably had built up in Julie for years. He wondered how André had spotted her, what he'd done to bring out the paranoia, the lust for power, the rage. Jack would probably never know.

Margarita Mariq had seen what was happening to her grand-daughter. She'd seen the danger. But what she couldn't *just see* was how to save her. Oh, she could have gotten her away from André, locked her up, worked on her. But the configurations might have refused to unravel.

Then the idea had come to her. Jack could only guess how desperate she must have been simply to consider it. Suppose she let Julie do it? Suppose she let her granddaughter find out just what it meant to kill her own mother. To become the Queen of Eyes and truly see what she'd done. Might the horror of it make her desperate to undo it? And then, if it could be reversed, if Mom and Grandma actually came back, would that open at least a small window of recovery?

Jack was pretty sure Margaret hadn't told Sarah. He shook his head at the thought of what *that* reunion must have sounded like. According to Carolien, Margaret had taken steps to make sure nothing would happen to Sarah's body until after the weekend, at which point, of course, Sarah would have come back to life again. He laughed a moment, imagining what a job it must have been for COLE, the good old Committee Of Linear Explanation, to cover that one up at the funeral parlor.

Serious again, he thought of the incredible risks Margaret had taken. The biggest risk was Jack himself. What if Sarah had never come to him? What if he'd never gone to the Risen Spirit Shelter, for Jeremy to spread his wings? *Oh, Jack, I knew I could count on you.*

Jack knew it wasn't random chance he'd found the Queen. André himself would have set up the pattern to create a search, to bring in John Shade. Jack was pretty sure it was André who'd given Jack's card to Julie and told her to set it up where Mom could see it. But what André could never have guessed was that he himself was being led, as surely as he was leading Jack. How could he? Who would imagine a woman would arrange her own murder?

Jack folded his arms and shook his head again. No matter how brutal a gangster André Matin was, no matter how ruthless—he was no match for a grandmother.

Jack didn't really know how long he stood there, just staring at the house. How long would it take? Years? Maybe just months. And then Julie would get to go home, reunited with her resurrected mother and grandmother.

And Layla Shade would still be dead. And Eugenia Shade would still be locked away in the Forest of Souls.

Possessed or not, Julie Strand had murdered her mother in full consciousness. In cold blood, cold as the frozen Hudson. And then Mom comes back, and Julie gets fixed, and life for the Strand girls resumes its generational path of seeing.

Genie Shade never meant to kill her mother. Oh, she'd liked the power the poltergeist gave her, the feeling that her mother couldn't control her. But on that day when the geist took over, and the knives flew all around the kitchen, that wasn't Genie. Not even the smallest part of her. But it made no difference, did it? Layla wasn't returning. And Jack still had no way to bring his daughter back.

He discovered he was shaking, whether from anger or grief or just the damp December twilight, he couldn't tell. He was about to get in his car when a woman's voice behind him said "You come here often?"

He turned and saw a tall thin woman in a dark green parka and green UGG boots. She'd left the parka hood down for her long black hair to bunch up around her shoulders. Jack said, "My first time. How about you? Are you a regular?"

She shrugged. "I hope not. But she *is* my niece. Step-niece?"

"Have you gone inside?"

Slight smile. "That level of involvement I can do without."

There was a pause. "You look different," Jack said.

The smile again, a little stronger. "You're awake."

Now Jack grinned back. "So I am."

Another silence, and then the woman said, "You did a great thing, Jack."

"Did I? I don't see that I had much choice. It was my fault she got killed." He paused a second, then said, "Even if it was her idea. Of course, I didn't know that at the time."

"And if you did? If you'd found out right away, would it have made a difference?"

"No."

"You saved her, Jack. If she'd come back with no one to help her . . . She trusted you. And she was right."

Trusted me, Jack thought. *Enough to pull me into a family murder. Why? Because I knew what it felt like?* But all he said was, "I don't know your name."

"Oh, I'm sorry," she said, and for a second he thought she blushed. "I'm Elaynora."

"Nice to meet you, Elaynora."

"I feel like I've known you—" She took a breath. "I've never had the chance to thank you, Jack. For that time on the beach."

"I didn't do anything."

"You tried. My mother and I—we'd been having one of our *difficult* moments. And the fact that someone would just come forward like that—well, it meant a lot."

"And your mother?"

Elaynora smiled. "Not quite so happy."

"So tell me, did she pull me into all this—" he waved a hand. "—to punish me?"

"No, no. It was more the opposite. She knew she could trust you."

"Huh. That's what she told me." He rolled his eyes. "Lucky me." To his surprise, they both laughed. He said, "Can I ask you something?"

"Sure."

"Who's your father?"

"Ah, of course. I could tell you his name but you wouldn't be able to pronounce it. I can hardly say it myself." She spoke a combination of clicks and whistles and liquid vowels.

"See what you mean,' Jack said.

She grinned. "I try to stick with Dad."

"Smart move."

"I came across his name on a list once. It was in a book of ethnology. The book described him as a minor sun deity of an extinct tribe."

"Lost his gig, huh? That must be rough, when all your worshippers die out."

"Now he operates an agency for dream hunters."

"Is that what he did for the tribe?"

"Kind of. They believed dreams come from the sun, so he made sure to supply them."

"And now he hunts down dreams for his clients. Pay enough and you can get any dream you want."

"Something like that."

"And you join the hunt?" She smiled, but didn't answer. Jack said, "I'm guessing Mom's not too wild about all this."

She shrugged. A tiny ripple of light moved off her shoulders and vanished in the growing dark. She said, "She considers it 'disreputable.'"

Jack laughed. "I'll bet. Families." He laughed again, and this time Elaynora joined him.

"Happy families are all alike," she said.

Jack finished the *Anna Karenina* line. "Unhappy families are each unhappy in their own way."

"Good old Tolstoy. Do you know, he hired my father once? He needed some dream help to finish *War and Peace*."

"Huh. I always thought there was something Traveler about him." Jack looked around. "Did you walk here?"

"Yeah. I'm staying in the village."

"Why don't I drive you back and buy you a drink? Are you allowed to drink alcohol?"

"When I'm off duty."

"And you're off duty now?"

"Uh huh."

"Good," Jack said. "Me too."

Just before they got in the car, they each stopped a moment and looked once more at the house. Then they got in the Altima and Jack drove them back to the world.

3

JOHNNY REV

That was your black double. You aren't who you think you are.

—Flannery O'Connor, "Everything That Rises Must Converge"

Prologue

I N HIS EARLY YEARS AS A TRAVELER, JACK SHADE, REBEL JACK, as people would later call him, studied with the legendary teacher known as Anatolie. He didn't really know her fame at the time, only that she was the one whose name he'd been given by the lion-tamer who'd first shown Carny Jack a glimpse of the Real World in the mouth of a lion.

In the years Jack studied with Anatolie, she annoyed him as much as inspired him, not least because at something like five hundred pounds she did not get around much, and Jack sometimes thought he was more errand boy than apprentice. One day he went to see her in her fifth-floor walk-up on Bayard Street in Chinatown, and as usual had stopped in at the Lucky Star restaurant to pick up the order she'd called down when she knew he was coming. Most of the time Jack didn't really mind bringing her food, but that day he decided he'd had enough. It was time to tell her some hard truth. "Why don't you get a ground-floor apartment?" he said as he arranged the food on a tray big enough to go across her belly. "Or at least one of those lofts with an old freight elevator."

"And why is that, Jack?" she asked softly, as her ancient bone chopsticks began to ferry *har kow* to her wide, flat face.

Jack should have recognized that tone and backed off but he was feeling reckless. Years later, a dealer in the Ibis Casino would tell him, "You were always Johnny Danger back then. Or maybe just Jack Crazy."

"So you can actually leave the house now and then," he told her. "Get out in the street. Experience picking up your own food."

"Oh, Jack," she said, "you still think things are as they appear?" As she moved on to shredded pork and puffed tofu in ginger sauce, she said, in that same bland voice, "Perhaps you should go. You don't seem in the mood for a lesson."

"Great," Jack said. "All this way just to drag your food upstairs."

"Oh, by the way," she said as he was about to leave, "pay attention on the way home. You wouldn't want to miss anything." Jack made a noise and slammed the door.

He was so annoyed he didn't notice anything strange until he was on Canal Street, heading for the No. 6 Subway, and a large woman in a bright red parka bumped into him. She was moving so fast, with heavy shopping bags in each hand like pendulum weights, she almost knocked Jack down. "Hey!" he yelled, and was about to add something very New York when he noticed the woman's gait and the set of her shoulders. "Anatolie?" he said, but not loud enough for her to hear him as she moved through the crowds of shoppers, tourists, and hucksters.

It can't be, he told himself. Even if she could get herself up and dressed and downstairs without his help, how would she have had the time to catch up with him? Distracted, he found himself going past a knock-off shop, the kind of place with oversize, over-bling watches and fall-apart luggage out front, but fake Prada hidden in the back for the right sort of customer. A skinny Chinese man with greasy hair was pretending to flirt with a trio of white teenage girls from the suburbs in hopes they might buy his phony Pandora bracelets. Jack paid no attention until the man called out, "Rolex watch, Jack. Look just like real."

Jack spun around, and in place of the Chinese hustler stood Anatolie, so large she filled the doorway. She held up the watch. "Good quality, Jack. No tell difference."

Jack wasn't sure he could breathe. He turned to the three girls to ask if they too saw the large black woman, only to discover that their skin had darkened and their over-gelled bleached hair had snaked into long dreadlocks. All three nodded and smiled at him.

Jack tried to escape into the crowd but it was no good. The old Chinese ladies with their net shopping bags filled with bok choy and tofu, the guys behind the fried-noodle stands, the homeless man pretending he had someplace to go, the art students with plastic bags from Pearl Paint—they were all *her*.

He did his best not to look at anyone, at least not close enough to see them change, as he rushed back to Bayard Street. For just a second he considered picking up a bribe at Lucky Star, but was pretty sure he couldn't take it if cheerful, loud Mrs. Shen became a five-hundred-pound black woman with dreads that wound around her waist like that Norse serpent that holds together the world. So instead he just ran upstairs, burst into her apartment where of course she was still lying on her oversized, reinforced bed, empty takeout cartons all around her, and he begged her, "Make it stop. Please. I get it, I'm sorry, I'll never say you can't leave your apartment again. Please. You can't be everyone."

She laced her hands across her belly. "Are you sure about that, Jack? Maybe there's just one person in the world, and we're all Duplicates." Jack stared at her, confused. Finally she smiled, and said, "You can go now. It's safe."

He hesitated a moment, then left. All the way home everyone remained themselves, but even so, he stood a long time outside his door before he went inside. For what if his wife Layla's olive skin had turned dark brown, or eleven year old Eugenia had put on four hundred pounds?

Now

J ACK SHADE WAS WALKING DOWN LAFAYETTE STREET, HEADING toward Canal, when the Momentary Storm hit. He was on his way to buy a stone frog from Mr. Suke (not his real name) as a present for Carolien Hounstra, Jack's colleague in the New York Travelers' Aid Society. Generous Jack, people called him, though usually not without a half-smile and a lifted eyebrow.

Carolien collected frogs, had many shelves of them in her West Side apartment. Some were netsuke, others jade or malachite or onyx, and a few were so old it was hard to tell what they were. There was a story people liked to tell about Carolien's hobby, that an ancestor had been turned into a stone frog by some malevolent Traveler, or maybe a vindictive Power, and Carolien hoped to find him and turn him back. Others claimed it wasn't an ancestor but an older, or younger, brother, and the enactment had retroactively aged the carving to make it harder to find him. Still others claimed it was Carolien herself who'd stoned her brother—or maybe a lover who'd jilted her—and had done too good a job, so that when remorse set in she couldn't locate him. This last group consisted mostly of people whose advances Carolien had rejected. "The Dutch Ice Queen," some called her, a term which always made Jack laugh or shake his head.

Jack doubted the truth of all these stories. It wasn't that he believed Carolien would not try to rescue a relative. He'd seen how she'd dropped her work at NYTAS and everything else, including Jack, when her teenage cousin from Rotterdam had come to New York for a couple of weeks. No, it was just that people liked to make up stories about her. Six feet tall, 185 pounds, and very Dutch, with long blonde hair, large breasts, and a tendency to say or do whatever she wanted, she was a natural target. She didn't appear to notice but Jack thought that might be an act.

If Jack doubted that Carolien had a relative who'd been turned into a frog, he strongly suspected that Mr. Suke was in fact a frog who'd been turned into a man. He just wasn't sure if the frog Suke had been alive or carved. Jack was wondering if he should outright ask him, and whether that might violate some code of privacy, when he felt something brush against his leg. He smiled, and looked down to see Ray, his reddish-gold spirit fox, moving his tail to get Jack's attention. No one could see Ray but Jack, so when he spoke he kept his voice low. "What is it, buddy? What do you want me to see?"

Ray lifted his head to point his snout downtown, and Jack followed the line of sight to the helix-shaped tower of the new World Trade Center. As Jack watched, a dark cloud rolled over it, until all you could see was gray sky. *Oh shit,* Jack thought, *not again.* But then he heard someone to his left say, "Jesus, look at that," and someone else say, "You can't even see it," and Jack let out a breath. Not an omen, then, or at least not just for his eyes only.

It would take a few minutes before he realized how wrong he was.

As Jack and everyone else watched, the dark cloud poured towards them. Soon it began to rain, hard slashing drops that sent umbrellas and coat collars up, and a few people scrambling into doorways. Jack just stood there, squinting at the rain as if the drops might form a pattern. He looked down and Ray was still at his side, body rigid, tail straight out, telling Jack there was something in the rain. Something about Ray . . . his tail was wet! How could—

A border storm! Half in this world, half in the Other. *Shit,* Jack thought. He didn't like border crossings, no one did. You could meet your mirror, your Traveler From The Other Side, and then things would get really tangled. Some people said that that was how Peter Midnight, all those years ago, had lost Manhattan to the Man in the Black Cravat.

Hold steady, Jack told himself. Even if it was a border crossing it was just a shower. And then the hail started. Not huge, about the size of a shooter marble, it came down heavy, and on wild swirls of wind, so that anyone who'd braved the rain now ran inside shops or doorways. Except Jack. Even Ray had vanished, but Jack knew he couldn't leave, there was something he was supposed to see.

The hail began to move around itself, separating, coming together, forming shapes, columns—a man. Vague at first, not as defined as, say, the Face on Mars (set up by some prank Traveler to embarrass NASA) but still clear. Tall, strong-looking yet somehow graceful, with the long, tapered fingers that marked a Traveler. Jack squinted at him, the posture, the shape of the head. "No," he whispered. Light appeared in the face. Whether from a flash of lightning, or the sun coming through a gap in the storm, it lit up the right jawline from the ear almost to the mouth, showing a surface smooth as melted gold. Down Jack's jawline, his scar throbbed.

"Oh fuck," Jack said, then loud, shouting, "You're dead! I killed you, goddamnit. I *killed* you!"

It took a couple of seconds for Jack to realize that the hail had stopped, and the sun now lit up the street and people had ventured back into the open, only to stare nervously at this man who'd just screamed about killing someone. Some already had their phones out, to call 911 or to take a picture. Either one was as bad as the other. Quickly, Jack glammed himself so that no one would remember him and any pictures they took would be blurred. Then he turned and headed uptown. Carolien's frog would have to wait.

Jack and Irene Yao were playing mahjong in Jack's office in the Hôtel de Rêve Noire. The office was really just a two-room suite several floors down from the larger suite where Jack had lived for the past nine years. Irene owned the hotel, but she and Jack had long ago become friends. Elegant as always, the fiftyish woman had let loose her long gray-black hair to flow gently down the back of her maroon linen dress. Jack himself wore a pale yellow shirt, collar unbuttoned, dark brown pleated pants, and a thin red silk tie draped around his neck.

They played with a three hundred year old set of ivory tiles backed with bamboo. Jack couldn't remember exactly when they'd started playing together, but it was always just the two of them, and never for money. Jack was a high-stakes poker player, and even though mahjong was closer to gin rummy, he didn't want to trigger his professional skills by letting the game get serious. At the same time, he kept wondering if Irene was setting him up somehow. The tiles had been in her family a long time.

Two soft knocks came at the door. Startled, Jack looked up from his hand to see that Irene was gone, her empty chair slightly away from the table. Another knock, just one this time, and Jack stared at the back of the door, eyes narrowed. He knew that sound, knew what it meant. He glanced once more at the empty chair, then stood up and went to open the door. Sure enough, Mrs. Yao stood there, dressed the same but with her hair up, and yes, she was holding the small silver tray with Jack's card on it. "Mr. Shade," she said. It was only *Mrs. Yao* and *Mr. Shade* when Jack was working.

Jack looked down at the card. *John Shade, Traveler,* it read, and the name of the hotel, and the black horse's head from the Staunton chess knight. Only, someone, the client, Jack assumed, had scratched a jagged line through the embossed head. Like a scar.

Jack didn't need any work at this point. A few months back he'd taken a case to find a missing woman who'd turned out to be the Queen of Eyes, holder of all the world's oracular power. Jack hadn't asked for a fee when the case ended, but a few weeks later his client, the Queen's daughter, had shown up with a check for

100K. Jack was pretty sure the money had come from *La Societé de Matin*, the international order of gangster magicians—his finding the Queen had helped them avoid a faction war—but that was okay. He'd earned it. So he didn't need to work, and didn't want to, but a curse Jack had foolishly put on himself years earlier gave him no choice. If someone showed up with Jack's business card Jack could not refuse the case. Travelers called this compulsory obligation a "Guest," after an old Irish term, *geass*.

Jack sighed. "Thank you, Mrs. Yao," he said, and took the card from the tray. It was cold.

When he looked up, Mrs. Yao was crying. Jack had never asked her how much she knew, but he suspected it was more than she let on. "It's all right," he said. "It's just a case."

She dabbed at her eyes with a fingertip. "I'm sorry," she said, then, "He's downstairs. In your office."

"What—?" Jack looked around, saw he was in the living room of his suite. Hadn't they been—weren't they—something was wrong. For a second, Ray appeared, fur bristling, then vanished, as if—as if someone was blocking him. But Ray belonged to Jack, who could interfere with that?

And then Jack was in his office, sitting at the mahogany table that served as his desk, and across from him sat a man who was hard to see. He looked around Jack's height and weight, six feet and 175 pounds, and was dressed in an open-necked black shirt, black jeans, scuffed cowboy boots, and a long, unbuttoned black leather coat. His face was hard to make out, sometimes blurred, at other moments deeply shadowed. Except—down his jawline, from his ear to his mouth, ran a jagged line of golden light. Only when Jack unconsciously touched his own face did he realize that the light followed the path of his scar.

Jesus, Jack thought. I'm dreaming. This was all a goddamn dream. He almost laughed. People could attack you in dreams, but it was easy enough to fend them off.

"I have a case for you," the man said, his voice a harsh whisper.

Jack leaned back in his chair. "Go ahead," he said.

"I have an enemy. Someone who wants to destroy me."

"Do you know why?"

The hidden face flashed brightly, then a moment later faded back into darkness. "It doesn't matter," the man said. "You've got to make him stop."

"How do I do that?"

"You'll find a way. That's what you do, isn't it? I'm hiring you to beat him. I want to win."

Jack said, "I can't just kill him."

"Why not? He tried to kill me, didn't he?"

"You haven't told me who he is," Jack said. "What's his name?"

The man shook his head. "No, no, no, that's the wrong question."

Jack felt his voice dry up, as harsh now as the man's rasping whisper. "What's the right question?"

"*My* name," the man said. Now he leaned forward, as if to bring his face into the light. "You're supposed to ask who *I* am. Isn't that right, Johnny? Isn't that the first step?"

Jack came awake in his bed with a shout. Despite everything, his Traveler training told him it was 4:17 in the morning. The narrow steel posts at the corners of his bed glowed slightly, as if heated. He lay there, unable to move or breathe. *It was him!* The Dupe. Jack Fake. Hidden Johnny. The Man Without A Scar. And now it turned out that the Dupe—the fucking Duplicate— was also a goddamn *Revenant*. Johnny Rev. The Man Who Didn't Leave.

"Goddamn it," Jack said out loud. What the fuck did he do now? His own Revenant had hired him. Did it make any difference that it was in a dream? Dream Johnny still had Jack's card, didn't he? And the man the Rev wanted Jack to kill? Well shit, that was easy enough to figure out. That could only be Jack himself.

People make Dupes for all sorts of reasons—to assist in some enactment, to take their place in a dangerous operation, to trick an enemy or escape a trap. Jack Shade was probably the only Traveler to duplicate himself to go speak to his mother-in-law.

On the worst day of Jack Shade's life, after the poltergeist that had possessed his daughter Eugenia had killed Jack's wife—after Jack himself had tried to save his daughter and ended up exiling her as the only living resident in the Forest of Souls, that dark woods of the unhappy dead—as Jack squatted next to Layla's body on the blood-drenched kitchen floor, rocking back and forth, howling—the doorbell rang.

Jack could never say for sure what drove him to answer it. Did he think it was the police and he should just give himself up? Did he imagine it was a team from NYTAS, the New York Travelers Aid Society, come to take him away for endangering Traveler anonymity? Or did he somehow hope it was Layla's remnant, come to forgive him, and together they would go to rescue Genie? But when Jack opened the door, barely conscious of the blood running down his face and neck from the knives the geist had flung at him, what he saw was indeed a dead person. Just not his wife.

Elvis Presley stood there, young and dangerous, with that lush Captain Marvel Jr. haircut, dressed in worn jeans and denim jacket and a dark T-shirt, and a pair of very scuffed blue shoes. Elvis looked Jack up and down, then cocked his head, as if to say *Yeah, brother, I've had days like that.* Instead, all he said was "Hey, man, my damn truck's gone and over-heated on me." Jack couldn't help himself, he glanced past Elvis to where a rusty old Chevy pick-up, from around 1955, was parked at the curb. It sure looked real enough, as oily steam came off the filthy hood. Elvis said, "Ain't nothin' I can do but let it cool down some. So I figured maybe I could go see if there was a friendly face around." He grinned. "And shit, maybe some beer and peanut butter."

Not sure he could speak, Jack just nodded and stepped aside for Elvis to enter the house.

Almost from the moment of his death, Elvis Presley had been a member of the most exclusive group of Friends and Helpers this poor suffering world has ever known, the Dead Quartet.

124

Except for its leader, the Quartet's personnel changed with the times. The current lineup consisted of Joan of Arc, permanent anchor and chief, plus Nelson Mandela, Princess Di, and Elvis.

Anytime someone new joined, he or she wiped people's memories clean of the person they replaced, but that didn't stop people whoknew from speculating. Carolien Hounstra had made it a kind of hobby to try to track down any traces of previous members. She was pretty sure that Joan had originally taken over from the Quartet's founder, the Virgin Mary. Mary had gotten sick of it and agreed to Joan's demand for a permanent slot. Di, Carolien said, had replaced Eleanor Roosevelt. She was less sure about Mandela, thinking Che Guevara or Gandhi. And Elvis, she suspected, had taken over from either James Dean or maybe Billie Holiday.

What the Quartet did was pretty simple. They helped people. People lonely, desperate, all out of money, friends, or hope. They were said to specialize: Joan to warriors, queer people, and the young whom everyone had deserted; Di came to the sick and abandoned; Mandiba to people in the low ebb of a long struggle; and Elvis to ordinary folks with weights that were too damn heavy, and no one to help carry the load. Jack Shade was not exactly ordinary, but he sure as hell qualified otherwise. In fact, since Elvis mostly showed up at gas stations and 7-Elevens, his appearance at Jack's door made it clear how much Jack needed him.

Jack said, "Come on," and headed for the kitchen with Elvis behind him, as if all that mattered was peanut butter and beer.

When Elvis saw the body he shook his head. "Jesus, man," he said. "You really are in trouble. You off your old lady?" Jack stared at him. "Hey," Elvis said, "wouldn't be the first time. People fight, they get carried away."

"Bullshit," Jack said. "You know what happened here."

Elvis looked at him a long time, then said, "Yeah, I guess I do. Thing is, man, not everybody can see like I can. Anyone who heard anything, anyone who just come up to the door, they're going to see shit they won't understand. You got to take care of this, man."

Jack found himself shaking so hard he had to grab hold of the kitchen table. When he saw that his hands were covered in blood his first thought was that he better not stain Layla's antique oak table, she'd be really pissed off. And then he wondered, was it his blood or hers? He remembered then, he'd been down on the floor, holding her, even as a stone door had opened in the air and a kind of wind had pulled his daughter into the Forest of Souls. He looked at Elvis. "What am I going to do?" he said.

Elvis nodded. "Okay. First thing you gotta do is cast one of them things around the house. What d'you call 'em?"

It took Jack a moment, then he said, "Oh, right. A glamour."

"Yeah. Funny word for it, huh?"

"It's old," Jack muttered. He closed his eyes to concentrate. A glam wouldn't solve anything but it would keep outsiders— non-Travelers, or "nons" as some people called them—from noticing anything.

It was a simple enough action, but it took Jack three tries to get it right. When he did, however, he discovered he felt a little stronger. No cops were going to rush in and take Layla's body away from him. He looked at Elvis. "Thanks," he said.

Elvis shrugged. "Sure. But you know, Jack—" Despite everything, a smile flickered across Jack's face, for he was pretty sure he hadn't told Elvis his name "—this ain't an answer. You're going to have to call those guys in." Jack looked at him. "What do you call them, COLE?"

Jack sighed. "Yeah, I know." The Committee Of Linear Explanation existed to clean up messes that the outside world couldn't know about. Without them, Jack could be arrested for killing his wife. And probably his daughter. God knows what the cops would think he'd done with Genie's body. He squeezed shut his eyes a moment, made a face and shook his head, like a child trying to banish everything. But that's what COLE would do, make it as if it had never happened, cast some alternate reality sheet over everything, so that as far as the outside world was concerned, Layla and Genie had just—what, gone on a trip? Left him? Died in some fucking tragic accident? "Shit," Jack said.

Elvis said, "I'll tell you a secret, man. I always loved his singing."

"What?"

"Nat King Cole. He could do that kind of velvety cat voice, but every word was clear as a bell. I always wished I could sing like that. Y'know, they called me 'King,' but he really was. I mean, he was colored and all, but the best goddamn singer I ever heard." Then he smiled sheepishly and waved a hand. "Shit," he said. "No offense, man."

Jack shrugged. "None taken." He stared down at his hands, at Layla's blood.

Elvis put an arm around Jack's shoulders. "Tell you what, man. It's gonna take awhile for my truck to cool down. What do you say we grab a couple of cold ones and you tell me about your wife and kid. COLE can fuckin' wait, right?"

So Jack Shade and Elvis Presley sat down at Layla's oak table, knives and cleavers scattered on the floor, with Layla's body at their feet and Genie gone where probably even Elvis and the whole Quartet couldn't find her. And Jack talked about how he and Layla first met, before he was even a Traveler, how he was a carny magician back then, making a few extra bucks doing tricks at a wedding where Layla Nazeer was one of the bridesmaids. They'd gone out for a while, and Jack was smitten, but then he'd lost track of her in the upheaval when he saw the stars and galaxies in a lion's mouth, and his life changed forever.

Jack found Layla again when his teacher, Anatolie, sent him on a training mission to de-possess a law firm. Jack always suspected that Anatolie knew that Layla was working there as a paralegal, but when he asked Anatolie, she accused him of "distraction," the great danger to apprentice Travelers.

When he told Elvis that, Jack had to stop a moment. *Not just apprentices*, he thought. *Distraction* was what had killed his wife. If he'd been paying fucking attention to the geist that was taking over their daughter, shit, if he'd listened to his wife's fears instead of telling her that poltergeists were harmless—

Jack threw his bottle against the wall. It didn't break. He was shaking now, staring at his wife's body.

Elvis said, "S'okay, man. There's more in the fridge, right?" He brought Jack a fresh bottle. Jack stared at it for what felt like a long time, then took a swallow and began to talk about what it was like when Genie was born.

They went on until dawn, and then Elvis stood up, rolled his head on his neck, as if to loosen his ghostly muscles, and said, "Well, I guess my damn truck's probably okay now. Maybe it's time you called COLE."

"Wait!" Jack said.

"C'mon, man. You can't just stay here in a glammed house. You've got to let her go."

Jack said "What do I do about her mother?" Elvis stared at him.

Nadia Nazeer had never liked Jack Shade. It wasn't an ethnic thing, or at least not overmuch. As Layla had said to him once, if he were an Arab but still himself, her mother probably would have felt the same about him. Maybe if they could have told her who Jack really was, what he did, Nadia might have felt less disappointed in her daughter's choice. Maybe not. Once, after a tense weekend at her mother's house, Layla had done an impression of how her mother might react to the idea of a Traveler. "Sorcery?" she'd said, in Nadia's cultured, scornful voice. "Seriously, darling? Does he go around trapping wayward djinn in old whiskey bottles?"

Jack had said, "Actually, Coke bottles work much better. So long as it's not New Coke," and the two of them had laughed so loud someone at a stoplight turned to stare at them.

Nadia never liked Jack. It wasn't just that she considered him a selfish, lowlife gambler who needed to grow up and get a real job—for after all, what could they tell her except that Jack made his living playing poker? As much as she could barely tolerate her son-in-law, Nadia's real problem was her daughter. A successful businesswoman who'd started out selling cheap jewelry, she'd wanted her daughter to "become something," and considered Jack, and even Eugenia, as Layla's retreat from the world.

All this, Jack poured out to Elvis, and more, things he'd never told anyone, not even Layla herself, like the day Nadia had summoned him to her grand office over-looking Lower Manhattan and tried to get him to leave her daughter. The whole time she was going on about "authentic love" and "sacrifice,"

Jack kept thinking of things he could do to make her stop. Seal her mouth, of course, but less drastically he could summon a Momentary Storm to drown her out with thunder. Or maybe animate the intricate little metal animals she kept on her desk, and send her screaming from the room. But he'd done none of those things, just sat there through the whole speech, even agreed to "give it your full consideration," because after all, she was his wife's mother, and what would Layla say if her mother reported to her some very strange things that had happened when she was talking to Jack?

"You know," Elvis said, somewhere around the sixth or seventh beer, "your pals in COLE could take care of it."

Jack shook his head. "I can't do that. Let them fuck with her mind, her memories? Even if I make up some lie—I mean, I have to, right, I can hardly tell her the truth—at least it will come from me, face to face. Not some fucking Traveler bureaucracy."

Elvis took a swallow of beer. "If you say so, man."

Only, when the time came, Jack couldn't do it. He kept bracing himself, swearing he would do it the very next day, before the funeral, after the funeral, and yet he just couldn't face her. Finally, he just decided to make a Duplicate.

There were two kinds of Dupes, momentary and "permanent." Momentary Dupes were little more than illusions, like a glamour. They faded as soon as their task was done. For something as complicated as talking to a mother-in-law, you needed the real thing, a replicant that actually existed in the world. Still, the process was stressful but not that difficult, a bit like making a golem, except with more exacting standards, since a golem didn't have to look or sound like anyone in particular. And where a golem could be made of pretty much anything—synagogue dirt, originally, but now garbage, junk mail, recycled cardboard, even plastic (but no Styrofoam), a Dupe needed "donations." Bits of skin from the palms (you had to be careful not to draw blood), clippings from the fourth toe of the non-dominant foot, blood from the little finger of your dominant hand, hair clippings, dirt washed off the body at dawn, sexual fluids taken at midnight, small amounts of urine and feces.

Along with all these physical traces, you had to include some favorite article of clothing or jewelry, money that had been in your pocket or wallet for at least forty-eight hours, and what the manual called "a life token," a photo from a special trip, a ticket stub, an old baseball cap, whatever you'd saved just because it was more than itself. There was a famous story of a woman from an abusive family who'd destroyed all the remnants of her childhood, only to become a Traveler and have to sneak into her parents' house to find something they'd kept that she could use to make a Duplicate. Finally, you were supposed to write fragments of memory, fear, and desire on bits of paper and then cut them up to sprinkle over the mix.

Jack did the operation on the roof of the hotel an hour before dawn, careful to glam the stairway so that any insomniac who'd taken it in his head to look at the city would change his mind and go back to bed. Carefully, he undressed and folded his clothes according to exact instructions, then placed them on a small metal table in the northwest corner of the roof. The Act of Assembly, as the operation was called, was not difficult but had to be done correctly.

It was late August. The night had been cool, and now a sharp breeze tingled Jack's skin as he set down his donations then drew a circle with blue chalk around the small pile and himself. He sat facing due east, his bits of self stacked in front of him. For a moment, he looked at the first glimpses of purple in the night sky, then sighed, and shut his eyes.

Step by step, Jack "closed the gates." Legs and arms crossed, he pressed his lips together, curled his tongue back against the roof of his mouth, stilled his ear drums, narrowed his nostrils, squeezed shut his sphincters. After several minutes like this, a figure began to take shape in the world behind Jack's eyes. The Unknown

Traveler, this visitor was called, and even though you could never see him or her, you somehow always knew s/he had your face.

Wholly in the inner world, without actually moving his lips or tongue, Jack said, "I thank you for your Presence. I, Jack Shade, have assembled these donations and fragments of my true self, inner and outer, that they may serve my needs, without selfishness or blame, with all honor to the Founders of our practice, the First Travelers, who opened the way and laid down the paths." There was a time when Jack might have wanted to roll his eyes at the language required for things like this. But not that day.

The Unknown faded, and something else began to take shape, little more than a shimmer of dull light. Now was the time to get to work. The raw form would assemble itself through the power of the donations, but it was up to him to shape it, to get it right. Jack had spent the past four hours staring at himself in the full-length mirror in his bedroom, noticing the tilt of his shoulders, the bends of his fingers, the length and roughness of his ropy hair, the turn of his nose, the left ear a bit larger than the right, the way his left big toe curled slightly inward, the dents in his rib-cage from old fights, the crease in his hips, the knife scar from his battle at the Bronx Gate of Paradise.

On the rooftop, he assembled his Duplicate step by step, detail by detail, getting everything exactly right—until the very end, when it came time to recreate the freshly formed scar that ran down Jack's jawline. He started it, could see it taking shape, almost there. And then suddenly he dismissed it, so that when he abruptly opened his eyes the figure that stood before him was his old self, Johnny Handsome, as Layla had once called him.

It didn't appear to make any difference. Jack spoke the Standard Formula to Activate a Duplicate, "I have assembled you and you will do my will," and the Dupe answered correctly, "You have assembled me and I will do your will."

Now, sitting alone in his bedroom, an hour after the dream had woken him, a glass of Johnnie Walker Blue in his hand, Jack wondered why the hell he'd done that, leave off the damn scar. To make it easier to talk to Nadia was the simple answer. COLE's cover story had indeed been a tragic car accident, and to keep things simple, Jack was supposed to have been far away when it happened, so how would he explain a scar? But he could have glammed the Dupe so that Nadia wouldn't notice. COLE had already set Nadia and everyone else at the funeral not to notice Jack's face, or wonder why Genie's coffin was sealed before anyone could ask to see the supposedly mangled body.

So was it just vanity? The desire to see himself as unspoiled one last time? Jack grimaced, took a sip of whiskey. He didn't like intro-spection, considered it an indulgence. "*Schatje*," Carolien had told him recently, using the Dutch word for *sweetheart*, "no one will ever confuse you with Hamlet." Now, however, he had no choice. If he was going to get out of this mess he had to know exactly how he'd gotten into it. Did he just not want to see what he'd become?

Looking at a copy of yourself is hard enough in normal circumstances, not at all like looking in a mirror. When we look in a mirror we automatically compose ourselves, turn or tilt our heads the best way, smile or open our eyes. Looking at a Dupe is like seeing yourself on video, only worse.

He got up and went to the window. The antenna on the Empire State Building flared red for a few seconds then returned to anonymous metal. No, not vanity. Because he remembered how after it was all over—or so he thought—he'd gone back to the house, to his and Layla's bedroom, where she'd kept her old-fashioned framed photographs on top of the dresser, and he remembered how he'd picked up a vacation picture of the three of them, back when Genie was seven, all of them laughing as they posed with some guy in a Batman suit. It wasn't vanity to make the Dupe like he used to be. It was nostalgia. Looking at Handsome Johnny, Jack could pretend, for just a moment, that none of it had ever happened. That it was all a dream.

And at the time it had seemed like no harm had been done. He'd taken care of Nadia, given her an outlet for her anger and grief, and then he'd gotten rid of the Dupe—or so he thought—and everything was good. Only—

The working to destroy a Dupe is called the Act of Dissolution. It's complicated but fairly straightforward, easier than the Assembly, for the Dupe is just a copy, with no will of its own, and cannot help but cooperate in the operation to collapse it into a kind of dust that will simply blow away. Unless the practitioner makes a mistake.

If you don't do it exactly right, if you leave even a shred of the construction untouched by the working, there's a chance the Dupe can reconstitute itself. Coalesce, people called it. Once it re-formed on its own it became a Revenant, a very different creature entirely, with a will to survive all its own. Revs sometimes tried to take over the lives of dead people, not realizing how disturbing that would be. More commonly, they attacked their originals, showed up at their homes, or work, and claimed they were the real thing. In rare cases, they killed the originals to make it easier. "Shit," Jack said out loud. As far as he knew, no Rev had ever hired the original to kill himself.

He took another sip of Scotch, vaguely aware he was hardly tasting one of the world's most expensive whiskeys. Down in the street, people rushed back and forth with that purposeful New York stride that never changed, day or night. They all looked the same. Maybe they were all Duplicates, Jack thought.

Jack made a noise, rolled his head around to loosen his neck muscles. He'd been up all night, partly to try to figure it all out, and partly to avoid any more dreams.

Why in a dream? If his Dupe had reassembled and wanted to attack its maker, why not just go at the body, Jack-in-the-world? Maybe the Rev wasn't strong enough. He might still be forming, and a dream body was the best he could manage. In that case, the answer was simple. No more dreams. Never go to sleep. Jack laughed and drank some Scotch.

There was another reason the Dupe might be using dreams, and it was one Jack didn't really want to think about. Two months before, Jack had broken up with a woman named Elaynora Hall. He and El had dated for nine months or so, after meeting outside a Traveler safe house in Red Hook, NY. It wasn't a nasty break up. No broken plates, no yelling, no spells directed at anyone's genitals. Just a generic two adults—this isn't working out—no hard feelings—standard issue. It made things a little complicated that Jack was a Traveler. It made them a little more so that Elaynora Hall was a Dream Hunter.

Elaynora's father was a dispossessed sun god. The tribe that had worshipped him had died out, their lands taken over by outsiders who'd brought in their own gods and astronomical spirits. The lost tribe must have spoken a weird language because Dad's true name was so filled with impossible noises that Jack just called him "Papa Click and Whistle." He had a human name, however, Alexander Horne. It was a professional name, really. Unlike some of his ilk, he did not just ascend to some higher realm to sulk for a few thousand years. And because the tribe who'd worshipped him had believed that dreams came from the sun (true, as far as it went, but they had to pass through the moon to reach us), Mr. Horne now ran a dream agency.

Dream hunters were an odd group. Some of their work was as simple as leading people to solve a problem or be inspired while they slept. Sometimes they helped Travelers get to places they couldn't reach awake. Or they acted as bodyguards against Nightworld mercenaries. Or took on mercenary work themselves. El insisted that she and her father never did that kind of job. "Why should we, Jack? We have a long waiting list."

Maybe El would not stoop to battle-for-hire, but what if she had a personal reason? Jack sighed. There was no way around it, he had to know.

He went over to the hotel desk and opened his laptop to log on to Jinn-Net. When the familiar flashes of fire and wisps of vapor appeared he clicked on an app titled Teraph.wiz. Soon a child's head appeared, milky face crowned ostentatiously with golden curls. It looked amazed, and frightened, as if it had just turned a corner and seen an angel, or worse. Except it couldn't have turned any corners, for there was just a head. No blood appeared—why be gruesome?—but vague tendrils hung down from the neck.

Originally, long before computer graphics, a *teraph* was an actual severed head. The action was so old no one knew its origins, but if you knew the spell—and had the stomach for it—you could find some kid at the cusp of puberty, behead it, and keep the poor head alive as an oracle. In 1434 the Travelers, and the Powers, and the Renaissance version of COLE had banned the practice. Jack knew of only one modern attempt to create a genuine teraph. In 1927 a sorcerer from *La Societé de Matin* kidnapped a twelve year old girl in Lyon. Though the *Societé* are an order of gangsters, they tracked down the renegade before he could really harm the girl—the spell takes nine days—sent her home glammed up to forget everything, then stuck the magician's own head on a pike outside the Lyon Gate of Paradise.

So no, there were no actual teraphim. But that didn't prevent computer simulations. Jack stared at the revolving image. Like its inspiration in the human world, the AI version of a teraph existed half in this world (or at least the online version) and half in the NL, the Non-Linear. Even though it was just a face on a screen, you had to catch its eye, which meant hitting control/enter the instant it looked at you. It took Jack three tries but finally the head stopped spinning.

Jack thought he saw the mouth turn up slightly as a high adolescent voice said, "Jack Shade. Time has passed since you saw us last." Like all oracles, physical or virtual, the teraph spoke in the "divinatory we." And was given to bad poetry.

"Yes," Jack said. "I rejoice to see you, and beg the blessing of your wise sight."

"Very well. You may speak your question."

Jack took a breath. "Is Elaynora Horne helping my Duplicate to attack me?"

The eyes rolled back, and a clicking sound came from the animated mouth. Jack waited for the inevitably vague answer, but when the face focused on him again it said simply, "No. New grass grows clean."

"Thank you!" Jack said. The eyes closed and the head began to spin, the signal that Jack's audience had ended. He turned off his computer. Okay, he thought. Whatever the hell was going on, El wasn't behind it.

Suddenly Jack was exhausted. He hadn't gone to bed until 2:30, and of had course woken up at 4:17. He squinted out at the sky. The sun had not made it over the buildings yet, but it was definitely morning. If you were under attack by dreams, mornings were a lot safer time to sleep than at night. Jack had no idea why. Maybe dreams were photosensitive and couldn't find their targets during the day. Or maybe they followed strict union rules and clocked out at dawn. Jack didn't care, he just hoped that with daylight, and the protection he'd put around his bed, he could sleep safely for a couple of hours.

Like most Travelers, Jack had aligned his bed on a strict polar axis, with the head at north. Four thin silver poles bolted to the floor at the corners created invisible walls around the bed. Now Jack had made those walls real by running copper netting from pole to pole. Dream net, it was called, and looked like mosquito netting, but with an even finer mesh. Some people said dream net was the origin of those New Age toys called "dreamcatchers," but instead of trying to grab hold of a spiritual dream (whatever that might be) dream net was meant to block hostile or dangerous dreams from getting to you.

Jack tossed off the hotel robe he'd been wearing since he woke up, then went to the closet to remove his carbon blade knife from its hidden sheath in his boot. A knife resting on your solar plexus, with the blade pointed up toward the heart, gave you added protection. He moved aside the netting on the west wall and laid himself down. Hands loosely on his knife, Jack closed his eyes.

—Ray was walking before him, moving with quick urgent steps, looking back now and then to make sure Jack was following him, letting out short yips, as if to say, "Come on, come on." Jack knew he was dreaming, but also it was safe, for Ray was there, and in his aspect, his red fur giving off flashes of light. Ray was a Fox of the Morning, a solar emanation, and had been with Jack for years, ever since Jack had found himself under attack by demonic chickens.

They were walking through one of the desolated neighborhoods on the outer fringes of the city, with boarded-up windows, urine stench, and doorways and any empty spaces strewn with needles, condoms, and what appeared to be fragments of bodies. Jack didn't look too close. "Hey, homey," a voice slurred, "you wan' some?" Jack couldn't tell if it was a man or a woman and figured maybe that was the idea. He just watched Ray.

The yipping noises speeded up until Ray suddenly stopped, right in the middle of the street, body all stiff as he stared at the courtyard of one of those gulag-like "projects" the city had put up back in the '50s and '60s with such good intentions.

It took Jack a moment to notice the old man picking up small objects, examining them, then throwing some away and stuffing the others in a large canvas bag. You had to look hard to keep track of him, for sometimes he became all shadows, then at other moments vanished in bursts of light. Half turning his head to the left and squinting, Jack managed to get a better view of the man. He wore an oversize dark green coat that might have come from some Soviet Army Surplus store out in the 'stans. It made it hard to see his shape, let alone his face. Jack started to move closer but Ray blocked him, yelping. "Just watch," Ray seemed to be saying.

So Jack stood on the other side of the street and leaned forward, trying to make out what he was seeing. The man picked up every-thing—crumpled newspapers, condoms, bone fragments, bits of clothing, bandages, a broken knife. Most things he threw away as soon as he touched them, but every now and then he found something he wanted—Jack had no idea why—and stuffed it into his bag. When he did that, he would wave his right hand over his find before putting it with the others. It was a large hand, thick with muscle. Jack could see some kind of marking at the base of the first finger, what people used to call the Apollo finger.

"What is he?" Jack whispered to Ray. "Traveler? Some kind of Scavenger elemental?" These days, Jack knew, there were elementals of everything, from garbage to obsolete video games to spy satellites. But why was Ray showing him this?

Enough sneaking around, Jack thought. "Hey!" he called out. "What are you looking for? Maybe I can help."

Startled, the man half turned without standing up. Jack caught sight of a grin, all sharp white teeth, and then a flare of light blinded him.

He came awake in his bed, gasping. "Goddamn it," he said when he'd caught his breath. He sat up, pressed his left thumb and forefinger against his closed eyes for a second, then made a face at the dream netting. "Lot of good you are," he said.

In the shower Jack turned up the hot water as far as he could bear it, and used lots of olive oil soap to make sure he got rid of any dream residue that might have passed through the net. The soap, made especially for Travelers from the two-thousand-year-old groves below Mt Parnassus in Greece, usually could be trusted to remove anything dangerous clinging to the skin. Jack was not so confident in this case.

As he dried himself off under the bright arc lamp in the bathroom he noticed his skin in the full-length mirror attached to the door. Jack didn't spend a great deal of time looking at himself. He knew he liked his slightly off-kilter face with all its small scars—he was never sure about the big one—his ropy hair that always looked like he cut it himself (actually it was cut by a hairdresser named Pablo, whose husband Jack had once rescued from a Red Dog pack)—his loose muscles, his long hands with their tapered fingers. He liked himself enough not to need reminders. But now something caught his eye, and he examined his skin, front and back.

There were marks on him, small sparkling dots of silver. Very few, and very small, unnoticeable except under the bright array of the arc lamp. He touched them. No pain. Hard to tell because they were minute, but they felt smoother than his skin. He scratched at one. It didn't come off, and he wondered what would happen if he tried to cut it away. Probably a bad idea.

The one thing he knew for sure was that he didn't like it. The marks signaled the start of *silvercation*, by which a Traveler eventually lost control of his body. If it went too far it could become irreversible, even if the cause—usually an enemy—was removed. Jack examined himself again. He found only four very small marks. Two or three, maybe four days, he guessed, before it became really dangerous. At least he hoped.

He walked over to his closet, where he made a face at the rack of clothes. When he was on a case, Jack dressed all in black—black shirt, black jeans, black boots. Otherwise, especially when he played poker, it was loose clothes and color. But was he working now?

He pulled on narrow black pants, primarily so he could wear his boots with the hidden knife sheath, and then a pale blue shirt untucked over the pants. He was half out the door when he turned around and returned to the closet, where he took down a long cardboard box from the back of the shelf. He examined the various things inside it, then selected a black spray can and a ragged red cloth with a frayed edge. He put them inside a black messenger bag and slung it across his chest.

Down in the hotel lobby, Jack saw Irene talking to Oscar, the night concierge. Jack hesitated a second. Should he warn her? Tell her to watch out for someone who appeared just like him, except without the scar? He noticed her looking at him oddly and feared the silver had spread faster than he'd thought. But then he realized it was the odd mix of clothes, black for work, color for time on his own.

She smiled, said, "Good morning, Jack. You're up early. Or are you just coming home?"

He smiled back. "Nothing so exciting. I've got to go see someone, kind of an early-bird type."

She gave a delicate shrug. "Enjoy the morning. Perhaps it will become a habit." Jack was about to leave when Irene said, "Oh, Jack, I almost forgot. I dreamed about you last night."

Jack managed to force a grin. "Really? What was I doing? Nothing too shocking, I hope."

She did not smile back. "I'm not sure, actually. It was all a bit difficult to see, somehow. You said you wanted to show me something. You lppked excited. Then we were walking down some long, dark corridor until we came to a stone door. It was a bit odd, really, it did not appear to be part of a wall. But you opened it, and I saw some dim shapes, and then there was a flash of light that hurt my eyes. . .and that was it. I woke up."

The door to the Forest of Souls. Was the Rev threatening to send Irene Yao to the Land of the Dead? Take away everyone Jack loved?

He said, "Sorry, doesn't ring any bells. Or open any doors." Then, as an afterthought, he said, "You know, I have this odd netting that I found once when I was traveling somewhere. Some sort of folklore thing. Anyway, it's supposed to protect you from bad dreams. Let me know if you want me to rig it up around your bed." Who knows, he thought, maybe it would work better for a Non-Traveler.

Jack expected her to smile, and say something like, "How could a dream of my favorite resident be bad?" but instead she nodded, and said, "Thank you, Jack. I may give it a try."

"Great," Jack said. "Let me know." He wanted to run up to her rooms and rig up the dream-net right now, in case she went for a mid-morning nap. But Anatolie always told him that when you deal with Non-Travelers you have to let them take the lead.

Outside, the sun had risen all the way and was shining thinly through strands of clouds. Jack was chilly without a jacket but knew it would warm up quickly. He walked over to 34th Street and raised his arm. Almost immediately, a taxi cut across three lanes of angry commuters to pull up in front of him. The ability to summon taxis on command was one of the minor perks of being a Traveler in New York.

Jack leaned back in the seat. "Broadway," he said, "between Eighty-eighth and Eighty-ninth, east side of the street."

The driver stared at Jack in the rearview mirror a moment before heading into traffic. He didn't say anything, but every half-minute or so he glanced in the mirror. It wasn't until Jack saw the grin on the driver's face that he realized he had to get out of the car, *right now*. He took hold of the door handle, prepared to roll into the street.

Too late.

"Hey," the driver said, "I think I dreamed about you last night." And then Jack was asleep.

—He was walking into the bling lobby of the Palace Hotel, behind St. Patrick's Cathedral. He was wearing a smoky brown silk suit and the oxblood wing-tip shoes he'd once taken off an investment banker who needed to follow his wife into the Shadow Valley where you can only go barefoot. Poker clothes.

His friend Annette was in town, from Vegas or Macau, and she'd set up a private game here in the Palace. Jack was excited as he walked up the wide marble staircase in the lobby. Then he stopped, confused. Something was wrong but he couldn't figure out . . . was that Elaynora, over by the wall, reading the *Times*? What was she . . .

And then he was in the elevator, and he didn't remember pressing a floor, but he must have, because it was rising. It stopped at Eleven, and when the door hissed open he headed down the hallway, as if he knew where he was going. "Move forward or get out," Anatolie told him once. "Never hesitate." And sure enough, when he got to 1121 he knew it was the room. Maybe Annette had mentioned it.

He knocked, and Mr. Dickens, Jack's favorite dealer, opened the door. Jack smiled, but before he could say anything, the dealer told him, "I'm sorry, sir, but this is a private gathering." He moved to close the door.

"Charlie," Jack said, "it's me."

The white-haired old man, dressed in a bespoke black suit and crisp white shirt buttoned to the neck but without a tie, only said, "I'm sorry, sir, but this is a closed event."

Jack wouldn't let him push the door shut. "This is crazy," he said. "Annette called me." He looked over the dealer's shoulder to where seven people were sitting around a conference table. All of them wore black, three of the men in Chassidic robes, two in business suits, and a sixth man in a black shirt and black jeans. The sixth man sat across from Annette, who wore a black dress with long sleeves and a low neckline. They appeared to be involved in a large pot, judging from the stack of chips in the middle.

"Annette!" Jack called out. "I got your phone call. Tell Charlie to let me in."

Annette glanced curiously at him for a moment before turning her attention back to the game. "Raise," she said, and pushed in nearly as many chips as were already in the pot.

"Call," the man in the black shirt and jeans said, and suddenly Jack realized it was *him*. The Rev.

"Annette!" Jack said. "That's not me. He's a Dupe. I'm over here." Now he could see that the Rev was wearing black boots along with the black shirt and jeans. Work clothes. *That's not right,* Jack thought, *you keep work and poker separate.*

Annette glanced again at the door, squinting, as if trying to figure something out. But then the Dupe said, "I called you," and her attention flipped back to the hand. As if Jack wasn't there, as if he'd never been there.

She turned over a seven, eight of hearts. "Flush," she said.

The Rev grinned. "Sorry, babe," he said, and turned over the jack, three of hearts. Higher flush. Laughing, he scooped up the chips. "It just gets worse and worse, doesn't it?"

No, Jack thought, you don't do that. When you win, you don't gloat. He would never do that. Not now, anyway. Maybe when he was younger. Before the disaster, before the geist took control of his daughter and killed his wife. Suddenly, Jack realized—the Rev wasn't just Johnny Handsome, the Man Without a Scar. He was Johnny Empty, the Man Without Pain.

Let him win, Jack thought, but it was almost like someone else speaking in his head, a message.

"No," he said out loud, "I can't do that." For if Johnny Empty won, who would rescue Genie from the Forest Of Souls?

Jack woke up to find the taxi double-parked on Broadway. "Twelve seventy-five" the driver said. He sounded annoyed. Tell a guy a weird story and the guy just falls asleep! Jack knew that by the end of the driver's shift the dream passenger falling asleep would become the punchline.

The taxi pulled away and Jack stood outside Kimm's Imports and Delicacies. Marty Kimm sold a mix of Asian groceries—dried mushrooms, packs of noodles, sauces—along with lackluster porcelain bowls, beginner Go sets, notebooks with children waving flags on the cover, cotton shoes, and toys so old-fashioned the neighborhood kids didn't even roll their eyes, they just stared in disbelief. People wondered how "nice Mr. Kimm" could survive in such a competitive high-rent street. It was only a matter of time, they told each other, before another Pret-a-Manger took over and sent "poor Mr. Kimm" to some Korean assisted-living home.

For Mr. Kimm was old, the kind of old that makes you want to guess his age, like guessing the number of jelly beans in a jar. Short and thin, with silver hair cut short, and a constant smile on his face, as if everyone he met was a cute child, he always wore an ironed white shirt, and creased khaki pants. Jack had no idea how old Marty Kimm was. He might have been older than the world.

Jack knew one thing, though. Kimm's Imports was not in any danger of closing. For while it was a genuine store—Jack and Carolien sometimes cooked dinners using only ingredients and utensils from Mr. Kimm—its reason for being there had nothing to do with noodles and chopsticks. Marty Kimm was a gatekeeper.

Every city has a range of gates, New York just has a few more of them than most. Along with the six Gates of Paradise (two in Staten Island, one each in the other boroughs), and most importantly, the Gate to the Forest of Souls in a garage on 54th Street, there were several minor gates, such as the Gate of Flowers in the Bronx, or the Gate of New Skin in a basement in Brooklyn. Marty Kimm was in charge of a Gate of Knowing. On the other side was a Living Archive, and if Jack could get through and consult her he would learn more about Dupes than in weeks of research. Most importantly, he would learn what *he* needed to know, though it might be his job to figure out why.

Mr. Kimm was playing with a child's abacus when Jack came into the shop. He looked up, nodded once, then said, "Hello, Jack. I trust you are having a good day?"

Jack said, "I'm having the kind of day where I need to find out things."

"Ah, of course. Do you have a gift?"

All gatekeepers required some sort of offering. For Barney, keeper of the Forest Gate on 54th Street, it was a stolen truffle. For Mr. Kimm it was a limerick, and it had to both say something and be "humble."

Jack recited

There once was a Traveler, Jack
Who everyone thought was a hack
He lost his old key
To travel for free
And now he can't find his way back

"Very nice," said Mr. Kimm, and clapped his hands once, the way you might for a four year old who's done a somersault. He nodded toward the back of the store. "She's waiting for you. Perhaps she will have your key."

Jack looked and saw a bead curtain over a doorway at the far wall. Was it there before? *Yes, of course,* his cortex said. His amygdala wasn't so sure. He glanced back at Mr. Kimm, who was once more playing with the abacus. The markers were just painted wood but they gleamed like bright marbles. For a moment, Jack thought they were entire worlds, and a dizziness came over him so that he nearly fell. But he looked again and saw they were just bits of wood.

He stepped through the curtain into a wide, bare room with a polished checkerboard floor. The walls were covered with mirrored panels, set off from each other by thin gold columns. It might have been an eighteenth century ballroom, except instead of perfume there was a sharp smell, and instead of the minuet there was a staccato of wings. When Jack looked at the back of the room he saw a woman covered by brown owls.

She appeared to be lying on a couch, though it was hard to tell because all he could really see was her face, round and kind, her unwrinkled skin a milky white. The owls, some with horns, others smooth, hid the rest of her. In front of her stood an old-fashioned black steamer trunk, the kind parents used to send with their kids to summer camp.

A Traveler with a strong need to learn about something had several options. The big city Travelers Aid Societies had old-fashioned libraries, complete with frail, ancient books bound in human skin, or even scrolls that might crumble if you tried to unroll them. More isolated Travelers, or just more modern, turned to the Cloud Archives maintained by Jinn-Net.

Of course, this particular cloud was not something you could reach via Google. But when even that wasn't enough, when you needed to *know, right now,* there was the Mother of Owls, and her treasure box of whispers.

"Hello, Jack," she said, her voice dry and precise and very old. "Mr. Kimm approves of you. I believe he likes you."

"I need help," Jack said. "I need to know."

"Of course. And the subject of your need?"

"Dupes. Duplicates."

"Ah. A tricky subject. So easy to get lost, for the road keeps turning back on itself. One's bird crumbs eaten by one's own mirror." The owls fluttered, lifted up and came back down.

Jack kept his eyes on their mistress. "Can you help me?" he said.

"Perhaps. And what of the other thing?"

"Other?"

"The Duplicate is only half of the quandary. Isn't that true, Jack?"

He found it hard to hold her gaze. "Yes," he said finally. "It's all taking place in dreams." He didn't want to tell her the rest of it, how his Dupe had come back as a Rev, and the Rev had invoked Jack's Guest.

But maybe it wasn't necessary. Mother Owl smiled and said very softly,

There once was a Jack who was proud
And believed he stood out in the crowd
Until an old dream
Held him down in a stream
And no one could hear him out loud.

Jack nodded, not sure he could speak. The old woman said, "You may open the box."

Jack stepped forward. Owls fluttered all around him, their teeth and razor-sharp claws showing, but he paid no attention. He took a breath and lifted the lid of the trunk.

There were stories of what happened when you released what was in the box. Carolien had done it, of course, for Carolien loved *knowing* more than anything else. She'd told Jack that a bright yellow *kabouter* in balloon pants and a party hat had leaped out and bitten her tongue, then spoke into her blood so rapidly she remembered nothing until suddenly she began to write it all down, filling up a three-hundred-page journal over four days. Others talked of voluptuous women who surrounded you, singing. None of this happened to Jack. Instead, whispers swirled all around him like smoke until he became so dizzy he had to hold on to the lid to keep form falling over. He could hear fragments of words and nothing else, and he worried it was all useless, he would learn nothing he could use against the Rev. Finally, he slammed down the lid and lay on the floor gasping while the ceiling spun above him. "Shit," he said. And then he grinned, for suddenly he realized he *knew* things.

He knew that four hundred years ago, Peter Midnight wrote "the strangest book in the Hidden Library," titled *The Book of Duplicates: A Natural History of Replication*, and to do it, Midnight had to travel back in time to the earliest days of the world. Travelers move through time constantly but usually return an instant before they left, so that they forget whatever they saw or did. Midnight broke the barrier by duplicating himself, transferring the block to the Dupe, and destroying it. And he still might not have known he had done it, except that he woke up in bed with a dead body next to him, and when he turned it over it was himself, with a rolled-up scroll in its mouth.

Jack learned that Dupes once filled the world. Originally there was only one person, amorphous and crude, spit out by the Creator, who'd gotten something stuck in Her teeth. This Original pestered its maker so much that He copied it and said, "There. Now talk to each other and leave me alone." But the two just stared resentfully at each other, each claiming to be the Original, the other a Dupe. To prove the point, one of them made a fresh copy and said "You see? That's how I made *you*." But the other only laughed and made hir own Dupe, sayin, "*This* is how it's done. You're just a copy, and a bad one. Look how much better this new one is." As they argued, the two new Dupes stared at each other. Then each of them made a Duplicate.

Some time later, the Creator stirred Herself from the place where She'd hidden from the world. To His horror, He discovered the world was full of Duplicates! They covered the mountains and valleys, they sat in the trees, they walked or swam in the waters. Furious, the Creator urinated across the world, sweeping the infestation away in the flood. At the last second She rescued the last two Dupes, held them in Her hand until the flood subsided, then made one a man, the other a woman. "There," He said. "Now if you want to make more you'll have to do it the hard way. But at least you'll enjoy it more." When She set them back on dry land She hid the secret of Replication so Dupes would no longer clog the Earth.

But the power wasn't lost, for as all Travelers know, *nothing* is ever lost. Hidden, blocked, but always there. No one knows who discovered it. Some say Peter Midnight, but of course, he wrote the book, and Travelers are notorious braggarts. Others—and this was a claim made in the fifteenth century—others say it was a Traveler named John Shade, who went back to The Very Beginning on a mission to rescue his daughter from The Green Dark Woods. No one knows if he succeeded, but he brought back the Great Secret, though he had to surrender it along the way, some thousands of years back. *No*, Jack thought, *that can't be right.* But he had to let the question go, for more and more knowledge came rushing through him.

He learned of a Traveler whose Dupe cut him up and baked him in a pie, or else swallowed him whole.

And another, who thought she'd dissolved her Duplicate, done all the steps, only to discover that when she looked in the mirror she could never see herself, only the Dupe, and when she tried to speak it wasn't her voice but the Duplicate's.

He learned of a Traveler whose Revenant begged to remain. "I won't challenge you," the Rev said. "I'll stay in the shadows. I swear by my maker." But they both knew that could never happen, for it was the nature of a Revenant to try to take over. And it was the nature of a Traveler to cling to the world. Finally, one killed the other, but then the survivor made love to the corpse and brought her back. For this, too, is the nature of a Traveler, to accept no limits, and to search for whatever seems lost.

He learned that certain Travelers have the power to Duplicate themselves in other people, take them over, at least for a time, and he remembered that day Anatolie had become an old woman on the street, a Chinese huckster, a trio of teenage girls.

He learned that the baby Moses who was found in a basket among the bulrushes of the Nile was a Dupe, and that the original was raised as a Traveler in the desert, waiting for the day when the Dupe would show up and the true Moses could cut his throat and set him on fire to ignite the Burning Bush.

He learned that long ago there lived a Traveler named Loud Sue. The name was a joke, for Sue was one of those obnoxious people who *say* that nothing worth saying can actually be said. One day, Loud Sue left home (maybe to avoid speaking) and traveled to an orchard where a pair of Shadow Dogs attacked her. To escape, she climbed a tree with ten branches, and on the third branch from the top found a bird's nest where she could lie down safely and fall asleep. She dreamed that she was not Loud Sue at all, but her Duplicate, Young Sue.

She woke up surrounded by chicks, their mouths open as they waited for their mother to feed them. When she heard a great flapping of wings she clambered down through the branches, back to the Earth. But as she moved, she wondered—was she Loud Sue, who had fallen asleep and dreamed she was Young, or was she Young Sue, even now dreaming she was Loud?

Avoid orchards, the Travelers say. And if you absolutely must enter one, never ever fall asleep.

He learned that sometimes the Dupe takes over—*I want to win*, the Rev had told Jack—for there was once a great Traveler who left the world and allowed her Duplicate to take her place.

He learned that some claim the universe itself is a copy, an unfinished Duplicate of a lost world, which is why so much of existence is *dark*—dark matter, dark energy, dark desire.

He learned that sometimes you can attack a Revenant by making more and more Duplicates, and for a moment he thought he had the answer, only to have the whispers tell him that a strong Rev can absorb the new copies into itself and become more and more powerful, until finally, when the original has exhausted himself, the Rev will eat him, and it will be as if he never existed.

The final revelation came not as a whisper but a vision. He saw a woman, barefoot in a loose white dress, standing at an old wooden table. She was dark-skinned, but with long straight hair. She had her back turned to Jack, bent over the table, writing with a long thin pen on small strips of paper. When she finished each one she folded it and inserted it under her a fingernail. Finally she stood up, and Jack thought she would turn and face him, but instead, she stood in front of an old full-length mirror, with her fingers at shoulder level, spread like the ribs of a fan. Under her nails the letters flickered and glowed. "Nothing is lost," the woman whispered.

—and then Jack was on all fours, on a damp concrete floor, an empty steam trunk open in front of him. For an instant he heard the flapping of wings, but when he looked there was no one there, no owls, no old woman, just rows of storage shelves, mostly empty. Jack stood up, shook himself, looked around one more time, then stepped through a dull bead curtain, back into Mr. Kimm's variety store.

The old man moved some counters on his abacus. Without looking up, he asked "Did you find what you need, Jack?"

"Not sure," Jack said. "Maybe too much."

"Ah. Too much, too little, all the same, yes?" His accent had gotten thicker. It was his way of saying goodbye.

"Thank you," Jack said.

"Always here for you, Jack. Always here."

Outside, the day had brightened, and a look at the sky told Jack it was just after 2:00. He glanced at his watch. 11:44. He wondered, not the first time, why Travelers bothered to wear watches at all. What day was it? He walked to a newsstand on the corner and glanced at the *Post*. Above the blaring headline, the date assured him he'd only lost a couple of hours.

He was about to hail a cab when he noticed the people on the street corner acting strangely. They were looking at their hands, turning them over, staring at the palms, the fingers. They didn't appear upset, just confused. That would change, Jack knew, and quickly. Sure enough, a man and woman, the man in front of a store selling "designer pet food," the woman crossing Broadway from the traffic island, became suddenly agitated. They looked all up and down their arms and legs and midsections, whatever they could see of themselves, and began slapping their bodies, as if to swipe away insects.

The woman stopped in the middle of the street, and stayed there when the light changed, oblivious to the horns and shouts and curses of the drivers swerving around her. The man was breathing heavily, raking his arms with his nails. This was phase two, Jack thought, the sense of attack. Invasion. As he took the spray can and the frayed cloth from his messenger bag he could guess what was next. What the Rev might do.

Sure enough, people began to stare at each other. They pointed and poked, saying things like "Why do you look like me?" and, "Why are you imitating me? *Why is everyone imitating me?*" In fact, they looked nothing at all like each other. They were young and old, male and female, different races, it made no difference. No matter who they looked at, all they could see was themselves.

Jack opened the fringed cloth until it lay in folds all about his feet. Then he shook the can and began to spray the material. He knew that for the best effect he should empty the whole can but there wasn't time, especially since he had to cover his nose and mouth to avoid inhaling. The spray wouldn't harm him but it would dull his senses until his Traveler metabolism shook it off. The formula in the can carried some fancy modern name, but like most Travelers Jack preferred the traditional—Spell-Breaker. If used in time it could nullify a casting, and without permanent damage to the victim. Not in time—the symptoms varied, but for these people, Jack suspected, a permanent state in which everyone looked like their double. They would spend the rest of their lives in isolation, sedated through a hospital ventilation system before a nurse or orderly could bring them food.

Don't think, Jack told himself. Thinking was distraction. Never get distracted, Anatolie had taught him. Jack dropped the cloth and grabbed hold of the smooth side. Then he flipped it open in the air.

A "spread cloth," as it was called, existed partly in this world, and partly in the "World of Extension." Inert, it looked about the size of a king-size sheet and folded down to a square foot. "Awakened," it could stretch so far it appeared to fade into the sky. Jack didn't need anything that radical, he just wanted the tendrils to be able to touch all those frenzied people filling up the street corner. Soon the filaments were snaking and twisting, making crackling noises as they searched for people to heal. They went into an ear, a mouth, an eye, and the people gasped, or sighed, as the ghost snakes entered their brains.

Jack waited until he was sure the tendrils had reached everyone. Then he snapped his wrists back. The snakes withdrew, the cloth began to shrink, and soon it was small enough, inert enough, for Jack to fold it again and put it back in his bag.

The people in the street stared at each other, then at their own arms and legs. Some touched themselves, their faces or chests, even their groins. Then they looked around, horrified or just furtive, suddenly aware they'd embarrassed themselves on the public street. Some said things like, "Oh my god, I'm so sorry, I don't know what—God, I'm sorry." Others moved away as fast as possible. A few looked breathlessly at the person next to them, and if they got the right look back, held hands and walked quickly away.

And beyond the crowd, hard to see in suddenly bright sunlight, a man in black stood, holding up a small rectangular object like a sacred relic. It was him, of course, and what he held was the marker, the Guest. Jack's card.

The Rev said something. Impossible to hear in the noise and traffic, but all Travelers are lip readers. Jack wasn't that good at it, but this one was easy. *I want to win*, the Dupe said. Then he turned and strolled away.

For a second, Jack considered running after him, but if he caught him what would Jack do? So he just stood there and pretended to himself he was being himself useful by checking there were no casualties.

From behind him he heard a woman, cold and stiff, like an old-fashioned pre-Siri computer voice. "John Shade," it said.

Oh fuck, Jack thought. *The last goddamn thing* . . . He sighed and turned around.

There were two of them, a man and a woman. They often did that, as if satisfying some government directive for gender equity. They were dressed in old-fashioned suits, the way the Supreme Court requires lawyers to appear, dull gray for the man, knee-length black skirt and low-heeled pumps for the woman. Gray and black were a pun, of course. The colors of *coal*.

For a second, Jack thought they might be the same two who'd come to the house that long night, after Elvis told him he had to call them. But no, efficiency just always looked the same.

The man's voice came out breathy, little more than a whisper. "This has to stop," he said.

"Yeah, well, I'm not exactly having a great time," Jack said.

"That's no concern of ours," the woman said. "What does concern us is that this feud of yours has begun to involve non-Travelers. That is not acceptable."

Jack glanced around, saw that no one was looking at them. Glamours. COLE was good at that. "It's not my feud," he said. "If you can tell me how to make the Rev go away, I'll be glad to do it."

Jack was surprised to see a half-smile twist the woman's mouth. "Dissolve it," she said.

"I did. Apparently, it didn't take." *No*, he thought, *I did it right.* He brushed the thought aside, for obviously he didn't.

"There are more advanced methods," the woman said.

"It's complicated."

The man said, "Your Guest."

Jesus, Jack thought, *do you people know everything?*

Her tone slightly less techno, the woman said, "We understand your dilemma. Unfortunately, it makes no difference. Preventing the outer population from discovering reality is our sole concern." She smiled, almost regretfully, but Jack got the message. They would do whatever it took to stop the bleed. *Exile*, Jack thought. He and the Dupe removed from the world. No passage back. Like his daughter.

"I'll take care of it," he said.

The man turned and walked away, but the woman hesitated. Sympathy seemed to cut through the mask for a moment, and Jack had the wild idea she would make the telephone gesture with her hand next to her ear and mouth, "Call me." But then she walked off.

Jack stood in the street a moment, head tilted to the left, as if trying to hear a whisper. There was something, some glimmer, in what had just happened. *I did it right.* But clearly he hadn't, there was the Dupe. Finally, he let it go and hailed a cab.

Before he got in, he sprayed Spell-Breaker over the car. He could see the driver make a face and reach for the gear shift, but managed to get inside before the taxi could pull away. *Trust me*, Jack wanted to say, *this is for you as much as for me.* But that never worked, so he just said, "Forty-Eighth St. between Ninth and Tenth."

No one was sure just how Carolien Hounstra could afford a six-room apartment in the newly chic Hell's Kitchen. Certainly not from her work at NYTAS, where she was everything from door watch to record keeper, two jobs that were a lot more complicated than they sounded. Nor did she freelance, like Jack. Family money, some said. Found a djinni in a lamp, others claimed. Jack's favorite story was that Carolien was unearthed in a coffin filled with pirate gold, in a crypt beneath Amsterdam's Moses and Aaron Church. She'd been asleep, the story went, until a nun kissed her awake. *Smart nun*, Jack thought.

The ride passed without any dream attacks, and Jack gave the driver a ten dollar tip. Before he could ring the bell for 6E, the buzzer sounded, and Carolien's voice came through the scratchy intercom. "Jack! Come up."

Carolien was standing in the doorway when Jack stepped out of the tiny elevator. She wore light green linen pants and a loose, dark green shirt that came down almost to her knees, but was unbuttoned enough to reveal the wondrous swell of her breasts. Her long, golden hair was braided in a triple pattern that made Jack think of the caduceus. She smiled like the sun breaking through the clouds. There were people who said that the dreary climate of Northwest Europe was a direct result of Carolien Hounstra moving to New York. The smile faded and the blue eyes narrowed as she looked him over. "So," she said. "Trouble. Come in."

Carolien's apartment was decorated in a variety of styles. The living room was '50's "modern," with kidney-shaped glass tables and uncomfortable chairs. Her kitchen was so full of gadgets Jack suspected it could cook a five course meal all by itself. Her bedroom featured elaborately carved dressers, an ebony bed—on a north-south axis, of course—and a large gold-framed mirror that could probably identify who was the fairest in the land. The hallway that connected all this would appear to any deliveryman (who was not staring at Carolien) as unadorned walls painted a pale yellow. Jack saw alcoves, some filled with clouds and hidden faces, others with faraway scenes, such as people in animal costumes dancing and laughing.

Without a word, Carolien led him to a closed wooden door at the end of the hallway. A wave of her hand and the door opened without her touching it. Jack followed her into what he called "the Reign of Frogs." Shelves of all sorts—polished wood, metal slats, stainless steel—covered every wall. And every shelf was covered with frogs. Most were stone, jade and malachite, but there were lots of wood and netsuke as well. The majority were squatting, but some appeared caught in mid-leap. With a jab of guilt, Jack remembered his abandoned errand to Canal Sreet. *When this is over*, he thought, but then found himself wondering, if the Rev took over, would he go get Carolien a frog?

The only carving not on a shelf was the largest, a big-bellied jade frog wearing a gold crown. About three feet high, "King Frog," as Jack called him, squatted on the floor in front of a shelf of stone subjects. Jack once asked Carolien, "Why don't you kiss him and turn him back into a handsome prince?"

Carolien shrugged. "Maybe he wouldn't like that. Or maybe I would become a frog."

Now they sat facing each other in the middle of a polished black floor. Jack said, "Thank you for seeing me."

She made a Dutch noise. "Am I a dentist now? Why wouldn't I see you?"

"Sorry. It's been a rough couple of days." He reached out and touched her cheek. Whenever he touched her, he was amazed that skin could feel so soft and strong at the same time. *Thank God for Dutch cheese*, he thought.

Gently, Carolien removed his hand. "Tell me what is happening," she said.

Jack took a breath. "I had a visit from COLE today."

"Ah. Were you naughty?"

"Not me. At least, not exactly." He paused, then said, "I'm in trouble, Carolien."

"Tell me."

Jack laid it all out for her, holding back only his errand before the Momentary Storm. She listened without moving, then suddenly leaned forward and kissed him. Surprised, Jack almost backed away before he held her face and kissed her back. *Jesus,* he thought, *maybe this is what I need.* To hell with dreams and Revenants. A wild thought surfaced that when they got naked they would discover his cock had gone all shiny, and he'd have to make up some line, "Once you've tried silver, there's no. . ." But he couldn't think of a rhyme and he gave his attention to kissing the top of Carolien's breasts, moving down—

And then suddenly it wasn't him. He could not have described how he knew, but it was like seeing yourself/not yourself in a dream. The goddamn Rev had his lips on Carolien's right nipple, his hand between her legs. With all his concentration, like some novice Traveler trying to psychically lift a fucking pencil, Jack managed to push the body, the Dupe's body, *his* body, away from Carolien.

And then he was back again, gasping for breath.

"So," Carolien said. "That bad, yes?"

"Jesus," Jack said to her, "that was a test?"

"Yes, of course. How else do we know?"

Jack shook his head. Usually he appreciated Carolien's Dutch frankness. "We are a small country," she'd say, "we have no room for embarrassment." But sometimes . . .

155

Carolien said, "Your scar is back. Good."

"It wasn't there?"

"For a moment, no."

"So it really was him. How did he do that?"

She sighed. "He operates in dreams, Jack. Dreams are like ooze. They can slide, and cover things. But you know this." Jack didn't answer. "Oh, Jack," Carolien said, "it's not me you need. It's *her*."

"Fuck," Jack said. But of course she was right. When you're hunted by a dream, where else do you go but a goddamn Dream Hunter?

Jack Shade's relationship / affair / fling / experiment / beneficial friendship with Elaynora Horne lasted a little over nine months. El's father may have been an ex-Sun god, but her mother was the Queen of Eyes, and Jack had met El through working that case. They didn't talk about Mom much. The Queen had never publicly acknowledged her, El being the product of a youthful indiscretion, which is to say the young queen-to-be trying to run away from her life. El was much closer to her father. She worked in his dream agency, after all, but it was more than that. You could say she idolized him, if that term wasn't so heavy with meaning in this particular instance.

The first time they made love, on a snowy December night, El had told Jack it had to be at her place, an elegant two-story apartment on the Upper East Side. That was okay with Jack, he wasn't wild about bringing girlfriends to his hotel room. In El's bedroom, he was a bit surprised to see black wooden shutters attached to all the windows, and more so when she systematically closed them all. *Privacy issues*, Jack thought, and then forgot about it as he began to kiss her lips, then her face, her neck, her breasts, and then her thighs as their clothes came off.

They made it to the high bed that looked half as big as a basketball court—no compass alignments, Jack noticed—and El was arching her back, and gasping, when suddenly she pulled away and held up her hand. "Wait," she whispered, "I need you to wear something."

Jack almost laughed and said, "It doesn't look like you need any help at all," but he'd been around long enough to know you didn't question or make light of these things. There'd been a woman in Denver who'd tied streamers on his wrists and ankles and scrotum, another in Paris who put makeup on him and called him "Jacquie," and a Japanese diplomat in Brooklyn who'd had him wear a Barack Obama mask. And once in Boston a woman had spent hours inscribing Jack's chest and thighs with words in some long-lost alphabet. "Messages home," she'd called them.

So he just nodded, waiting for whatever strange thing she would give him, and almost made a noise in surprise when all she did was hand him a pair of dark wraparound sunglasses. But he just put them on and went back to kissing her, though it was a bit strange because he could hardly see. We may think we close our eyes during sex but we actually depend on them much more than we realize.

Jack had once made love to a blind woman, who'd seduced him by telling him that she could see when having sex. What she didn't say was that he would become blind. At first he'd gotten angry and started to push her away, but she clung to him, saying, "Please, Jack, let me have this. Your sight will come back, I promise." So Jack had discovered what it was like to make love entirely by feel. After, he lay in bed while his partner got up, and for a moment he panicked when sight did not come flooding back. But soon flashes came and went, and then glimpses. He saw her standing in front of a full-length mirror, staring and touching, urgently connecting finger knowledge to shapes she would try to memorize. Jack didn't get up until his sight had fully returned. Then he walked over to where she still stood before the mirror, her blank eyes weeping. "I'm sorry," he said, and tried to hold her, but she pushed him away.

"Go," she said. "Please."

"We could do it again. If not now—"

"No! It only works once. Then—then I have to find someone else." Jack had gathered up his clothes and gotten dressed in the hallway before he let himself out.

Now, as he made love wearing glasses so dark he could barely see his partner's outline, he remembered that other time, and closed his eyes to better feel his way around El's body. He began to get hints of why the glasses—and the shutters—as El began to vibrate toward orgasm. Faint flashes filled the air, then died out. Jack could feel them even with his eyes closed, and when he opened them it looked like parts of the room were flaring up, then disappearing.

El began to shudder, and grunt, and the flashes came faster. And then she cried out, and Jack, who'd been using his fascination with the lights to hold himself back, let go so he would come with her. In the midst of that perfect moment, a blast of fiery light flooded the room.

Jack made some kind of noise but held on, unwilling to cut short the experience. When the moment came to separate he fell back on the bed, only to cry out and sit up when he realized how hot—how sunburned—his back was. Gingerly he touched his chest, winced, for it was worse. Made sense, since he'd been facing her. He pointed to the glasses. "Is it safe?" When she said yes, he took them off to look down at the worst sunburn he'd had since he was five and ran away from his parents so he could build the world's biggest sand castle.

"I'm sorry, Jack," El said, but he could see her fighting a grin. "I guess I should have warned you."

"You think?" Jack said, and then they were both laughing.

"It'll wear off," she said, and kissed him. "The sunburn, I mean."

So sex with Elaynora was, well, complicated, though they worked out ways to manage it. Unfortunately, other problems began to surface. Jack got a sense that she considered the work of a Traveler undignified, if not downright low-class. At first she sounded fascinated, wanted to know everything. Then she began to make comments about the tricks Travelers liked to play on each other, such as sending someone through the wrong Gate, so he ended up in Pigworld rather than among the Messengers Of Light, or some of Jack's clients. She began to talk of the valuable work the Dream Hunters did, the scientific breakthroughs they inspired ("It's not just the benzene molecule, Jack"), the important clientele, the need to police the dream borders and catch illegal aliens before they could take root. "Dream Hunters matter," she would say. "What we do is important."

It all came to a head about eight months into their time together, the day Elaynora took Jack to meet her father. She looked flustered, excited, which made Jack nervous. Was he supposed to ask Papa Click and Whistle for his daughter's hand? El didn't seem the type, far too modern. But what did Jack know? He asked her if they were going to meet Alexander Horne at home or at work. She laughed, a little too loudly. "At work, Jack. Believe me, you don't want to see where my father lives."

The Horne Research Group occupied a suite on the eighteenth floor of an innocuous office building on 45th Street, between Lexington and Park. Jack noticed that the floor-to-ceiling windows in the reception area looked out on the Chrysler building, and if you glanced up you could see the gargoyles looming above you. A Korean woman in her twenties sat behind a long empty desk. At least, she seemed like a woman. Standing before her while El said they were there to see "Mr. Horne," Jack caught the faintest aroma of Other about her. Maybe she was a dream.

Alexander Horne came out to welcome them and lead them into his office—the corner, of course. He presented himself as a large man, a couple of inches taller than Jack. Probably that would have been the case no matter how tall Jack was. Probably he appeared two inches taller to everyone. He had a barrel chest and large, strong hands with prominent veins and muscles. His face was wide, with a high forehead, a prominent nose, and a long, thin mouth. His thick silver hair was swept back. He wore a conservative gray suit with a maroon tie.

"Jack!" the ex-deity said. "It's great to meet you. Elaynora can't stop talking about you."

She laughed. "Hardly. Make one vaguely complimentary comment . . ."

They sat down at a circular table made of bone or ivory. A moment later, the receptionist—"Wondrous Jessica," Horne called her—came in with coffee on a polished silver tray.

For the next half hour Alexander Horne questioned Jack about his work as a Traveler. He pretended it was chatting, but Jack could recognize an interrogation, and found himself becoming more and more annoyed. And yet, it still amazed him when Horne said, "So El tells me you might be ready for something new."

"What?" Jack said. He looked at El, who glared at her father, then told Jack, "I didn't say that. Really. That's not what I said."

"Oh?" said Jack. "Then what exactly *did* you say?"

"Just that—that the life of a Traveler is uncertain. And as long as you have that Guest, your life isn't really your own. Anyone at all could hire you. But maybe if you did some other kind of work the Guest wouldn't apply anymore."

Jack stared at her. "You told him about that?"

Horne chuckled. "Don't be angry at her, Jack. Believe me, I've tried and it doesn't work." He sipped his coffee. "I understand. The last thing a guy wants is for his girlfriend to interfere in his career. But do me a favor, Jack. Just think about it, okay? What we do here is challenging and exciting. And it helps people. I know Travelers do that as well, but we get under the surface of things. We don't just fight reality, we shape it."

He paused, put on a serious face. "And something else, Jack. What my daughter said about your—spiritual obligation. The Guest, as you call it. And this comes from me, not Elaynora. We can do more than set this thing aside. If you decide to work with us, we can nullify it."

"What? What the Hell are you talking about?"

"The dream world is a threshold, Jack. It's the only place where true change can occur." He sighed, held up a hand. "Look, let's table this discussion for now. You're angry, I understand that. I've ambushed you here, I apologize. Why don't you take a few days to think about it. No pressure. Just know that this is not an empty promise."

Jack stood. El started to get up as well but Jack turned and walked out before she could say anything.

For the next few days Jack went over Papa Click's offer again and again. He avoided sleep and protected himself with dream net when he had to close his eyes for fear Alexander—or Elaynora—Horne would try to influence his decision. Freedom, he told himself. No more slavery to anyone who showed up with his goddamn card. He thought of creeps like William Barlow, who almost got Jack killed. Or his fear that someday some gangster from *Le Societé de Matin* would show up with Jack's card and hire him to do something truly vile.

Jack had actually tried to break the Guest on his own once. It was early, his third case since making the disastrous promise. A prim middle-aged woman named Amelia Otis placed Jack's card on the table and said, "I suspect my husband—Mr. Chandler Otis—of demonic copulation. I want you to find out if it's true."

"Do you know what sort of demon?" Jack asked.

"Incubus."

Jack had to stop himself from smiling. "I think you mean succubus."

"No," Mrs. Otis said, and cast her eyes down. "Incubus," she repeated more softly.

Jesus, Jack had thought, *it's not the demon part that bothers her, it's the gay!*

After the client left, Jack wondered, was this his life now? Hostage to every sleaze who showed up with his business card? He decided he would unswear his oath. He would say three times, "I, John Shade, absolve and abjure all vows and obligations surrounding my card." As he said it, he would cut the card Otis had given him. The first time he tried it his hand slipped and he sliced his thumb. The second time, his voice became a whisper and he felt like he'd been stabbed in the stomach. The third time, his throat seized up and his whole body seemed to break into little pieces. He managed to throw away the scissors and fall on the floor.

When he got up again he discovered the card was unharmed, as bright and fresh as if it had just come from the printer.

A couple of times Jack simply tried to ignore a client, and became so sick he ended up in the ER. Only taking some small action to begin the case broke his symptoms. So the one thing he knew was that he couldn't break the Guest on his own. Then why didn't he leap at Horne's offer?

He told himself that he didn't like coercion. Or that he liked being a Traveler. But there was something else, he could feel it. Finally, he went up on the hotel roof just before moonrise, and did a simple enactment to ask the moon to show him the thing he was missing. He expected the light to fall on something, but it was the moon itself that gave him the answer. Just for an instant, as it came into view above the low buildings across the East River, the face in the moon was Eugenia Shade. The image collapsed back into the usual vague form, but for that second it was Jack's daughter, as clear as the picture on the corner of his desk.

He understood now. The Guest came from the worst moment of his life, it was part of his terrible mistake—but it was also his last link to his daughter. He couldn't just throw it away.

Jack showed up at the Horne Research Agency at nine the next morning. Walking past Jessica's protests, he went straight to Horne's office. "I'm not interested," he said, and left before Horne could say anything.

Things were never the same with El after that. She tried to apologize but Jack told her it wasn't necessary, he knew she meant well, but it wasn't going to happen and he didn't want to talk about it, it was okay. Jack knew that was a shit thing to do to her, but he didn't care. For awhile they pretended they could just go back to how things had been, but they got together less and less often, and for shorter times.

One night, as they were about to make love, and El went about closing the shutters, Jack had the sense she was simply going through the motions. Just as he felt her approach orgasm, he took off the dark glasses. Brightness indeed filled the room, but just for a moment, and barely enough to scatter a few dots across his field of vision. When they separated, El smiled with supposed satisfaction until she saw the discarded glasses. "Hell," she said, and lay on her back staring at the ceiling. Jack got dressed and left, and that was the last he'd seen of her.

And now—now he was supposed to go ask for her help. He glanced at Carolien.

"Oh no, *schatje*," she said. "This is one you're going to have to do without me."

Jack made a face. "Maybe she won't be home."

Carolien looked over at King Frog. The eyes glowed red for a second, then returned to dull stone. "Sorry," she said. "She's home. Better hurry." Then her voice got serious. "This is real, Jack. The Revenant is not going to stop. And he came with your card. You need all the help you can get."

Jack nodded. He could hear that voice again, the angry parody of himself. *I want to beat him. I want to win.*

Elaynora met Jack at the door to her apartment. She was wearing a white linen pantsuit with wide legs and an asymmetrical jacket, the left side longer than the right. Her hair was shorter, layered and blow-dried to look like she'd just stepped out from a swim under a waterfall. Jack glanced at the windows, saw the shutters were open, and hoped she hadn't noticed him checking.

"Jack," she said, with what sounded like real concern, "what's going on?" For a second, he wondered again if he could trust her. The oracle had said so, but then her mother was the Queen of Eyes, maybe she had rigged the answer. *New grass grows clean.* No, Jack decided. It wasn't just the Teraph app. Carolien and her frogs would have caught something if El was dangerous.

He said, "Let's sit down, okay? It's kind of a long story."

"Of course." She led him into the living room, where they sat down at opposite ends of her off-white couch. When Jack had told her everything she said, "So all this is because you didn't dissolve it properly?"

Jack found himself shaking his head. "That's the thing. I keep thinking I did."

El frowned. "Maybe that's why it came to you in dreams. Perhaps you did it right in the physical world, but some fragments remained in your skeletal dream frame."

Jack guessed that was Dream Hunter tech talk. He thought a moment, said, "So part of the Dupe remained hidden in my dreams and that's where it reassembled itself?"

"Yes. And since your card, like everything of significance in your life, has its counterpart in the dream frame, the Revenant was able to get hold of it and present it to you."

"Jesus. And now it's starting to break through into the physical." He hadn't told her about kissing Carolien, but the scene on Broadway was enough. El nodded, her lips tight. Jack said "Can you help me? Show me what to do so I can block it? Maybe if I can get the Dupe out of my *frame*, the card, and the job—you know, killing myself—will go with it."

She sighed. "I don't know, Jack. I'm good, but I suspect this is beyond me."

"Fuck," Jack said. He knew what was coming next.

El looked down, then forced herself to meet his eyes. "Jack—I'm afraid we're going to have to ask my father."

The Horne Research Agency was closed for the weekend but its owner opened the office for them. He was dressed casually, an old-fashioned red and black checked flannel shirt, khaki pants, and plain black sneakers. Despite everything, Jack almost smiled at the thought of Papa Click and Whistle jogging in Central Park. Down in the street it was a dull, cloudy day, but Jack had assumed the office would be bright and sunny. Instead, everything looked dull, lifeless, and very old. A day off is a day off, Jack figured.

He said, "Thank you for seeing me. I know the last time we talked—"

Horne waved a fleshy hand. For an instant, Jack thought he'd seen that before, the hand, the gesture. But the moment passed as Horne said, "Forget it, Jack. I made you an offer and you weren't interested. What's past is past." He turned to his daughter. "Now tell me the problem."

She looked at Jack, who nodded, then she told her father what she and Jack had figured out.

Horne sat down on the edge of his desk. "This is serious," he said.

Jesus, Jack wanted to say, *you think so, Sun boy?* He kept silent.

"As I understand the situation," Horne said, "there are really two problems here." As if running a meeting, he held up his left hand with the first two fingers extended. There were deep indentations at the base of the first finger, like tattoos dug deep into the flesh. He said, "First, obviously, is the Duplicate itself. The Revenant, as you term it. Jack, if there were no other complications, do you think you could successfully repel it?"

"I'm not sure," Jack said. "It's in the dream world, or half in it, and I don't have a lot of experience there. That's why I need your help." *Something's wrong*, he thought.

"Ah, but now we encounter the other problem. Are you even allowed to overcome it? Doesn't your curse, your Guest, as you call it, require you to do its bidding?"

Jack sucked in a breath. "Yes. That's the other reason I need your help."

Horne's eyes narrowed. "What do you mean?"

"You told me once that you knew a way to remove the curse. I know I turned you down, but that—"

Horne slapped his desk, and a gust of wind stopped Jack's voice in his throat. "What?" Horne said. "That was then, this is now?"

El stepped toward him. "Please, Daddy," she said, "he needs our help."

Horne stared at her a moment, frowning. Then he sighed and shook his head. "It was never that simple. If you had joined us, if you had come to work as a Dream Hunter—"

If you'd married my daughter, Jack thought.

"—then over time, gradually, we could have worked you free. But even in the best of conditions it would have been a slow process. No one, neither you nor I, can simply wave a hand and make it go away." As if to demonstrate how hopeless it was, he moved his left hand in the air. To Jack it appeared in slow motion, the tattooed finger like a painting in the air.

And suddenly Jack remembered where he'd seen that before. The dream. The one Ray had shown him. The old man in the projects—picking up odd bits and pieces—waving his hand over them—the indentations at the base of the finger—

Horne said, "I just don't know what we can do, Jack. It's very possible that you simply cannot beat him, that he's going to win."

I want to beat him, the Rev said. *I want to win.*

Softly, Jack said, "Sonofabitch." Then louder, "It was *you*!" And louder still, "You bastard! It was you!"

Horne's eyes caught fire, then immediately went back to normal as he turned to his daughter. "El?" he said. "What is he talking about?"

"Jack?" Elaynora said. Jack could hear the tremble in her voice, the fear of someone who understands but doesn't want to.

He kept his eyes on Horne. "I didn't do it wrong. Not in the awake world or the fucking dream world. The pieces didn't just drift back together again. *You* went looking for them. You gathered up the shards, re-join them, like a broken vase. You gave it my card, and then you told it what to say."

Horne glared at Jack, and once again light like fire came from his eyes, but Jack was ready, his own eyes narrowed to the thinnest slits. His face grew hot, but he could still see. Now Horne looked back at his daughter, his face and voice softer, pleading. "Elaynora," he said, "I'm your father. I've taken care of you all your life. Are you going to believe him over me?"

Without taking her eyes off her father, Elaynora held out her hand toward Jack. "Give me your coins," she said. It took Jack a second to realize what she was doing, then he reached into his pocket and pulled out all his change. Three quarters, a nickel, and four dimes. $1.20. Jack hoped that was an auspicious amount.

El shook the coins in her hand, tossed them on the desktop. She looked, made a noise, did it again, then once more. For a second, she just stared at them, then turned on her father, her fists up as if she wanted to hit him. "You goddamn sonofabitch!" she yelled. "How could you do that? What's *wrong* with you?"

Horne just stared at her, confused. Finally, as if desperate, he looked Jack. "What did she do?"

Despite everything, Jack had to hold down a smirk. What he wanted to say was, *Asshole*, but instead he said, "What do you think? She asked her mother."

Horne didn't get it. "What?" he said.

Now El threw up her hands. "She's the Queen of Eyes, Daddy! Holder of all the oracular power in the goddamn world. Did you think you could *hide* anything from her?"

His voice suddenly small, Horne said, "I didn't know you could—"

"What? Talk to her? Of course I can. She's my mother! I could have used playing cards, matchsticks—coins are just the easiest." Suddenly, her anger all gone, she said, "Why, Daddy? Why did you do that?"

Horne stood up. Jack braced himself for another flare, but nothing happened. At least not inside. Out in the street, what was an overcast day suddenly brightened. Horne said, "He deserved it! He refused an offer other men would crawl for. I was going to make him my apprentice. Have you any idea how special, how rare, that is? But no, none of that was good enough for him. He paused, then said, "And on top of all that, he cast *you* away."

"*What?*" El said.

Horne went on, "And all because he thinks he's so damn important. Friends with the Queen of Eyes. Student of Anatolie the Younger. Even the murderers in *La Societé de Matin* love him. Well, it was time someone taught him a lesson."

Outside, the sky had gotten still brighter, bursts of light bouncing off the buildings. Jack was sure that if he went to the window and looked down he would see people running indoors. He kept his eyes on Elaynora and her father.

El said "*He cast me away?* Jesus, Daddy, I'm not some spurned maiden. We broke up. That's it. And he didn't want to work for you? So what? You think he's one of your tribesmen who used to worship you? You think you had a right to *smite* him? Grow the fuck up!"

Outside, the Chrysler Building gargoyles looked to have caught fire. Jack touched El's shoulder. "What?" she snapped, still glaring at her father.

"Look out the window," Jack said.

She turned to him for a moment, then to the glass. "Oh my god," she said. She stepped to her father, began to hit his shoulders, his chest. "Stop it!" she yelled. "You'll kill everyone!"

Suddenly, all the fight drained out of Alexander Horne. He sat down hard on his desk, his head bowed. Outside, it looked for a second as if night had fallen, but it was just the ordinary day returning. "I'm sorry," Horne muttered. He looked up, his face in pain. "Really, sweetheart. I don't—I don't know what came over me."

El crossed her arms, refusing to let him in. "You're going to have to fix this," she said. "Break down that—that *thing* you assembled and scatter the pieces."

"But that's just it," Horne said. "I can't. It's too late."

"What?"

"It's nearly out of the dream world. I can't contain it."

"Then kill it."

"That's not possible. Not until—not until it becomes completely physical. And that means. . ." He stopped, but Jack knew what came next. The Rev taking over. Horne turned to Jack. "I'm sorry," he said. "Please believe me. If I could—he's going to win, Jack. I don't know how to stop him."

Jack's mouth opened, but nothing came out. Instead, he heard the dupe. *I want to beat him*, Johnny had said. *I want to win.* Jack had assumed that meant he would have to allow his own death since he had no choice but to do what the client asked. But nothing was actually said about Jack dying. He looked now from Horne to Elaynora.

"Jesus," Jack said. "I know what to do."

Jack Shade—*Original Jack, accept no substitutes*—stood naked in front of the mirror in his room at the Rêve Noire. This was the second time in two days he'd done this. It reminded him of Layla examining herself on her thirtieth birthday, turning, frowning, pinching, pulling. This was different. Jack wasn't assessing, he was memorizing. Every part of himself, every fold of skin, every kink of muscle, the palms and backs of his hands, the turns and knots of his hair—even more than when he'd made the Dupe, he had to get it all clear.

The back was the worst, of course. Jack had bought some cheap mirrors at one of those Walgreen's drugstores that could pass for a small town and set them up to reflect his back to his front, but it was still tricky. An old Traveler motto: Where you've come from is always more dangerous than where you're going. You can *see* where you're going.

The silver had spread—a big shiny patch on his upper right thigh, another over his left kidney. He couldn't let himself worry about it. He just had to take it in as more details and make sure he got them right.

Next to him stood the room's mahogany table. He'd moved it from the wall and stacked it with very thin sheets of rice paper and a Subtle Pen. The Pen looked like a thin metal stylus with a very sharp point. In fact, it was a border crossing device, using ink from the Other Side. Subtle Pens were very rare—Jack had borrowed this one from Carolien—and used mostly for the kind of contracts that could never be broken. The quality Jack needed was simpler, however—the ability to write very, very small, in words that couldn't fade or be erased. Everything Jack saw he wrote, and still it all took up less than two sheets of paper.

Once he'd gotten down everything he could see, Jack used his black knife to cut out every written segment. When he'd finished, the table looked littered with the discarded carapaces of minute insects. Jack placed his palms on the table. A breeze stirred the fragments. They swirled an inch or two above the table, and then, slowly, they drifted over to Jack's hands—and slid under his fingernails.

The sensation caught him by surprise, very soft yet somehow a jolt. Jack gasped, held up his hands at eye level. He couldn't really see the pieces of paper, only a faint shimmer, yet there was a kind of heaviness. Not weight, really, more like a shift in his center of gravity, as if—as if he was doubled. *Just what I need*, he thought, then reminded himself that in fact it was exactly what he needed.

Painstaking as it was, the physical part was easy. The memories, however . . . Someone once said that to set down all your experiences would take longer than it did to live them. But neither could you consciously decide on the important ones. You had to allow them come to you. So Jack closed his eyes, let out a breath, and invited his life to parade before him.

There were things he would have expected—the lion's mouth, his first meeting with Anatolie, the first time Ray came to him, finding the Queen of Eyes. And of course Layla and Eugenia. So many moments. Precious, angry, stupid, frightened, triumphant.

And then there were the things long forgotten. Stealing a pack of gum when he was seven and being terrified a cop would kill him. Wandering into some gang street where a group of older boys, in colors he'd never seen, taunted him, only to suddenly run away for no reason Jack could figure out. His thirteenth birthday, after his parents had bought their own home in a safe area. Jack had slipped out at night, just to walk around, and one by one, all the dogs in the neighborhood began to follow him. A fight with Layla so ridiculous that neither of them could stay angry. Genie's third grade report card, when she got straight A's except for a B- in PE that made Jack love her all the more.

When he'd let everything come to him that wanted to, he wrote it all down, cut the strips, and then these too took their hiding places under his fingernails.

He was ready, he told himself. Now he just had to wait until the meet time. So why did he feel like he'd missed something? He stared in the mirror. What the hell was it?

He felt woozy, his eyes heavy. *Oh, you gotta be kidding,* he thought. He'd cast dream net over the whole damn room, emptied a fresh can of Spell-Breaker covering every surface. Then his eyes returned to the mirror and he saw Ray, walking toward him as if out of the glass, and he realized it was all right. There was someone behind Ray, a child. Jack squinted, trying to focus, before he realized it would better if he sat down and closed his eyes.

It was Genie, of course. Not as he'd last seen her, fourteen years old and sprayed with her mother's blood, but younger, sweeter, in jeans and a Girl Power T-shirt. Dream Jack made a noise. The photo. This was Genie from that day at the theme park. In fact, it was the actual moment the picture was taken, with that spray of hair lifted by a gust of wind. "Daddy," she said. "You can't go away."

"I'm not—"

"Don't let him get rid of you, Daddy. *Please.* You have to come save me. I want to go home."

Jack looked around. They were in the hotel room, only now there were trees all around, thin and gnarled and leafless.

"Sweetie," Jack said, "it's going to be fine. But even if I screw up, which won't happen, you'll still be okay. Because he'll still be me. So *he'll* come save you. I promise."

"No!" she yelled, and her fists came up in front of her like a shield. "He's *not* you, Daddy. He's nothing like you. *He doesn't have the scar.*"

Jack came awake so suddenly he nearly fell backwards. Of course she was right. Jack had made the Dupe—the original copy—as if the disaster had never happened, and that didn't change when Horne put him back together again. He wouldn't care about Genie, not like Jack did.

He walked over and picked up the picture from that faraway day. He looked at it for what felt like a very long time, then brought it to the table, where he removed it from the frame. Now he went to his night stand and took out a vial of contact dust. He scattered some on a fresh sheet of paper, then pressed the photo onto it. When he picked it up, the image was gone from the photo, while on the rice paper Layla, and Genie, and he himself stared up joyously. He took out his knife and began to cut the picture into pieces small enough to fit under his fingernails.

Once Alexander Horne realized he was caught, and more, that his relationship with his daughter depended on him trying to undo the damage he'd done, he switched completely and just wanted to help. Jack believed him. You probably didn't last long as a former god if you couldn't adapt. He still didn't trust him, of course, but there were ways Jack could use him. Two things, actually, one simple, the other more tricky. And neither of them involved telling Horne, or even El, exactly what he was trying to do.

The simple task involved taking over a New York City street in the evening. For the street, Jack chose the block on Lafayette where the Momentary Storm had opened the border and allowed the Rev to make his first appearance. He got a certain satisfaction at seeing Horne wince when Jack told him the location. The Big Kids hated it when some short-lived human saw through their tricks.

The standard way to take over a city street, day or night, was to fake a movie. So many films were made in Manhattan that people hardly stopped to look anymore, just rolled their eyes in annoyance at the roped-off area and the detour. Jack could have glammed the fake permit and the police barriers himself, but as a businessman, Horne was more connected to the city's power structures. Besides, it gave him a stake in what they were doing.

Jack stepped over the barrier on Lafayette at 9:30. He smiled at the small tech crew hovering around the lights and camera. The equipment was real—NYTAS kept a supply of such things—but the people running it were phantoms. Digital golems, Carolien liked to call them. Jack's smile broadened when he saw the name Carolien had given their supposed film-in-progress: *The Frog Prince of Manhattan*.

For the frogs were there, or at least fifty or so, lined up, some on benches, outside of a retro-80's coffee shop, a "pointy-shoe boutique" (Carolien's term), and a hipster pet store, with King Frog in the front. Jack nodded to him. Hard to tell, but he thought he saw a light flicker in the king's eyes.

Standing in the middle of the street, Jack looked around. Everything seemed in place. By his request, Carolien had set up the frogs and left. El wanted to come but Jack told her it would work best if no one else was there. They weren't far away, he knew, and that was all right. If it worked he'd be happy to see them. And if not—well, maybe they could try to contain the Rev. Or rather, Jack Shade, version 2.0.

He was just about to get started when two actual people, a man and a woman, stepped over the rope and came toward him, right past the phantom film crew. He had a moment of alarm until he recognized their stern gray and black suits. The man spoke first, in that flat Voice of Authority. "John Shade. Whatever you are doing had better not involve outsiders."

"Of course not," Jack said. "That's the point of the barrier. The one you just ignored?

The woman said "COLE knows what it's doing." Despite her flat tone and blank expression, Jack caught that hint of interest. Not his concern, he thought.

The man said, "You know that it doesn't matter to us which version survives."

"Yeah," Jack said. "I get that."

"So long as nothing leaks."

Jack said, "Just seal the barrier after you leave and everything will be fine."

When the pair of them had stepped over the ropes and back to the world, they paused for a second to glance up and down the street, and then they left. At the corner, the woman looked back at Jack, nodded slightly, then followed her partner.

Jack stood in the street, facing the World Trade Center, just as when the whole thing had started. He was dressed all in black, partly because this was work—the Rev was still his client—and partly because he knew that's how Johnny would be dressed. The only unusual thing he had on was a small leather pouch hung from a long cord around his neck.

He took a deep breath. "Ray," he said. His fox appeared, tail curled up, face tilted toward Jack. He said, "Tell Horne I'm ready." Ray's tail jerked, and then he vanished.

This was the tricky part. Horne's second task was to bring the Rev. Papa Click was the one who'd created the damn thing, so Johnny would believe him when he said Jack was down and now was the time to strike. But could Jack trust him? He hadn't told Horne what he was going to do, but Horne could still warn the Rev to watch out. Jack didn't think he would. El was watching through her mother, and this was Horne's only chance to get both of them off his back. Jack shook his head. A pussy-whipped god.

There was a kind of crack in the air, something you couldn't really see or hear, and then *he* was there. Dressed all in black, head slightly cocked to the side, a grin at the corner of his mouth. *Jesus*, Jack thought, *do I look like that?* Maybe the Rev was thinking the same thing.

Somewhere behind Jack, a man said, "Holy shit! Did you see that? That guy—"

Another man said, "Dude, it's nothing. Just special effects. You know, CGI."

"CGI?" his friend said. "This is the fucking street, man. That guy came out of nowhere."

"Forget it," the other said. Jack knew that in a second or two they would do exactly that. The barrier didn't stop people seeing things, it just stopped them remembering.

Jack moved a couple of steps closer. It felt like pushing against something—the dream interface, Jack realized. The Rev was still not entirely here. Jack stopped now. Let him make the next move.

The Rev began to circle him, slowly, in long loops. That shimmer continued, and a couple of times Jack realized it was he himself who was flickering. He thought for a moment of something Anatolie suggested once, that there was only ever one person and all the rest of us were Dupes. *Not this time*, he thought. *One of us has to go and one of us has to stay.* It was that simple.

Johnny jerked his head toward the frogs. "Brought an audience, huh? Or maybe Carolien just wanted to have her friends watch me beat you. They were watching when I kissed her. You remember that, right? We're going back to that pretty soon." Jack didn't move.

The Rev gestured toward the pouch around Jack's neck. When he pointed his finger, it was like a stab of light that quickly vanished. "What the hell is that?" he said.

"Dragon seeds."

The Rev looked shocked for a moment, then laughed. "Oh, man," he said, "you that desperate? You're gonna sow a race of warriors to try and beat me? Come on, that never works."

Every Traveler knew the ancient Greek story of Kadmos of Thebes, who created an army by planting the teeth of a dragon. They knew what the story was actually about, and why it was a really, really bad idea.

"Not exactly," Jack said. He lifted the pouch off his neck and emptied the contents into his left hand: six dark brown seeds, smooth and round. Jack was pretty sure the Rev would focus on what Jack was doing, and not on the fact that now they looked completely alike. Except, of course, for Jack's scar.

Jack threw three of the seeds to Johnny's left, the others to his right. Instantly, Duplicate Jack Shades sprang up. They were simple, more like sketches than a finished product, but they were there.

The Rev laughed, clapped his hands. "Wonderful," he said. "Just like our old carny days. Not an army of warriors—a platoon of fake Jack Shades." He looked at them all. "Come on," he said to them. "I'm your brother."

Jack had thought he might have to fake nervousness at this point, but the Rev wasn't even looking at him. The six low-level Dupes ran at Johnny as if to attack him, until the Revt opened his arms wide then clapped his hands. There was a flash, and suddenly the Dupes were gone. For a few seconds, small lights, like fireflies, danced around the Rev's body. "Best you got, Jack? You know what they say—what doesn't kill me.."

Nietzsche?" Jack said. "You do a lot of reading in the dream world?"

The Rev laughed. "I was thinking G. Gordon Liddy."

He's drunk, Jack thought. Drunk on the energy Jack had just fed him. *We're almost there, and he's not thinking.* Because if he did think about it, the Rev would realize that Jack *couldn't* attack him. Not with cheesy Dupes or anything else. Jack had no choice but to let the Rev win.

So he had to keep him off guard, rile him up. He said, "How can you take my place? You're not me. You're not even a real Duplicate. You're just a badly made copy."

"Bullshit!" the Rev said. "I'm you because you made me. Only I'm better than you. I'm you before you fucked yourself up. That's why I'm taking over. To save you. To redeem you."

"Face it, Johnny. You're nothing but broken-up pieces. You were never meant to exist, except a down on his luck sun god managed to dig through the garbage and find enough junk to slap you together."

"Fuck you! He saved me. From your hatred. You tore me to pieces but he found me and brought me back. He filled me with holy light."

"There," Jack said. "You see? That's him talking. I would never say shit like that."

The Rev let out a cry of rage, then charged at Jack. He hit him in the face, the stomach. Jack made a show of fighting back, because the Rev would expect it, and it would feed the Rev's desire to win, but it just an act, for what could he do, he still had the Guest.

And it was all so strange. The blows were real, his face and body could feel every one of them, and at the same time they seemed far away, something Jack was watching. Like a dream.

And then all his observations, all his analysis, ended, along with any pretense of fighting. He was on the ground now, broken, his lungs on fire, blood all over his face. The Rev reached down and yanked him to his feet. He held Jack's face next to his, said, "See, Jack? You thought you could beat me. But you're the one who's done. Finished!"

"Bullshit," Jack managed to whisper. "I'm still here. And you're still a fake."

"Not for long." The Rev pulled Jack's limp body against his, wrapped one leg around Jack to hold him in place, and then he opened Jack's mouth and placed his own mouth tightly against it.

It wasn't a kiss, no matter what it looked like. It was more like an extraction. Jack could feel himself pulled inside out, everything that was Jack Shade sucked out of him. Strangely, the last thing he remembered was a man's voice, an onlooker. "Christ," the voice said, "I'm all for marriage equality and shit, but this is *freaky*." In a second or two, what the man had seen, what he'd said, would all be gone. Forgotten, as if they never existed.

Like Jack Shade. Sucked away, pulled into his enemy, nothing left of him. Like a forgotten dream.

Jonathan Marcus Shade, the *new* Jack, former Duplicate, former Revenant, the Man Who Came Back, the Man Who Took Over, stood in the middle of Lafayette Street. "I did it," he said. He turned around, looked at the golems pretending to film it all, looked at the ropes and the stragglers on the other side who would never have the faintest idea of the incredible thing that had just happened here. "I did it!" he said again, "I beat him. I won."

"Horne!" he called out, and looked for his Dream Hunter benefactor. "Are you here? Did you see?" No response. He looked for Carolien too, but all he saw were rows of frogs lined up like spectators. Maybe that's why she'd brought them, so they could watch and report back to her. He imagined how he'd show up at her place later, how she'd greet him with champagne. Or Dutch beer and cheese. He laughed. Maybe he should go see Irene Yao first. Have a cup of tea from that fifteen hundred year old teapot. And then—then he would go to his room. *His* room. *Jack Shade's* room. He laughed. "I won!" he shouted.

He looked down at the street. Just as he thought, there was nothing left of that other one, the so-called original. Not even a blood-stain. In the end, once he came out of the dream world, there could only be one of them. He was never just a Dupe. From the very beginning he was better, Jack Shade without all that suffering.

He was here. He'd made it all the way through. He began to touch himself just to feel that solidness. His sides, his arms, his legs. He reached up and touched his forehead, his eyes, his hair. And then he froze. For his right hand had come up against a gnarled, twisted line of hard skin. A scar.

"No," he said again. "That's wrong. I don't—I'm Handsome Johnny. I can't—." He jerked his hands away from his face, held them in front of him, palms out, fingers spread wide. *It must be a mistake,* he thought. *A residual memory.* In a moment he would check again and it would all be fine, the scar gone, banished like its owner.

Something—something was happening to his hands. They were shaking, tremors he couldn't control, couldn't even lower them. And light filled them. No, not the hands, the fingernails. New Jack stared at them, confused, and suddenly scared. And as he did so, the light lifted off his fingers and into the air, moving like a swirling cloud. No. It was paper! Hundreds of cut-up bits of rice paper glowed and danced around each other in the air. It was right then that Johnny Rev, the Man Who Thought He'd Come Back, realized exactly what Jack Shade had done to him.

He lunged for the papers, the Cloud of Knowing, but it was too late. The papers coalesced into a stream that flew through the air to travel in a great swirling arc—right into the mouth of King Frog. For a moment there was a low grinding noise, and then a multicolored flash of light shot back across the street at the Traveler who just a moment ago had been staring at his hands.

It hit him in the forehead, enough of a jolt to unbalance him, so that he fell backwards. He managed to turn in the air and land on his hands and knees. Somewhere behind him, a man who would soon forget he'd even been there yelled, "Cool!" and a woman, his date apparently, whispered loudly, "Shh! You'll ruin the shot." She too would forget, though at the end of the evening, when her friend would try to kiss her, she would turn away, annoyed with him for no reason she could figure out.

Shade was still on his knees, catching his breath, when a woman who never forgets anything came and crouched alongside him. "Jack?" she said. "It is you, yes?"

"Yeah," Jack said. "I'm back."

"Ah, thank god," Carolien said, and when they stood up she kissed him.

When they'd separated, Jack asked, "Was that a test?" Carolien nodded happily, and Jack laughed.

It was Alexander Horne who'd given Jack the clue, when he inadvertently reminded Jack of the Rev's actual words. Not kill Jack, just beat him. If the Rev could somehow win, only for a moment, that would satisfy the Guest. The other clue was the fact that Johnny was not an actual Duplicate, he was a dream of a Duplicate. He could enter the hard world the tough way, step by step—or, take over Jack's body. If Jack could vacate it for a while the temptation would be too much to resist. Johnny would leave the dream world by entering Jack's body and believe it was his own.

The question was, of course, how Jack could return. His final vision in the Court of Owls had shown him how you could transfer your memories, your physical knowledge, your loves and everything that mattered onto scraps of paper hidden under your fingernails. King Frog was the final trigger that would bring him back to his body.

Carolien put her arm around his shoulder to steady him. "Come home with me," she said. "The golems will take care of everything."

He moved away from her and stood up straighter to look around. There, just at the edge of the ropes, stood Elaynora Horne. Jack went over to her. "Are we good?" he said.

"I'm the one who should ask you that. It was my father that did this."

"Screw your father. You and me—are we good?"

She took a deep breath, let it out. "Yes."

Jack nodded, then kissed her lightly on the lips. "Thank you," he said. Then he limped over to where Carolien already had a taxi waiting just beyond the ropes.

Tomorrow, he thought. Tomorrow he'd finally go get her that frog.

Epilogue

JACK SHADE, ORIGINAL JACK, STOOD A LONG TIME BEFORE THE scuffed brown door on Bayard Street. There was something invisible about the doors to the upstairs apartment on this busy street of stores and restaurants. Invisible and all the same, each one a copy of all the others.

Did she know he was there? Probably. If she cared to monitor the street. If she cared to monitor him. Or maybe it wasn't caring, just keeping track. *Pay attention*, she used to tell him. *Don't get distracted.*

He turned away from the narrow apartment door and stepped through the open doorway of the Lucky Star Restaurant. It all looked the same—the worn linoleum floor, the old wooden chairs, the white bowls of *sambal* next to the aluminum napkin dispensers. And at the far end, standing behind the wooden order counter with its stack of paper menus, stood Mrs. Shen, her hair a little grayer, her fingers a little more gnarled, but otherwise unchanged.

There were only two occupied tables in this middle of the afternoon, one where two young neighborhood guys were silently eating a large plate of *guy laan* in oyster sauce, the other with a middle-aged white woman who'd pushed aside the remains of some noodle dish and was writing in a large green notebook.

Mrs. Shen looked up, about to recite some innocuous formula, then her mouth fell open and a second later she clapped her hands. "Jack!" she said. "What a nice surprise."

"Hi, Mrs. Shen," Jack said. "It's nice to see you."

"Are you back?" she asked. "More study?"

He smiled. "Just a visit, I'm afraid."

"Oh, a shame. We've missed you, Jack."

"Me too." He paused, then said, "She like anything special these days?"

"Seaweed and jellyfish salad in sesame garlic dressing."

"Sounds good. Give me a double order, okay?"

"Of course."

When Jack stepped outside again, the door to the upstairs apartments stood open. He smiled and began to walk up the five flights of stairs. At the top, her apartment door was open as well. Jack suspected it was the only door in Manhattan without multiple locks. Without any locks, actually.

"Hello, Jack," she said as he walked in. She looked exactly the same as when he'd last seen her, stretched out on her reinforced bed, hands resting on the rope of dreads that crossed her belly.

"Hello," he said. "I brought you some seaweed and jellyfish."

"Thank you. Please put it on the chair, if you don't mind." Jack nodded, and set the brown bag on the plain wooden chair next to her bed.

Silence a moment, then Jack said, "I was talking to Alexander Horne recently." A smile flickered across her face, so quickly no one but Jack would have noticed it. He said, "He mentioned you. Called you Anatolie the Younger." No reaction. Jack took a breath. He said, "Are you a Duplicate?"

"Yes."

Jack's eyes closed a moment, then he said, "Were you always my teacher?"

"Yes."

"Did I ever meet the origi—Anatolie the Elder?"

"No."

"Is she alive?"

"Yes."

"Where is she?"

"Not here."

Jack was pretty sure he knew what "here" meant. He said, "Is she ever coming back?"

"I don't know."

There was a long pause, then Jack nodded and said, "Thank you." When Anatolie didn't answer, he went back down the stairs.

4

HOMECOMING

.

We want what is real
We want what is real
Do not deceive us

—*Bald Eagle Song,* from Crow Indians

I.

AROL ACKER SAT ON THE OTHER SIDE OF THE TABLE FROM Jack Shade, her eyes downcast on the smooth mahogany surface as she tried to keep her hands from whatever nervous habit she didn't want to display. This was Jack's office, but really it was just another room in the Hôtel de Rêve Noire, Jack's home for the past twelve years. Carol had come to the hotel because that was the address on the card that began *John Shade, Traveler.* The hotel owner, Irene Yao, had brought Jack first the card, and then the client.

Now Jack wondered what Mrs. Yao had thought of Carol Acker. Would this prim old–fashioned white woman seem as out of place to elegant Mrs. Yao as she did to Jack? Jack's usual clients included seers, sorcerers, dream hunters, even an occasional golem. Carol looked as small-town normal as you could get. Hair cut in a style that was pretty enough but you'd forget it the moment you walked away. Face and makeup the same. She wore a gray wool dress with a round collar, long sleeves, and a hemline that reached a couple of inches below her knees. Her left hand bore an unadorned wedding band and a narrow engagement ring with a small but well-cut diamond, yet Jack found himself looking at a ring on her right hand, silver with an unshaped lump of black onyx set on top of it.

Jack said "Mrs. Acker, what can I do for you?"

She had trouble raising her head to meet his gaze, but when she did, her gray eyes appeared to have a greater depth than Jack might have expected. He felt a slight relief when she looked away. She said "I'm—do you think I could have a cup of coffee?"

"Sure," Jack said, and dialed room service. "Milk and sugar?" he asked, and she nodded. When he'd placed the order he told her "They'll be up in a moment. Why don't you start by telling me what's going on?"

"Well, that's just it," she said, eyes once more cast down towards her hands. "It's nothing, really. It's . . . just a kind of feeling."

"What kind of feeling?"

"That something is missing. I'm sorry, I know how vague that sounds."

"That's all right. It's a start. Tell me about your life, about what's missing."

"I don't *know*. I mean, I like my life. I've been married thirty years, I have two wonderful children, and three beautiful grandchildren. I'm active in the church and I enjoy it. Just a couple of months ago they actually gave me a small award. For my volunteer service. It's a good life, really it is."

A knock at the door signaled the arrival of Carol's coffee. Room service was always fast when Jack had a client. After he'd tipped the waiter and closed the door, Jack said "Let's cut to the chase. Carol. Just what is it that's troubling you?"

Staring down at the cup in her hands she said again, "I keep feeling like something is missing."

"What kind of something?"

"I don't—just some part of me, something very deep."

"How long have you felt this way?"

"As long as I can remember. And now that I'm getting older it feels more urgent. Like time is running out on something very important. Does that sound . . . foolish?"

Jack guessed she meant "insane," but all he said was "Not at all. It's what you feel." *Jesus*, he thought, *I'm turning into a therapist.*

She sipped her coffee. "I keep wondering, maybe something terrible happened to me. When I was very young. I've read about that. Something bad happens to a child and they send part of themselves away. The part that remembers."

Jack nodded. "I know. It's called dissociation."

"No, no," she said, and annoyance briefly flickered in her face. "That's—that's psychological. I'm talking about something . . ." She stopped and looked directly at Jack. "Mr. Shade, do you know what soul retrieval is?"

Jack thought, *How do I get into these things?* He said, "Yes, of course. It's when a—when someone journeys—(*was that the right word?*)—and brings back a missing piece of someone else."

"Yes, that's it." She nodded, with a flush of excitement. "That's what I think I need."

Jack sighed. "Mrs. Acker, I know what it is, but I'm not—I don't specialize in that. I'm sure there are better people. If you like, I could get you a referral."

"No!" she said, with more animation. "My—my husband's cousin said you were the person."

"Your husband's cousin?"

She looked down again. "Yes. I asked him to do it, and he said no."

"Why did you ask him?"

Eyes still down. "He, um, it's what he does. He's an urban shaman."

Better and better, Jack thought. He said, "Then why'd he say no?"

"Well, I guess maybe I wasn't always as supportive as I should have been."

So, Jack figured, the church lady was a bit scornful of hubby's weird cousin, with his drums and rattles and New Age jargon. Now suddenly she wants his help. He said, "If you don't mind, Carol, how did your cousin know of me? Was he the one who gave you my card?"

She looked up at him now, hopeful. "Yes, that's right. Jerry—my cousin-in-law—he said he couldn't do it, the retrieval, but then he said he knew just the person. And he got your card from a drawer and gave it to me."

Oh shit, Jack thought. *Acker!* He should have realized. *Jerry fucking Acker.*

It was not long after the death of Jack's wife, and his daughter's banishment to the limbo of the Forest of Souls. He was Crazy Johnny back then. He'd moved into the hotel and had the cards with his new address made, but really, he had no fucking idea what he was going to do. He'd been at some party—couldn't even remember how he got there—and he'd had too much to drink, and some asshole named Jerry Acker was holding forth on his mystical journeys to the spirit world, where he hung out with angels and power animals, and other great stuff. Finally, Jack decided to teach him a lesson. He turned Jerry's cocktail glass into a pair of snakes entwined together. It was quick, and Jack made sure no one else could see it, but as poor Jerry stood there, mouth open as if he couldn't decide whether to scream or vomit, Dumbass Jack stuck one of his brand-new cards in Acker's pocket, and whispered to him, "If you ever need the real thing, Jerry boy, come find me."

And now here was Cousin Carol, who was so fucking nice she figured she must be missing some part of her goddamn soul. And she didn't even know that she had come armed with one of the world's most potent magical weapons: Jack Shade's business card. Because of a self-imposed curse—a *Guest*, the Travelers called it—Jack could not refuse anyone who had his card and wanted to hire him.

"Can you help me?" Carol asked.

That was the question, wasn't it? Maybe she'd been so pressured as a kid to be a proper young lady that some part of her had said "Screw this. I'm out of here," and Jack could go find it and bring it home. He said "If you really are missing something I can locate it and return it to you."

"Thank you!" she said. Then, nervously, "Umm, can you tell me how much this will cost?"

Of course, Jack thought. That was one way to get rid of her, tell her some huge amount she couldn't possibly pay, and then it would be her who turned away, not him. And it wouldn't be entirely a lie. Jack's fees ranged from nothing to tens of thousands of dollars. Somehow, he could not bring himself to do that to her. He said "Five hundred dollars."

She gulped, then nodded. "When can we do it?"

"Can you come tomorrow afternoon? Three o'clock?"

"Yes. Yes I can. Thank you."

Carol walked stiffly to the door, her hands clutching her purse in front of her like a shield. At the door she turned her head and said again, "Thank you," then quickly left, as if afraid she might embarrass herself with all that emotion.

Jack looked at the door for a moment after she left. Something felt off about this situation. Was Jerry Acker setting him up in some way? He made a face. Poor Jerry was just too much of a jerk, he couldn't have any idea of the power hidden in Jack's card. Carol herself? Jack was pretty sure her meekness was not an act, any boldness in her soul was probably the part that left. And yet—

"Ray," he said, "what did you make of that?" Ray was Jack's guardian fox, mostly invisible even Jack, but always around. Only this time, no golden-haired sharp-nosed fox appeared. "What the hell?" Jack muttered, then louder, "Ray? Where are you?"

Over the next few seconds Ray flickered in and out of existence, as if he couldn't hold on. Or maybe he didn't want to be there, for when he finally manifested, his whole body was shaking. "Hey," Jack said, and knelt down to put his arms around his friend. "It's okay." He couldn't imagine what this would look like to any Linear person who happened to step into the room. Only Travelers and Powers could see creatures like Ray. "I'll be careful," Jack said. "Really I will." He let go, and Ray disappeared.

Carol arrived precisely at three the next day. She was dressed more casually, the same proper coat, but under it a light blue sweater, gray wool pants, and running shoes without any brand marks. Jack wondered if she'd read some book on soul retrieval, and it advised comfortable clothing.

Jack was dressed for work, for *travel*. He wore loose fitting black jeans, high black boots with his carbon knife hidden in its sheath along the right calf, and a long-sleeved black canvas tunic buttoned to his neck. The tunic had a lot of pockets, and Jack had spent a couple of hours choosing what to put in them. He ended up with charms and small carvings, a bone flute, Monopoly money, a nineteenth century London Bobby's police whistle, a miniature blow gun with darts, and a couple of (forged) letters of recommendation from high level Powers. Ray's strange behavior had made Jack realize this job might not be as simple as it looked, and he better prepare himself.

Carol stared at him, then blurted "You look darker." Immediately she gasped, and actually put her hand over her mouth, a gesture Jack found sweet. "Oh, I'm sorry," she said, "I didn't—I mean—"

Jack said "I put a line of charcoal down the center of my face, and on my cheekbones."

"Oh," she said, not sure if she should be relieved, or more embarrassed. She let her attention shift to the room, where a single wooden chair stood in the center of a wide ring of rose petals. "Is that for me? Am I supposed to sit there?"

"Yes."

"It's . . . it's lovely. Thank you."

What it was, Jack thought, was a pain in the ass. The petals came from a pair of bushes that grew on either side of the Manhattan Gate of Paradise. They were probably the only roses outside a florist's shop in late November, but even if it had been July it wouldn't have made a difference. In New York, if you wanted to form a Whisper of Protection, as the circle was called, the petals had to come from that one Gate. And unlike the five Gates of Paradise in the other boroughs, the Manhattan Gate *moved*. It had taken Jack nearly three hours to track down its current location, in a non-descript stone archway at the eastern end of Broome Sreet The whole time he was searching he told himself how ridiculous it all was, he was over-doing a very simple job. But then he thought of Ray and kept at it.

Carol asked, "What do we do?"

"*You* don't have to do anything, but sit in the chair. Though you probably should take your coat off and set down your purse." As Carol moved to the table, Jack said "Do you have the fee ready? You might be emotional later and want to go straight home."

"Yes, of course," she said, and reached in her purse for a check, which she waved in the air, as if to say, "Ta da," before laying it on the table.

"Thank you," Jack said.

"And now I sit?"

"That's right." Jack watched her step carefully over the rose petals to take her place, back straight, hands folded in her lap. Jack suddenly hoped that whatever he returned to her would make her as happy as she seemed to expect. He noticed again the onyx ring on her right hand and thought how it might help, how the missing piece might appear as someone wearing the same ring. He said "How long have you had that ring with the black stone?"

She opened her eyes to look at it. "Oh this? I don't know, a long time. I found it in a thrift shop when I was just in high school."

Jack nodded. "We're going to start now." He stepped inside the circle.

"I'm so excited," Carol said, and closed her eyes again. "Should I meditate or something?"

"No, you just have to sit there." That sounded kind of dismissive, he thought, so he added, "I'll tell you what. Keep your eyes closed and breathe deeply, and, um, focus on welcoming home the missing part of yourself. Imagine a joyous reunion party. With a cake and candles."

Carol smiled. "That's lovely."

Jesus, Jack thought, *there are people who make a living saying shit like that?*

Eyes closed, Carol said "Are you going to drum now?"

"No, I don't do that. No natural rhythm."

"Oh," Carol said, and blushed.

Enough, Jack scolded himself. It was time to stop screwing with the client and get serious. He said "Carol, it's best that we stop talking now. I won't be able to answer soon." Carol nodded, and

Jack added, "And if you hear or even feel anything a little strange, it's okay. Just keep your eyes closed and breathe naturally." Another nod, a little more tentative this time.

Jack began to circle her, slowly, bent towards her—and sniffing. He tried to keep it quiet but it was the only way he could find the place where the soul-piece had left the body. Carol tensed, but didn't move or speak. Jack really hoped it wouldn't be anywhere too embarrassing. Once—

Focus, he ordered himself.

Most of Carol just smelled suburban. Cheap perfume, deodorant, kitchen aromas, air freshener, body waste, and traces of male sex, but not female. Her husband had probably screwed her a couple of days ago and she'd faked orgasm. But there wasn't—there! It was just a faint acrid smell at the opening of her left ear, like a long ago cut that looks fine but has never really healed. She must have been very young, Jack thought.

He stood up, took a breath, then blew his police whistle, softly, into Carol's ear. Once, twice—

—and he was falling. He passed through layers, places, unable to hold onto anything. A café in Brooklyn where people laughed and applauded as he went by. A cheap hotel room that stank of illegal surgery. A cowboy town that might have been a movie set. A lecture hall where a group of professors were shouting at each other but turned and stared at Jack as he passed. He fell through rock walls covered in lichens as sharp as barnacles. Finally, Jack discovered he still had the police whistle in his hand. *Fuck this shit,* he thought, and blew the whistle as hard as he could.

Just before he crashed he heard, then saw, a great wind. It whirled and whirled around itself, not funnel-shaped and black like a tornado, but a hurricane that had reduced itself to ten feet high, with its eye just two or three feet across. For an instant Jack thought he heard a voice inside all that noise, a child calling to him. He almost reached into the wind, but then it was gone.

Jack fell hard on a damp and dirty city street, at nighttime. He grunted and got up, then looked around. West Street down in the Village, he realized, for there was the Hudson, just beyond the West Side Highway, and across the river, Hoboken. Only, it looked like the old days, before the city got around to cleaning it up and raising the rents. Stores were empty, or even boarded up, with not many lights on in the apartments above them. *What the hell?* he thought. *There's no one here.*

Then he looked a little further down the street and saw, in fact, a whole group of people, neatly lined up and waiting to get inside some dimly lit club. A crude sign above the door declared it "The Iron Cage." Jack stared at the line and realized they were all men, and all dressed in black leather. "Oh, you've got to be kidding me," he said out loud. "A leather bar?" Jack had been a kid when that scene was going on, but he remembered hearing about it. And he knew a Traveler who'd come from that world and liked to talk—in way too much detail—about the "good old days."

He shook his head. Maybe Carol Acker was meant to be a transman heavy into bondage, and her parents, or just society, drove it out of her. Now how would that work when he brought it back? Talk about getting more than you bargained for.

With a slight limp Jack made his way towards the bar. The men in the line glanced at him as he approached, then looked away. They all dressed the same, tight black leather pants, padded to make their cocks look bigger, muscle shirts to show off all that work at the gym, leather caps worn over short haircuts and neat mustaches. Jack remembered they were called clones, all those men who'd been bullied in high school and were now trying for the same hyper-masculine look.

Then he got closer and saw that they didn't just look the same, they *were* the same. Same height, same face, same body. Not clones but duplicates, used as extras to make the whole scene more real. He ignored them and went up to the bouncer. At least he looked different, which meant he wasn't just a prop. Dressed in leather pants and a leather vest with no shirt, he was bigger than the dupes, bulkier. No cap on his shaven head. A red bulb over the door made his scalp glow. Half a foot taller than Jack's six foot two, he crossed his arms as he looked Jack up and down, lingering on the tunic. "Sorry," he said, "we don't do drag here, *girlfriend.*"

"My name is Jack Shade," Jack said, "and I need to go inside."

Behind him, a couple of the clone dupers snorted, while another yelled "Get to the back of the line."

The bouncer snorted a laugh. "Do you think so?" he said. "Tell you what, Mary, get in line and maybe I'll decide to let you in when you reach the front. Don't bet on it, though."

Jack considered a glamour to make the bouncer look the other way and forget he'd ever seen the oddly dressed customer. But then he reminded himself that the bouncer was not some non-Traveler whose Linear senses could be easily shifted. He stared hard at the tall figure, then closed his eyes. He opened them as narrowly as he possibly could, and for just a second saw the bouncer in his true form. Bright sunlight obliterated the gray street, the bar, the line of men. A giant cheetah stood on its hind legs in front of Jack. Or rather, an image of a cheetah, with exaggerated whiskers, huge round eyes, large spots that looked painted on in thick daubs, and claws that curved out from human-like hands. Jack whispered, "You're a long way from home, aren't you?"

Jack blinked and the bouncer was back, but now he stared at Jack with a strange look, his mouth slightly open. Jack reached into one of his side pockets and pulled out a charm, a frog carved from an antelope bone. He held it out in his left hand. "Here," he said, "maybe this will help you when you get home. After all this is done." Sometimes, he thought, you bring something and you have no idea why until you need it. The bouncer took the charm in his huge hands and held it up before his eyes. His mouth opened and closed, and he said something Jack couldn't hear. Jack slid past him into the bar.

Bare red bulbs hanging from the ceiling lit up a crowded room. A rough wooden bar ran across one wall, with men who looked just like the ones outside leaning against it and swigging beer from unlabeled bottles. Behind the bar, a shirtless bartender handed out more bottles, his face glistening with sweat. Some kind of heavy metal band blared from loudspeakers suspended from the ceiling. Jack found himself longing for Judy Garland. Or *The Sound Of Music*. A thick layer of sawdust covered the floor. If it was supposed to absorb any wetness or stains it wasn't doing a very good job. Jack could see blood, and brown spots, and could smell other things. When he got back, he thought, he was definitely charging extra.

He looked around, first at the men by the bar or on the dance floor, then at the ones along the walls and in the corners, most of whom were doing various things to each other in improbable positions. Would he have to go examine each one of them for Carol's onyx ring? He imagined walking up to someone and asking, "Do you mind removing your fist for a moment?"

No. He was being too literal. The scene jarred him, and it was meant to do that. Meant to make it hard for him to think. If these men were all dupes they couldn't all be Carol. He needed to find someone who was different. As he thought this, he noticed a slight change in the men. They didn't stop what they were doing, but shifted, as if to keep watch on him.

Ignore them, he thought, and closed his eyes. He couldn't block the noise, or the smells, but underneath it all, faintly. . .he opened his eyes to focus on the wall furthest from the door, where a man was spread-eagled against a large wooden X, his wrists and ankles manacled to the ends. Two other men were lashing him with bullwhips that struck him almost horizontally, so that he was criss-crossed with lines, his t-shirt and jeans in shreds. His cries of mixed pain and pleasure sounded like others around the room, except that faintly, underneath them, Jack could hear the tears of a child. It was then that he realized. Whatever had happened to drive Carol Acker's soul piece from her body, her soul wasn't hiding. It was being held prisoner. He studied the man through slitted eyes. There it was, on the right hand. The onyx ring.

And something else. If he turned his head to look at an angle, so that he could barely see the figure on the wall, the whip marks became lines that swirled and moved all on their own, like the winds that Jack had seen before he fell into the street. A cage, he thought. A cage of wind.

As Jack began to move towards the man on the X the clone tried to block him. Some made crude passes at him, grabbing or rubbing his crotch, others pretended to dance in front of him.

He tried to push his way through to the prisoner but more and more of them crowded him. Finally, he took out his police whistle and blew a loud blast. The clones fell back, holding their ears. Now Jack held up one of his forged documents. Covered with a script unknown to language scholars was a painting of a beautiful young man flying naked above a mountain range. "My name is John Shade," Jack called out, "and I come under the banner and protection of Cthermes, Lord of Travelers!"

Whatever their true nature, the men in the bar were real enough to what they were supposed to be that they let him pass. Some stared at the picture, with hunger or a deep sadness. Jack moved quickly, but didn't run, to the wall.

The men with the whips were bulkier than the dupes, more like the bartender, and Jack wondered for a moment if they too were exiled cheetahs. It didn't matter, he had no more antelope charms, and besides they'd already turned to face him and raised their whips. Jack reached down towards his right leg, and his knife jumped into his hand. With two quick slashes he cut off the thongs. To his surprise, what he'd assumed were just leather sinews writhed along the floor, and the guards doubled over in pain, their whip hands held tight against their bellies. Tentacles, Jack realized, but he didn't care. The man on the wall raised his head to look at Jack with hope. "Please," he whispered, "you don't know how long they've held me." What had been whip marks now moved in swirls around the body. Within them, the onyx ring flared as Jack stepped forward.

Still on his knees, one of the guards said "Shade, stop!" and the other added "You don't know what you're doing."

Jack ignored them as he moved towards the figure on the wall. The whips were gone, but he still needed a way to break through the swirling lines. As he looked the man became a girl in a torn red dress, her body covered in angry slashes and what looked like dirt and pieces of stone. "Hurry," she begged. He held up the knife. Would it cut through the lines?

As Jack was about to try, one of the guards gestured with his good hand. Jack braced himself for an attack, but to his surprise the swirls and lines vanished. Amazed, he rushed forward to free the prisoner, only to realize that she was gone too. For a second, he saw a crude painting on a stone wall—some creature, or spirit, with whirling lines all around it. Then that too vanished, and Jack found himself falling . . .

He crashed hard, on his side, on what turned out to be a highly polished stone floor, lit by flickers of fire. He looked up and saw a layered chandelier with as much as a hundred candles. Sconces along the equally polished walls held five more candles each.

Strangely, Jack heard the music and saw the musicians before he noticed the dancers all around him. At the end of the room, on a low pedestal, eight men in blue velvet waistcoats and breeches, with white wigs on their heads, were playing some ornate but repetitive dance music on what today would be called "early instruments." Jack recognized the odd tinny sound from concerts he'd gone to with his wife.

Finally, he saw the dancers, and just in time, for a line of them was coming towards him as if they'd trample him and not even notice. He rolled out of the way at the last moment. The men wore black waistcoats and breeches, with white stockings and patent leather shoes with gold buckles and one inch heels. Their wigs were shorter than the musicians, but looked more finely woven. The women also wore wigs, high elaborate concoctions apparently inspired by the chandelier. Their gowns, pale blue with small pearls and jewels sewn into them, had long sleeves, a bodice that flattened the breasts, and wide flounced skirts. Their faces were powdered white, their lips dark red.

Safely by the wall now, Jack studied the dancers. As he'd guessed, there was only one couple, duplicated to fill the floor, which meant he could rule them out. The orchestra, too, were all the same. But when he looked at the wall opposite the musicians he saw something different. A young woman in a pale green dress that was more flowing than the dancers' gowns, was sitting in a high-backed wooden chair with her white-gloved hands folded in her lap. On either side of her stood a wide middle-aged woman in a long black dress buttoned up to the neck. With their arms crossed over their wide bosoms, and scowls on their faces, they looked more like harem guards than chaperones. Each had a long beaded purse on her arm, and Jack imagined them drawing out scimitars if he got too close.

He stared at the girl's right hand. It was hard to see through the gloves but Jack thought he saw the rough shape of the onyx ring.

Jack started to make his way toward the young woman. With each step, however, the dancers, seemingly oblivious to his presence, managed to step in front of him. He tried to slide through them, but more appeared in his way. Shoving them aside brought the same result. Jack wondered if they multiplied, like amoebae. When he glanced back at the orchestra he saw that their faces, impassive and calm, were all turned towards him. Now more and more dancers moved around him, in tighter and tighter rings. Soon they would trample him.

He took out his bone flute and began to play a simple five note tune, over and over. The musicians scowled, the dancers hesitated, even stumbled. As he continued to play the tune, Jack began to beat out a counter-rhythm against his thigh with his free hand, as complex as the tune was simple, but in a completely different pattern. What he'd said to Carol was true, that he had no natural rhythm—he suspected nobody did—but he'd once spent a year studying with a master drummer in Burkina-Faso.

The effect was immediate. The dancers fell to their knees and pressed their palms against their ears. The musicians played louder, but off-key, the violins and violas sounding like cats in an alley fight. Jack moved in and out of the stricken dancers as he made his way to the girl and her chaperone guards. When he got closer, however, something changed. The music became smoother and harmonious once more, though not the same melody. Jack glanced back at the orchestra. They still looked in pain as they compulsively tortured their instruments. The music here must be coming from the air or the walls, Jack thought. It swirled around and around itself, and as Jack stared at the young woman the music became visible, that same cage of spiraling wind that had trapped the man in the leather bar. Jack wondered how the hell he could cut through music.

He moved forward, and as he did so, the two women stepped towards him. Jack braced himself. They opened their purses, but instead of swords they took out large hand mirrors, one backed with gold, the other with silver. When they lifted them light poured out from the glass like a great wave. Jack's black clothes, and the charcoal on his skin, would protect his body, but he had only a few seconds to save his eyes. And more, for he knew that "baby starshine," as Travelers called the light, would go straight for his brain. He could already feel the fire through his closed eyes as he fumbled in his pockets for the polished coins from the Shadow Roman Empire. He pressed them tight against his eyelids. The chaperones cried out, and a moment later Jack heard the thud of the mirrors hitting the floor.

He removed the coins and opened his eyes just enough to check that they weren't faking it. Their eyes looked completely blacked out, almost gouged from their heads. In a high quavery voice one of them said "Shade, no. You don't know what you're doing."

Fuck, Jack thought. *I'm getting sick of hearing that from people who've just tried to kill me.* He looked past them to the girl. She seemed unable to get up from her seat, but her eyes were wet and her voice tight as she said "Please. You don't know what they do to me. Every night when the music stops . . ." Her voice trailed off into sobs.

Jack made himself look not at the girl but at the energy that swirled around her. In the leather bar it had been whiplashes. Now it was sound. Circular melodies and harmonies impossible to decode moved all around her to form a spiral prison. Jack took out his bone flute again. It was such a simple instrument, just five notes, but maybe if he found the right pattern . . . He began to play, tentatively at first, but then he let his instrument lead him. Like a skeleton key, it weaved through the harmonies, finding places to unlock, the way a master thief can open a set of tumblers, one by one.

The lines began to drop away. "Hurry!" the girl called to him. "You don't know how long I've been here, what they do to me."

He thought of his daughter, trapped in the Forest of Souls. For him, years had passed, but for her it could be decades, maybe longer . . .

Any moment, Jack thought. Just a little more open passage. *Now.* He braced himself and leaped for her, but even as he moved, one of the women called out some words in a language that almost cracked Jack's head open. And then, just as with the man on the X, the girl turned into a rough painting on a stone wall. Jack crashed into it—and through it—

—and fell onto a wooden floor, in a dark room that smelled of old sweat, older books, and whiskey. He saw a plain wooden table with ten old chairs around it. There were ten shot glasses on the table, along with a bottle of Schnapps, and a plate of small cakes that looked much older than the liquor.

Jack heard a murmur of voices in some language he couldn't quite catch. When he glanced around he saw a half-open door, with light and what he realized now was chanting on the other side. He walked through into what looked like a small makeshift synagogue, with a few benches, a plain wooden ark on the far wall, and ten old men who swayed and sang in Hebrew. They had come in suits but had taken off their jackets and rolled up their right sleeves of their white shirts so they could wrap the leather cords of *tefillin* around their arms. The small leather box attached to the cords gleamed slightly on their biceps, as did the matching box on their foreheads. There were ten of them, the number for a *minyan* that would allow a service to take place. And of course they were all the same person. Jack wondered if that counted for a prayer session.

The thing was, there was no one else. None of the dupes could be Carol, so where was someone different, with an onyx ring and trapped behind swirls of energy? Swirls. He looked again at the *tefillin* straps and realized they wrapped around the men's fingers and up their arms in a spiral. Was Carol's soul trapped in one of those little boxes? In all of them? Would he have to rip

THE FISSURE KING

them off each man's arm, take them apart, and put all the pieces together, a jigsaw soul? Or search for the ring, like a prize in an old crackerjack box?

Then he looked again at the front of the room and realized there was a larger box. The ark. Usually an ark held one or more Torah scrolls, which made them big enough to hold a child, or even a small woman. He stared at the wooden structure. Unlike the ones he'd seen in richer congregations, it was unadorned beyond a peaked cornice at the top. No carvings, no velvet curtain, just two doors that opened from the center. As he continued to examine it Jack thought he could see faint lines, swirls like the leather on the men's arms, but thinner. And alive. They moved all by themselves, round and round the ark, like chains.

He took a breath of the stale, sweaty air and stepped forward. Without a break in their prayers, or even a turn of the head, the congregants moved to block him. He shifted in a different direction and they followed. *This is getting seriously old*, Jack thought, and tried to shove them aside. Instantly the *tefillin* straps sprang off their bodies and wound around Jack's arms and legs so he couldn't move. They held him so tightly he couldn't even strain or push against them. If he could reach his knife— useless. Same with his charms and tricks and whistles.

Now what? Would they dismember him? Would the straps get tighter and crush his lungs? Instead, the men began to argue. It was in Yiddish, of course, Hebrew being only for prayers, and it took Jack a moment to catch what they were saying. It was about someone they called the Rescuer, and ancient texts detailing what to do to this person if he ever showed up. Kill him? Let him live but never release him? It didn't take Jack long to realize the Rescuer was himself.

One said the Rescuer was innocent because he did not understand his crime. Another claimed that only actions matter, not knowledge or intent. A couple then said they themselves were the guilty ones, for they did not try to correct him. But still another said to tell was useless. "As it is written," he said, " 'You shall hide your treasure from the stranger, for the stranger will come with eyes painted over, and ears filled with stone.' "

Enough of this bullshit, Jack thought. The treasure they were holding was a woman's soul. He couldn't reach any of his weapons or tricks, but he didn't need to. He had something better. Jack had once met an old-fashioned golem, the kind made out of dirt by some rabbi. The thing is, the rabbi got so excited, or maybe guilty, that he fell down dead of a heart attack just after the creature came to life. With no master to obey, and stuck in a room full of books, the golem began to study. There were Talmudic texts, but also books on magic. By the time Jack had met him, the golem had become a world famous scholar. Kabbalists, Sufis, and others would travel thousands of miles to study with him.

Jack had come for something simpler. Names. Jewish magic was based on the secret names of God, and just knowing one or two could give you great power. Jack served the golem for twenty-eight days. The idea of a human taking orders from a golem amused the creature so much he kept thinking of new commands just to watch Jack obey them. Finally, the Mud Rabbi, as some called him, gave Jack three names. One to create, one to destroy—and one to escape.

Jack called out the escape name. To his surprise, it hurt his throat, but the effect on the men was more extreme. They cried out and fell to their knees, hands over their ears and yelling curses at him. "*Schwartze* sorcerer!" he heard, but ignored them as the leather straps fell from his body. He weaved his way through the men to the ark.

Finally he opened it. At first it looked empty, and Jack felt ready to smash something. Then he looked again and saw a small figure, a girl about three inches high. She sat on what looked like a stone chair, with her hands folded in the lap of a shapeless dress that might have been made from animal skin. Despite her tiny size the onyx ring shone brightly on her finger. "Please help me," she said. "They've kept me here so *long*." Jack could hear the tears rather than see them. Once again, he thought of Genie.

"It's all right," Jack said, "I've come to take you home."

"Hurry," the girl said.

But before Jack could reach for her, a strong woman's voice called out, "Shade. You don't know what you're doing."

What the fuck now? Jack thought. He wanted to grab the girl and run, but didn't dare, so he turned and saw what he first thought was an old man in a white robe of heavy wool, with a long white beard, and white hair down his back. Then he looked closer and saw it was a woman. He thought for a second of Abby, the Bearded Lady at the carnival where Jack had worked long ago. Jack had dated her for a while, and when they kissed, Jack sometimes felt like Abby was the man, and Jack the woman, a sensation he found oddly exciting.

In the room, the dupes, still on their knees, called out "*Der Wisser Rebbe! Der Wisser Rebbe!*"

Jack looked at this "White master" and wondered if he could ignore her, or shove her aside if she tried to stop him. Probably not a great idea, he decided. He had a vial of Vatican holy water in his tunic, maybe he should douse her and announce her baptized in the name of Christ. Instead, he said "I know exactly what I'm doing. Bringing back a soul that was taken a long time ago."

In the ark, the girl pleaded "Don't listen to her. She's crazy! She holds me and hurts me."

The Rebbe said "Mr. Shade, this is your last chance. Please. Turn back."

"Tell me why I should do that," Jack said.

Sadness, and maybe fear, clouded her face a moment, then she said "I cannot. The Ancient of Winds has ordered silence."

"Well, that's fucking convenient."

The Rebbe closed her eyes and began to sway, as if in prayer. Suddenly, images, sounds, smells swept through Jack's senses. They came and went so quickly he couldn't really identify anything, but there was a great wind somehow smashing into a stone wall, and blood, and burnt meat. And laughter. Then it was all gone, and Jack found himself staggering back from the Bearded Lady. "What the hell was that?" he said. "What did you do to me?"

"More than I should have. More than I'm allowed."

Jack glanced at the miniature child on her chair in the Ark. Why didn't he just take her and run? As if she could sense his confusion the small voice pleaded "We have to go. Now! She's trying to take over your mind. *Please.* No one's ever come this far before."

Jack shook his head a moment. *No one*—had Carol Acker hired someone before Jack? Did cousin Jerry actually try before he gave Carol Jack's card? Something was wrong—he looked at the White Rebbe. Her eyes stared at him, unblinking. Of course. The girl was right, the old woman was trying to hypnotize him.

He closed his eyes and grimaced, then shook his head. When he looked again, the Rebbe seemed to have shrunk slightly, her gaze more sad than dangerous. Jack said, "Actually, it doesn't matter if I believe you or not. I have a kind of curse. It's called a Guest. I cannot refuse anyone who brings me a special token. A woman hired me to find her missing soul and bring it back to her."

"Her *soul*?" the Rebbe said. "That's the word she used?" She inclined her head towards the ark. "For *that*?"

"Yes. And it doesn't matter if she got it right or wrong. I have no choice."

The woman said something in Hebrew. Then, "So. You took a vow, and now it holds you prisoner."

"That's pretty much it."

She glanced at Jack's right boot. "You have a knife. If you cut your throat your Guest would have to leave."

"Don't bet on it."

"Ah, but even if your curse torments you beyond death you would no longer be able to do what should never be done."

And no longer able to bring back my daughter, imprisoned in the Forest Of Souls. Jack moved his eyes from the Rebbe's stare, and suddenly he was sick of all this. These creatures, or Powers, or whatever they were, had taken part of a girl's soul and locked it away behind layers and layers of illusion. It was time to take her home.

He took a golden needle from his survival tunic and moved it across the doorway, conscious all the time of the Rebbe standing motionless alongside him, the dupes behind them. If the end of the needle turned to iron Jack would have to identify whatever was dangerous before he could reach inside. With a smugness that made Jack want to slap her, the Rebbe said, "Don't worry, your Dialectical Needle will stay pure. It's not the ark that threatens you."

Jack finished his examination then put the needle away. Finally he reached inside the box. He didn't realize he was holding his breath until his arm didn't burn up or turn to stone. "Hurry" the girl said. "You don't know what they do."

"It's okay," Jack said. "I won't let them hurt you anymore. I'm going to put my hand around you but don't be scared." The last thing that Jack saw before he took hold of the girl was the White Rebbe, her eyes closed, her mouth set in a smile that seemed to express the sadness of centuries. Then the whirlwind hit.

Tight swirls of power, so intense they felt more like wires than gusts of wind. The room was gone, and there was stone all around. But Jack couldn't worry about that. He managed to get the hand holding the girl next to his face, and said above the screeching winds, "There is a tree in my pocket. When I put you there hold on tight to the tree and you'll be safe." The tree was a six-hundred-year-old sequoia Jack had gotten as a gift in the Miniature Forest. He'd thought he might plant it somewhere as an offering, but this was the best use for it. Now they had to get out of there.

There wasn't much time. He could feel the lacerations on his face and wrists, anywhere that wasn't covered. Jack closed his eyes and mouth and didn't dare breathe. Somehow he managed to reach a hand into a long shallow pocket and take out a crow feather. Every year, on no set day, thirteen such feathers appeared on the unmarked grave of Peter Midnight, the early New York Traveler buried in Manhattan's Inwood Hill Park. There were people who spent weeks camped out in the park in hopes of getting one, but Jack had received a message this past year from the Queen of Eyes, telling him the exact moment the feathers would drift to the ground from a high-flying murder of crows.

With his left hand Jack moved the feather counter-clockwise, in flat horizontal circles. At first he could only do it right in front of him, but slowly the winds backed off and he could turn his whole body around. He stopped when an opening appeared in the air. It was clearly a way out but all it led to was some kind of cave, and Jack was done with hopping world to world. Using the feather as a kind of paintbrush, he drew a doorway where the rough opening was. At the same time he called out a set of numbers. They were like GPS coordinates, except they included more dimensions. And were much older, invented by an Italian Traveler who'd had to rescue a foolish poet who'd accepted an offer of a tour of Hell.

Jack's office materilized on the other side of the doorway. The air appeared thick, almost congealed, but Carol Acker was there, still on her chair in the circle of roses. A couple of hours must have passed, because he could see it was dark outside the windows, but Carol looked peaceful, her eyes closed, her hands in her lap

Though Jack knew the tiny figure in his pocket couldn't hear him above the angry winds, he said "Be brave, little soul. You're almost home." With a twist of his body he propelled himself through the doorway.

He landed hard on the floor, just outside the circle. "Jack?" Carol asked, and lifted her head but kept her eyes closed.

"Yes, it's me. Don't open your eyes just yet." He turned on a desk lamp so he could see her more clearly. When he glanced at the digital clock on his desk he discovered even more time had passed than he thought, for it was nearly nine o'clock. He frowned. Had she been sitting there all that time?

Carol said, "Did you—"

"Yes. I have it." Jack hoped these were not empty words. What if the girl—Carol's soul—had not survived the winds? When he reached in his pocket he could feel her still clinging tightly to the sequoia, so he lifted out the tree, with her attached, and set it on the table. He whispered to her "It's okay. You can let go now." As gently as he could he pried loose her arms, then placed her on his left palm. She looked up at him with a mixture of hope and fear. "Get ready for something wonderful," he whispered to her, then louder, "Carol, something's about to happen. It may feel like a jolt, but it's okay."

"I'm ready," Carol said.

As Jack moved his hand closer to Carol, the girl on it became even smaller, no more than a quarter-inch tall as he brought his palm close to Carol's ear. With a sharp puff he blew on the girl and she vanished into Carol's ear canal.

Carol spasmed, and gasped, but she kept her eyes closed, and her hands clasped. And then she didn't move. Jack pulled up a chair to face her, then waited a full three minutes before he said softly, "Carol? Are you all right?"

For a another twenty seconds or so she didn't answer, but then the left side of her mouth turned up a slight smile, and she said "Oh, yes. That's *much* better." The voice sounded the same as before, but with more notes and undertones. Still in her seat, Carol opened her eyes. They were the same as before, only deeper, with new subtleties of color. Jack found that if he looked long enough he could see flickers of red deep inside her.

She sat back and looked at Jack, a slight smile on her face. "So," she said, "you met *Der Wisser Rebbe*." He must have looked startled because she laughed and said, "Did she make you feel like a young girl again, Jack? That delightful beard. She really is quite old, you know. Well, not as old as me, of course. But all those *rules*. Things you can say, things you can't say, how does she keep track? I wonder, dear Jack, my hero, my rescuer— if she'd allowed herself to tell you the full truth, would it have made a difference? I doubt it. I imagine plucky Jack Shade still would have brought back timid Carol's missing soul." She stood up and stretched.

Jack tried to stand, but she flicked her fingers and he discovered he couldn't move. When she picked up her purse she said, "Did I pay you? Yes, of course, prudent Jack got his fee up front. Maybe I should double it. You did go through a lot. And I certainly won't want for money. But no. A deal is a deal, and we wouldn't want to spoil you."

At the door she stopped and said "Oh, and Jack? Remember how you told me to envision a homecoming cake? I just want you to know—I blew out *all the candles*."

And then she was gone.

Jack stayed frozen in his chair a long time. The night passed and the dawn came and still he couldn't move. When he was finally able to get up it was seven in the morning. He raced to the bathroom, then ignored all the debris and went straight to his laptop. Usually, if he needed to know what was going on, he opened Jinn-net, the dark web service for Travelers and Powers. But something told him he needed the outside world, so he went to the standard Internet.

It didn't take long to discover what he didn't want to know. CNN.com burst forth with the headline, "Breaking news! Grisly Double Murder In New Jersey Suburb!" The live feed showed an ordinary ranch house surrounded by police cars. In front, a young correspondent, her face set to "grim" to hide her excitement, said "We still don't know much yet, Wolf. The police have released the names of the victims, Jerry and Marjorie Acker." Jack began to shake. The woman went on, "According to one policeman I spoke to—and Wolf, I have to tell you, he looked very shocked— the bodies were, quote, 'torn to pieces.'" She paused, as if to convey her own horror, then added, "And one strange detail. Apparently, the killer, or perhaps killers, used the blood, maybe even body parts, to write a cryptic message on the wall of the murder room. Just two words, Wolf. 'Much better.'"

Jack closed his laptop. Still shaking, he reached for the phone.

2.

"F"EEBIE" Sam Harwin and Dean "the Fed" Margolis, so-called because of their ability to impersonate FBI agents, showed up at Carol and Bob Acker's home on Long Island only half an hour after Carolien Hounstra had called them. Though Carolien had said she did not expect Carol to be there, she also told them to bring every level of protection they could manage—etheric body armor, spells written on their faces, clothes, and genitals in invisible ink, entire cans of demon repellent sprayed on their bodies, and whatever charms and weapons they could carry in their conservative FBI suits. Sure enough, however, it wasn't Carol who opened the door, but her grief-stricken and confused husband.

"Is this about Jerry?" Bob Acker asked, and Sam said yes. "But why would I—I haven't seen Jerry in months. Well, Carol—" He stopped himself.

Dean asked, "Is Mrs. Acker here, sir?"

Terror crept into Bob's eyes. "No, she—she was so upset—hearing about Jerry and Marge's death—she said, she said she needed to be alone for awhile."

The two Travelers looked at each other. Sam turned to Bob and asked "Did she say anything else?"

Bob looked down. "Yes—she said, she said I and the kids and our grandkids would be safe. That no one would *bother* us." Now he raised his eyes. "What did she mean? Officer, I mean agent, how could she know that? I mean, did the killer *speak* to her? Was she going away to save us somehow? She's not—she's not going to get hurt, is she? He's not going to do to her what he did to—*oh God*."

Dean cast a glamour over the poor man to erase such thoughts from his head. In a voice enhanced by Basic Persuasion, he said "There's no need to worry, Mr. Acker. These kinds of cases never work that way."

Acker looked confused. "These kinds of cases?" he said, but then his voice trailed off, and a moment later said, "Oh, thank you. That's so good to hear."

"We're sorry for your loss," Sam said, and then the two men headed for their car.

"Oh, excuse me," Bob Acker called after them. They stopped, turned. "Do you guys have an agent named Jack Shade?"

"Fuck," Dean said, under his breath. All they knew was that Carolien had called them at the New York Travelers Aid Society and asked them to check on this Acker guy. Something to do with his cousin's death. And that they should protect themselves, and if the wife was there, to be prepared for trouble.

To Bob, Dean said, "Yes, we do. New York office. Do you know him?"

"No, no, but my wife asked me, she said if anyone came asking about her, to find out if they knew this Shade person. And if they did, to give them a message for him. For Mr. Shade, that is."

"So what's the message?"

"She said to tell him she was just getting started. Warming up."

"Were those her exact words?"

"Yes. Yes, I think so."

"Thank you," Dean said, and then, "Mr. Acker, look at me, please." Acker's face slackened. "Good. Now this is important. It's for your country. You do love your country, don't you?" Acker nodded. "Good. You will forget the name Jack Shade. You will forget *us*. You will forget your wife's message. All you will remember is that you and your family are safe. Will you do that for me? For your country?"

"Yes," Bob Acker said.

"Very good." Dean walked to the car, where Sam already had the engine running.

As their black Altima jerked away from the curb, Dean said, "Jesus fucking Christ. *Jack Shade.* What the goddamn hell has Johnnie Reckless done now?"

Jack's phone call to Carolien had been only three words. "I need you." When she arrived, seventeen minutes later, and saw Jack just sitting there, so clearly frightened, and the other chair inside the remains of a rose petal circle, she grabbed a third chair to sit down right in front of him, and took his hands. "Tell me," she said.

A long shuddering breath ran through Jack, and then he said, "A woman named Carol Acker—or some *thing* inside her—has just slaughtered her cousin and his wife in Teaneck. She might go for her own family next. We have to protect them."

Carolien said, "Do you know where they are?"

Jack got up and retrieved the check form the table. As he'd figured, it was from a joint account with her husband and displayed their address. "Here's the husband," he said, as he sat down again. He added, "Carolien, it was her cousin who gave her my card. The one she just killed."

Carolien was wearing a navy pea jacket over paint-spattered overalls. She took a cell phone from her jacket pocket and speed-dialed a number. "Sam," she said, "I need you and Dean to go check on someone." When she'd given them the information— and added that they should protect themselves—she hung up and focused again on Jack. "Now," she said. "Everything."

Carolien was Dutch, six feet tall, one hundred sixty-five pounds, with long blond hair, and the whitest skin Jack had ever seen. He found it hard to look at her without thinking of milk, or vanilla ices, or some other ridiculous food cliché. Maybe it was because that was how most of the males, and some of the females, from NYTAS talked about her, as a wondrous meal they'd like to devour. Jack knew that part of their hostility to him came from the fact that Carolien had turned them all down and chosen him. He and Carolien were still more friends than lovers, a relationship that suited both of them, Carolien most of all.

It was only as he talked about it that Jack realized how little he understood. "What was that *thing*?" he said. "Was it really a lost part of a suburban housewife who'd always been too nice all her life? And what was holding it prisoner?"

"It may be," Carolien said, "that this is something much older than Mrs. Acker."

"Then what's her connection to it?"

Carolien closed her eyes and let her head drop, something Jack had seen her do just before she came up with some link no one else would have found. Sometimes she would sit like this for a long time, hours even, but now it lasted only ten or fifteen seconds. When she opened them again she said, "*Schatje*— (Dutch for "little treasure," or sweetheart)—tell me again, please, when you saw this *thingetje* on the stone wall, what did it look like?"

"Like some kind of beast surrounded by coils of wind."

"Ah," she said, and reached for his laptop. "Password?" she asked.

Jack looked down and mumbled "Carolien." She laughed and began to type.

A minute or so later, she turned the screen around and held it up to him. "Is this it?" she said.

Jack found himself staring at what looked like a cave painting of some kind, like those in Lascaux or Altamira. Only, where those were mostly realistic images of bulls and horses, this showed a demon or monster, upright like a man, yet wild and ferocious, with long claws and teeth, and arms that looked like it was trying to break free of the world. Or the lines that swirled around it like a cage. "Yes," Jack said, "that's it. What is this?"

She set down the computer but didn't close it. "The pre-historians call it 'the Whirlwind Enigma.' It is strange for them because it seems wrong in so many ways. This, you know, is how they understand things. By making categories."

216

"Carolien," Jack said, "we have no time for this. I need to know what I'm facing. What I've done."

"No," she said firmly. "We cannot simply rush ahead. We must understand."

Jack looked down, nodded. Carolien didn't need to say that rushing ahead, *his* rushing, had killed Jerry and Marjorie Acker. And they were probably only the start.

"First," Carolien said, "the painting, if indeed that is what it is, is sixty-five thousand years old. Much older than any other complex cave art. The paintings in Le Chauvet are only thirty-five thousand. Second, all the caves with advanced paintings have many examples. Here there is only one. And the cave is very hard to reach, so much so that it was only discovered ten years ago. Third, the great cave art shows almost all animals, and with great realism. Here we see a monster. *Fourth*." Her voice was rising. "The paints. There is the usual ochre and other mineral pigments, but also something else. And that something is very toxic. The scientist who scraped a sample used gloves, of course, but a very little bit fell onto his arm. In the next hour his skin began to itch, and then an hour later he collapsed, and two hours after that he was dead."

Jack waited a second to make sure she was done, then said, "And this Enigma thing—you think it's a picture of what I brought back to Carol Acker?"

She shook her head. "No, *schatje*. Not a picture."

"Fuck," Jack half-whispered. She was right, of course. Not a painting. The thing itself, imprisoned in that wall for sixty-five thousand years.

Softly now, Caroline said, "Do you know Johannes Ludann's theory of cave paintings?" Jack nodded. Ludann was a Danish Traveler who became obsessed with cave art. Instead of the usual academic belief that they were magical attempts to benefit hunting or fertility, Ludann claimed they were trapped hostile Powers that had preyed upon humanity until it figured out how to imprison them. In 1987, Johannes Ludann disappeared after declaring that he would "find clear proof and bring it back."

Jack said, "So you think this thing, this fucking Enigma, is what Ludann was talking about?"

Carolien nodded. "Possibly. Look." She grabbed the laptop and ran her fingers over the keyboard. Then she turned it around so he could see the screen where a news article declared *Mysterious Cave Painting Vanishes From Rock Wall. Scientists Stunned, Angry.* She said, "I saw this just before you called me. It was how I knew."

"Christ," Jack said. "Are you telling me this—*this thing*—was trapped in that wall, and I fucking *released* it?"

Carolien said, "Yes, that is possible."

Jack discovered his nails were digging into his palms. He spread his fingers, breathed deeply, then said, "But what does this have to do with Carol Acker? She was just some bored housewife."

"Who knows?" Carolien said. "Maybe that creature reached out to her. Maybe it searched the world until it found what it needed, a possible vessel. . ." Her voice trailed off.

Jack said, "And a Traveler who didn't think to ask questions."

"No," Carolien said sharply. "To worry about such things will only waste time." Her accent always became stronger when she was being stern. "There is a more important question."

"I know," Jack said. "What does she do next? And how do I stop her?'"

Jack's phone buzzed. He'd set it on the table after calling Carolien, and now it vibrated towards him. He reached across the table for it. "What the hell?" he said, when he saw the display. "Margaret Strand," it read. Now he looked up at Carolien, somehow more amazed by this than everything else that had happened. He said "It's the Queen of Eyes!"

Carolien, too, looked startled before she quickly said "Then you had best answer it, yes?"

Jack touched the connect button. "Margaret?" he said, then put it on speaker.

A strong yet distant voice said, "This is Margarita Mariq Nliana Hand." Jack nodded. "Margaret" was her everyday name. She was in her aspect now, her power. The Queen of Eyes was the holder of all oracular power in the world, an office that had passed from mother to daughter for far longer than anyone knew. Some time ago Jack Shade had brought the Queen back after an assassination attempt, and he knew she liked him, but still, the Queen rarely spoke directly, let alone called someone on the phone.

"I am honored," Jack said.

"You have asked, and I shall answer." *Asked?* Jack thought, then realized he'd spoken aloud his question about what happened next and how to stop her. Did she hear everyone's questions, all over the world? She said, "And you must listen."

Jack sat up straighter, as if she could see him. "I'm ready," he said.

"You have two days, Jack Shade. There were three, but the first is gone." Jack sucked in a breath, thinking of all those hours stuck in his chair. The Queen said, "Two days before it truly begins. Then it will be too late. *Haarlindam, 1132.*" Before Jack could say anything, she hung up.

"Wait!" Jack said. "What about Carol Acker? Damn!" He hit the callback button. After a few rings a pleasant voice said, "Hi. This is the voicemail for Margaret Strand. I'm sorry I'm not—"

It was only after he put down the phone that Jack saw Carolien's reaction to the Queen's message. She was sitting forward on her chair, her back a straight line, her mouth half open, her eyes fixed on the phone. Jack got up to squat before her and take her hands. She didn't seem to notice. "Carolien," he said softly, "what is it?"

She looked at him, almost surprised, as if she'd forgotten where she was. Then she closed her eyes for a moment, and when she opened them, swore softly, "*Godverdamme.*" Then louder, "Haarlindam!"

"What?" Jack said. "What is Haarlindam?"

"A very old *Nederlandse* city. Every Dutch Traveler knows of it."

"I'm sorry, Carolien, I've never heard of it. And what does—"

"Ah, but you won't have, dear Jack. This is something the *Nederlands Reisen Associatie* keeps very much to itself. In the year 1132—" She stopped and crossed herself, something Jack had never seen her do. "—the Travelers and the Powers joined together, and they—what is the word, oh yes, *obliterated*, they obliterated the city of Haarlindam, and everything and every person within it."

"Jesus," Jack said, "Why? What the hell was going on there?"

"No one knows. The Travelers of 1132 time-sealed it."

"Shit," Jack said. A time-seal was a kind of bubble, a force-field to use the modern expression, that prevented any information from a place or an event from leaking out to the future, or even the past. "Does anyone have a clue?"

"Only that something *verschrikkelijk*—terrible—had become free in Haarlindam, and no one could stop it. In this case, some small details, stories perhaps, escaped the seal. Preserved, maybe, by the sealers. Bodies, and body pieces, strung like decorations for *Carnaval*. Lines and line of black poles with human heads on top. Heads that could see, and hear, and smell. And of course, scream." She gripped Jack's arm now. It always surprised him how such soft hands could be so strong. She said, "Jack, if this *thing* you brought back to your client, your Carol Acker, is anything at all the same as what happened in Haarlindam, and we have only two days, we *must* stop it. *Before.* Before it completes its so-called warming-up."

Jack took a breath. "I did it, I'll stop it."

She shook her head. "No, no, no. Not alone. Even you will need help this time."

"Where do we go? The Queen has obviously said all she's willing to say."

Carolien smiled slightly, just for a moment, but it thrilled Jack to see she could do it. "Where else? We are Travelers, *ja*? Then we must go to NYTAS."

"Oh, great," Jack said. "Arthur!"

The New York Travelers' Aid Society had existed, under various names, from long before there was a New York, or a Nieuw Amsterdam, for that matter. Carolien had once traced it back to an alliance of the Mannahasset and Wampanoag Indians, but it went back much further than that. Under the current Chief, however, an erstwhile surgeon named Arthur Canton, it had become something of a showcase—for Canton himself. He'd moved the Chief's office to a former ceremonial chamber and made sure that all group actions, communications, and requests for the help of NYTAS's vast resources must go through him. He assisted those he liked, and blocked those he didn't. Canton liked Carolien, everyone did. Jack, on the other hand—Canton considered Jack arrogant, selfish, a loner who never helped the group and considered himself above everyone else. All true, of course, which made it that much harder for Jack to plead for help.

They found the Chief at his great ebony desk inlaid with gold and silver to show the Planetary Palaces and diamond arrows to chart the pathways between them. Canton wore a charcoal suit with a black tie containing bits of light that represented some constellation or other. His chiseled features and lush hair always made Jack suspect he'd cast some George Clooney glamour over himself, and if they ever saw the real Arthur he'd have a sloping forehead, a rat nose, and a receding chin.

Canton sat with the air of someone who expected a summons from the White House at any moment. The real White House, of course, not the showpiece in Washington. He said, "Carolien, it's lovely to see you as always. Your unruly pet, on the other hand—"

"Enough," Carolien said. "We know you dislike Jack, of course you do. Everyone does." Jack struggled not to stare at her.

Canton smiled. "Except you, apparently."

"I vacillate," Carolien said, and then, before Canton could answer, "Arthur, believe me, please. We come with something so important we must set aside any personal matters." She looked at Jack. "Tell him."

Jack described Carol Acker's "soul retrieval," condensing his struggles in the different worlds and going straight to what happened afterwards, especially the slaughter of the man who'd given Jack's card to his cousin Carol. Then he told Arthur about the telephone call from the Queen of Eyes, and let Carolien explain about Haarlindam. He could see it hurt her to do this, reveal a Dutch Travelers' secret to Arthur Canton, but she did it anyway,

For what felt like a long time, Arthur stared at Jack through narrowed eyes, while the fingers of his left hand drummed slowly on the tabletop. "So," he said finally, "we seem to be driving down an old road. Mr. Lone Wolf Shade, who has no use for his colleagues until *he* needs something, has once again—how shall I say this—Oh right, fucked up. And now he expects NYTAS to save him. Ah, but this time he brings his mommy to plead for him."

"Arthur, please," Carolien said, "this is not about Jack."

"No? I got an interesting call just before you arrived. From Dean Margolis and Sam Harwin. They were not terribly pleased to discover they'd been used as Jack Shade's errand boys."

"Jack did not do that," Carolien said, "it was me. We needed to know if Mr. Acker was safe."

"Well good news, then. He's fine, apparently. But his wife did leave a message. Just in case someone showed up. A message for a certain Jack Shade. She wanted you to know that she's, quote, 'just warming up.' And now the message has been delivered." He inclined his head and rotated his hand in mock servitude.

"God damn it," Jack said, "can't you see that—"

Canton waved a hand and Jack's mouth locked so he couldn't speak. The position of Chief carried certain powers, which probably was why Canton rarely left the building. To Carolien, he said, "I've made my decision, Carolien. You may go now. And take your dog with you before he soils the floor."

Carolien looked about to try again, but Jack took her arm and led her out. When they had left the building, Carolien let loose a stream of Dutch that Jack figured would burn his ears if he knew what it meant.

It didn't matter, Jack knew. He looked around at the street. NYTAS was on Madison Avenue and the passersby were mostly office workers and executives, well-off shoppers, people on their way to appointments with clients, lovers, or therapists. The sun had come out but the air had turned chilly, and some held their light jackets tightly against their bodies. *Haarlindam*, he thought. What if she chose New York this time? He looked at a man who'd just bought a hot dog from a cart and was happily taking his first bite. For an instant, Jack saw the man turned inside out, his body parts strewn across the Art Deco relief of an angel on the building behind him.

Jack took out his phone and began to dial. Carolien asked whom he was calling, and he said "COLE."

COLE stood for the Committee of Linear Explanation, and no Traveler liked to call them, though every Traveler knew their number. When an action spilled over to the outside world COLE stepped in to clean things up, to restore Non-Travelers' trust in their limited reality. Jack had only ever called them once, the night his daughter's poltergeist killed her mother and then his daughter had left the world entirely, pulled into the dead zone of the Forest of Souls.

The phone rang once, and then a woman's voice said, "You have reached the offices of COLE. All our agents our occupied right now, but if you stay on the line—"

"Fuck!" Jack said, and almost threw the phone at NYTAS's oak door. Instead, he just put it back in his pocket, and told Carolien, "I have to go do something and it has to be alone." She started to speak but he said, "There's no time. I need you to head back to your place and monitor the news, track any activity that might tell us what she's doing, where she is. The Queen said two days, but she's already started. Warming up. Will you do that for me?"

She nodded. " Call me," she said.

"When I can." Jack stepped into the street and raised his arm. Instantly, a taxi pulled to the curb and the cabbie ordered the confused couple in back to get out. When they tried to protest he yelled "Emergency! No charge, okay?" Jack took their place the moment they stepped out. The ability to command taxis was one of Jack's favorite perks of being a New York Traveler, but now all he cared about was getting where he needed to go. "The Public Library," he said. "And I'll pay their fare as well as mine."

The scene on the Library steps might have been summer, with people sitting on the cold stone, or the small slat chairs on the sidewalk, some reading but most talking, eating street food, playing games or texting on their phones. Two young women in tight jeans and sweaters, and wearing clunky Ugg boots leaned against one of the stone lions, talking intensely about some boyfriend, while in front of the other lion a young white guy was doing card tricks to impress a couple of middle-aged marks.

Okay, Jack thought, *where to start?* He gestured at the two women. Both of them gasped, then laughed with delight. "Mr. Kewpie!" one of them said, and patted the lion's mane, which had become soft and silky. "What are you doing here, little one? So far from home! Did you follow me? Who let you out?" She began to pull on the stone head, which didn't move but let out a low growl. "Come on, sweetie," she said. "When did you get so heavy?"

Jack pointed at the card sharp. The eight of hearts flew out of his hand and began to loop around the heads of the older men. Soon other cards followed it. "What the fuck?" one of the marks said, and the two of them hurried down the steps, swatting at the cards, while the sharp stared after them and made strange noises.

Come on, Jack thought, *who do you have to screw to get some attention in this town?* He went back to the two women, gestured again, and a deep voice boomed out of the lion. "Riddle me this. What creature walks on four legs in the morning, two legs in the—"

That was as far as it got. Everything froze, the lion, the people, even the cards in the air. Jack closed his eyes. *Finally*, he thought.

Behind him, a firm man's voice said, "John Shade!" He turned and there they were, a white man and woman in black suits and white shirts. An old Traveler joke went "Nothing is ever just black and white. Well, except for COLE, of course." Jack wasn't sure, but he thought they might be the same two who'd confronted him some months back, when he was fighting off his dream duplicate. Maybe he'd become their special assignment. Or maybe all COLE teams just looked alike. The man said, "John Shade, you have violated—" but the woman interrupted him.

"Jesus, Jack," she said, "what the fuck are you doing?"

"I needed help," Jack said, "and nobody was answering the phone at your headquarters.

The man ordered "Move!" Jack had never heard so much fury in one syllable. It was just standard procedure, get the bad boy Traveler away from the scene before the weird memories could take hold in the witnesses' minds. As he began walking east, towards Grand Central Station, he saw that two more agents had arrived to glam the witnesses' minds. Jack thought how he'd often pitied Nons—non Travelers. They knew so little of reality, and were so easily put asleep. Now he envied them.

They didn't talk until they stopped at the main entrance to the train station, under the statue of Mercury in flight above the doors. Before the agents could accuse him, Jack told them what had happened. "Look, I need help. I ony staged that scene so I could talk to you. I've got to find that, that *thing*, and stop it, and I have just two days. Maybe just today, maybe tomorrow will already be too late. And I don't think I can do it alone."

The woman looked from Jack to her partner. "What do you think? Maybe the satellite system?"

"No," the man said.

Startled, the woman let some color show in her face. "But you heard what Nliana Hand said. Haarlindam was almost a thousand years ago. We were in that seminar together, Paul. Think how much bigger the targets could be today."

"Stop," the man said. "This is not our responsibility. It will only become so if Mr. Shade reveals things to the outside world. And then our task will be to remove Mr. Shade."

The woman stared at her partner. "Don't you think mass slaughter will *reveal* things?"

His shoulders moved in the slightest of shrugs. "Not necessarily. The outer population will no doubt cast its own interpretation. Disease or terrorism, most likely." He waved a finger and a white Lexus illegally parked in front of the Grand Hyatt Hotel next door to Grand Central glided forward. As the man got in the car the woman said to Jack, "This isn't over. He's letting his dislike of you cloud—" And then, as if realizing she'd said too much, she ducked into the car.

She would try, Jack thought, but her partner—whatever he thought about Jack—represented the agency's mission. Don't save the world, just keep it ignorant. He watched the Lexus get absorbed in traffic. So many people, he thought. In trains, on the street, in stores and offices. *Tell Jack I'm just getting started,* Carol Acker had said. Warming up. *And two days,* the Queen had said. And Jack Shade had no idea what to do.

He stepped inside the train station to reduce the traffic noise, and called Carolien. "COLE's a wash-out," he said. "All they'll do is cover it up after it happens."

She made some kind of Dutch noise, then said "Maybe I should speak to Arthur alone."

"Don't bother," Jack said.

"What are you going to do? You cannot act alone this time. You must understand that."

"I know. There's another possibility."

"Possibility?"

"An ally. Someone who owes me."

"What? Do you mean your Dream Hunter friends?"

"No. I'm talking about someone with real fire power."

"Who—Oh no. No, Jack, you cannot—*La Societé*?"

"I told you, they owe me."

"And what will you owe *them* if you do this? You know what they are! Jack, please."

"I don't have a choice, Carolien."

"*Godverdamme*, Jack. That's what you told yourself when you freed that—*thing*. You always have a choice."

"Not this time."

"Maybe we can petition the Powers."

He made a noise. "Come on. Even an emergency request would take four or five days just to get a hearing."

"Perhaps they could undo any damage done between the petition and their acceptance."

"Maybe. But what if they can't? Or won't? And suppose they don't grant the petition? Without NYTAS behind me they could say I don't have standing. You know what they're like. Fucking divine bureaucrats."

He could hear tears in her voice now. "Please, Jack, think of what you're doing. Think of who they are!"

"I'm sorry, Carolien, I just can't worry about myself in all this."

"I can't let you—"

"I have to go, Carolien. I'm sorry." He ended the call, then switched off the phone. It was time to move.

He hailed a taxi and had the driver take him to 67th and Lexington. The building on the northwest corner housed a high end Islamic couturier on the ground floor with long silk dresses and hijabs so elegant that Carolien had once said she might convert for the fashions. Above the shop rose faceless offices, whose entry door, gray and anonymous, bore only one logo, the initials "S.I." in gold letters, and to the left of it a keypad of numbers. There was no bell to ring, no intercom. Either you knew the number code or you didn't. The code was simple but impossible to guess. It was the birthday of King Solomon, according to the ancient Hebrew calendar.

Suleiman International, originally headquartered in Baghdad but for the past ninety-two years in Geneva, had diversified in recent times, like all wise conglomerates. And SI was nothing if not wise. If you knew of their existence, and had the money, you could hire them for cross-world quantum encryption, nano-possession of troublesome clients, Akashic data protection (guaranteed for up to one hundred past lives), or emergency exorcisms of politicians in danger of foreclosure by their operational hosts. But if you knew they existed, you also knew their original and primary function—controlling, and selling, the services of the Djinn.

Jack tapped in the king's dates. The door silently opened, then closed behind him the moment he entered. There was only one elevator in the narrow lobby and Jack rode it to the third floor, where a young white woman in a pale blue dress sat at a crescent-shaped cedar desk. Judging by her uncovered long blonde hair she was not a believer. *Nice to know*, Jack thought, *that S.I. didn't discriminate.* Before Jack could say anything, the woman told him, "Welcome to S.I., Mr. Shade. How may we help you?"

Jack had often noticed the proclivity of powerful organizations to flaunt their intelligence. He was not in the mood to play, however. "I need a flask," he said.

"Ah," the woman said, "I'm afraid that service is restricted, and most likely—how shall I put this—beyond your financial resources."

"Please tell Mr. ibn Hakeem that Nadia Nazeer's son-in-law is here."

Jack thought he saw just a flicker of surprise before she smoothed her face and said, "A moment, please." She stood up and gestured towards a red leather chair and a small table with various newspapers scattered around it. "Please have a seat," she said, "this won't take long." Jack sat down and immediately felt like he'd returned to his favorite chair. It was so comfortable he had to remind himself it had not existed thirty seconds ago.

The receptionist returned a minute later with a middle-aged Arab man dressed in the sort of suit whose price Jack could not even try to guess. Of course, he thought, if you control a Djinn tailor you might not have to pay anything. Jack knew of a prince who went through the Seven Trials just to acquire a Djinni who would craft the robe for the prince's coronation. "Jack!" Mr. ibn Hakeem said, and took Jack's right hand in both of his. "It's good to see you. Sandra tells me you've requested one of our higher end services. Come. We will discuss it over tea."

Years ago, Abdullah ibn Hakeem had dated Nadia Nazeer, Jack's mother-in-law. They met at some Arab-American fund-raiser and went out for about a year, until Nadia had seen something, just a hint of something, that was not supposed to exist. Jack had stepped in to help ibn Hakeem cover it up and change Nadia's memories. Ibn Hakeem had ended the relationship, but he'd told Jack not to hesitate if he ever needed a favor.

Jack said, "I'm sorry, sir, I would love tea, but my time is not my own right now."

S. I.'s man in New York looked startled for a moment, though not as much as Sandra, who actually stared at Jack, mouth open, for a few seconds before she composed herself. "Ah," ibn Hakeem said, "everyone is so busy these days. Perhaps when your time returns to you."

"I would like that very much. Thank you."

To Sandra, Mr. ibn Hakeem said, "Please tell Mr. Hakami in Resources that Mr. Shade will be coming down, with my personal request for all assistance." He led Jack to the elevator, or rather *elevators*, for now a second door had appeared, narrower, with discreet glyphs in the corners. He held it open and Jack stepped into a varnished cedar chamber, with a gold plate that held only one button, marked with a *tav*, the final letter of the Hebrew alphabet. Jack wondered if the wood came from the Temple— the first one, of course, the real one, built by Solomon and a work crew of Djinn.

He didn't feel the elevator descend but a moment later it opened to reveal a vast room of eight foot high metal cabinets that went back as far as Jack could see, perhaps even across borders between worlds. A small man in shirtsleeves stood before the elevator. He was bald, with a neat mustache. He didn't look Arabic, but not exactly European either. Of course, he might not have been human. He said softly, "Good afternoon, Mr. Shade. My name is Hakami. I am happy to assist you."

"I need a flask."

"Yes, of course." He turned and set off down the central corridor. "This way, please," he said. They rounded various corners, until Jack wasn't sure he could find his way back alone. Finally, they came to a stop before a cabinet that looked exactly the same as all the others, except that the gray metal appeared slightly newer, shinier. "This will do," Hakami said. He smiled at Jack. "You know, I presume, that they come in two sorts, those who accepted the Messenger and those who remained infidels. I am sure Mr. ibn Hakeem would prefer the former for you. Much easier to control. For a beginner, of course." He slid open one of the cabinet's ten or so metal drawers. Inside was what looked like a rectangular steel thermos with a black screw-on cap. He smiled as he lifted it out. "As I am sure you know, Mr. Shade, the smoky glass bottle with the ancient cork has gone out of fashion." He began walking back, and Jack followed.

At the elevator, Hakami somehow produced a clipboard with a sheet of paper and attached pen. "Please," he said. Slight smile. "There are no hidden clauses, I assure you." Jack read the paper which acknowledged his receipt of "Container RS-42," and his acceptance that any unfortunate side effects of his "desired grantings" would be solely his responsibility. Jack took a breath and signed. Hakeem took the clipboard and handed over the container.

It felt warm, and slightly heavier than Jack had expected, but otherwise unremarkable. "You might want to open it outdoors," Hakeem said as he pushed the elevator button. "This is not to imply any danger, or indeed issues of size, but only that clients sometimes mis-speak—from the surprise, you understand—and their first grantings become, well, a bit untidy. Not that such a thing would happen to you, I'm sure."

"Yeah, thanks," Jack said. He was getting a little tired of the guy.

There was still only one button in the elevator, but now when Jack pushed it, it returned him to the lobby. Back in the street, he hailed a cab and took it to the garage where he kept his Altima. As he drove up the West Side Highway he found he kept looking at the clock, and then the flask. 1:45. Only two days, and the first was half over. Maybe he was mistaking a mistake. He had gone to Suleiman International for quick transportation to where he needed to go, but maybe *they* were what he needed. He went over the meeting with ibn Hakeem again and again, and each time he decided he'd gotten all he could have expected. And who knows, maybe the flask would be enough? But he didn't think so. At least this way he could go get the help he really needed.

Jack continued north as the West Side Highway became the Henry Hudson Parkway. Just past the city line he pulled onto a local road, then a dirt road marked "Private Property." It ended at the edge of a meadow. As Jack stepped onto the grass he felt the crackle of the NYTAS shield that protected the place from nosy hikers, dog walkers, and real estate developers. "Okay," he said to the flask as he set it down on the ground, "let's see what I've got here." He unscrewed the top.

Jack had expected to see great swirls of smoke pour out, but instead he felt a twisting inside him, as if he himself were the one changed. His eyes stung, and he blinked, and when he opened them again, an Egyptian-looking businessman in a pinstripe suit and shiny black shoes, with slicked back hair and manicured hands, stood calmly before him. Slightly taller than Jack, the Djinni raised an eyebrow. "Nice place you have here. Do you know that Dr. Canton brings acolytes here for what he likes to pretend is sex magic?"

Jack just stared at him.

"What?" the Djinni said, "Did you expect a twenty foot tall fellow in a loin cloth with a booming laugh?"

Jack said, "Nah, that's a great movie but I'm no little Indian kid." The looked at each other a moment, then Jack said, "So what happens now? You say you're going to turn me inside out and set me on fire, and then I say I don't believe you could ever fit inside that tiny flask—"

"No, no, we'll just skip to the wishes. I might add, though, that we were never actually that stupid. The routine used to be part of the standard contract—let the clients think they've gotten the better of us—but in recent years, I'm happy to say, Suleiman International has modernized."

"Glad to hear it," Jack said. "Do you have a name?"

"Of course I do. Do you wish to know it?"

Jack laughed. "No thanks. I may not have done this before, but I know the rules. You'll know when I use up any of my wishes. Three of them, right?"

The Djinni pressed his palms together before his heart and bowed his head. "Certainly, effendi."

"How about I call you Archie?"

The Djinni smiled. "An honorable name."

Jack looked him up and down. Was it possible this creature could take on Carol Acker? Would he waste a wish if he tried it?

The Djinni dropped his subservient post and said, "Mr. Shade—my contract indeed requires that I attempt to fulfill whatever you wish. However, even we must know our limits, and your—problem—is older even than the Djinn. I would greatly prefer it that you not waste your opportunity, and that I remain—intact."

"So you know," Jack said.

"Of course I know."

"Do you know my plan?" *Plan* was stretching it.

"No, only your dilemma."

"All right, then. First wish. You ready?"

"Always, effendi."

"I want you to take me to the Old Man of the Woods."

The Djinni smiled. "Ah. This will, of course, require flight. You had best step back."

"Wait," Jack said, "why not just, I don't know, magically transport me?"

"We say teleport these days."

"Teleport. Fine."

"But you did not wish that, effendi. Your wish is my command. *As stated.* If you prefer, we can consider your 'take me' wish as granted, and initiate a new—"

"Forget it," Jack said. "Flight it is." He took a few steps back. "Do what you need to do."

The Djinn inclined his head once more, and then grew larger. One moment he was a little taller than Jack, the next he was some thirty feet tall. Jack half expected the Djinni to boom at him like low-level thunder, but the same smooth voice as before said "I apologize for the lack of a pigtail to cling to. I suggest you ride in my pocket, though again, I am sorry I did not think to bring along a Sequoia tree. If you like, you can wish for one—No? Then I suggest you hold onto the flap." He knelt down and held out his palm. Jack climbed on, and a moment later was gently deposited in the jacket's right-hand pocket. The silk lining felt oddly pleasant.

Jack was one of those people who when asked what super-power they would most want, answered "Flying, of course." So when they lifted into the air he stuck his head out to look. But it all went by so fast, trees, houses, whole towns, and the air was so cold, that he quickly sank down again. He did see enough to know they were following the Hudson River north, but that was no surprise, for the one thing anyone knew about the Old Man's house was that he lived near the Canadian border.

Jack wasn't sure how long the journey took, probably no more than fifteen minutes. When he felt the Djinni set down he was so grateful to be out of the cold that he forgot, just for an instant, why he was there. And then it was back, and all he could think about was how much time had passed, and whether he was even making the right choice. The Djinni said, "Effendi, I suggest you emerge before I resume my normal size." Jack lifted himself out of the pocket and jumped onto the giant hand which then set him on the ground.

Jack realized he'd had no idea what he would see when he arrived at the home of l'*Homme Ancien de la Bois*. If he'd expected anything it might have been some grand Versailles mansion surrounded by elegant guards. Instead, he found a one-story wooden house with a plain porch and a dormered attic. It wasn't exactly a log cabin but it wasn't too far above it. He thought for a moment of the suburban house where the Queen of Eyes lived, and then of the cocktail party Carolien had taken him to at Arthur Canton's two story apartment overlooking the Hudson, with its grand piano and marble statues.

He turned to the Djinni. "I may want my second wish when I'm finished here."

The Djinni inclined his head. "Very good, effendi. And how might I spend my time in the interval?"

"I don't know. Become a tree or something."

"As you wish, Master." He pressed his palms together.

"Bullshit," Jack said quickly. "You know damn well that wasn't a wish. I don't give a fuck what you do."

The Djinni said, "It is a pleasure doing business with you, Mr. Shade." And then, with a slight smile, "I don't care what anybody says." Jack laughed but the Djinni had already become a young maple tree.

3.

A S JACK WALKED UP THE LEAF-STREWN STEPS TO THE PLAIN
wooden door he thought how maybe it wasn't too late. He
could use wish two to return to Suleiman International,
then three to gain temporary access to the Undeniable Voice,
and use *that* to persuade ibn Hakeem to grant him an army of
Djinn. But Archie had already told him there were things even
the Djinn couldn't fight, so what difference would numbers
make?

He knocked on the door. A dry precise voice with a slight
French accent said "Come in, Jack." Shade took a breath, turned
the knob, and stepped inside. Once again he realized he'd had no
idea what to expect, either of its interior or its famous occupant.
And once again, it all appeared so ordinary—a comfortable
living room with a fireplace and well-worn leather easy chairs,
simple lamps, an oak table and chairs, a cabinet with glass doors
showing wine and liquor glasses of various sizes, and alongside
it two shelves with wine bottles, most without labels. An iPad
lay face down on a side table It was the only intrusion of the
modern world. Here and there were small glimpses of luxury. A
Persian rug of subtle reds and golds lay between the easy chairs.
There were two paintings on the walls, Rembrandt's old Jewish
couple and Caravaggio's gamblers. Jack assumed they were the
originals, and that the Rijksmuseum In Amsterdam, and the
Kimball Museum in Fort Worth, were proudly displaying fakes.

As for the Old Man himself, he stood around 5' 10", thin, wearing jeans and an old-fashioned red and black flannel shirt. His high brow and aquiline nose and thin lips struck Jack as very Gallic, perhaps even aristo. He was clean-shaven, and wore his silver hair short and parted on the left. His skin had that look of thin, almost transparent leather that could sometimes be seen in the very old and very rich. His left ring finger displayed a wide gold band with some sigil Jack couldn't place. *Is this what he really looks like?* thought Jack. *Alone in his house? Does this house even exist?*

No one knew the actual age of the Old Man of the Woods, but everyone who knew the title also knew what he was—the Grand Master of the Society of the Morning, an ancient order of gangster sorcerers. In their present configuration they began in France in the eighteenth century, and were said to have gained a foothold in the Americas via Benjamin Franklin, though many believed them to have been much older, possibly as old, or even older, than the Travelers themselves, which would make them very old indeed. Jack had no opinion. He only knew that the Travelers Aid Society, and even COLE, were frightened of them. They were said to exert influence, or raw power, at every level, from the demon nano-worlds all the way up to the High Orders of Angelic Light.

Jack knew all this but he knew something else as well. The Old Man of the Woods owed him. When Jack saved the Queen of Eyes he also blocked an attempted coup against the leader of the Society. "Jack," the Old Man said, "it's good to finally meet you." He offered his hand, and Jack knew he had no choice but to shake it. The handshake was firm and dry. It reminded Jack of an ancient parchment he'd once dug up in the Negev Desert.

The Old Man waved Jack to one of the leather chairs. "Would you like a drink?"

"Sure," Jack said.

"Perhaps whiskey. You look like you could use some warming up."

Jack thought of his frigid ride in the Djinni's pocket. Did the Old Man know about that? Probably. "Sounds good," he said.

The Old Man took two tumblers from the cabinet and a dark green bottle from one of the shelves. "Do you want water, or ice? I recommend straight, if you don't mind my saying so."

"Straight is fine," Jack said. The Old Man poured Jack's tumbler a third full and handed it to him. For just an instant Jack hesitated—what was the old story? Never eat or drink anything in the Land of the Dead?—and then took a sip. The taste was dark and smoky, and seemed to permeate his body all at once.

The Old Man smiled. "I assure you, Jack, the people who distill that for me are quite alive. Do you like it?"

"It's amazing."

"Good. Then I will send a case to your hotel. Perhaps Miss Yao will like it as well."

Jack stared at him. "She knows nothing of this. Of any of it."

The Old Man waved a hand. "Of course. I simply thought you might wish to share it with her. And the remarkable Ms. Hounstra."

Jack thought of how Carolien had begged him not to do this. He leaned forward in his chair. "Let's stop the bullshit," he said. "I appreciate your hospitality, it's great, but I came here to ask for some serious help."

The old Man sipped his whiskey. "Of course," he said. "And I will offer any assistance I can. And not just because of the debt I owe you. This *creature* endangers all of us. These things that we do, you and I, they are very different but they depend on the world remaining stable. And more, ignorant. Unaware of itself."

"So you know what's happened."

"Not everything. Tell me about the host, please."

"Host?"

"The human who wears the ring."

"Right. The ring is the key." Jack told him about Carol Acker and her desire for a soul retrieval. "Was it fake?" he asked. "Was she playing me the whole time?"

"No, no. I see I must explain about the host." He sipped his drink, then set it down to lean forward slightly. To Jack it felt like something had shifted in the room, a subtle mass moving towards him. "The creature came to life long ago, before humanity, quite possibly one of the First Incursions. For millenia it fed on whatever wretched creatures stumbled before it. I suspect it always felt there was some lack in its existence, though of course there is no way to know. I doubt that even your Peter Midnight could have traveled back that far, if he were foolish enough to wish to do so." Jack nodded. Peter Midnight was from the eighteenth century but he was said to have mastered moving through time. Though he was buried in that unmarked grave, Jack always half expected to meet him. Is a time traveler ever really dead?

The Old Man went on, "Then the Powers seeded awareness and culture into the world. As always with our benevolent Friends, their good intentions brought unwelcome side effects. For now the creature discovered something new and wonderful. Group suffering. As humanity became conscious, so did the enemy."

Enemy? thought Jack, *isn't that you?* But all he said was, "Let's cut to the important part. What stopped it? What will stop if now?"

"No one knows precisely, who, or what, imprisoned it. It is possible that the Travelers came into being for just this purpose." Jack did his best not to react. No one really knew the origin of the Travelers, though most believed that the Powers (or a Power) imbued a few early humans with knowledge and ability, and the desire for more. He said, "So the Travelers did it?"

"Rather an alliance. The neo-Travelers, certain Powers, and quite possibly the White Ravens. Now Jack's eyebrows went up. The White Ravens very rarely ventured from their own world, usually content to interact with this one through their dark children. The Old Man said, "It would make sense, for the Ravens control the winds."

"And so the whirlwind cage."

"Precisely. First trap it, then imprison it in the wall. Only—it found an escape hatch. Somehow it managed to break off a piece of its own prison, the wall, and send that into the world. The wall contained onyx—another indication that the Ravens were involved—and so the black stone became the link."

"Was it always a ring?"

"No, no, that is a relatively modern configuration, an adaptation, we might say, to cultural adornments." Jack knew that by "modern" he meant the last five thousand years or so. The Old Man said, "In one form or another, the link attached itself to a possible host. This human would know nothing of this, only an intense experience of something missing. Almost all have simply died, and then the link found its way to someone else. Did your Carol Acker say where she got the ring?"

"A thrift shop."

"Yes, that would work. Anonymous, unassuming."

"So let me see if I get this, "Jack said. "The link—the ring, or whatever—goes from one host to another and each one dies with no harm done. Except every now and then some asshole decides to help one of them resolve that awful feeling of something missing Is that it?"

"Yes."

"So now it's up to me, the current asshole, to destroy it."

"That cannot be done. What you can accomplish is to re-imprison it. And soon, before it becomes so strong that we have another Haarlindam. Or worse. But you cannot do this yourself, it is already too strong."

"So you're offering to help me?"

"Yes."

Jack leaned forward. "And then what—at some future time you show up and remind me that I owe you?"

The Old Man shook his head. "No, no, I am already in *your* debt. Besides, having this creature loose in the world doesn't suit me any more than it suits you."

"Okay then. Where do we start?"

"I can offer you two things. A tool, and firepower." He opened a small drawer in the end table next to the couch and took out a lump of black rock. As he handed it to Jack he said, "Like the ring, it comes from the cave wall. This will help you transport Ms. Acker to the cave, and then to separate her from the parasite and force it back into its prison."

"Just like that, huh?"

"No. You will have assistance. Frank? Benny?"

The door at the back of the room opened, and two men stepped into the room. Had they been waiting on the other side, or had the Old Man used their names as a summoning spell? Didn't matter, Jack decided. They were white, and both around six feet tall, but there the resemblance ended. One was thin and handsome, with curly black hair, and dressed in high end jeans and a navy blazer over a pale red polo shirt. The other was stocky and muscular, with wide shoulders, a face that was broad and hard, a nose that had been broken more than once, and brown hair thinning on top. He wore old jeans, heavy shoes, and a leather jacket over a dark T-shirt. The Old Man said, "These are the Pope brothers." He extended a bony finger, first toward the thin one, then the other. "Frank, Benny."

Frank Pope nodded and said, "It's an honor to meet you, Mr. Shade." His brother—if in fact, that was true—said nothing, only nodded. Frank added, "My brother doesn't talk much, but he's quite useful, especially in a fight."

Jack said, "Frank Pope, Benny Pope, are you guys named after—"

"Actually," said Frank, "I'm afraid it's kind of the other way around."

Jack glanced at the Old Man, who allowed himself a momentary smile. "Sure," Jack said, "I guess it figures. So they're, what, backup?"

"Don't underestimate them," the Old Man said.

"I won't. When do we start? How do we find her?"

"I'm afraid that won't be a problem." The Old Man reached for his iPad and opened it to show Jack the screen. The sound was off, but a streaming banner on the bottom read *Breaking News: Brutal Attack On New Hampshire Town—No Claim of Responsibility—Mysterious Message—'Warming Up, Jack.'*

The shaking was back. Jack tried to control it, but it only got worse. *Fuck it*, he thought. He said, "The Queen told me three days."

"And she was right," the Old Man said. He set down the iPad. "This is just a practice session."

"So what, I go there—with your Pope boys—and we take her on? How do we know she'll still be there?"

Softly, the Old Man said, "Because she's proud of her work, Jack. She wants you to see. You are her rescuer, after all."

Jack clenched his fists to keep from hitting him. Or trying to. "All right," he said. "I guess this is our shot. How do we get there?"

The Old Man smiled for a moment, then said "I'll take care of that."

"I should have realized," Jack said. Then, "I have to go outside for a moment."

"If you're going outside to ask Archie for increased strength that'd probably be a good idea."

"Christ," Jack said, "is there anything you don't know?"

"In *my* woods? Please. Do you think your Djinni is the only entity disguised as a tree? Perhaps I myself am a tree and you are talking to a puppet. Perhaps, unlike Archie, I have always been a tree. Perhaps that is the true meaning of the Old Man of the Woods."

Jack stepped out without answering.

Outside, it had gotten dark, and Jack swayed with a moment's vertigo. How much time had passed? He remembered the Sun in the sky as he'd approached the porch. Was it even the same day? It had to be. Why would the Old Man offer to help him, then speed up time so Carol Acker, or the thing inside her, would reach full power before Jack could get there?

In the dark, it was hard to tell the trees apart, so that Jack finally had to say, "Archie. Show yourself, please. And that's not a wish, it's a request."

The Djinni's voice came from the left. "And my pleasure to grant it, effendi."

Jack turned to face him. The Djinni stood motionless, with his hands clasped loosely in front of him. A quarter Moon had risen, which it was well into the evening, and there was just enough light to show Archie's hair stirred slightly by a breeze. Jack said, "The Old Man knows you're here. Knows you were a tree."

"Of course. These are his woods, after all."

"Yeah, kind of what he said. Look, is there a way you can block him hearing what we say?"

"I believe so, yes."

240

"And can we do that without it being an official wish?"

The Djinni smiled. "Perhaps I myself do not wish to be overheard."

Jack smiled back. "Thanks, Archie."

Archie's face became serious. "But please understand, effendi, there is a limit to how many favors I may grant. I remain under contract, after all, to Suleiman International, and the terms do not just govern the clients."

"Don't worry," Jack said. "I'll need my second wish soon enough. I'll even tell you what it is. Power. It's what the Old Man thinks I came out here for, but I'd rather wait until I really need it. So when I say 'Now,' I want you to give me energy to resist whatever Carol acker throws at me. Agreed?"

"Of course. But if all you wanted was to adjust the timing, why close off our conversation?"

"Because that's not the reason. I need to ask you something. Can you tell if the Old Man is lying? Does he really want to stop Carol, or is he playing me? I don't know if you realize it, but he's done this thing with time. Speeded it up." The Djinni nodded. "So I need to know, is he actually going to help?"

The Djinni closed his eyes and bent his head forward. When he looked up again slight stress lines had formed around his mouth and eyes. With what seemed a conscious effort he smoothed them away. He said, "It is—difficult to venture too deeply into such a convoluted mind. There are—traps. If you will, effendi, tell me, please, how much time has passed since you asked me that question?"

"Only a few seconds," Jack said.

"Ah. Thank you. Let me say that as far as I can discern, the Old Man did not lie to you. He does indeed wish to help you. He does wish to see the creature returned to its confinement. Only— and I cannot be certain about this—he may wish to delay that confinement until the last possible moment. Exactly why I could not say."

"And that moment would be?"

"Shortly before it reaches full power. Sometime in the next several hours."

Jack made a noise. "Okay. Thanks. And the Pope brothers?"

"They are sincere. They wish to follow their Master's orders and do not seek to understand his motives."

"All right, then," Jack said. "I guess that's as good as I'm going to get." He started to head for the porch but turned and said, "Oh, and as long as you grant my second wish at the moment I need it, you're free to do what you like for now. Roam the world, see the sights."

The Djinni smiled. "That would be most pleasant."

Once again, Jack stopped himself before going inside. "Oh, and Archie?"

"Yes, effendi?"

"Thank you. And call me Jack. If that doesn't break your contract."

"You are most welcome, Jack."

Inside, the Old Man stared at Jack for a few seconds before he said, "Very well, then. Are you ready?"

"That thing you did with time," Jack said. "Speed it up. Why did you do that?"

When the Old Man didn't answer, Frank said to his boss, "What's he talking about?"

Jack told him "We had a whole day left to stop Carol—that thing—before it reached full power. But your Chief accelerated time while we were chatting, so now it's down to the wire." He stared at the Old Man. "Right?"

The Old Man sighed. "There would have been no point in sending you too soon. The creature simply would have gone dormant, hidden away inside Ms. Acker. You would have thought yourselves victorious while merely teaching it to be cautious."

Frank and Benny looked at each other, then Frank said, "We could have just killed her. The Acker woman."

"You do not understand," the Old Man said. "Once it's out it's out. If you'd killed Ms. Acker it would have jumped into someone else. Perhaps Mr. Shade. They have a bond, after all." Before Jack could say anything, the Old Man went on, "It needs to fully expose itself, to be *almost* ready. Only then can you return it to its prison." He looked at Jack. "That is what Margarita Mariq meant by three days. Not a time frame, but the moment at which to act. That was the reason for Haarlindam. The Dutch Travelers and their allies knew they had to allow it to reveal itself before they could send it back to the cave."

Frank said, "What the fuck is Haarlindam?"

The Old Man shook his head. "Of no importance. You had best be going. I pushed time to bring you to the correct moment, but if you delay . . ."

Jack said, "Where is she?"

"I just showed you. Willowtown, New Hampshire is the name, I believe."

"She hasn't left."

"Oh no, Jack. She wants you there. To witness. You're her rescuer."

"Can you send us there?"

"Of course." He pointed to a plain wooden door to the right of the bar. Jack could not swear it had been there before. "You'll find that opens to where you want to be."

Jack looked at Frank and Benny. "Ready?"

Benny grunted, and Frank said, "Let's go."

4.

THE NOISE AND THE LIGHTS HIT JACK THE HARDEST. Helicopters, vans, bullhorns, armies of police and FBI, and all the media, all of them struggling for control, for something they could understand. And then the smell—blood, organs, slaughter. There were bodies, and pieces of bodies, everywhere, on the streets, the lawns. They were in some well-trimmed neighborhood, neat rows of two-story houses, lawns raked free of leaves, glassed-in porches, all set for an early New Hampshire winter.

And oddly, the first thought that came to Jack was not about the dead, or the cops, or even Carol Acker, but rather *COLE's not here.* He knew what they would do, of course. Mind slam everyone—cops, media, survivors—so it all became a terrorist attack, and the pols could make speeches, and the people could light candles and vow revenge. There were Travelers who believed that COLE had created and maintained a Jihadist group and a couple of right-wing militias just so they could have people to take credit for things no one would understand. So where were they? Maybe they'd already been and gone. Maybe they wouldn't even have to do anything, the Linear world would just believe what they needed to believe about something so terrifying. Or maybe—maybe COLE was keeping away because they were scared.

Frank Pope said, "Jack! Where is she? Can you see her?"

But before Jack could even look around some guys in suits—FBI? NSA?—spotted *them*, and came running, guns out, yelling, "Who the fuck are you?" and "On the ground! Now!" and "Where did you come from?"

"Shit," Frank Pope said, and turned to his brother. "Benny, shut them up, will you?"

Jack saw Benny reach under his jacket, and from some holster Jack was pretty sure hadn't existed a moment ago, take out a gun. It looked a little like Dirty Harry's .44 Magnum, but the cylinders were different colors, and the barrel was shorter and thicker. Jack knew what it was, though he'd never seen one up close before—a Gun of the Morning, the weapon of choice for *La Societé de la Matin*. "No!" Jack said, "They're innocent. COLE will—"

"Fuck COLE," Benny said, in a voice softer and higher than Jack would have expected. He fired once, a silent blast of blue light that filled the air, bright as the Sun if only for an instant. Everyone froze—the cops, the agents, the media people, even the helicopters in the sky. They might have been a frame from some big budget zombie apocalypse movie.

"There," Frank said, "Now we can goddamn think."

And then *she* was there, weaving her way slowly through the bodies on the ground, the frozen mob of outsiders. She wore a black dress with no coat, and high red boots (absurdly, Jack thought how that was smart, she wouldn't have to worry about staining them with blood), and she'd cut her hair shorter, the sides angled longer from back to front, and she, or some salon person, had made her up in a way that was both subdued and sharp as a knife.

As she approached them she raised her hands and clapped, three times. "Oh Jack," she said, "you came. My hero, my rescuer, and now my witness. Sweet loyal Jack. I can't tell you how good it is to see you."

Benny fired again, black light this time. It surrounded Carol, and for a second she swayed, and looked about to fall. But then she shook herself, and the light cracked like a thin shell and fell in actual shards that vanished as soon as they touched the ground. "Seriously?" she said. "Against *me*?" Benny didn't answer. She turned to Jack. "Your new homies?"

"We're here to take you back, "Jack said.

"Oh, but sweetie, you just set me free."

"We all make mistakes," Jack said.

"Not you, Jack. You did it exactly right. And you know what? Because of you, and your steadfast loyalty, I'm almost ready. You should be proud."

Frank Pope said, "Shade! She's mind-fucking you. Do it!"

Jack looked at him, then back at Carol, who tilted her head slightly, still smiling at him. "Do what, Jack?" she said. She spun her head around on her shoulders, Linda Blair style, and when it was facing him again, she said, "Would you like me to devour you?" She opened her mouth, and it seemed to get larger and larger, the teeth like sharp mountains and beyond them black smoke that swirled endlessly into darkness.

Jack didn't realize he was moving towards her until Benny yanked him backwards. "Archie!" Jack called out. "Now!"

Fire surged through him, a holy flame that burned out any confusion or fear. He laughed suddenly as he remembered that the Djinn, for all their ability to take on human form, were made of "smokeless fire," offshoots of the Original Flame. He reached inside his jacket and took out the black stone. "You've used Carol Acker long enough," he said. "It's time to go home."

For a moment, Carol's face twitched and changed shape, becoming larger and more ferocious at first, then almost formless, made of nothing more than teeth and wind. Then it was Carol again, and she screamed at him, "Where did you get that?"

"An old man gave it to me," Jack said. He stepped towards her, holding the stone in front of him. She began to spin, faster and faster, and Jack became scared she would escape them. But then Frank and Benny each fired their guns, blasts of light the color of a bruise, and the air itself screamed, and Jack wanted to drop the stone and cover his ears, but the Fire inside him held on. Carol stopped spinning and fell to the ground, on all fours on the blood-soaked grass.

And then they were falling, all of them, plummeting through worlds, one after another, some familiar, like the leather bar and the minuet, some new and strange, and so quick Jack couldn't make out what they were. In a few the little girl was there, begging Jack not to send her back, *please*, she said, she trusted him, he'd saved her, how could he give her back to the torturers, didn't he know the terrible things they would do to her? The Fire in Jack's arms held on to the black stone, and his ears of flame refused to listen.

They landed heavily, off balance, in a dark cave lit only by Jack's Fire until Frank found the switch for the lights the French archaeologists had set up along the walls. It was smaller than Jack had expected, only about twelve feet long, and three feet wide at its center, narrowing at each end to low tunnels. Carol Acker was on all fours, crumpled and scared. She looked up, her face frightened and wet as she stared at Jack who was still holding the black stone before him. His whole body was shaking but he refused to let go.

"Why are you doing this?" Carol said. "I don't understand." She looked at Frank and Benny, who stood on either side of her and fired dark purple light at her from their Guns of the Morning. The light became spiraling strands, winding tighter and tighter. Carol Acker's pleading voice said, "They're hurting me, Jack! They want to *kill* me. They're evil, can't you see it? You're not like them. You're not like them. You're better, Jack. I *know* you are. Make them stop. Please!" She sounded like a child who'd been viciously abused and just tasted freedom, only to have her rescuer inexplicably return her to her tormentors.

Jack didn't listen. If the memory of all those bodies hadn't been enough, if he might have weakened, the Holy Fire of the Djinn kept him strong. It wasn't just Archie, it was all of them, they were one being, one flame. Armed with that Fire, Jack Shade bore down on the crumpled, bleeding woman.

And then something lifted out of her. It wasn't really a creature, though it appeared to take the form of a squat beast with thick legs and arms and a narrow triangular head. Whatever it may have been originally it was so old and ferocious that it couldn't really hold its shape but kept twisting and stretching as it tried to fight its way free of the swirls of energy from the two guns, and the eternal Fire of the Djinn that pushed it back, back to the wall—until finally there was only one escape. With an agonized cry it retreated into the rock.

Light still filled the cave, and a scream of rage and pain, and in that moment two figures suddenly appeared, causing a puff of wind as they displaced the air around them. One was a bearded woman in a long white robe, and the other was an old man wearing a black shirt, black pants, and black shoes. They looked at each other and smiled, and the light and the fading scream of the beast filled their bodies. They became radiant, younger, more upright, and their eyes—their eyes were filled with love.

The two brothers looked frozen, unable to move or speak as their guns fell to the floor. Jack held the stone in front of him, the way he'd done with Carol Acker, but all the energy had gone from it. He threw it at the Old Man and the Rebbe, only to watch it break up in the air before it could touch them. He tried to use the Fire but that was gone too, and he realized he'd only asked for power against the creature, and that was done. Wish granted.

Der Wisser Rebbe and the Old Man of the Woods held hands and smiled at each other. Jack half-expected them to start necking, like teenagers in the back of a car, but instead the Rebbe smiled and said something in Yiddish—Jack couldn't make it out, but he was pretty sure it was something like "See you next time"—and then she was gone.

The Old Man turned towards Jack now, his face serene.

"You sonofabitch," Jack said. "You used me."

"Of course," the Old Man said. "That time you rescued the Queen of Eyes—what was it she said about you?"

Jack stared at him a moment, confused, then he made himself remember. Softly he said, "She told me 'I knew I could count on you.'"

"Exactly."

"So she was part of this too?" Nausea rose up in him at the thought.

"Not at all," the Old Man said.

"Then why didn't she warn me? She didn't say anything about you."

"You didn't ask. The Queen only answers questions. Indeed, she cannot do anything else. She cannot *see* anything but answers. All you asked about was the creature."

"And the Rebbe—her attempts to stop me—that was all for show?"

The Old Man smiled. "Child psychology. You're stubborn, Jack. Your best incentive is to tell you no."

Suddenly, Benny Pope lunged at his master, arms out as if to strangle him. He never made it. The Old Man gestured and Benny was flung back against the wall, landing not far from Carol Acker's unconscious body. Frank bent down to put his arm around his brother, but he kept his eyes on the Old Man.

"All those people," Jack said. "That whole town."

"Seriously, Jack? You would complain to me about a few hundred dead? When you've lived as long as I have—do you know that fifty-five million people died in World War Two? And poor little Willowtown was nothing compared to Haarlindam."

"You were there," Jack said. "You staged it, just like you staged this. You and your bearded girlfriend."

"Of course. But seriously, Jack, you did a good thing today. If you hadn't stopped it, if the creature had truly reached full strength, I assure you, a great many more would have perished."

"If we'd stopped it right away—if Carol hadn't come to me with my card—no one at all would have died."

"Ah, but then there would have been no benefit."

"Benefit?" Jack said, his voice almost a whisper.

The Old Man sighed. "You have done me a great service, John Shade. And now I will make you a promise. Neither I, not any of my followers, will ever come to you bearing your card. You will never be compelled to serve *La Societé de la Matin*."

"Right," Jack said. "You'll just use another Carol Acker."

"No. My vow extends to any third parties. I know you have feared this, Jack. That fear is over."

"Go to Hell," Jack said.

"Oh, not yet. And not for some time. Thanks to you. Goodbye, Jack." And then he was gone.

Jack just stood there, staring at the space where the Old Man had been, feeling suddenly how cold the cave was. He might have simply done nothing for a long time if Carol Acker hadn't moaned to his left. He turned and she said, "Jack, where am I?" She tried to get up but winced, and leaned against the cave wall, underneath the "painting." Jack glanced at Frank and Benny, saw that Benny was still dazed and Frank was staying with him. He went over to squat beside Carol.

"It's okay," he told her, "I'm going to take you home." Unconsciously her left hand covered the ring on her right, as if to protect it. Jack wondered if it was true that she'd found it in a thrift shop. For all he knew, Carol Acker hadn't existed before the ring. Maybe it grew her, the way those night plants in Bolivia grew pseudo-human beings to defend them. He decided it didn't matter. It wasn't Carol who killed all those people, it was that thing now back safely in the wall. The Whirlwind Enigma.

"Jack," Carol said, "did I—I dreamed—did I hurt Jerry? And Marjorie—and—" She began to shake.

Jack put his arm around her. "No, no," he said, "that wasn't you. It's okay." Behind him he could hear Frank and Benny getting to their feet. He said to Carol, "I'm taking you home, remember?" She nodded against his shoulder. "But first, you have to do something for me, okay?" Another nod. "I need you to give me that black ring."

Carol scrambled back away from him. Again her left hand covered her right, which now was a fist. "No!" she said. "I can't."

Jack said, "It's just a ring, Carol. Just something you found in a thrift shop."

She shook her head. "It's mine. I've always had it."

And it's always had you, Jack thought, but he said, "Tell you what. You give it to me, and I promise to take care of it."

Carol just shook her head.

Frank Pope touched Jack's shoulder. When Jack turned his head, Frank said, "I need to tell you something."

Jack looked from Frank to Carol. "It's okay," he told the shaking woman. "I'll be right back. Nothing's going to happen."

He stood, and moved to where Frank was waiting for him, a few feet from Carol, alongside the cave painting. Benny stood behind his brother. Frank said, "Jack, look at the creature. Do you see the way it's pulsing?"

It took Jack a moment to see it, but Frank was right. A faint energy, like an old light bulb, was pulsing on and off behind the swirling lines.

"Now look at the host," Frank said. "Look at its hand." Jack stared at Carol. Every few seconds a faint flash of red showed between the fingers of her left hand, which still covered the right. Frank said, "The connection's still alive. If we destroy the ring, right now, we might break the connection for good. No more host."

"She won't give it up," Jack said.

"So we cut off its hand. Who the fuck cares?"

"None of this was her fault. Look, I can watch over her, catch her just before she dies, and get the ring before it has a chance to find a new host."

Frank made a noise. "Give me a fucking break, Shade. *You* watch over someone? *Seen your daughter recently?*"

Later, Jack wondered what he might have done if nothing else had happened. Would he have tried to kill Frank Pope? And if he had, what would he have felt? Shame? Satisfaction? But he would never know, for it was right then that Benny Pope shot Carol Acker in the face.

The light was yellow and blue, and so hot Jack had to move away from it. Carol tried to scream but before any sound could come out, the skin on her face peeled back, and then the muscles, and in a second her face was on fire, a napalm-like flame that poured down her body, burning clothes, skin, organs, even the bones. The onyx ring didn't so much slip from her hand as the hand disappeared from inside it. It fell to the floor among Carol's ashes and almost immediately began to fade, seeking escape, seeking a new host. Benny fired again, at the ring now, a blast of dark purple light. The ring lifted off the ground and spun in the air so fast Jack could hardly see it. His breath stopped as he feared for a moment it would escape. But then it fell to the stone floor, dull and gray. Benny stamped on it, and when he lifted his boot there was nothing but dust.

The creature in the wall made no noise but rage vibrated through Jack's body. He doubled over in pain, and when he looked up again the Whirlwind Enigma had become an old worn painting, the swirls of energy mostly gone, the twisted face dull and chipped away.

"There," Frank Pope said. "It's done."

"Archie!" Jack called out. "Get me out of here!"

He discovered himself on all fours in the NYTAS meadow, a few feet from his car. As he stood up he saw the Djinni, a polite distance in front of him. "Thank you," he said. "I just—" He couldn't seem to finish.

Archie inclined his head towards him. "It has been an honor to serve you, Jack."

"So that's it, right? Three wishes, three grantings?"

"I'm afraid so, yes." His eyes darted to the car.

"What?" Jack said, then, "Oh, right." He went over and took out the metal flask and cap. "Not allowed to hang around, huh? Go for a drink?"

"Sadly, no. And now, if I might make a suggestion, you might want to set the flask on the ground and stand back."

"Just one thing," Jack said.

"Quickly, please," the Djinni said. He looked in pain.

"If I'd saved a wish—that was my plan, you know."

Archie nodded. "Yes."

"And I'd asked you to bring back my daughter from the Forest of Souls—could you have done it?"

"No, effendi. We are not permitted there."

"Yeah," Jack said. "That's what I thought." He put the flask on the grass, the top alongside it, and moved away.

The Djinni's form wavered and flickered, like some primitive movie, and then gave way entirely to a stream of fire that poured into the flask. Jack wondered if he was supposed to screw on the cap but the thing lifted off the grass and settled on the opening, where it turned swiftly until it locked into place. Jack walked over and touched the flask gingerly to see if it was hot, but if anything it was a little cold. He picked it up in both hands and brought it to the car, where he set it down upright on the front passenger seat. Then he got in and began the long short journey to Suleiman International.

Epilogue

F JACK LOOKED CAREFULLY FROM THE END OF THE CEMETERY he could just make out the top of the George Washington Bridge. He was glad the place was quiet on this chilly cloudy afternoon, and that the grave he sought was at the edge of the grassy necropolis. He had no desire to glam any curious mourners who'd strayed from a boring funeral. He reached in his car, parked at the end of the lane, and pulled out the small flat drum and deer antler.

It had taken him three days to make the drum, following an instruction video he'd found on a Facebook shaman group. He'd gotten the wooden frame, deerskin, and antler stick from a shop on East 9th Street. They sold readymade drums, of course, but he'd wanted to do it himself, and without any Traveler shortcuts. Briefly, he'd considered going out and hunting a deer, skinning it, drying the hide, the whole deal. But besides the time it would take he remembered how much Genie had loved seeing deer, and how upset she'd gotten when she found out there were men who waited all year for the chance to kill one.

Now he squatted by the double grave with the simple headstone. "Jerome Acker," the left side said, and "Marjorie Acker" on the right, with "Beloved Husband/Wife, Father/ Mother" as the only epitaphs. *So they had kids*, Jack thought. He wondered how old the children were. Full grown, he hoped. Like Carol Acker's children.

There were no religious symbols on the stone, no five-pointed star, no lunar crescent on its side to resemble cow's horns. Maybe not all urban shamans were Pagans, he thought. What the hell did he know?

With as much reverence as he could muster, he laid the drum on the grassy grave, with the antler stick on top of it. "I'm sorry, Jerry," he said. "You didn't deserve what happened to you, you and Marjorie. I was an asshole and you suffered for it. Like Carol." He sighed and stood up. He took a moment to set a long-standing glamour on the drum so that no one would notice it and take it away. And then he walked back to his car.

5

THE FISSURE KING

PART ONE —THE PAST

Jack Shade, Runaway Jack as someone later called him when she heard the story, was sixteen when he did that thing lots of people talked about but never did—he left home and joined the circus. To be exact it was a carny outfit, Green's Midway, and it would be another couple of years before he found himself part of a real (dis)honest-to-God circus, complete with clowns, a trapeze act, and in particular a lion tamer.

Young Jack didn't run away because of any particular trauma, or crime. Mostly he just felt like he didn't belong. Actually, he'd felt that way all his life, though as an infant he had no way to explain that to himself, all he could do was stare at these two big people who hovered around him, making noises and feeding and cleaning him. As a kid, he learned to move through the rules and patterns of his urban neighborhood, school, and the other kids, though still it never felt like it had anything to do with him. It all got a lot worse when some wannabe gang took shape on Jack's street, and Jack's parents panicked and uprooted them all to the suburbs. Some other new kid from the city might have put together a gangsta act and taken over the local scene. But Jack Shade just felt out of place. Or maybe in the *wrong* place, for there was always the feeling he was supposed to be somewhere else.

The funny thing was, he knew how easy it would have been to do some street routine and rule the high school. At times he even wanted to and made some half-hearted attempt. But he couldn't bring himself to follow through with it. He told himself it was too easy, these suburban jerks weren't worth it. But the fact is, he was Johnny Lonesome even back then, though nobody would call him that for a very long time.

His parents loved their new home. They would go on and on about how quiet it was, no car horns all night, no shouting and fighting. To Jack the neighborhood seemed like a funeral home after hours. About the only noise ever heard was a dog barking.

One night, late, he got so bored he himself started barking out his bedroom window. To his surprise, all the neighborhood dogs joined in. Then he switched to howling, and all the dogs followed that, too. Jack figured his parents would storm in at any moment and yell at him to stop making trouble and go to sleep, but they didn't, so he decided to step out the back door in his pajamas and see if he could push things to an even higher level. But when he opened the door he just stopped. There on the lawn, just past the concrete steps, sat a pair of dogs, huge, with thick shoulders and narrow heads, the jaws slightly open, the eyes bright as the full moon. All the neighborhood dogs were still howling away, but these two just stared at Jack. Shaking, and holding his breath, he backed into the kitchen and closed the door as quickly as he could without slamming it.

He made his way upstairs to his bedroom, where he lay on his bed, breathing hard. The howling stopped, but Jack lay there for an hour before he dared to turn off his reading lamp and try to sleep. He knew, it wasn't a question or a guess, that his little game with the neighborhood pets had summoned those two great beasts, and more, that this summoning was something you really really didn't want to do. When morning came—he'd only slept a couple of hours—he got dressed for school and nervously made his way downstairs, where his mother was making French toast, while his father drank coffee from his "World's Best Golfer" mug. Jack managed to act natural as he went to the back door and looked out. The dogs were gone, though he thought he spotted paw prints in the grass.

Years later, Jack would learn that the great dogs were named Lily and Sam, and that they went back a very long way, possibly

Before the Beginning. He also would learn how *lucky* he was that he didn't speak to them, not so much as a "Shoo," or a "Good doggie," for then he never would have made it back into his house. Some people thought the dogs were blind, and needed your voice to find you, but most thought that anything you said, even a "By all the Powers, I command thee, begone!" came across to them as "Hey, you hungry? Here's dinner."

Once, a long time ago, there was a man named Joseph of the Waters who tried to force the world to change. He didn't do it for himself, this was not some World Emperor thing. Instead, he wanted to end pain and suffering, which apparently had gotten even worse than usual in Joseph's time. There is, in fact, a way to do this, every Traveler learns about it, just as they all learn what a bad idea it is to try. But Joseph of the Waters was a proud man. People around him said he was different, and wiser, and stronger than everyone else. Joseph thought so, too.

Instead, Sam and Lily got him. They tore him apart, yet somehow he didn't die. Instead, he became stranded between life and death, a creature of borders, and cracks in the world.

Jack never tried that trick with the dogs again, and for a month he did his homework and watched TV with his parents and went to bed early. He even went to some asshole school dance and made out with Becky Coonan, a girl he knew from geometry class. Jack was good at geometry, so good that it annoyed him other kids didn't just get it. Later, he would learn that that was an "indicator," but back then it just added to his feeling that he didn't belong, or rather that he belonged somewhere else, he just didn't know where.

He went out with Becky a few times after that, but soon he got bored and dropped her. She was angry, but he didn't seem to care. He didn't think he was cold, though Becky and all her friends seemed to think so. It worried him a little that he didn't care. You saw kids like that on TV shows, or in commercials for anti-depressants or help lines, and Jack was scared he'd become an adolescent cliché. But he knew that this need he had, to be somewhere else, to *do* something, was real. And important.

School ended, and he didn't have to see Becky every day, which was good, but now there wasn't even geometry class to interest him. There were guys he could hang out with. No matter what he did to discourage it, they still saw him as big city tough. He just didn't care.

One night in July he felt too hot to sleep, even with the A/C, or maybe he was restless and called it hot. He found himself throwing on some clothes from the floor and stepping quietly downstairs. At the front door, he stood awhile, his hand reaching out to the doorknob, then pulling back. What if those dogs were there? *Shit,* he thought, *I'm losing my fucking mind.* He meant it as a joke, but the fact was, he'd been reading up on crazy, and they said it often started at his age, especially in boys. "Bullshit," he whispered, "there's no giant dogs out there. And even if there were, fuck 'em." As quietly as he could he turned the knob and stepped outside.

His father had built a small covered archway, his mother's idea, to set the house off from all the others, and now he stood there and looked around. No people, no cars, and no giant dogs. Only one or two houses had a light on, but they were pretty far down the street.

He walked left, the longer direction, and the one that didn't come to a dead end, but curved round and met up with an older street, from an earlier development, with brick houses instead of the wooden ones he sometimes thought of as his parents' 'hood. When his family had moved in, and Jack had seen the older houses around the corner, he'd told his parents that those were the ones that would stop the Big Bad Wolf, who would then turn around and make his huffy-puffy way back to their wooden shack. His parents hadn't found the joke very funny, and now neither did Jack.

Just as he approached the point where he could see around the curve, Jack heard noises. There were shuffling sounds, and faint clicks, and whispers, and a hissing noise that took Jack a moment to realize was laughter. *The dogs,* he thought, and almost ran home, but then he realized, no, it had to be people, and he was too curious to turn back. If he'd been in the city he might have stuck to the sides of buildings as he moved forward, but here there was nothing but lawns, and if he did try to slink from house to house probably some insomniac racist housewife would call the cops.

As soon as he saw the women in the road, he just stopped and stared. Three of them, old, he thought, though they were dressed so strangely, and had their backs to him, so it was hard to tell. They were skinny, but had big asses, accentuated by their bending forward as they moved, a sideways shuffle with frequent stops. They all wore long tattered dresses with fringes, like something a bunch of hippies had thrown out as too old and embarrassing. Two of them wore flat sandals with woven thin straps, the third went barefoot. It was hard to tell what color they were, though their arms were bare, or mostly. They could have been light-skinned black, or Hispanic, or maybe even Arabs. One had long flyaway hair, another had clumps of curls that bounced and tossed every which way, while the third, well, her hair was such a mess it seemed to have gathered twigs and leaves and bits of paper, and even insects that couldn't work their way out. Jack half-expected to see a family of mice poke their heads up.

Every few steps the women would cast some stones or pebbles on the ground, stare at them and whisper or laugh, then scoop them up and do it again some seconds later. At another time in his life, Jack would learn that they were called the Old Ladies, and they were old indeed, possibly even older than Sam and Lily. And he would learn how very rare and special it was to see them, that even people who had studied about them, and spent years tracking them down, would miss them entirely, or find them and not even know it.

In fact, Jack discovered it was indeed hard to see them. They kind of flickered in and out, like the hologram princess in *Star Wars*. No—it was his mind that flickered. It kept trying to insist there was no one there, the street was empty, even as he stared right at them. Suddenly, he just couldn't help himself. He had to know if they were really *there*. So he called out, "Hey! What are you doing?"

The three straightened up and turned around to look at him with as much surprise as he was staring at them. In a voice that was weirdly young and even sexy, the one with the rat's nest hair said, "Oh my. A natural. And a strong one too." Unconsciously, Jack touched his hair, which in those days he cut short in what he considered "Denzell-style." But he knew they didn't mean his hair, even if he wasn't sure just what they meant.

Silver-hair lazily twirled a finger towards him. "Go home, boy," she said. "There's nothing here. You're just dreaming. Sleep-walkin' and dreamin'."

Jack felt his eyelids falling, his body about to turn, but he shook himself and held steady.

The curly-haired one said "Oh my," and rat-hair said "I told you he was strong, didn't I?"

Suddenly they chanted at him, a nursery rhyme or something, and then broke out laughing. "O live! O live!" two of them cried, and the third answered, "and I'll anoint you with aleph oil!"

Fucking crazy, Jack thought. *That's all they are, a bunch of crazy old bitches.*

And then they did the strangest thing of all. They quoted, or slightly mis-quoted, a folk song Jack's father used to sing when Jack was seven or eight. Jack had always thought that this was the single most humiliating thing his dad had ever done. It would have been bad enough if his father had gone around mangling Marvin Gaye or something, but a *folk* song? And here were these weird women repeating it. In a tuneless rhythm they recited,

If you want to be a traveler too
Run inside and bar the door
Nail your shoes to the kitchen floor
And thank the stars for the roof that's over you.

Jack did, in fact, run home right then, and he certainly locked the door before he dashed up to his room, where he lay in bed and stared at the ceiling until morning. But he knew he wouldn't stay there. At home. For that night Jonathan Michael Shade had discovered the single most important lesson any of us can learn in this life. *The world is not what we think it is.* And once you know that, what else can you do but *Travel*?

Jack's opportunity to make a move in his life came a few weeks later, when the County fair opened about twenty miles north from where Jack lived. In the years since he'd lived in the area he'd never gone. What did he care about a bunch of hicks showing off their favorite cows just before bludgeoning them into Big Macs? Or the contest for best daisy grower. There was even some contest where they dressed pigs up in little costumes. And the food—people went on for weeks about fried bread, and shit like that. But it also had games and rides and contests, and Jack figured it wasn't local people who did that, and maybe when they moved on he could move with them.

So he joined some guys he knew from school, two of whom had cars, and rode up on opening night. His friends went straight for the rides and the fried bread, but Jack mostly walked around, checking everything out, especially the games. There were some where you threw things, baseballs or rings, and tried to knock something over or circle it, and win a prize. It didn't take Jack long to figure out they were rigged, one way or another, and people only won when the guy who ran the game wanted it.

There were other games that were more like gambling, though officially "games of skill." And there was even a fortune-teller, "Mme. Clara" the sign said, in a small metal booth painted with stars and hands and cards with names like "The Lovers," and "The Tower," and one called "The Juggler," though he wasn't tossing things in the air, he just stood behind a table with some dice and a knife and a few other things. A velvet curtain served as a doorway and Jack considered having his fortune told, but he just kept moving around.

Just before closing time his friends found him watching a game where you put quarters through a slot onto a tray that moved back and forth, and if your quarter was the trigger point a bunch of quarters would fall into a cup where you could get them. He'd been watching it for a while to try and figure out how it was rigged to prevent more than a few bucks being paid out over the evening when his friends came up. "Christ, Shade," one of them said, "you're gonna stand here all night? Come on, we're going."

Jack went back every night after that. He told his parents the guys were going, and his folks didn't question him, since they were glad he'd found some friends, but he took the county bus or hitchhiked. The second night he walked around again, saw little tricks he hadn't noticed the night before. A kind of current ran through the place—or maybe slithered, since he couldn't feel it all the time, but when he did it didn't move in a straight line. He tried a few rides, both to avoid suspicion and to see if that current might run stronger in moving objects, but he couldn't feel it at all. It only showed up in the rigged games and the fortune-telling booth.

The fair lasted six nights, Tuesday to Sunday. On the third night Jack worked out who ran things, a tall white man, skinny, with thinning hair and black-rimmed glasses. He wore black jeans and a white shirt, unbuttoned at the neck, and with the sleeves rolled up. A lot of the time he sat on a wooden stool near the ring toss, but every now and then he would stroll around the booths and machines. He had a trick of seeing everything while looking at nothing. Some of the workers called him "Marty," but most said "Mr. Green."

On the fourth night, with half the crowd at the costumed pig contest, Jack went up to Marty Green, who was sitting on his stool, looking at spread sheets. "Excuse me, Mr. Green?" Jack said.

For a couple of seconds Green seemed not to notice, then he slowly lifted his head. "Yeah?"

"Umm, there's a guy in a brown suit walking around. I think he's a cop."

"Really? You don't say."

Shit, Jack thought. Green knew that, of course he did. Like all sixteen year old boys, the one thing Jack hated most was humiliation. He was about to leave when Green asked "What's your name, kid?"

"Jack. Jack Shade."

"Huh. Sharp-eyed Jack. You're okay, kid. Thanks." He went back to his spread sheet. Jack didn't know what to do, so he started to walk away. Without looking up, Green said "Did you get your fortune told?"

"Nah," said Jack, "I don't believe in that stuff."

"Yeah? Well, you might want to try it. And tell Clara it's on me."

"I can pay for it."

"That's not the point."

"Umm, okay. Thanks."

He didn't visit Clara until the next night, the fifth. It was Saturday, and crowded, and Jack had to wait online behind a group of white girls his age—they managed to shoot glances at him, and he managed not to notice, and a middle-aged grim-faced Latina woman. Jack tried to guess what she'd come to ask, and almost immediately he could hear her tight voice: "I want to know if my husband is cheating on me."

Finally it was his turn through the velvet curtain. The booth was flimsy, aluminum sides and roofs that could be set up easily and taken down, but the walls inside were covered with the same symbols as outside. Mme. Clara herself was a short dark-skinned white woman in a shimmery long blue dress, with several fake silver necklaces and a transparent blue scarf draped over her dyed black hair. Jack figured she was supposed to be a Gypsy, but she looked a lot like Mrs. Parke, his homeroom teacher, who was a light-skinned brunette, so he figured Clara had dyed her hair and used a tanning bed. He kind of liked the idea of a white woman who made herself look darker. On a small wooden table in front of her, covered in a black cloth with yellow stars, sat a small crystal ball on a white cushion, a teapot and an empty cup, some thin sticks, and a pack of cards face down. A sign pinned to the cloth declared "Mme. Clara, Sees All! Tells all!" and then in smaller letters, "For entertainment purposes only."

As Jack sat down on the wooden chair across from her the woman said, in an obviously fake accent, "Good evening. How may Mme. Clara help you?"

Jack said "I want to know what I should do."

She nodded, "Ah. I sense a girl is involved."

"What? *No.* That's not—I just—some weird shit has been happening, and I want to know what to do about it."

She looked a bit uncertain, then said, "Do you wish tea leaves? Or the palm? With such a deep question, perhaps only the cards will do."

Jack guessed that the cards cost the most. "Sure," he said. She was just picking up the deck when he added, "Oh, Mr. Green, Martin, he wanted me to tell you that this was on him."

She hesitated a second before picking up the deck. "Very well," she said. She began to mix the cards.

Jack said "Shouldn't I be doing that?"

"Oh no," she said, her accent thicker than ever. "Only reader must touch cards." Quickly, as if she wanted to get it over with and return to people who were paying, she set down six cards. Some of them just looked like a collection of swords or cups, but the others looked like old-fashioned paintings, with titles he could read, even upside down. One, called the Lovers, showed some guy standing between a couple of women, with Cupid about to shoot an arrow at the poor sucker. The second, called the Wheel of Fortune, showed a bear turning the crank on a big wooden wheel, with monkeys in clothes going up one side and down the other. Jack wondered if it was a circus act. The third was that "Juggler" guy.

Carla just glanced at the cards and then said, "You are a good person, brave, but the people in your life do not understand you. They do not see the true you. You will face many hardships in life, but also joy. You will find a great love, lose it, and find another."

"What?" Jack said. "You're talking shit. You could say that to anybody."

Clara glared at him. "How dare you? I have told fortunes for the great and powerful. I—"

"There's a cop walking around outside. You want me to get him and tell him you're scamming people?"

She crossed her arms and smirked. "Go ahead," she said, her accent slipping. He got his cut already. Besides, how could I scam you when you didn't pay anything?"

"That's right," Jack said. "Mr. Green sent me here. How do you think he'll like it if I tell him you just used your standard shit on me?" He leaned forward. "Do it for real. Come on."

Her hands trembled slightly as she picked up the cards she'd turned over, put them back, shuffled the deck, cut it into three stacks, put them back together, and shuffled some more.

"Quit stalling," Jack said.

"Shut up. You want this 'for real,' you have to let me do it." Finally she turned over four cards. The Juggler was there again, and the Lovers, but now Death, which showed a skeleton wearing a cloak and wielding a scythe, and then the Moon, with a couple of wolves or dogs howling at the Moon. She stared at them, then murmured "You have abilities you might not know about."

"I'm starting to guess."

"You will learn. Someone—someone will train you. And then you will find love. And believe you are happy."

"Love." The idea seemed remote to Jack. He just wanted to know where he belonged.

She said, "But you will lose almost everything. I'm sorry." Jack shrugged. "And wander. In . . . strange places." Now her hand hovered over the deck, uncertain, it seemed, whether to turn over another card. Finally, she did, then jerked her hand away as if the card had caught fire. "Fuck!" she said.

"What?" Jack said. "What's wrong?" He stared at the card. It was called "The Drowned Sailor," and showed the body of a man washed up face down on a beach. "What is it? What does it mean?"

"No, no," she said. "It's not what it fucking means. It just shouldn't be here."

"Why not?"

"Because it doesn't exist! It's not part of the deck."

Jack frowned. "What do you mean?"

She placed a fingertip on the face down pile. "This is the Tarot deck. Seventy-eight cards. Four suits of fourteen cards each, plus twenty-two extras. Got that?" Jack nodded. She held up The Lovers. "See this? Number six. Six out of twenty-two." She reached for The Drowned Sailor, but only pointed at it. "What is this one? What's the goddamn number?"

Jack leaned over to see better, and noticed that Clara pulled back, as if afraid he'd touch her. "XXV," he said, "twenty-five."

"Right! But there's only twenty-two of them! It's not part of the deck."

"So what? You slipped it in with the others."

"No, no, no. It doesn't—Please listen. This card, this *thing*, was not in the deck when we started. And if I put it back, and we look through the whole deck, it won't be there. I swear."

Jack said, "But what does it mean?"

Carla pulled away. "Oh no," she said.

"What? Tell me."

"You didn't say 'that's ridiculous,' or call me a liar. Or a crook." Jack stared at her. "Oh Jesus," she said, "you're one of *them*, aren't you?"

"One of what?"

"A Traveler."

If you want to be a traveler too . . .

Jack said, "What is a traveler?"

"You think *I* can tell you that?"

"Then you're not—"

"I'm just a fucking fortune teller." In her fake accent, she said "Knows all, tells all."

"Then tell me what this means. This card you say you've never seen before."

In her normal voice again she said, "I didn't say that. I've seen it once. And before that I heard about it. From other readers. I didn't believe it, of course. I figured they were screwing with me. And then there it was."

"So what does it *mean*?"

She closed her eyes a moment, concentrated. "There is someone—someone you need to find. Not now. You will know when it happens. Something with water. And loss." She stopped.

"Great. That's it?"

"I'm sorry."

"Take another one."

"What?"

"Another card. Come on."

She sighed. "I don't think that it will—" She stopped as she picked up the next card, looked at it, then dropped it as if it was on fire. "What the fuck?" she said.

"Christ," Jack said. He looked down at an ornately dressed woman riding in a chariot drawn by a pair of swans. A crown adorned her head, and in her outstretched hand she held an enormous eye that seemed to stare at the viewer. "Don't tell me," he said. "Another card that doesn't exist?"

"Yes," she whispered. Then, her voice rough, "I don't know what this is. I've never even heard of it."

Jack said, "Well, gee, let me guess. She's wearing a goddamn crown, and holding an eye, so maybe she's the Queen of Eyes."

Clara said "*What did you do to my cards?*"

Jack threw up his hands. "That's it. Enough of this shit. You can't tell me anything, can you? But even as he got up to leave, he knew it wasn't true. In his mind, he heard her say "You're one of them. A Traveler."

Outside the booth, a small line of people were waiting for their fortunes to be told. "Don't waste your time," he said. "She's nuts." They all stared at him but didn't step from their places.

Jack found Mr. Green standing next to one of the rides. Green smiled at him. "Well? Did Clara give you a reading?"

"Oh yeah. It was terrific." He took a breath. "Look, um, Mr. Green." He almost added "Sir," but stopped himself. "I want to go with you. Tomorrow. When you leave. I want to *travel* with you." He waited to see if Green would react to the word, but if it meant anything, Green didn't show it.

Instead, Green looked at him a moment, then said "How old are you, kid?"

"Eighteen."

Green laughed. "First rule of carny life. We con them, not each other."

Jack said "Sorry," but he didn't look away from Green's sharp eye.

"Here's what you have to do. We leave tomorrow, nine AM. Get back here by then, with a letter signed by each of your parents, saying it's okay for you to ride with us."

"What?"

"You heard me. And no forgeries. I want their real signatures."

"Why can't I just stay here and help you pack up, then take off with you? I could write them or something, tell them what's happened."

"And get us all busted fifty miles down the road? No thanks, kid."

"But how am I supposed to—" Jack stopped. He saw Green's eyes on him and realized there was more going on here than legal issues. It was some kind of test, though he wasn't sure about what. He said, "Sure thing. I'll be back to help you pack up."

Green nodded. "Good." As Jack turned to go, Green said "One more thing. Am I going to have trouble with Clara if she finds out you're coming with us?"

"How should I know? She's the fortune-teller. Ask her." Green laughed.

Jack caught the bus home, which was good, since he didn't want to hitchhike. He needed to think how he would get his parents to sign that letter.

At home he said a quick "Fine" to his dad's "How was the fair?" Ignoring his mother's offer for something to eat he went up to his room and typed the letter he'd been composing on the bus. In high school that year they'd learned how to write a proper business letter, and Jack now made it as correct as he could, with a letterhead on top, a "To whom it may concern:" line, and at the bottom two signature lines, with his parents' names typed under them. He'd decided to keep the content simple. No mention of dropping out of school, but no mention of coming back either. Just permission to go with the carnival, right now. When he'd finished he packed a small duffel bag with some clothes and a few things he figured he could not just pick up along the way.

He went downstairs, set the bag quietly by the door, then went and stood in front of the television. His father said "Hey!" and tried to look around him. His mother said "Jack? Is something wrong?"

Jack said "I want to travel with the carnival for awhile. It leaves tomorrow and you have to sign this letter." He handed it to his father, and his mother leaned over to read it with her husband.

Jack's father said, "Is this some kind of sick joke?" and his mother joined in, "Why would you want to travel with a carnival?"

"It's just for awhile," Jack said, and "There's nothing to do here."

"Then get a damn job," his father said. "A real one. Here in town."

"Is there something wrong?" his mother asked him.

Now came the tricky part. He closed his eyes a moment, trying to remember just what those women in the street had sounded like when they told him to leave, and he immediately ran home. It wasn't just the tone, it was a kind of . . . *undertone*, a level of assurance that left no cracks for resistance. He said "Mom and Dad, this is something I need to do. And *you* need to sign this letter. *Right now.*"

Later, Jack would learn that this voice was called Basic Persuasion, and people trained for years to do it correctly. Right now, all he cared about was that it worked. His parents tried to say something but couldn't seem to do it. They looked confused as they signed the letter, and even more so as Jack took it from them and went over to pick up his duffel bag. "Jack?" his mother said. "You'll be back home for school, won't you?"

"Sure," he said. He didn't like to lie to them, but he was afraid that when the hypnosis, or whatever it was, wore off they would come after him. And besides, it wasn't entirely a lie. Maybe whatever he was looking for, he'd find it by the end of Summer.

Jack traveled with Marty Green and the carnival for six years. For the first couple of months he kept waiting for some kind of revelation about why he was there. He would glance at Mr. Green, or some of the older workers, but all he ever got was orders and instructions. The obvious person to ask was Clara, but she wouldn't even look at him if their paths crossed, so he left her alone.

Over time he just seemed to settle into life in the carnival. He set up and took down the rides, he helped with the booths, he cleaned up. He shared a trailer with a man in his forties, Bernardo, who seemed to like Jack well enough, which was how Jack felt about him.

That first Summer he called his parents often enough that they wouldn't send the cops to drag him back, but not enough to encourage fantasies he was homesick. As the Summer wore on, they began to talk about when he would come home. The last week end of August his Dad told him he had to stop fooling around, and come home right away. *This is it*, he thought. He said he wasn't returning, he would get his GED later and go to college, but right now he was where he "needed to be," and would stay.

His mother cried, his father yelled "Enough is enough!" and similar things, and Jack realized he would have to do that trick again, with his voice. He was scared he wouldn't remember how to do it, or it wouldn't work over the phone, but it actually came easier this time. "Mom, Dad," he said, "It's all right. I need to do this now."

Sounding a little dazed, his father said, "Oh. Well, I guess that's okay then. I mean, it's good, I guess. If it's what, you know, you need."

His mother was crying, but decorously. "Will you promise to take care of yourself?" she said.

"Of course," Jack said.

"We love you," Mom said. Jack said he loved them too, and then it was done.

Calls from the staff were made from a phone in Mr. Green's office. It was a cell phone, rare in those days, and it had some kind of lock on it that meant you had punch in your personal code before and after use. That way, Marty knew who was racking up minutes. The first time Jack had used the group phone to call his folks, they'd offered to buy him a phone and send it to him, but he managed to convince them it was impractical.

Now, as he logged out of the phone, Jack wondered about what he'd told his parents. It was true, he realized. He did need to be there. He just didn't know why. Well, at least it was better than school.

Much better, he decided over the next few days, as Green asked the guys who ran the games to show Jack how they worked. Jack had already figured out most of it, but he'd learned it was not good to be a smartass. The Summer season of state and county fairs was ending, and soon things would slow down enough for Jack to learn the practice as well as the theory. There would still be things like town festivals, and church carnivals, especially in the South, but more time off. Jack discovered he enjoyed the gimmicks and tricks that made it all look natural. Soon Green began to let him run a couple of the games for short periods, to give the regular guys a break.

One night Green called Jack into his trailer. The trailer was divided into Green's bedroom, which Jack had never seen, and his office, which was bare and simple, just a wooden desk, a few chairs and lamps, and a large file cabinet. The only decoration was a framed poster from some old carny freak show. This evening, however, Green had set up a small wooden table in front of his desk. A Green and black checkerboard cloth covered the surface and went down to the floor. On top of the cloth lay a group of small objects—three small metal cups turned upside down, a gold-plated metal star small enough to fit under one of the cups, three old-looking cards—a queen of hearts and the two red jacks—a large white feather, a black knife, and a pair of antique dice. Jack stared at it all, trying not to look nervous. He had no idea what this was, or why Green was showing it to him.

Green said, "Ever see a set-up like this before?"

Jack was about to say "No," when a memory clicked into place. "That card," he said. "When Clara did that reading for me. This stuff's like what he had on the table." He concentrated a moment. "The Juggler. That's what it was called."

Green looked at him a moment. "I wondered if that might come up." He waved at the table. "This is the classic Juggler's set-up. And by the way, that word didn't use to mean someone who threw things in the air. It meant this, moving things around so people can't follow where they are." He turned the cards face down and slid them in and out of each other. "Which one's the queen?" he said.

Jack pointed to the card on the left. When Green turned it over, and it was indeed the queen of hearts, Jack realized he'd been holding his breath—not for fear he'd get it wrong, but that it would turn into that *other* queen, the one with the giant eye.

"Very good," Green said. "Let's try again." He shifted the cards much faster this time, and meanwhile kept looking at Jack and talking to him, about the carnival, the people, asking questions— suddenly he stopped and said, "Where's the queen?"

Jack realized he had no idea. He was about to guess the one on the left when he stopped, and for no reason he could have explained, closed his eyes a moment, then opened them and pointed at the middle card.

Green looked at Jack so intently, Jack found it hard not to look away. Green said, "You didn't know, did you?" Jack didn't answer. "Your hand knew, but your brain had no idea, right?" Jack hesitated, then nodded. "What matters is that you trusted your hand."

"I guess," Jack said.

"Okay," Green said. "Now pay attention. The cards are important because they're on the up and up. A good juggler can make it difficult by doing what I did, distract the mark by talking, sometimes using subtle aggression or flirting, but essentially the game is straight. So people trust it, even if they lose. And sometimes you want them to win, especially if there's a crowd watching." Jack nodded. "But this—" Green pointed to the cups. "This is different." He put the star under one, moved the star around a little, then said "Which one has the star?"

"Huh?" Jack said, "it's the middle."

"Lift it up."

Jack did and discovered it empty. "What the fuck?"

"Lift up the others." Jack did so, and the star was nowhere to be found. He could feel his mouth hanging open, and shut it.

"Come round this side," Green said. When Jack did so, Green lifted the curtain to show him a foot pedal attached by a pair of cables to the underside of the table. Green moved the middle cup aside and stepped on the lever. A small trap door opened to reveal a narrow chute. Green reached under the table and palmed the star.

Jack realized that the pattern of the table cover concealed the very fine cuts that hid the trapdoor. "Cool," he said.

Green laughed. "Lining up the cup and opening the trap is half the skill. Lift up the cup on your right." Jack did so and saw the star. Or rather, another star because Green still held the original one. Green said, "That's the other half, slipping another star from your hand to another cup. The mark's confusion helps."

Jack didn't like being called a mark, but he only said, "Why are you showing me this?"

Green said, "I'm not sure. To tell you the truth, we usually don't run this. Too easy for some smart cop, or one who's been around, to catch on. But something—fact is, a good Juggler is hard to find, and I just have a feeling about you."

Jack tried not to swell up with pride. "Thanks," he said, "so I'm going to do this?"

"We'll see."

Jack nodded. "Okay." He was about to leave when he asked, "What's the other stuff for? The knife and the feather and the dice."

Green frowned. "To tell you the truth, I don't actually know. It's kind of a tradition. Give the crowd something to look at beside the juggler's hands."

Around that time Jack started playing poker with some of the guys. He'd played a little in school and usually won, but he expected that the guys who played a couple times a week would think him too young. But in fact they welcomed him, made sure to get a chair for him, even offered him beer. He soon figured out why. The first night he played he lost his entire week's pay in just under an hour. "Come back next week," one of them called after him, and everyone laughed. To their surprise he did, and that time he lasted most of the evening, and the time after that he broke even. He was starting to get how each one played, the hands they went for and the ones they folded. And he became aware of his own tendencies, his tells and his blind-spots. Slowly he began to win, steadily enough that he had to back off at times to make sure they would let him stay in the game.

And he began to see someone as well. Green didn't go much for the old-fashioned freak acts—"People see weirder stuff on television" he liked to say—but he did feature one sideshow marvel, "Edwina, the Bearded Lady." Her real name was Abby Borger, and she usually sat in a small booth between the roller coaster ride and the games, as a way to lure people towards the money-makers.

When Jack first met her he assumed the beard was fake. She grinned and let him pull on it, then explained it was some kind of hormone thing. When it started, she and her mom had freaked out. She'd tried pills, electrolysis, shaving and plucking several times a day. Finally she became sick of fighting it, and when she saw the signs for a carnival coming to town she let her beard grow in, dressed up in her hottest, shortest dress, and went to find the boss to tell him he needed her. "I'm a tradition," she said. "What kind of carnival is it if you don't have a bearded lady?" Green hired her on the spot.

The thing was, apart from the beard, Abby was sweet, sexy, with long blond hair, a cute smile, and a great body. And she was smart. That was the thing that really drew Jack to her, that he liked to hear her talk. Science, politics, art. . . She seemed to respect his intelligence even if he didn't know that much. She was also older than him, by seven or eight years, so he figured she just saw him as a mascot. Then one evening, when they'd been drinking wine and talking about some book, she suddenly said, "Have you ever been kissed by a girl with a beard?"

"Uh, no," he said, feeling like a jerk.

"But you're curious, aren't you? What it feels like?" He stammered something and she laughed, then pulled him to her. The beard was softer than he'd expected—if he didn't shave for a couple of days his face felt like it could sharpen knives—and when she opened his mouth for her tongue, and pressed her breasts against him, he understood exactly why he'd dumped poor Becky Rubin.

Later, when they were lying in Abby's bed (she had her own trailer) she looked at him and giggled. "Hey," she said, "I just thought of something."

"Yeah? What?"

She whispered into his ear, "Once you've tried beard, nothing else is as weird." For a moment Jack didn't know how to react, and then the two of them started laughing, and soon they were starting everything else all over again.

Jack did well as a Juggler. They set him up in a booth with a backup of magical symbols, shooting stars, a silly-looking red devil kneeling down before a magician, and a sign that read "Do you dare to try your luck against Xoltan the Younger?"

"Xoltan?" Jack said, when Mr. Green showed him the sign. "Really?" And then, when he saw his costume, a dashiki and a turban, he almost said "No fucking way, man." But then he noticed Abby trying not to laugh, and he thought of the fake tiara she would wear, and the low-cut dress and push-up bra to show up the contrast with the beard, and how she had to let little kids pull on it sometimes, and he just grinned and said "Xoltan the Younger it is."

Jack had been doing his Juggler act for most of a year, and had gotten so good Green had to remind him to lose now and then, when one night Green summoned everyone to a meeting outside Green's trailer. It was late April, and they'd just finished a church fair in Georgia. Some of the guys looked nervous, Jack thought. It was too early to gear up for the county fair circuit, so what was this about? He said to Abby "What's going on?"

"I don't know," she said, "but I think people are scared we're closing down."

"Jesus," Jack said, "what will you do?" Being part of the carnival was important to Jack, though he couldn't say why, but for Abby it was her life.

"Oh, I don't know," she said, not looking at him. "Probably join some feminist empowerment freak show." She turned to grin at him, and a moment later they were both laughing.

And then Mister Green came out of his trailer, and instead of death he brought new life. Green's Midway was being taken up by an old-fashioned, balls-to-the-wall circus. Billington's Big Top, one of the last remaining touring circuses that actually played in a tent, had decided they needed a carnival sideshow.

The circus could use the extra revenue from the rides and games, while the carnival would benefit from the larger crowds. "There might be some adjustment," Mr. Green said, and the nervous looks remained. "But we'll work it out," he promised. People walked away, bolstered by Green's confidence. When just about everyone had gone, Jack said to Abby "I'll see you back at your trailer, okay?"

She kissed him lightly. "Sure."

Jack went up to Green. "What about Xoltan?" he said. "Do you think the Billington Circus will like having a juggler fleecing their customers?"

"Fleecing? When did you get to be such an old time carny man?"

"I'm serious," Jack said. "I like what I do, I'd like to keep doing it."

"Are you sure?"

"Of course I'm sure. I just said so, didn't I?"

Green sighed. "So you did. Don't worry, Jack. You may have to let a few more lambs keep their fleece, but you're good."

"Thanks," Jack said. He stood there for a moment, with Green waiting for him to leave, then he said, "What about Abby? Will she be okay?"

Green laughed. "don't worry about Edwina. She's a rock."

Jack nodded. "Okay, then. Thanks." He turned to walk off. He was a few steps away when Green called, "Hey, Jack."

Jack turned. "What?"

"You know you don't belong here, right?"

"What the fuck?" Jack said. "You just told me I was okay, now you're kicking me out?"

"I didn't say that. As far as I'm concerned you can stay and fleece the rubes until we're both old and gray."

"Then what are you talking about?" Jack thought how this was the first place he ever felt he belonged. Stupidly, his eyes got moist, and he hoped the lights from the trailer were dim enough that Green didn't see them. "This is my home," he said.

"Well, that's okay, then," Green said. "See you tomorrow, Jack," and he stepped inside his trailer. Jack stood for a moment, letting his heart settle, then he walked—casually, he hoped—to where Abby was waiting for him.

The first time Jack saw the Billington Big Top he thought how "Small Top" would have been more accurate. He remembered his parents taking him to Barnum & Bailey's at Madison Square Garden when he was nine, and this outfit could have fit in a corner of it. They had all the right acts, just on a small scale. A handful of clowns (none of them very funny), a husband and wife trapeze act that played it pretty safe, an actual juggler, the kind that tossed things in the air—Jack thought maybe they should meet, but when the Great Santini, whose real name was Sam Epcott, showed no interest, Jack let it go—a sequined woman who did simple dance steps on the back of a (slow) running horse, a top-hatted barker who somehow always seemed like he should be running a funeral home—and a lion tamer. There were no elephants, which Abby said was good, since circuses treated elephants like shit, but there was a hell of a lion tamer.

Anastasia, she called herself, and for all Jack knew that was her real name, he never heard anyone call her anything else. A white woman nearly six feet tall, she performed in a one-piece purple outfit that clung to her from her toes to her neck, with no boots or shoes. Long waves of thick black hair would flow down her back then snap in the air as she turned to gesture to one of her cats. There were only three of them, two leopards and a lion. Like everything else in Billington's the act was small, but it never felt that way. Anastasia's proud stance, her struts and pirouettes, and above all her intimacy with her animals captivated the audience. The leopards looked like twins (they were, in fact, mother and daughter), and people loved it when they played together on the tent floor.

But it was the lion who was clearly the star. A tawny gold body and face, with a thick black mane, Nero, as Anastasia called him, seemed the hugest creature Jack had ever seen. He found himself wishing the lion could have been there that night the dogs showed up at the back door. Years later he would realize that Sam and Lily could have torn Nero to pieces, but in the circus Nero seemed invincible.

Though Anastasia had no private name, the way "Edwina" was really Abby, Jack was sure, though he couldn't say why, that

"Nero" was not the lion's real name. In one of the rare moments when Jack dared speak to Anastasia one on one, he asked what Nero's "original" name had been. It was offstage and Jack had followed Anastasia to a hillside, where she sat on the grass and looked at the sky. She had changed to street clothes, jeans, sneakers, and a hoodie. Jack thought she looked just as amazing in a blue sweatshirt as in her purple suit. "Can I join you?" he said.

She glanced up at him. "Sure," she said. Jack thought she looked amused, and wished he hadn't come.

He sat for a moment, then said "What are you looking at?"

"Oh, just the usual."

Jack had no idea what that might be so he said nothing. When the silence became uncomfortable he said "Can I ask you something?"

She turned to smile at him. "Sure," she said.

"What's Nero's real name?"

"What makes you think his name isn't Nero?"

"I don't know, I guess because I'm Jack, not Xoltan, and Edwina is really Abby."

"I see. Well in that case, Nero's name is—" Jack half expected something in Swahili, or a growl. Instead, she made a sound that Jack could not have imitated, or even remembered. All he knew was that it hurt his ears and the back of his head.

"Wow," he said. She didn't answer. "Don't worry, I won't tell anyone." He laughed but she had already turned back to the sky. "I guess I should go," he said, and stood up. "Um, thanks. For answering my question." When she said nothing he turned and walked stiffly back to Abby's trailer.

When he got there he found her sitting by her small metal table, leaning back with her arms folded. "Well," she said, "how was Mees Ah-na this evening?"

"What?" Jack said. "If you think there's something going on between me and that lion tamer you don't know what you're talking about."

"If there isn't it's only because *she's* not interested. You're not man enough for her."

"That's bullshit," Jack said.

"Is it? I don't know who you're lying to, Jack, me or yourself. Or which is worse. Either way, I think you should sleep in your own trailer tonight."

"C'mon, Abby, you're making stuff up that isn't there." He would have said more, but she began to cry. "I'm sorry," he said softly. He thought of explaining that this thing he had about Anastasia was nothing at all like what he had with her, but he was pretty sure she didn't want to hear it. And even if she did, and asked him to explain it, he knew he couldn't have answered. So he left.

Jack had not shared the trailer with Bernardo since he'd taken up with Abby. Bennie, as everyone called him, drank and snored, and rarely washed, and Jack had to brace himself to return there. When he stepped inside he was glad to see Bennie already asleep in the narrow bed built into one side of the trailer. But just as Jack sat down on his own bed and started to take off his shoes, Bennie opened his eyes and said, "Huh. Look who's here. What happen, Beard Girl kick you out?"

Jack was about to make up some bullshit about needing space but instead said, "Yeah. I guess so."

Bennie laughed softly and said, "You gotta keep away from lion chicks, kid. They'll fuck you up every time."

Before Jack could say "It's not like that" Bennie turned on his side and went back to sleep.

For a while Jack did his best to ignore Anastasia, hoping maybe Abby would take him back if he could show her nothing was going on. And then for a while he was distracted by an outsider. A college girl named Layla Nazeer came to the circus with a group of friends. But when the others went inside to the main show, Ms. Nazeer stayed to watch Xoltan the Younger. The next night she came alone and invited him for coffee after he finished. The night after that she drove him back to her dorm room, where he stayed until it was time to go back to work.

Soon it was Summer, and Layla was free to follow the circus, finding a motel near wherever the circus stopped for a few days. Some of the carny guys, especially the older ones, didn't like it.

They would say how dangerous it was to fuck outsiders. Most, however, just looked once at him, smiled, shook their heads, and walked away. Jack didn't care. As far as he was concerned, he and Layla were just having fun.

When Labor Day came she began to seem distracted, uncomfortable. It annoyed Jack at first, then he got it. "Classes starting soon?" he asked.

"In a couple of weeks."

He made a noise. "Then you better take off. Get yourself ready."

"Jack—"

"Hey, it's cool. We both knew this wasn't your life, right?" She began to cry. "It's okay," he said, "really it is." He kissed her, and they made love, and the next morning she drove him back to the circus, and then she was gone. He would not see her again for several years, and when he did he was a different person.

With Layla gone, Jack discovered he hadn't lost his fascination with Anastasia, he'd just been distracting himself. He would close down his act to watch her perform, and if she happened to walk past him he would stare after her until he heard people laughing, and then he looked away.

Then one night, when the circus was set up outside a town in southern Ohio, Jack couldn't seem to fall asleep. It was five in the morning and he was lying on his bunk, staring at the dull ceiling, and feeling like he used to feel in his parents' house, like he needed to go somewhere, do something. He thought of Mr. Green saying "You don't belong here," and it made him angry, but also scared. He liked it here. He liked his role as Xoltan the Younger. Maybe if he could get back with Abby—

"Fuck," he whispered to himself, and swung out of bed to put on his shirt and jeans and sneakers and step outside.

He took a deep breath. He could feel, rather than hear, a low hum in the air. Or was it the ground? The sky was just getting light, and as far as Jack could tell, everyone was asleep. He glanced over at Abby's trailer and surprised himself with the fear that she might not be alone. The hum grew stronger and he began to walk, certain somehow that it would guide him. The air was chillier and damper than he expected, and he almost went back for a jacket, but decided not to chance it. Chance *what* he couldn't exactly say. He left the camp to walk over a low hill, and then across a short meadow to the edge of a lake.

Later he thought how he should have spotted the lion first. How could you miss a lion as big as a fucking house, sitting right there by the water? Or he should have noticed Anastasia. After all, he'd pretty much been stalking her for the past month. But instead, it was the guy. White, dressed in a tight-fitting black jacket that flared at the waist, with actual ruffles at the cuffs, black pants, and a white shirt with a lace collar, and shoes with gold buckles, and a tall black hat, he looked like he'd stepped out of some colonial re-enactment. Jack hoped the guy wasn't there to recruit a slave for his show. And then it was like something clicked, and he saw Anastasia, dressed in her usual offstage outfit of jeans and a hoodie, and next to her, sitting peaceful and quiet, Nero—or whatever his "true" name was.

Jack realized suddenly that it was hard to *see* them. It was just like those women around the corner from his parents' house, they kind of flickered, and you had to concentrate, and fight the urge to turn around and forget you ever saw them. He didn't move.

Anastasia and the man were squatting on the ground and playing some kind of game. Dice, he realized. They took turns tossing a handful of dice, five, Jack thought, but he wasn't sure. He thought of the antique dice on his Juggler's table. These looked even older. With each throw, they would stare at them, and maybe nod or make a noise, then the other would pick up the dice and throw them again.

It made Jack dizzy to watch. It was like—like the sky re-arranged itself after each toss of the dice. *I'm going nuts*, Jack thought, and *I better get out of here.* But he didn't move. Underneath all those thoughts was a small voice saying, *You have to stay. This is important.*

It was Nero who saw him first. The lion flicked its tail, looked at him, then growled. *Fuck*, Jack thought, but still he didn't leave. And then it was the man, who looked up at Jack, then said to Anastasia, "It appears we have a visitor." He rolled his r's in a way Jack would later recognize as Dutch.

"Good heavens," Anastasia said, and laughed. "Johnnie Shade, what are you doing here?"

"Um, it's Jack" Jack said.

She ignored him. "Go back to bed, Johnnie Dream. In the morning you'll forget all about this."

Jack swayed, and had to fight to keep his eyes open. But he stayed.

Anastasia and the man looked at each other. "Oh my," Anastasia said. "The Old Ladies told me a natural might be coming my way. But I had no idea it would be such a boy."

"I'm not a boy," Jack said.

She inclined her head. "My apologies, Johnny Natural."

Jack was about to say that that was not his name, but instead asked, "Who's your friend?"

"Who indeed?" she said, then turned to the man and smiled.

"My name," he said, "is Peter Midnight."

Later, much later, Jack would know that the man he met that night was, in fact, long dead, buried in that unmarked grave in Inwood Hill Park. The grave was hidden, but everyone who mattered knew the area, if not the exact location. The area was, in fact, marked by a plaque, proudly set up by the New York Historical Society to immortalize the most famous and most misunderstood real estate deal in history, the sale of Mannahatta Island for a bag of beads. Those historians who like to reveal the "truth" behind commonly accepted stories sometimes point out that the Indians who made the trade did not actually live on the island, but were just traveling through, so that they did not give anything up in exchange for that handful of trinkets.

But as Jack would later learn, the woman who sold Manhattan—there was only one, not a group—was indeed a Traveler, and she knew exactly what she was doing. For she was that rarest of Travelers, a Bead Woman, and with that pouch of colored glass, seed pods, and bits of stone, she could see the Hidden Lands, and open roads beyond even the range of Midnight himself. To this day, no one knows where—or when—Midnight acquired those beads. Some believe he'd gone All The Way Back, but no one actually knows. And how would they find out?

And Jack Shade—he didn't know anything at all that night, except that a lion tamer sat huddled with a man in a weird outfit and a huge fucking lion who should have been asleep in his cage.

Or was that really . . . the more Jack stared at Nero the less certain he became that the huge beast was actually there. It didn't move, just crouched like the goddamn sphinx, front legs out, body facing its mistress, but with the head slightly turned towards Jack. It too seemed to flicker, like those women, what did Anastasia call them, "the old ladies?" At times the lion's mane seemed to flow into the sky, blotting out the stars, and then the golden coat would come alive, like a burst of sun. Somehow it all made him want to do just what Anastasia had said, turn around and run back to his bunk to close his eyes, and in the morning wake up and say, out loud, "Wow. What a wild dream." But instead he stood there, and kept his eyes on the lion.

Softly, Anastasia said "Come here, Johnnie. I want to show you something."

The man said, "Stasia, what are you doing?"

"It's all right, Peter," she said. "I suspect it's why we're here tonight."

Jack took his eyes from Nero to look at the man and woman. What should he do, obey, leave? Somehow everything depended on what happened next, but if anyone had asked him what "everything" was, he'd have had no idea.

In his harsh accent, Peter Midnight said, "Come, boy. This boon she is granting you is like no other."

Jack wanted to say not to call him "boy," but instead he moved forward. When he'd come to within a couple of feet of the lion, Anastasia said to him, "Now look at ____" She said that name that hurt Jack's ears. He turned his head just as the lion opened its mouth.

At first all Jack could see was that wide pink tongue, and all around it a jagged mountain range of teeth. But then he looked deeper, and the mouth became a cave, the walls darker and darker, until darkness swallowed Jack, everything. It went on and on, then, slowly, Jack began to see tiny flickers of light, followed by swirls that came and vanished like brief glistening clouds. And still deeper he looked, so far that he could never find his way back, but it didn't matter, for he was seeing—seeing—an overwhelming flash of light hit him, and at last he staggered backwards, and would have fallen if Peter Midnight hadn't caught his shoulders and held him up.

"It is good," Midnight said. "You *saw*, yes?"

Jack said "That—was that—really—?"

"Yes. I told you, a boon like no other."

Jack looked at Anastasia, who was writing something on a small notepad with some sort of antique gold fountain pen. She tore off the paper and handed it to Jack. An address, he saw. He said "This is New York? Chinatown?"

She smiled. "Yes. On the ground floor you will find a restaurant, the Lucky Star. Inside you will find the owner. Her name is Mrs. Shen. Tell her you have come to see Anatolie, and that you would like to bring a gift. Mrs. Shen will prepare two or three takeout dishes. When you have paid for them you will step outside and open the door to the left. It will not be locked. Not for you. There will be stairs in front of you. Five flights, I'm afraid, but you are young and strong. At the third floor you may feel dizzy, or even a desire to drop the food and run away, but keep going, it will pass. Do you understand?"

"Yes," Jack said.

"Good. At the top of the stairs open the door. Inside you will find the largest woman you have ever seen. Go to her, do not be afraid—"

"Why would I—"

"—and tell her that Anastasia the lion tamer sends her greetings. She will nod, and then you will say 'If you will grant it to me, I would like to serve you and become your student.'"

"What?"

"Repeat that, please." A sharpness had come into her voice.

Jack said "If you will grant it to me, I would like to serve you and become your student."

She nodded. "Good. Now go."

"What? Now?"

"Yes. Your time here has finished."

"But how will I get to—"

"Do you have money in your trailer? For a bus?"

"Sure. But we're out here—"

"Go get your money, and anything essential, then go to the road and put out your thumb. A truck will stop for you and take you to the bus station."

"What? You can't—" He stopped, for he realized that he did not doubt her, not for a second. He looked at the lion, resting on the grass, and the man and woman, standing together, watching him. "Okay," he said, and turned to walk back to his trailer.

Before he'd gone more than a few steps the man called after him. "*Mijnheer* Shade." Later, Jack would learn that the odd word was Dutch for "Mister." Now he just turned and stared. The man—Peter Midnight—said "I too will grant you a boon."

Jack waited. When there was nothing else, he said, "Yeah? What's that?"

"Not now. When you need it, I will come."

Jesus, Jack thought. He said, "Sure. Thanks."

Now he looked at Anastasia one last time. He said "My name's not Johnnie."

She smiled. "Yes, Jack, I know."

PART TWO—THE FUTURE

I.

JACK STOOD BY THE WINDOW OF HIS HOTEL ROOM A LONG time, it seemed, before he made the phone call. The northwest view allowed him a glimpse of both the Empire State Building and the gargoyles on the Chrysler Building. He thought the gargoyles might be singing to each other but it was hard to tell over the traffic noise. If so, they were doing it for their own amusement, for the Empire antenna did not seem to be broadcasting anything that Jack could sense.

He went over and picked up the hotel room phone. He could never say just why he used that for certain calls rather than his cell, but it seemed right. He found himself holding his breath until a quiet voice said "Hello, Jack."

For a moment he thought the Queen had answered in her aspect, that she'd known he would call. But then he realized it was only caller ID. He said, "Hello, Margaret. How are you?"

"Alright."

She was bracing herself, he could tell. "Listen," he said, "I need to talk to—Margarita Mariq." He'd almost said "your other self," but realized how rude that would have been.

"It's not that simple."

"I know."

"Do you?"

"Look, Margaret, I don't want to cause any trouble. I'm only asking because I need to find the Nude Owl, and it's very urgent."

"The what?"

Shit, Jack thought. This was worse than he'd expected. He'd assumed Margaret Strand might not like him asking her to summon her aspect, but it hadn't occurred to him she wouldn't just know everything the Queen of Eyes knew. He should have realized, of course. How could she get through the day with all that awareness? He said, "The Know-It-All. The Knowledge Elemental."

"Oh."

"Please, I've tried everything and I can't locate her. It's really important, Margaret."

Pause. "I'll see what I can do."

Jack put down the phone and stared at it. *I'll see what I can do.* What did that mean? What if she couldn't? He realized he'd tended to think of Margaret as a kind of disguise, like Clark Kent. But instead they were two separate beings, the Margaret Strand who'd grown up knowing she would one day become the Queen of Eyes, and the actual Queen, Margarita Mariq Nliana Hand, who emerged for the first time the moment Margaret's mother died.

He thought of a Traveler he'd met once in New Zealand, Julietta Calvino, who was not actually one person but a community in a single body. "Multiple Personality Disorder" the psychiatrists called it, and maybe for some people that medical gobbledygook meant something. But Judith was a Traveler, and so were most of the others who from time to time inhabited the body (he'd asked if Judith was the "original" and was told that that was rude). Those who shared the Traveler's knowledge and skills used them according to their own temperament. It was a good arrangement, Jack thought, much better than Dupeing yourself. A Dupe was just another you, an extra body, but suppose you could become something else entirely, and all in the same shell?

Jack smiled as he recalled the time he went to a bar in Auckland, expecting to meet Julietta, and instead "Marcus" was there. Same face but somehow sharper, more defined, with the long hair pulled back into a biker ponytail. Same body underneath the denim shirt, leather jacket, and loose jeans. And yet, there was no sense this person was, or ever had been, female. It wasn't a trans thing. As a Traveler, Jack had met plenty of transwomen and men. They actually formed a kind of elite, with a few claiming you couldn't *really* be a Traveler if you hadn't changed sex at least once. Marcus was not a male version of Julietta, he was a completely different person inhabiting the same body.

Jack had assumed any callback would come from the hotel phone, and it took a moment to realize his cell was buzzing. He grabbed it and saw the text message, officially from "Margaret," but obviously from *her*. It read: *Feb 9, 8 PM, Poughkeepsie, Hudson Walking Bridge. Look for the murder in the middle. Nliana Hand.*

Murder? Jack thought. Was someone planning to kill the Nude Owl? Was that even possible? And was the Queen sending him to stop it? He wanted to ask more but figured she wouldn't reply, so he just keyed "thank you" and sent it off.

Feb. 9. Two days. It would take two hours to drive up to Poughkeepsie, but he'd want to get there early. That gave him just over a day and a half to figure out how someone might kill an Elemental, and how to stop it. He called Carolien. He'd already asked her how to find the Nude Owl and she'd come up with nothing. Now he hoped she could tell him how to save the Owl's life.

Jack's search for the Know-It-All had begun three days earlier, but his need to find her went back a couple of weeks. It began with dreams. Dreams of trees, and destruction. For several nights Jack had dreamed of terrible things happening to forests, groves, individual trees. One night he dreamed of a fire that engulfed an entire mountain. Another time a tornado swept through a small town shopping street and left all the stores and cars and people, but uprooted all the trees. Another night he'd watched the people in a small African village wail and tear their clothes because the giant Ancestor Tree in the town square had been struck by lightning.

Carolien did her best on this one, too. While Jack ran errands—bringing her stacks of manuscripts, running searches on Jinn-net, serving her cups of coffee and bags of trail mix, Carolien ran through all her sources, from Mesopotamian dream manuals to Travelers' accounts of tornadoes and fires, and just getting lost in dark woods. She exhausted every source she could. "We are doing this wrong," she said finally. These examples and such—what you dream, *schatje*, is about you. You know what you need."

They were deep in the NYTAS archives, and now Jack slumped down in his wooden chair at the end of a white marble-topped table. "Yeah," he said. "Get a dream hunter."

They had to walk up several floors before Jack could get a signal for his phone, so he decided to wait until he was out in the street. He didn't know for a fact that Arthur Canton had filled the walls with surveillance elementals, but why take a chance? On the corner of Lexington and 45th he dialed the number.

A pleasant female Caribbean voice said, "Horne Agency."

"Hi, Aruna," he said, "this is Jack Shade. May I speak with Elaynora, please?"

A pause, then "Yes, sir. I'll check."

Jack hoped that El's father wouldn't get on the phone. Jack hadn't spoken to father *or* daughter since Daddy had tried to use Jack's own dream duplicate to kill him. He let out a breath when El came on the phone. "Hello, Jack," she said.

He decided it was best to jump right in. "I need your services," he said.

There was a pause, then "My services? As a dream hunter?"

"Yes. I've been having—strange dreams. I need to know why. We've—I've been searching for days, but nothing's come up."

"And by 'we've' you mean you and Carolien?"

Fuck, Jack thought. "Yeah, sorry. I'm being an asshole. It's just—well, she's the best researcher."

"Oh, I'm sure she is." Then he could hear her smile on the phone. "I'm sorry, Jack. I was just giving you a hard time. Of course I'll hunt for you."

"Thanks. Seriously. One thing more. Can we do it outside the office? Maybe at your place?" *Oh Jesus*, he thought right away. Bad move. Dream hunt where they used to screw?

"I'm sorry," she said. "That's not possible. I don't hunt at home. We have to do it here."

For a second, Jack considered asking her to make sure her father wouldn't be there, but then a better idea struck him. He said, "That's fine. When can I come over?"

"It sounds pretty urgent. If you can make it right now, I'll clear the space."

"Great," Jack said. "Thanks. I'll be there as soon as I can."

"Good. See you soon," she said, and hung up. Her voice had taken on a professional tone that Jack had never heard before. For a second it worried him, then he decided he liked it.

Jack stood in the middle of the room. "Okay," he said out loud. "Next stop, Papa Click and Whistle." That was Jack's name for Alexander Horne, El's father, whose real name Jack couldn't pronounce. It was the name Horne's worshippers called him, before they all died out and left him a dispossessed Sun god.

Jack closed his eyes and said, "Ray, I need you." When he opened his eyes, the fox was there, head tilted up to look at Jack, his thick tail curled in a golden question mark. Jack said, "You remember Alexander Horne, right?" Ray didn't move. Suddenly embarrassed, Jack thought how of course Ray remembered Horne. Ray was a Fox of the Morning, and Horne a Sun god. There'd been a moment when Ray had had to choose sides, and Jack had been very grateful that Ray had stayed loyal to him.

Now he said "I need you to get him out of his office. Just long enough for me and El to work together. Can you do that?"

Jack didn't know if a fox could smile, but Ray gave that impression.

Then suddenly they were down in the street, in front of the hotel. "What the fuck?" Jack said. A couple of tourists about to enter scowled at him, and he realized it was his language, not his sudden appearance. As for Ray, of course, the visitors didn't see him at all.

A good thing, because suddenly Ray *grew*. He became as large as a wolf, then a lion—he looked a bit like Nero, Jack thought—and then a horse. As Jack stared, amazed, Ray gestured with his head for Jack to climb on. Jack nervously mounted the giant fox. Though he'd touched Ray many times, he still worried he'd fall right through to the sidewalk. Instead, he nearly fell *off* when Ray took off at a run west on 34th Street. "Fuck!" Jack said, and held tight to Ray's fur.

They moved so fast the people and cars, and even the buildings, became streaks moving away from them. When they reached the building that housed the Horne Agency they went through the street door as if it wasn't there, then bounded up the stairs, stopping finally in the Agency's reception office, where Horne himself stood, talking with some gray-haired executive type in an expensive suit.

It wasn't until Jack got off Ray's back that Horne seemed to notice him. "Jack?" he said. "What are you—it's good to see you." Neither the client nor the receptionist sitting behind her desk acted as if anything unusual had happened.

Jack glanced at Ray, who nodded. "You've met Ray, I believe."

Again Horne looked startled, as if he'd just noticed the huge fox. Then he smiled, and inclined his head like a gracious king. "Of course," he said. "Thank you for bringing him."

"Actually, he brought me. I think he wants to show you something."

"Really?" He looked at Ray and smiled again. "Very good. I'm ready."

Ray glanced at Jack, who said "I think he wants you to go with him." Ray shook his head, then looked from Jack to Horne. "Sorry, I think he wants us both to go." Silently, he told Ray *You're supposed to be getting him away from me, remember? So I can work with El?*

And then he was moving, running, downtown, no longer on Ray's back but propelled effortlessly alongside him. On the other side, not exactly running, but moving in a kind of streak, was Alexander Horne. Only, now he was dressed in a kind of robe formed from beams of colored lights, and his face was too bright to look at.

Jack was so fascinated by what was happening that he didn't notice the other strange thing until they'd crossed Houston

Street, following Broadway south and east. Ahead of them they should have seen the single sculpted "Freedom Tower" of the new World Trade Center. Instead, two clunky identical rectangles rose up from the squat buildings of lower Manhattan. They hadn't just run downtown, they'd run down*time*, to some point before September 11th, 2001.

They moved through the lobby door of Tower One without opening it, up the staircase and out onto the observation deck. No one saw them, yet people facing them squinted and turned away. Jack had just enough time to remember how he used to take Genie here, how it felt so much safer than the Empire State Building because you couldn't look straight down but instead at an extension of the rooftop a couple of stories below, where the government had set up weather instruments and other devices. But now, instead of machines, he saw a small tribe of people, dressed in dyed animal pelts, their Central Asian faces marked with scars and red ochre.

Suddenly, the tribe seemed to notice Horne, or rather Papa Click and Whistle, for those were the noises they suddenly made, a clamor of impossible sounds as they waved their hands above their head. *Perfect*, Jack thought. How better to distract Horne than to bring his worshippers back? Sure enough, the Sun god floated down to walk among his people, who threw themselves face down on the concrete ground as he passed.

Brilliant. Except, how was Jack supposed to return, for as he might have guessed, Ray had gone to the lower roof as well, to walk alongside the re-established deity, leaving Jack with no way to get back uptown, let alone uptime. He was about to shout at Ray when he heard a voice.

"Jack? Hello?"

Jack saw an ordinary human hand waving in front of his face. He looked around. He was back in—or more likely he'd never left—the lobby of the Horne Agency. El stood in front of him, squinting at him as if he'd done something strange. Which of course he had. He'd Traveled, and left his body behind, something you're never supposed to do. "I'm okay," he told El, and hoped it was true.

296

El said, "So what's the urgency? What is this dream you need me to hunt?"

As Jack described the dreams of trees burnt or flattened, El led him to a room with thick curtains on the walls. They reminded Jack of the first time he and El had made love, when she'd given him dark glasses to wear and blocked the windows with heavy shutters. He looked from El to the single person wooden bed that stood against the wall on carved feet. El rolled her eyes but he could see her blush. "For god's sake, Jack, this is our primary induction chamber. You can't dream unless you're asleep." She pointed to a wingback chair at the foot of the bed and said, "This is where I'll be. Now do you want to do this or not?"

"Of course," he said. "How do we start? Do I need to take my clothes off and get under the covers?"

"You can keep your clothes on. It would be nice if you removed your shoes. Helps with the cleaning bills."

"Of course" he said, then hesitated as he took off the right boot, with his knife hidden in the leg." El pretended not to notice.

She said, "I've never worked with a Traveler before. Normally we use hypnosis, chanting, or even mild drugs to induce dream sleep, but I assume that's not necessary here?"

"No. Shall I start now?"

"Please." Just before Jack closed his eyes he saw El do so as well. There was something surprisingly intimate about that moment, the way a woman closes her eyes as she's about to be kissed.

Travelers tend to see dreams as dangerous landscapes that might be useful. They learn quick dream induction to get in, find out what they need, then leave. Jack glanced over at Elaynora Horne, who seemed to stare at him through her closed eyes. Then he shut his own, and a moment later was gone.

He was standing on a wide hilltop. All around him were the wrecks of trees, some as stumps, some as burnt-out trunks, others covered in some yellow fungus, with all the leaves gone and the branches broken or twisted. As he studied them he saw a shadow figure move quickly through the desolation. Now and then it would come close to him, linger for a moment, then dash off again. "El?" he called, but there was no answer.

He looked past the destruction to notice a small cove of healthy trees, each one wth flowers or fruit. There were magnolias and dogwoods, cherry blossoms and pomegranates. Jack found himself breathing easier, his heart rate slowing. And then the ravens attacked.

As if spit out from a tornado, the swirled down in a tight pattern to beat their wings at the branches and slash the fruit with their beaks. *Murder*, he thought, then *no, that's crows.* Ravens were something—parliament! That was it, a parliament of ravens.

And just as he thought that, he woke up. He gasped and nearly leapt off the bed, then sank down again. "Jesus," he said. He looked at Elaynora, who sat stiffly in the chair, hands on her knees. "Did you see that? The parliament—those ravens attacking the trees?"

"Yes."

He sat up, faced her. "What the hell does it mean?"

"Jack," she said softly. "You know what it means."

"What? No. Why would I—" And then he stopped. "Fuck," he whispered. For of course she was right, he'd known all along. Carolien couldn't see it because she was researching the history of dreams about trees. But these were *Jack Shade's* dreams, and it needed a hunter to get him to see it. "It's the Forest of Souls," he said. "Something's destroying it." And with it his daughter?

El shook her head. "No, nothing can actually destroy it. But it's being culled."

"What does that mean?"

"It gets too crowded. Too many people who die and get stuck as trees. They need to make room, so some of those wretched souls just get destroyed. For them it's as if they never existed."

She's wrong, he thought. She had to be. "How do you know this?"

She looked down. "The ravens told me. Just before you woke up."

That's why, he thought. Why it was so important that he remember the name. A parliament *speaks*. And now Jack had to make El speak to him, because he couldn't bear to put it together himself. So he asked her, "What does it mean? Why am I dreaming this?"

As she spoke he realized this too was what a dream hunter did. Tell people the things they don't want to hear. Elaynora said "Jack, it's your daughter. You have to get her out. Once the culling starts . . ." Her voice trailed off and she looked away.

"How?" he said. "How do I do it? *Look at me.*" She turned her head back and he could see she was crying. *Fuck that*, he thought. "Did you ask them? The ravens? Did you ask the fucking parliament what I can do?"

She whispered, "It doesn't work that way. I can't ask what the dream doesn't tell me. Jack, I'm sorry."

"How much time do I have?"

"I don't know."

"*Why* don't you know? Couldn't they at least tell you that?"

"It's jus—just soon. Weeks. Maybe even days."

Jack pulled on his boots and stood up. He was almost out the door when he stopped and looked back. "El—" He took a breath. "Thank you."

The next day Jack Shade stole a truffle from a shop in Greenwich Village. There was no fooling around this time, no temporary Dupe to cover his embarrassment. He waited outside "Marie Chocolaterie" on West 10th Street until 9:10, when Marie (or whatever her name was) opened the door, then he stepped inside, pointed his knife at her throat, and told the terrified woman that he wanted one, and only one, dark chocolate truffle, wrapped in a gift box, don't bother with the sticker on top. When she'd given it to him he stowed his knife then walked over to Sixth Avenue, where he raised his arm for a cab, and told the Nigerian cabbie to take him to the Empire Parking Garage on 54th Street.

Jack nodded to the Latina woman sitting in the pay booth, then walked past a couple of young white guys hanging around waiting for a car to show up, or someone with a ticket. The garage looked and operated pretty much the same as at least a hundred other small operations in mid-town. In fact, another was just a block down on the other side of the street. If anyone at Empire, employees, customers, or even the owner, had any idea that this place was different, that it was, in fact, one of New York's prime non-Linear locations, they didn't show it. One of the young drivers started to say that customers couldn't go get their own cars, but Jack waved a hand as he passed, and the young man looked confused a second, then went back to talking to his friend, who didn't seem to notice anything at all.

Jack pushed open the gray "Employees Only" door to the stairway, then took the steps two at a time to the second floor. And there he was, the Doorman, in his steel chair next to the anonymous red metal door, the only New York gateway to the Forest Of Souls. Barney looked the same as always, in his blue "Empire Garage" uniform, his white hair neat and short, his face a map of delicate lines. He smiled slightly, nodded. "Hello, Jack," he said.

"Hi, Barney." Jack held out the neatly packed stolen truffle. "I brought you something." Barney glanced at the little box with a mixture of desire and regret, but he didn't move. "Come on," Jack said. "Take it. I need to go inside."

"Oh, Jack" Barney said, with a sad shake of his head. "You know I can't do that."

"Why the hell not? This is the price, right? A goddamn stolen truffle?"

"Oh sure. And believe me, there's nothing I'd like more than to take your kind gift and send you on your way."

"Then do it."

"It's not the price, it's the mission. You know that, Jack. You think I don't want you to rescue that sweet daughter of yours?"

"You know about her?"

Barney rolled his eyes. "Of course I know. I'm the Doorman."

"Then you know I've got to get her out. Now."

"What I know, Jack, is that your own damn stupidity put her there, and you can't just stroll in and take her home."

Jack couldn't decide whether to get down on his knees and beg, or slam Barney's head against the wall. Instead, he just said "Barney, there's going to be a culling. The Forest has gotten too fucking crowded or something."

"Yeah," Barney said softly, "I know."

"Goddamnit, then you know my Genie might not survive. *You've got to let me inside.*"

Barney's voice rose as he crossed his arms. "And what do you think that will do? Even if you find her, you seriously believe the Forest will let you just take her hand and waltz out of there?"

"I have to at least try."

"No! You've got it all wrong." Barney sat up straight and pointed a finger at him. "Listen to me, John Shade. Your problem has always been that you *act* without *knowing*. That's what got you and your daughter in this mess in the first place. You have to *know* before you can help her."

"Then tell me."

"I'm not the one. I'm just the Doorman, for God's sake."

Jack was about to yell something when he stopped. *Of course*, he thought. Barney was just a Gate Keeper. If what Jack needed was knowledge, then he had to find the one person who could give it to him. The Knowledge Elemental. The Know-it-all. The Nude Owl.

Over the next couple of days, with that constant sense that any moment might be Genie's last, Jack and Carolien tried to find that most elusive of Elementals. While Carolien searched the Travelers' Archives, including the recently digitalized seventh century Mongolian accounts, sometimes called the Golden Age of Travelers (a Mongolian was the first to come up with fake money to bribe the Border Guards), Jack went through all his contacts, in this world and any others. Nothing. No one had seen the Owl or knew anyone who had. He tried Mr. Kim but the shop was closed, with a cartoon on the door of a smiling rat and the words, "Gong Hay Fat Choy! Happy Rat Year!"

He went to Suleiman International and offered to indenture himself for seven years in exchange for one wish from Archie. He didn't get past the receptionist. He swallowed some snake blood to understand the birds, but none of them could tell him anything. He even tried to see the Old Man of the Woods, but all he managed was to locate Frank Pope, who told him, "I don't know where that fucker is, and I don't care."

Finally, Jack did the thing he should have tried first. He called Margaret. And now he knew where to find the Owl, at least in a couple of days, and he had to hope that wouldn't be too late.

And hope indeed that if someone did indeed plan to murder the Know-it-all Jack could somehow stop them.

But Jack didn't even know that someone *could* kill a Prime Elemental. Some of the modern ones, like the Selfie Elemental, you could more or less take apart (except the Deconstruction Elemental, which the French Traveler/philosopher Michel Foucault was said to have brought into—or out of—existence). But Knowledge was basic. Carolien told Jack of a Traveler monk who tried to imprison (not kill, just imprison) the Darkness Elemental, and all he did was bring the Darkness's sister, Light, who surrounded the monk with so much brilliance he simply disappeared. "Yeah," Jack said, "it's like the old saying, the Big Kids stick together." Maybe the Ignorance Elemental could protect his little sister.

Late morning on February 9th, Jack gave up looking for answers, though Carolien said she would keep searching and call him if she found anything new. Jack armed himself as best he could without knowing the threat, then got his black Altima for the drive up to Poughkeepsie. He would get there early but he wanted to avoid the rush hour traffic out of the city. He drove up the West Side Highway, and as it turned into the Henry Hudson Parkway he raised a hand towards Inwood Park, and the grave of Peter Midnight.

The night before, Jack had dreamed of his daughter. He'd been sleeping fitfully ever since Elaynora had told him about the Culling, scared that any dream might reveal he was too late. But in this dream Elaynora was standing in a quiet grove of trees. She spoke to him, without sound, but for once he could read her lips clearly. "I love you, Daddy." He'd woken up with a gasp of relief. She was still alive. But for how long? He told himself that the messages had come to him—the dreams, El's hunting, the Queen calling him—because he had the chance to save her. The first step, however, was to save the Nude Owl.

The Hudson Walkway lay on top of an old unused railroad bridge that ran from Poughkeepsie to the small town of Highland on the west side of the river. The bridge had stood unused for decades until the State had covered the rails and wooden slats with a wide concrete surface and put up brightly painted railings with occasional signs and photos that detailed the river's history. Or at least the history that Non-Travelers could understand.

Jack and Elaynora had gone there once, as tourists, back when they were lovers. El's niece, via her half-sister Sarah, was being held in a safe house in the town of Red Hook, about twenty miles north of Poughkeepsie. El never actually visited her niece—she really had nothing to do with Sarah, or what Carolien once called "the world's most dysfunctional family." But El's mother the Queen of Eyes, often went to Red Hook to visit her grand-daughter, and sometimes she and El would meet afterwards. Jack was never present at those meetings, but he knew how hard they were on Elaynora, so he'd done his best to help her.

On the day they'd visited the Walkway, Jack had dropped her off near the Red Hook house, then came back for her an hour later. Her face was wet and she was shaking. Jack knew better than to ask about it, so instead he took her to lunch at the Silk City Diner, then drove down to Poughkeepsie, and the walk across the Hudson. They'd had fun that day—El had even played with someone's Labradoodle puppy—but it was a sunny afternoon in May, and now, well now it was a cold night in February, and Jack had gone there to save the life of an Elemental in the desperate hope that she could tell him how to break into the Forest of Souls and bring out his daughter.

The Walkway was closed in the evening, but for Jack that just meant less interference. At 7:30 he left the Altima in the empty lot on Parker Avenue, then walked up the path to the Walkway entrance. There was a locked fence that was easy enough to climb over, and a pair of surveillance cameras Jack could glam so they would never register him. He remembered how surprised he'd been when Anatolie had told him you could cast a glamour over electronic devices. Until then he'd assumed a glamour was a kind of instant hypnosis, a mental parlor trick. But if you could glam a machine . . . He smiled slightly as he remembered how unnerved he'd been when his teacher had said, in that mild voice he had not yet learned to fear, "The real question, Jack, is whether a machine can cast a glamour over *you*."

A nearly full Moon shone down on the concrete walkway, and beyond it, the large slabs of ice floating in the Hudson. January had been unusually warm, but as soon as February hit, the temperature had dropped to only a degree or two above freezing at mid-day, and down near zero at night. There was no wind, at least. Jack had on a long gray coat over his Travel tunic, with all its pockets, a black woolen hat, and thin woolen gloves with silk thermal liners.

The gloves allowed easy access to his knife, but also his bone flute, a roll of spell tape, his black feather from Midnight's grave, and various other tricks. Would it be enough? Would he be enough? If someone had the power to kill a Prime Elemental, could Jack Shade stop it? He had to, he told himself, and then immediately wondered if he should have borrowed Benny Pope's Gun of the Morning.

Jack had stationed himself about a third of the way from the Poughkeepsie entrance, but the Walkway was over a mile long, and there was no way he could see the whole length. So earlier that day, as soon as he'd arrived in Poughkeepsie, he'd set up surveillance stones every thirty-three steps. The small quartz pebbles would pick up any movement or sounds and relay them back to a larger stone in Jack' s coat pocket.

At 7:49 the quartz warned Jack of someone coming, and an instant later a police car drove up the Walkway from the Highland side. *Cop=gun*, Jack thought. Would a cop somehow kill the Nude Owl? She looked like a vagrant, and could say things that sounded pretty crazy. Or maybe she'd tell the cop some secret about himself that he couldn't bear to hear. Then, as the car pulled up alongside Jack he thought how maybe it was *his* murder Margarita Mariq had warned about. With all the dangers Travelers faced, racist cops seemed pretty low down the list. But still.

The car bore the words *New York Park and Bridge Authority*. *Good*, Jack thought. Probably less gun happy than a trooper or a local badge. The driver rolled down his window rather than get out, another good sign. "Sir," he said, "the Walkway is closed."

"Yes, of course," Jack said, and let his voice slide into Basic Persuasion. "I'm actually here as part of a meteorological study.

We're stationing people on all the bridges along the Hudson for first-hand observations."

The Park Ranger looked doubtful. "I don't think I've heard of that," he said.

"No, you wouldn't. It's just a pilot study."

"Do you have any ID?"

"Yes, of course. It's in my inside coat pocket." Jack moved his hand slowly and produced a fake ID he'd prepared, and charged with belief, before he left the city.

"Well, okay," the ranger said, and handed Jack his paper. "Good luck, Dr. Simpson." Jack never used his real name for fake ID. You could inadvertently trap yourself in a made-up world. So tonight he was "Lucas Simpson, Ph.D." The ranger smiled at him. "I don't envy you standing out here in this cold."

Jack laughed. "Well, we'll see how long I last. Right now I envy you being able to go somewhere for a hot cup of coffee."

The ranger blinked a couple of times, then he grinned. "You know," he said, "that sounds like a great idea." He rolled up his window and drove off. "Dr. Simpson" let out a breath and checked his watch. 7:56.

Two minutes later the quartz pinged him again. Very slight this time. A pair of crows landed on the concrete surface about ten feet in front of him. A little odd, Jack thought, since there were no scraps of food that he could see. But he was certainly no expert on crows. A few seconds later another five crows showed up, and when he looked at the sky he saw a swarm of them, a black cloud about to descend on the Walkway. Jack braced himself for an attack. But they ignored him and instead formed a thick column, about three feet wide and six feet high. Jack tried to look around them, frightened he'd somehow miss the Nude Owl.

No, he thought suddenly. Not a "cloud," or a "swarm." *Murder.* The collective noun for an assembly of crows was "murder." That's what the Queen had meant. To find the Know-It-All look for the *murder of crows.*

"Owl?" he called out. "I'm here. Show yourself."

The crows parted, and there she stood, in all her homeless, street crazy splendor. She wore a long and filthy overcoat over a sweatsuit and Green rubber boots that appeared stuffed with several layers of socks. Her matted hair was pushed under one of those Russian Army hats with fur earflaps. Thick mittens covered her hands.

The soft androgynous voice said "Hello, Jack. I'm told you wanted to see me."

Jack wanted to ask who told things to a Knowledge Elemental but his curiosity would have to wait. "There's going to be a culling in the Forest of Souls."

"Yes, I know."

"Then I'm sure you also know I've got to get inside and bring out my daughter. Barney—the Doorman—"

"I know who Barney is."

Jesus, Jack thought, *how do you talk to a fucking Know-It-All?* He said "Yeah, well, I gave him the damn truffle, or tried to. He wouldn't take it. Said he can't let me in."

Underneath the street grime, the Owl's mouth twisted in a quick smile. "Barney has always been a man of integrity."

Barney's not a man, Jack wanted to say, but instead just said, "I need to know how to get inside. I tried the Archives, I tried Mr. Kim, no one can tell me anything. Please."

Her voice even softer than usual, the Owl said "You're wrong, Jack."

"What?"

"You don't need to go inside the Forest. You just need to bring her out."

"What? You mean there's a way to do it from here?"

"Oh, Jack, if everyone tells you cannot do something, then surely you need to find someone who can."

"Who? Tell me. Please, Owl, there's no time."

"Try to think, Jack. If your child is separated from you by a boundary that cannot be crossed, then what do you need?"

"Someone who can cross any boundary."

"No! Someone for whom a boundary is not a wall but a crack. Every barrier a door." Behind the Know-it-all the crows began to move. At first they just swirled in the air, but then they started to close towards the Owl.

Jack said "No, no, you can't leave. Send them away!" But the crows were starting to obscure her. Jack charged at them, waving his arms. They squawked and flew at his face, but he ignored them. He tried to reach inside the murder, grab the Owl and pull her out, but his hands just slid free of the layers of clothing. "Tell me who it is!" he cried. "Tell me!"

"Follow the waters, Jack."

"*What* waters?"

"Follow the waters."

"That's not enough. I need to know—" But it was too late. The crows swirled around her, and when they lifted into the sky there was no one there.

Jack stared down at the slabs of ice in the Hudson. " Follow the waters," he whispered.

2.

J ACK CALLED CAROLIEN AS HE WAS LEAVING THE WALKWAY. He told her about the crows, the Owl, the idea of someone for whom a boundary is a crack, and "Follow the waters."

"It's a fucking riddle," he said. "all that trouble, just for a riddle."

"No!" Carolien said, in her firm Dutch voice. "A direction. The Know-It-All has given you a command. To find this person you are to follow the waters. You are at a river, yes?"

"Yes."

"Then follow. Stay as close to the water as you can. I will go to Tarrytown and check in to the motel. Maybe you find something tonight. If not, tomorrow we continue together. Okay?"

"All right," Jack said. He hung up. For a moment he stared at the Hudson, hoping for some clue. But just standing there was not following. He left the Walkway and headed for his car. He was almost there when he turned back.

There was a small park at the base of the Walkway, a few trees and a couple of picnic tables at the edge of the river. He went there now, and crouched by some rocks, as close as he could get to the water. For several minutes he scanned the flow, the ice, the choppiness from the slight wind. He was about to leave when he spotted several white objects just a couple feet away from the damp stones.

Jack couldn't tell what they were until he managed to snatch them from the river. When he held them in his hand they turned out to be bones and feathers, three of each. The bones were shorter, only about five inches, with the feathers about seven. All Jack knew about anatomy he got from watching crime shows on television, but he somehow knew the bones were human. And the feathers—he got out the black feather he'd found at Peter Midnight's grave, held the two of them up together. Identical. Was there a bird that had both black and white feathers? Or came in two versions?

He put away the black one and stared at the white. It reminded him of something . . . Xoltan! His Juggler's table at the carnival had three white feathers, and Jack was pretty sure they were cousins to this one. As far as Jack could remember, no one, not even Mr. Green, had any idea what they were, or why they were there. "Tradition," was the best Green could offer. Jack had tried waving them over the cards for show but quickly decided it was too corny.

And the bones? The dice, he realized. The dice on the table, that he never used in his act, they were really old and carved from actual bones. What were they doing there? And why had the river given him these gifts? He looked at them some more, then put them in his coat pockets, the bones in the left, the feathers in the right, and headed for his car. Follow the waters.

The Metro-North commuter railroad ran along the Hudson, which meant that every ten or fifteen miles there'd be a small station with a parking lot near the water. Jack developed a kind of rhythm, finding the station, making his way down to the river and getting as close to the water as he could, squat down and stare at the choppy water, the chunks of ice (smaller as he went downriver towards the city), the trees and weeds and rocks, any birds that flew overhead. There were none with white feathers, but at three places, Garrison and Cold Spring and Peekskill, he found that same combination, in twos this time, a pair of bones and a pair of feathers. The feathers were all identical, the bones varied slightly in length, but he still had no idea what they meant.

He found himself angry at the Nude Owl. For a Knowledge Elemental, she sure held things back. *More like a Riddle Elemental,* he thought. *Someone for whom every wall is a crack.* He studied the bones and feathers for cracks but didn't find any. Ice was filled with cracks, and a river was like a giant crack in the land. And if feathers were torn from a bird, or bones from a body, were those cracks?

There was a word that seemed just beyond him—another term for a crack—and he could feel it had something to do with the bones, but couldn't seem to get it. At Ossining he saw a pair of fish, sturgeons, he thought, leaping in the water. In the 19th century, he knew, sturgeon fishing was a major industry along the Hudson—King Sturgeon, they were called, but he'd thought they'd all died out. A fish leaping made cracks in the water. Bones and feathers had to be taken out through cracks in the body. *Damn.* He just couldn't get it.

He arrived at the Sleepy Hollow Motel outside Tarrytown a little after midnight. Jack and Carolien had stayed there once over a weekend, when Carolien had gone to meet the Council of Frogs. He spotted Carolien's Altima outside room thirty-two, but did not find a spot alongside her, so parked by the office. He was about to walk to the room when a tenor voice behind him said, "Excuse me, sir, have you checked in?"

Jack turned and saw a white man no older than twenty, dressed in black pants and a white shirt buttoned to the neck. Jack said, "I'm meeting Ms. Hounstra in thirty-two."

"Oh, sorry, Mr. Hounstra," the young man said, then "Your wife registered but I'm afraid you still need to sign in."

Jack considered glamming the kid to get rid of him, but remembered how Anatolie would tell him "Save your special skills for when ordinary wit will not suffice." So he just said, "*Ja, natuurlyk,*" then, "Sorry, I mean yes, of course." In the office he signed the register as "Johannes Hounstra" and said "*Dank je wel.* I mean, thank you." The clerk nodded and said "Your wife has the keys."

When Jack let himself in the room Carolien was lying on the bed, wearing only her painter's smock, and reading a book. Jack said, "Married? Really?"

She smiled that dazzling smile, so vast and soft all at once. "I thought a little amusement might help."

He sat down beside her and said, "Come here, Wifey," and kissed her. What are you reading?"

She held up the obviously ancient volume, probably "borrowed" from the NYTAS library. Chief Arthur did not like anyone taking NYTAS property off the premises, especially when that property originated in the "extensions," that is, rooms, or vaults, or even woods that existed "outside," as the Travelers said. The NYTAS Library was housed in a building at least three times the size of headquarters, even though you entered it through a door down the hallway from Arthur's office. Not even Carolien knew its full size.

Jack looked at the gold letters of the title. "The Emptiness of the Waters." He made a noise. Anatolie had mentioned the book to him once, told him not to read it, it would just confuse him. He felt a sudden regret that he'd never introduced Carolien to his teacher. He said, "Anything?"

"Only if you find *this* of deep meaning. 'At the back of the head the Sky is Blue. Fill your face with Fire and your mouth with dust.'"

"Yeah, that helps a lot," Jack said. "I want to show you something." He slid back to make room on the bed, then set out the bones and feathers and told her how he'd found them.

She ignored the bones for a moment and held up the nine feathers before her. Softly she said "These are raven feathers."

"What?" Jack said. He took out the Peter Midnight feather and said, "Ravens aren't white. They're—" He stopped, then said "Jesus. The White Ravens. These feathers are not from this world. They've crossed over."

Carolien said "Find a man for whom every wall is a crack." She picked up the bones in her hand, studied them. "These are human," she said.

"Yes. I thought that, too."

"I think—I think they are from the one you seek."

"Please don't tell me he's dead!"

"No, no. He's—*Verdamme!* I know *who*—*what*—this is, but I cannot—"

He stood up. "Then we just have to keep looking. Follow the waters."

"*Schatje,* you are too tired. You would miss any signs or messages. You need to rest, at least until dawn."

Reluctantly, Jack let the sense of what she was saying overcome his guilt. And there was another layer to the question of time. Genie was only in such danger *now* because Jack had let her linger there for so damn long. Or so it seemed, so it felt emotionally. But in the Non-Linear world of the Travelers things very often happened in their own time. He had tried to rescue his daughter. For the first three years or so he'd driven the people and other beings in his life crazy by begging, demanding, and scheming to try and do this thing that couldn't be done.

And other times, too. This wasn't the first time he'd pressured Barney, with no greater luck than now. He'd asked Margaret what to do, tried to insinuate that she owed him for dragging him into her crazy arrangement of her own death. She didn't actually refuse him, only said she could only discover information that was hidden, not something that didn't exist.

So what had changed? The Nude Owl indicated that there was a way to get Genie out. Had the Forest actually shifted in some way, due to the Culling? Was that why this mysterious figure, for whom every wall was a crack, was suddenly a possibility? As Jack slid towards sleep he thought how this crack person wanted Jack to find him. But he couldn't just reveal himself, he needed Jack to search for him, to become truly desperate. But why? There was only one answer to that one—there was a price. If the situation was dire enough, and Jack had looked hard enough to find whoever it was, then Jack would be willing to pay. *Fuck,* Jack thought. He should tell Carolien. But as he turned towards her she put a finger over his mouth, and a moment later he'd closed his eyes, and was gone.

He woke a little after five to find Carolien dressed and packed. Before Jack could demand instant action, she used her firmest Dutch voice to say, "First we have breakfast. Then the sky will be bright enough so we do not miss clues, or make mistakes." Jack looked out the window, saw it was still mostly dark, and nodded. Had he missed anything last night? He didn't think so. He was pretty sure he was meant to find the bones and feathers, and had gotten them all so far. Still, he knew he needed to eat, and as he got dressed a sudden urge for coffee shot through his body.

They went to a twenty-four hour diner they remembered from their previous visit. At this hour, it was empty, except for a straight couple in their thirties, apparently getting an early start on some family journey, and a couple of men, one black, one white, in camouflage outfits, sitting at the counter hunched over coffee. To Carolien, Jack said, "Hunting season's over, right?"

"*Ja*," she said, "and they are not military."

"Powers? The unfriendly sort?" Jack imagined a boulder blocking the doorway, or a sudden copse of trees grown up around their car.

"*Neen*," she said, the Dutch word for "No," pronounced *nay*. "I think maybe they are messengers but do not know it."

"Then what's the message?"

The middle-aged waitress, a blond woman with an old-fashioned punk haircut, came and took their orders. She looked already tired, with a long day ahead of her. When she'd gone, Carolien said, "What does camouflage do?"

"It hides you. Lets you blend in with your surroundings."

"Exactly. So you do not belong firmly in one world or another."

Jack said, "Huh. Like someone for whom every wall is a crack." Carolien smiled. Jack stared at the men's backs. He said "Do you think one of them is the person I'm looking for?" He half rose from his seat.

Carolien held his right hand in both of hers. "No, Jack. I am sorry. We would feel it."

He sank back. "Then what are they doing here? Are they Travelers."

"*Neen*. I think—I think they are puppets." Puppets were non-Travelers who did something for no apparent reason, at least not apparent to themselves, like wear camouflage outfits to a diner early in the morning. Carolien said "They are sending you a message. Or they *are* the message."

"Message of what? To keep away?"

"The opposite, I think. That you are getting closer. Jack—I think he or she wants to be found."

313

"Then why not send a real message, like where to find them? I don't have time for fucking hide and seek."

She shrugged her beautiful soft shoulders. "Maybe they can't. if you do not live in a fixed world but only in borders you cannot take action. You cannot seek but only be found."

Jack closed his eyes a moment. *I know this,* he thought. *I know who it is.* He just couldn't seem to bring it forward. Every wall is a crack—not in one world or another . . . His hands tightened into fists. *Goddamnit,* he ordered himself. *Figure it out.* Something from years ago, something he'd seen. "Damnit" he said.

"*Schatje,* what is it?"

Jack threw a twenty on the table. "Come on," he said, "we've got train stations to visit."

They used Jack's car, leaving Carolien's at the motel. The evening before, Carolien had downloaded a Metro-North Hudson Line timetable that listed the stations. From Tarrytown there were four express stops, Ossining, Yonkers, 125th Street, and Grand Central. But there were quite a few local ones, most of them just a platform and a ticket machine. The next was called Phillipse Manor, even though it served the village of Sleepy Hollow.

Phillipse Manor station was actually more elaborate than some others, a small but classic nineteenth century two story building of brownstone and oak timbers to hold up the slate roof. From the station you crossed a bridge over the tracks to the river side. Jack and Carolien walked to the end of the platform and climbed over a short fence to get to the water. As with most of the other stations, the river bank here was rocks and weeds. They separated by ten feet or so and squatted down to scan the water.

"Jack!" Caroline called, "To your left." Jack squinted, then jumped up to wade into the shallow water and snatch up the three feathers that were rising and falling on what Jack realized was the tidal current. The Hudson River flows from its source in Canada down to New York harbor, but several times a day the saltwater tides from the Atlantic push back upstream. The people who lived there before the Europeans, mostly Munsee to the south and Mohican to the north, called it Mohicanichtur, "river that flows two ways."

Jack scanned the water for bones or more feathers. When he didn't see any, he brought the three to Carolien. "Notice how dry they are," he said, as he held them out. Jack's hand was wet but the feathers looked like they'd been drying in a warm sun.

"May I?" Carolien asked and put out her hand.

Jack smiled at the formality. "Of course," he said as he handed them over.

She lifted them up to eye level, two in her left hand, one in her right. She said, "They are warm because they do not come from this world. Perhaps in the world of the White Ravens it is Summer now." She gave them back to him. "So. You said last night that you found three feathers the first time, and after that only two. Yes?" He nodded. "And now three again. This place is special."

"But no bones."

"No. Perhaps the specialness belongs to the Ravens. It is they who want you to take notice."

"Notice of what?" When she didn't answer, he began to walk back to the fence. Suddenly he stopped and turned to her. "Why is it called Phillipse Manor? Shouldn't it be Sleepy Hollow? All the other stations are named for the towns they serve."

She frowned a moment, then smiled. "Ah, of course. *Eigenlijk*—sorry, actually—it's named for a Dutchman. Frederick Phillipse." She pronounced it in the Dutch way, with rolled r's.

"Who was he?" Jack asked. He could feel excitement creep up his spine.

"He was a *patroon*." She pronounced it "patrone,' which made Jack think of some mafia boss. "In Nieuw Amsterdam, the original colony. When the British took over and made it New York, Heer Phillipse behaved like a good capitalist and switched sides. His new masters rewarded him with large parcels of land. So I suppose this area was indeed Phillipse manor before it became a setting for a silly story." She paused, then said, "So. Do you think he is the one? Not one side or the other? Like the camouflage men?"

Jack frowned. "No. He's not between, he just switched sides. Is there anything else about him?"

She frowned, concentrating. Carolien could travel in a way no one else could, not even Anatolie. Her *mind* could travel, leave her body and enter vast libraries. Now she went blank for a moment, and Jack reached out to catch her in case she fell. But it wasn't necessary, for a moment later she was back. She blinked, then stared at him with a kind of amazement. "*Spuyten Duyvil!*" she said. "Frederick Phillipse built the first canal at Spuyten Duyvil. Follow the waters!"

Spuyten Duyvil, Dutch for Devil's Spit, was the northern tip of Manhattan Island, where the Hudson River on the west met the Harlem River on the east. Add the tidal estuary and originally the short turn around the island's end was wild and dangerous. Though the canal tamed it, the place retained its original—Dutch—name.

The waters may have calmed, but Spuyten Duyvil was still a borderland, not exactly one thing or another. And there was something else about this place. The shape of the land, the path the Metro-North train followed, because the Spit gave it no other option, formed a snake curve, an undulating S. On December 1st, 2013, an accident happened at Spuyten Duyvil. The train's engineer was supposed to brake the train to take it through the turns. Instead, he kept it at full throttle. The train derailed, killing four commuters on their way to the office. When the investigators interviewed him the engineer insisted he could not remember anything, and he had no idea why he didn't slow the train. He'd gone into a "daze," he'd said. When they tested him for alcohol and drugs he came out clean, and people assumed he'd fallen asleep.

The Travelers knew different. *La Societé du Matin* had taken over the engineer's body and made it impossible for him to slow the train. Spuyten Duyvil was a place of natural power, and every time a train formed that undulating serpent it raised energy. Once the train straightened again the energy dissipated, and all but a handful of passengers—the people the Travelers call "Naturals"—never even noticed it. The accident changed that. Power surged from the broken train, and especially the dead.

That surge was *La Societé's* goal. Just why they wanted the energy no one knew, but for awhile it looked like they had gone too far. COLE seemed ready at long last to take them on, to call on the Powers to help them bring down The Old Man Of The Woods. In the end, COLE did what it always does, cover it up. They made sure the police and the insurance companies accepted the engineer's claim of innocence. The families buried their dead, helped by pay-offs from the Metropolitan Transit Authority which then installed automatic braking systems, and everyone went back to their daily commute.

Jack stared at the river. The water that flows both ways. The Devil's Spit. The snake curve where the land itself raises power. He looked at the ice floes, cracked, with thin lines, like—like fissures. A man for whom every wall is a crack, every barrier a door. Follow the waters. That feeling of having seen something. He turned toward Carolien. "Jesus," he said, his voice strange in his own head. "I know who he is." He stopped, and Carolien didn't prod him.

He was remembering now, the one time he'd truly surprised Anatolie. She was telling him about the Great Dogs, Sam and Lily, and he suddenly said, "Oh, I think I've met them." Anatolie had stared at him, her mouth half open, as if ready for one of her beloved har kow dumplings. So Jack had gone on to tell her of his bored trick as a kid, when he'd riled up the neighborhood dogs and then went downstairs and opened the kitchen door to discover the monsters.

Very softly, Anatolie had said, "Ah. I take it you did not speak to them?"

"No. I closed the door and ran upstairs."

Her mouth had twitched, the hint of a smile. "Then it seems, John Shade, that you are a very *lucky* young man." Later, Jack would understand that this was a kind of joke, for Travelers considered "luck" an illusion, a dangerous one, borne of ignorance. At the time, though, she just went on to tell him the story of who had met the Dogs, and what had happened to him.

Now Jack grabbed a handful of the bones from his pocket and held them out. "Carolien," he said, "*I know whose bones these are.*

The man who is not one thing or another. It's *him*, Carolien. It's Joseph of the Waters!"

"Oh, *verdomme*," Carolien cried. "*Natuurlijk!* The one person for whom every wall is a crack. The Fissure King!"

3.

EVERY TRAVELER KNEW THE STORY OF JOSEPH, THE MAN WHO wanted to change the world. They knew it because their teachers told it to them as an object lesson against what they considered the greatest danger to Travelers, not enemies or hostile Elementals, but what Anatolie called "aggrandizement," and what Jack simply thought of as "over-reaching." Joseph didn't think of it that way. After all, he did not do the working for himself. He had decided that the Original Powers, the ones who set up the world, had made things far too rough for wretched non-Travelers. Anatolie had surprised Jack with the expression, "rigged the game."

Lots of people thought this—how could you miss it?—but Joseph decided to do something about it. The OP had put a kind of escape clause into the structure of things. Anatolie had told Jack she suspected it was a kind of trap, a way to tempt Travelers who would go too far. Whatever the reason there was an enactment you could do that would require the Powers to hear your petition and make a change.

It was called The Way Of Force, and the preparation alone was rigorous. It involved eating strange combinations of food for weeks, as you found some remote frozen place, where you would walk out naked onto the ice and squat down, head between your knees, and speak strings of apparent nonsense syllables directly into the Earth. Then, once it actually started, you had to dress in white rags, tilt your head back until all you could see was the sky, and chant certain formulas over and over for three days, without sleep. During those three days not only must you not eat, you mustn't touch even a scrap of food.

Joseph went to the coldest loneliest place he could find. He did all the preparations, and while at first he told himself that this was crazy, arrogant, how could a lone Traveler force himself upon the Powers, slowly he became more confident. Energy surged through him and by the time he began the actual enactment he shook with strength. Head tilted back so that all he could see was a gray sky and a washed-out Sun, he called out the formulas, over and over. Three days, the archives said, and after the first, the sky began to brighten. On the second day the ground shook, and the Sun seemed to appear in several places at once. On the third day, light blazed across the sky, and it seemed to Joseph that the whole Earth vibrated underneath him, so violently it would swallow him up, but he kept on. Light blazed across the sky. It separated, first into sheets of flame, then columns of concentrated energy. *It's them*, Joseph thought. *I've done it.* His voice got stronger. The columns began to take shape, animals or people.

Suddenly Joseph heard a sound, the whimper of a creature in pain. For just an instant he looked down, then brought his eyes back to the sky. With relief he saw that the columns hadn't broken apart, if anything they had gotten clearer. And yet, he could not forget what he'd seen—two emaciated dogs, close to death from starvation, their eyes pitiful and desperate.

Joseph made his voice even louder than before but he could not drown out that wretched sound. His eyes still on the sky, his voice like a trumpet, Joseph continued, but he felt around him for a few scraps of meat and bone left over from his last meal. When a fingernail grazed something he tried to mentally tell the dogs to take it. The whimpering just continued.

It doesn't matter, Joseph told himself, *I've done it. There's no stopping it now.* He glanced away to pick up the food and toss it to the animals. "Here," he said. "Eat."

But when he looked back at the sky the light had started to dim. "No! This can't be right!" he shouted at the columns that even now were beginning to fade, then break apart.

"This isn't the end!" he cried, more to himself than the Powers. "I can do it again." And then he heard the growls, one low and thunderous, the other almost a shriek. He looked down and saw the dogs, changed now, their bodies large and thick, their fur layers of sharp scales, their teeth like jagged mountains from the first days of Creation. For of course they were Sam and Lily, the watchdogs of the Powers, who above all else did not like to be pushed around. Just before they leaped at him, Joseph called out the Words Of Departure, the formula that all Travelers memorize for the moment of their death.

Only, Joseph didn't die. They tore at his skin, his muscles and organs, even his bones, and yet he continued, not alive but not dead either. He had become a Border Elemental, caught between worlds, master of openings—the Fissure King, for whom every wall becomes a crack, every barrier a door.

Carolien touched Jack's shoulder. "He's waiting for you, *schatje*." Jack nodded. "In Spuyten Duyvil. Come on, let's go."

As they made their way back to the car they debated whether they needed to stop at the rest of the stations, one by one, to Spuyten Duyvil. "Make sure we have all the bones," Jack said.

"I don't think so," Carolien said, as she strode to the car. When Carolien moved quickly, Jack had to hustle to keep up. She said, "The bones were a puzzle, and an invitation. You've solved the puzzle. The invitation is complete."

"And the feathers?"

"Ah." She stopped at the car door, made a face. "I do not know." Jack almost smiled. Carolien hated not knowing something. Now she said, "But I do not think they come from him. They are connected to him but they come from something else. I am sorry, Jack. This is just a feeling."

Jack touched her cheek. "I'll take that," he said. "Then all that matters is that Joseph is waiting for us. Fuck the feathers. Time to go meet the King."

They drove down to Spuyten Duyvil using the Travelers' Siren, a device secretly built into black Altimas that emitted a psychic alarm so that all cars, including cops, would make way for them and not realize they were doing it.

When they arrived at Spuyten Duyvil Station they discovered that the railroad had set it on the Bronx side, rather than on the northern tip of Manahatta. So they got back in the car, drove over a short bridge, and looked for a place to park. The neighborhood of Spuyten Duyvil had gone upscale, they discovered, with townhouses and apartment complexes, and the kind of school that draws double career parents with school-age kids.

Jack searched for a parking spot that was close to the Spit, and hopefully not so tame and modern. He found it in front of a three story building made of large weathered stones, and a roof part slate, part copper. It bore the name "Villa Charlotte Bronte," and it really did look like something you might see at the edge of the moors two hundred years ago.

"Come on," he said, and they set off for the trees at the end of the street, where the land tilted down toward the water. As soon as they left the paved road the fragment of woods began to change. They didn't notice right away, but then it became too strange to miss. The ground became overgrown with winter weeds and brambles, the leafless trees more crowded together, so that they had to push branches out of the way. Ahead of them they could hear the sound of angry waters, the Hudson and the Harlem fighting for control of the point.

Jack turned around and saw that the Villa Charlotte Bronte was gone, and so was the street and all the other buildings. He said, "We've gone back in time. Before the British. Before the Dutch. Before Frederick Philipse dug his canal to tame the waters."

Carolien looked around again, then nodded. "*Ja*," she said, "How else to make a border, a place not one thing or another? The land has invited us backward."

"No," Jack said. "*He* did it. He promised me he would come when I needed him, and now he has." He pointed up the hill to where a tall man stood motionless. He wore a wide-brimmed black hat, a black jacket, yellow leggings and gold-buckled shoes, and around his neck a kind of ruff of black feathers.

Carolien gasped. "*Peter Minuit!*"

"Yes," Jack said.

322

"But he's *dead.*"

"Well, of course he is. His grave's not far from here. You know that."

"*Neen.* You do not understand. I saw him die."

"What?"

"*Alle Nederlandse Reisers*—sorry, all Dutch Travelers—must witness Peter die. That is the moment we become a Traveler."

"Jesus," Jack said. For a moment he remembered Benny Pope shooting Carol Acker in the face. And then his wife, lying in blood on the kitchen floor. But all he said was, "He's a time traveler, Carolien. Time travelers can die, but they're never dead."

He took a step towards the apparition on the hill. "*Dank je wel!*" he shouted, then bowed. When he stood up, the man was gone.

Carolien said, "*Schatje,* we need to work on your accent. But first, we must save your daughter." Together, they headed down the hill to the end of Manhattan Island.

The dense trees gave way to a small triangle of dirt and stones where the land met the water. Jack spun around, searching. "Where is he?" he said, feeling desperation creep up his spine. Had they done it wrong? Did he miss something? "Joseph!" he shouted. "Where are you?"

Carolien held up a hand. "No. You must not show disrespect. Please. Give me the bones."

Jack grabbed the collection from his pockets and handed them over. Carolien set them down, one by one, near the edge of the water. Then she backed off and got down on one knee. "Your majesty," she said, "we come, not for ourselves, but for an innocent. Eugenia Shade is trapped where she does not belong, in the Forest Of Souls. You alone can save her. We beg you to reveal yourself." She stood up.

As Jack held his breath, the air seemed to thicken, become a swirling column, dark, like a miniature tornado. Then it congealed, thick, hard, and at the very moment it became firm, like a pillar of ice, it began to crack. Small fissures opened up and down the surface. Then all at once they cracked open and showered to the ground. And then *he* was there.

Jack had never seen anything like it, gnawed bones and tissues somehow holding together in the shape of a man. Even the face was half eaten away, a skull with about a third of it gone, and the rest covered in strips of skin. Now it was Jack who got down on one knee. "King Joseph," he said, "we bless you and thank you. We know that nothing we have done deserves your precious intervention." Anatolie had taught this to Jack in one of their first lessons. It was called the Standard Formula of Recognition, to be used in the unlikely event of coming face to face with a Power.

When the King spoke, his voice seemed to come from far away, dry and hoarse. "Standard," he said. "I am not—one of *them*."

Fuck, Jack thought, and he got up. Did he blow it? Would the Fissure King leave? Or refuse to help him?

The skull moved slightly, tilting forward, then upright. Jack realized that Joseph was examining him. The voice said "You've met the dogs."

"Yes," Jack said. "When I was young and did not know what they were."

"But you didn't—speak to them."

"No."

The assemblage of bones and meat tilted back slightly. Jack worried it might tip over and break apart, but it stood upright again. The distant voice said "If only—" He stopped himself.

It took Jack a second before he realized the Fissure King was waiting for him to speak. "I need your help. My daughter is trapped in the Forest of Souls." Joseph stood motionless, silent. Jack said, "There's a culling. I don't know when, but soon. If she's still there she won't survive." He took a breath. "For all I know, it's already happened." *While I was collecting your goddamn bones*, he thought.

"No. It has not happened yet."

Jack's heart leapt. "So you know."

"Of course I know."

"Then you know I can't save her. I've tried everything I could, but I can't reach her. But you can. You can bring her out."

The King said, "There is a price."

Jack wanted to grab that loose assemblage, shake it, scream at it, *There's always a fucking price!* Instead, he just said, "Tell me."

The skull moved again, a kind of nod. Joseph said, "I want to die."

"What? You want me to kill you?"

The whole upper skeleton moved now, and Jack had the horrible thought that the Fisher King was laughing at him. "Kill me?" Joseph said. "*You?*"

Jack's fists clenched. He never knew he could hate someone as much as he did that moment. He opened his hands and said, "Then what can I do? Tell me."

Silence for a moment, and in that pause Jack realized that Carolien was looking from him to Joseph, her mouth open, her face pale. "Oh no," she whispered. "No."

Joseph of the Waters said, "I can only die if someone agrees to replace me."

Jack heard Carolien's gasp, heard the sob in her voice as she said, "Jack! You can't do this. *Please.*"

Jack kept his eyes on Joseph. "I'll do it," he said. "If you save my daughter I'll take your place." He expected Carolien to protest again, but she just stood there, staring at him. To Joseph he said, "How do we do it? Do I have to become like you?"

"No. The dogs did this. And you never spoke to them. You never offered them meat."

"Then what? What do we do so I can take your place?"

"*We* do not do anything."

Jack controlled his rage. "Okay, then who does?"

"The Ravens."

"What?"

"Do you have the feathers?"

Jack grabbed them from his pockets, held them out with both hands. "Here," he said.

"Ah. Twelve. Good. You got them all."

Jack thought, *Thank God*, though he had no idea what was going on.

The King said, "Set them on the ground in a circle. Not touching, with the pins inward." Jack began to put them in a curved line, end to end. "No!" Joseph said. "With the pins inward."

Jack just stood there, shaking. *What does he mean?*

Carolien touched his arm. "*Schatje,* he means like the spokes of a wheel. The pins are the hard part at the bottom. The part that sticks into the bird's body."

Jack grabbed the feathers from the ground and started again. In a few moments he had indeed made a wheel, with an empty center. He stepped back, looked at the Fissure King, who didn't move, but kept his body turned toward the feathers.

A thin band of light shimmered above each feather. It became wider, more substantial, columns of white light so strong and pure Jack could hardly look at them. He must, he knew. He remembered back when he saw the Old Ladies, how he knew he mustn't look away. And the dogs—he'd backed up, but didn't move his eyes until he'd closed the door. And Nero, when Jack stared into his mouth. The one unbreakable rule, the thing he'd learned on his own, even before Anatolie taught him True Sight. Don't look away.

They were taking shape now, twelve huge birds with their heads bowed, their brilliant wings folded over their bodies.

The Fissure King said, "Miss Hounstra, you who know so much. Do you know the collective name for Ravens?"

"Parliament," Carolien said.

Jack kept his eyes on the birds, but he thought, *It's a parliament? They're going to hold a debate while my daughter is dying?*

"No!" Joseph said. "That name belongs to their children, the meager black ravens of your world. The true name, the name for the Twelve White—is *Jury.*"

The Ravens lifted their heads and Jack saw that one stood taller than the others. *The foreman,* he thought. Whatever its title, the larger Raven said, in a voice that made Joseph's seem friendly, "Carolien Hounstra. Child of the Council of Frogs. Will you speak for the defense?"

Child of the Frogs? Jack thought. He promised himself he would ask her about that later. Then he realized there might not be a later.

Carolien said, "Always." Though he didn't look, Jack could hear the shaking in her voice.

"Then Lord Joseph," the Raven said, "Please state the charges."

The Fissure King said "Abandonment."

"What?" Jack said, still focused on the Foreman. "What the hell are you talking about?"

Joseph went on, "He has abandoned everyone who ever cared about him. He left his parents, he abandoned his first lover, Abby."

Jack said, "*She* broke up with *me*."

Carolien touched his arm. "Shh," she said. "Let your lawyer speak for you."

Joseph said, "He abandoned Xoltan the Younger."

"That was *me*," Jack said. "How could I abandon myself?"

Carolien whispered, "*Quiet*." Out loud she said, "My lords, Mr. Shade thinks he has a fool for a client. But he makes a good point."

"Your turn will come," the Foreman said. To Joseph, "Continue."

Jack wondered why Joseph, who clearly wanted Jack to succeed, would make the case against him. But then he realized that the Ravens would not allow the switch any other way. Joseph said, "He abandoned Layla Nazeer, the first time in the circus—"

Before Jack could interrupt again, Carolien touched his arm, whispered, "Don't speak."

"—and then again," the King continued, "when the geist entered his daughter and his wife begged him to help, he abandoned both of them."

Carolien said, "No, no, no. It was Miss Nazeer herself who returned to her life the first time. And as for the second, the last, Mr. Shade did not abandon her, he made a terrible mistake. Stupidity is not abandonment."

That's my defense? Jack thought, then immediately, desperately, hoped it would work

The King said, "He abandoned the carnival and his benefactor, Mr. Green."

"Only to apprentice himself to Anatolie the Younger."

Joseph said, "And then he abandoned his teacher as well."

"You know how that happened," Carolien said. "You can't blame him for that."

"He abandoned Elaynora Horne." Pause. "And Carolien Hounstra."

Jack thought, *What?* He waited for Carolien to object, but when she didn't he realized it was true. He'd left Carolien the moment he'd said *yes* to the Fissure King.

Finally, Joseph said, "Most of all, he abandoned his daughter."

Carolien said "*Nooit*. Never. He has never stopped trying to help her. To bring her out."

"No?" the King said. "Then why did he wait until now, the desperate hour, to find *me*?"

Jack wanted to yell at him "Because I didn't know about you!" but even to himself it sounded weak. *I'm losing*, he thought. *They'll find me, what, unworthy? I won't get to take Joseph's place and he won't rescue Genie. It's all over.*

And then that voice came. Stronger, more terrifying than any of the times Jack had heard it. A sound that could shatter the world. "I am Margarita Mariq Nliana Hand! I have come to speak for the defense."

The Ravens lowered their heads. "Your majesty."

Jack turned to her, then cried out. This was worse than that first time, at the Forbidden Beach. Then she kept changing form, now she seemed little more than an outline, but within that sketched body the whole world moved. Images appeared, then vanished, like electrons in a cloud chamber, replaced by a flood of others. People being born, dying, loving, hating . . .

Don't look away, Jack thought, but he had to. He focused on the Ravens as the Queen said, "John Shade has never abandoned me. I did not foresee this through my powers. I knew it. I knew John Shade, and I knew that whatever happened, whatever he witnessed, he would not give up on me. That is why I chose him to be the instrument of my death."

"Margaret," Jack said, and braced himself to turn towards her and thank her. But she was already gone.

When he turned back to look at the Ravens they stood absolutely still, their heads bowed, wings folded. Then all at once they opened their wings. Though they stood together their wings somehow didn't touch each other. Instead, they filled up the sky, like ladders to the nothingness beyond the world. The Foreman's voice came from high above. "John Shade, you have been found innocent, by virtue of the Queen of Eyes. Joseph of the Waters. Your petition is granted. John Shade may replace you. You are free."

At last, Jack thought. He turned to Joseph. "Now," he said, "your turn." But instead of answering, instead of any action at all, Joseph of the Waters simply crumbled. The rags of meat disintegrated, the bones clattered to the ground, some of them chipped and broken. Then a moment later they turned to dust and were washed away by a surge of water.

"No!" Jack said. "Come back here. You have to save Genie. *We had a deal.*"

Carolien's voice cut through his terror. "Jack," she said, "You don't need him."

"Of course I do. He said he would save her. Now he's gone."

"Jack. Look at your hands."

"What?" He held his hands up in front of his face. At first he just saw the lines, the ones palmists talked about. Lifeline, heartline. . . But then he realized they were something else. Cracks, openings. Fissures, not just in his hands but all up and down his body. Through them he could see—lights, flickers, people, animals, flashes of other worlds. For a moment he saw swirls of fire and knew they were the Djinn. But then they were gone, drowned in the flood of openings.

Staring down at his body, his legs, the endless cracks and ruptures, he managed to call out, "Carolien! Help me. I can't find her. I don't know where to look."

He managed to see Carolien standing in front of him, but seemingly separated by layers of fractured glass. He could hear her, though. Her lips moved, and the words wound their way through the cracks, the fissures. "Jack," she was saying, "Please. You must listen to me. Use your hands. Ignore everything else. Let your hands find her. Remember what they taught us. What every Traveler learns. *The eye can't hit what the hand can't see . . .*"

His voice somehow distant, he answered, "Dream like a butterfly, search like a bee." He raised his palms to his face. The cracks kept opening and closing, glimpses of worlds, but he paid no attention. "Genie," he said. "Where are you? Show me. I'm coming to get you."

And there it was. A shimmering wall of energy that flickered in and out of existence. On the other side of it, a forest, the branches of each tree twisted, the trunk contorted. And all of them on fire. And pressed against the wall, a girl. She looked exactly the same as the last time he'd seen her, fourteen years old, terrified in a red dress and worn-out black Mary Janes. She was saying something, and though he couldn't exactly hear her he knew what it was. "Daddy! Where are you? Help me."

At one time he would have thought nothing could penetrate that wall. But he was the Fissure King now, for whom every barrier is a door, every wall a crack. He reached out and felt the flickering energy. As he touched it, it hardened, only to break into countless lines and fragments. And now that he had cracked it, he could reach through it. He saw her gasp at the hands that appeared from nowhere, take a step back. Could she hear him? Could he still speak? "Genie!" he called, his voice strange in his own head. "It's me. I've come for you."

"Daddy?" she said, then "Daddy! Help me."

"Take my hands. Whatever happens, don't let go." She did it, and even though it had been years since he'd touched her he would have known those hands anywhere. "Get ready," he said.

When Eugenia was nine she made up a game in the park. She would get on the swing and go higher and higher, and then call out, "Hey ho, what d'you know? Better get ready, cause here I go!" Then on the next upswing she'd let go and fly through the air until Jack caught her. She always said she would knock him down, but she never did.

Now Jack called out to his daughter, "Genie! Remember this? Hey ho, what d'you know? Better get ready—"

Genie's tight voice said, "Cause here I go?" Jack pulled hard now, and suddenly the fissures opened wide, and his daughter came through the barrier, so hard he nearly did fall. But he held her.

"Daddy!' she cried, her face against his chest. Beyond her, the cracked wall, and the Forest itself, had vanished.

"It's okay, I've got you," he said. *How long?* he wondered. How long before it became impossible, even dangerous, for him to hold on to her?

He never found out, for she stepped back to look at him, then gasped. "Daddy? Your face. Your—what's wrong with you?"

"Sweetie," he said, "listen to me." He glanced at Carolien, and gave thanks she was there. He said, "I'm going to have to go away for awhile."

"No!" she cried.

He went on, "But you're okay now. You're safe. This woman is named Carolien. You can trust her. Trust her absolutely."

"Please, Daddy, don't leave."

"I'm so sorry," he told his daughter. "I love you. I will always love you." To Carolien he said, "Take her to Irene. My rooms are paid up at least for a year. She can stay there for now."

"Of course," Carolien said. "Or with me, as long as she likes."

Jack was fading now, more and more of him slipping through the cracks. He saw that the modern world was coming back. The fierce waters had softened, the trees were neater, he could see streets and cars and buildings.

Carolien called out to him, "Jack! Ik hou van jou." *I love you.*

He said, "Ik hou ook van jou, lieverdtje." *I love you too, darling.*

Just before he fell out of the world he thought, *Fucking hell. I can speak Dutch.*

And then he was gone.

EPILOGUE

EUGENIA SHADE STOOD A LONG TIME OUTSIDE THE LUCKY STAR restaurant. She would take a step towards it, then back. She looked at the blank apartment door next to it, then again at the restaurant window. Finally, she went inside.

It was just the way Carolien had described it. Long, narrow, a few tables on either side, the counter at the far end. The woman sitting on a stool, reading a newspaper. Three customers, all Chinese men, different ages, on their own.

She was suddenly conscious of how she looked, the way she hid herself. Jeans, sneakers, a black sweater, a long green coat, her hair pulled back and held with a clip. She could have cut it, of course, but if she did it herself it might come out terrible and people might stare at her, and if she went to a salon she would have to come up with some idea of what she wanted. When Carolien had taken her shopping, Eugenia had been afraid the Dutchwoman would want her to buy pretty things. To celebrate. Or something. But Carolien wasn't like that. Carolien never pushed her. Whenever she thought about that she wanted to cry, so she pushed the thought away. Stay focused, she told herself.

The thing was, Eugenia knew what she *looked* like. As far as she could tell she looked exactly the same as when—Fourteen. Fourteen years old.

She sure as hell didn't feel fourteen. She had no idea how old she felt. Carolien had told her how long she'd been inside, but it didn't mean anything. Twelve years. Twelve days. A hundred years. What difference did it make? Carolien had told her that a black guy had been president. Two terms! And now he was gone, replaced by some orange-haired white dude. She'd missed the whole fucking thing.

She reached the counter and the woman said, "May I help you?"

"Umm—are you Mrs. Shen?" The woman nodded, looked at her with curiosity, maybe suspicion. Genie took a breath. Caroline had offered to come with her, but she'd wanted to do it alone. Maybe that was a mistake. She said, "Uhh, I'm Eugenia Shade."

For a moment Mrs. Shen stared at her, then her whole face changed. "Oh!" she said, "you're his daughter. Welcome!" She looked past Genie, to the door. "Is your father coming too?"

"No. No, he's—out of town. For awhile."

"Oh, a shame. Too long since we see him. Tell your father we miss him."

Genie almost ran outside right then, but she managed to say, "Sure."

"You want lunch? Whatever you like. No charge."

"No. Sorry. I mean—Carolien—my father's friend—"

Mrs. Shen grinned. "The big blonde lady."

"Yes, that's right. Carolien said I should ask you what she wants."

"Ah. Of course. Yes." Mrs. Shen took a moment, and when she spoke again, Genie could hear a sadness inside her cheerfulness. She said, "Sea cucumber and tree fungus. And har kow, of course. You sit. Ten minutes, no more."

Genie sat at the nearest table. Across from her, one of the Chinese men, younger than the others, looked up at her, then went back to his noodles.

Soon, Mrs. Shen gave her two cartons of food. "You give her this," she said. "She likes it."

"Thank you. How much—"

"For you, nothing. "

"Thank you. Umm, is there a doorbell or something? I looked,

RACHEL POLLACK

but didn't see—"

"No need. Door is always open. For Jack, now for you."

For some reason, Genie bowed slightly, then felt herself blush. She said, "Thank you, Mrs. Shen," then rushed out.

When she tried the door it was indeed open. Careful not to spill the food, she climbed the five flights. At the third landing she became dizzy, but Carolien had warned her about that, so she kept going. At the top she saw a metal door. She was about to knock when a sonorous woman's voice said, "Come in."

Genie pushed the door open and stepped inside to see the largest woman she'd ever seen. The woman sat propped up against pillows on a thick mattress atop what looked like a reinforced steel bed. Genie wondered that the woman and the mattress didn't just fall through the floor. The woman wore a thigh-length dark red dress, silk maybe, and had thick dreads that came down the sides of her head, alongside her massive breasts, and somehow coiled together—like snakes, Genie thought—across her belly.

Genie said, "Umm, I'm Eugenia Shade."

"I know who you are."

"And you're Anatolie."

"Yes. I know who I am as well."

"I brought you some food. From Mrs. Shen."

"Thank you." She nodded at a wooden chair next to the bed. "Set it there, please." Genie did so, and found herself backing away. Anatolie said, "What can I do for you, Miss Shade?"

Genie's hands were shaking, but she willed them to stop. She said, "I want to study with you. I want to become a Traveler."

There was a long silence, and Genie had to fight an urge to run downstairs and not stop until she got to Carolien's house. Finally, Anatolie said, "Why do you wish to become a Traveler, Eugenia Shade?"

Genie said, "I want to rescue my father."

334

The End.

Acknowledgements

My deep gratitude to Gordon van Gelder and C. C. Finlay, who first gave Jack Shade a home in *The Magazine of Fantasy And Science Fiction*. Thank you as well, to my agent, Martha Millard, and my editor, Mark Teppo, for their amazing patience and forbearing. And to Zoe Matoff, for always being there, especially when things got hard. Finally, to Paula Scardamalia, writing coach extraordinaire, for catching the small things, and keeping me focused on the big ones.

About the Author

Rachel Pollack is the author of forty books, including *Godmother Night*, winner of the World Fantasy Award, *Unquenchable Fire*, winner of the Arthur C. Clarke Award, and *Temporary Agency*, short-listed for the Nebula Award. She is also a poet, a translator, a comics writer, and the author of a series of best-selling books about Tarot cards, including *78 Degrees Of Wisdom*, in print continuously since 1980. Her work has been translated into fifteen languages and sold around the world. She has lectured and taught on five continents.